What was it about this abrasive man that made her heart speed up and her breasts ache with longing? What was it about him that made her hungry for sensations she hadn't known she was missing? What was it about him that made her want to cast caution to the winds and explore all that he was . . . ?

Everything about Jake Dolan intrigued and, heaven help her, turned her on.

She stared at his mouth and ached to taste him.

She looked at his long hair and longed to bury her fingers in the silken threads.

She wanted to touch his broad chest and feel his arms around her. She wanted to—

He scowled. "Why are you looking at me like that?"

"Like what?" she asked innocently.

"Like I'm a food product."

Oh, Marnie wanted to taste him all right.

She felt bold, daring, and giddy with want.

Poor Jake was struggling like the fish on the end of a hook. . . .

KISS AND TELL

Cherry Adair

IVY BOOKS • NEW YORK

An Ivy Book
Published by The Ballantine Publishing Group

www.randomhouse.com

Library of Congress Catalog Card Number: 00-106524

ISBN 0-449-00683-2

Manufactured in the United States of America

First Edition: September 2000

10 9 8 7 6

For the Ladies on board the BICC train—
if friends were flowers, I'd pick you.

For Rose Lerma, Susan Plunkett,
Pamela Britton, and Jennifer Skullestad.
For great memories, and lifelong friendships.
You are the best.

And always for my flyboy, David, with all my love.

Chapter One

The perimeter alarms were set to go off when anything heavier than a hundred pounds crossed the almost invisible breakers. At first all Jake saw on the monitor was the fawn-colored Great Dane. The damn thing was a mean-looking bastard and as big as a house.

"Where the hell did you come from?"

The dog's large, square head and pointy ears swiveled, as if it could smell him down here, twenty feet below ground level. Jake stuck his size fourteens up on the counter and took another swig of soda. His eyes narrowed as he scrutinized the flat-screen monitor before him.

A second later his feet dropped to the floor at the same time his fist crushed the empty can. "Shit."

The dog had been hiding her.

For a split second . . .

Jake absently touched the scar on his throat and ignored the from zero-to-eighty acceleration of his blood pressure. He leaned forward to adjust the focus and shifted closer to get a better look.

A slender blonde, drowning in a green down jacket, sat not thirty feet from the front door of his cabin on the tree uprooted by last year's storm. Fair hair, all the colors of the sun and fingered by the breeze, danced in joyous spiral curls around her face and hunched shoulders as she concentrated on something in her lap.

Her skin was fair instead of dusky, her hair silky, not coarse, the angle of her head unfamiliar. She was no ghost from the past. Thank God.

Nevertheless, he didn't want her here.

Jake didn't know who she was or what she was doing in the high, remote Sierras at the nose of winter. Her mere presence was suspect. Not that she appeared to be anything other than a cute blonde on a solitary mountain hike. But then looks could be deceiving.

Neither the girl nor the dog was welcome.

He didn't like dogs. In his line of work they tended to be unpredictable. As for the fluffy blonde . . . Jake slam-dunked the squashed can into the trash, then leaned forward for a better look. He definitely didn't like *that* breed, either.

Closer inspection didn't improve her one bit. Unfortunately he hadn't had a woman in nearly a year, and this cupcake made his mouth water. Too bad. Like a mouse to an elephant, like David to Goliath. She was exactly the type of woman he avoided like the plague—petite, blonde, and delicate.

He was bone exhausted from an assignment in a small, forgotten Middle Eastern country where all hell had broken loose. All he'd wanted to do was take a break. Instead he'd come home to find the shit hitting the fan, his sixteen-year career in the toilet, and the vacation he'd wanted being enforced.

He had no time for the blonde outside.

Most likely a strong "boo" would send girl and hound running for town. After they left he'd get back to figuring out who was screwing with his life.

Marnie Wright wished she'd brought along a warm cap. Cold air nipped at her ears, making them sting. Dismissing the discomfort, she focused on the sketch pad in her lap.

It had been a bonus finding this old cottage tucked into the hillside. She'd hate to waste the light walking the mile back to her grandmother's cottage just because she was cold. She flipped up her collar and hunched her shoulders.

Only the front walls and the peak of the shingled roof showed through the surrounding trees, shrubs, and piles of deadfall. It was in better shape than Grammy's. While rustic, the wood siding and front porch had recently been repaired. The roof appeared solid, the windows intact.

Marnie flexed her fingers, narrowing her eyes at the log cabin before she continued drawing. The little house was perfect for the creepy Halloween story she was working on. All it needed was a little atmosphere. She shaded a curved whisper of smoke above the chimney, elongating dark shadows to make the small house unwelcoming and sinister. The fluid black lines of her charcoal pencil skimmed the page. Beside her, Duchess's head swiveled.

"What're you listening to? A chipmunk?"

Her dog made a low sound in her throat and wagged her tail.

Marnie laughed, her breath misting in the frigid air. "Don't go far." She put her hand behind her pet's massive head and looked her sternly in the eye. "And don't *play* with it, you hear me?"

Duchess bounded to the closed door of the empty cottage. She settled her backside on the front step, ears perked. Marnie smiled. Duchess loved her creature comforts. Rather than frolic about in the cold, she wanted inside.

"That's not home, goofus. Give me a few more minutes and we'll pack up and go, okay?"

She had lugged her sleeping bag and supplies to her grandmother's cottage before she and Duchess had taken a stroll, ending up at this isolated place. The exercise, and the cold, had made her hungry, too. She smelled rain and wanted to be back before it started pouring.

With a frown she considered for half a second going home to Sunnyvale. The river had a tendency to flood, making the bridge impassable. Leaving would be the prudent, safe thing to do.

But she didn't *want* to be prudent and sensible anymore. The decisions and choices she made in the next couple of days were going to change her future. After a lifetime of playing it safe, she needed to learn to take the chances life presented her.

Some of her happiest memories had been made up here at Grammy's cottage. And here was where she was going to decide the course of the rest of her life. A little rain wasn't going to deter her.

She'd almost forgotten what a pain in the butt it was to get up here. She'd left her car at the end of the narrow mountain road, then crossed the skinny footbridge fording the river, passed over another bridge spanning the ravine, and *then* had a three-mile hike up the mountainside. As kids, she and her brothers hadn't noticed such minor inconveniences. It had always been a grand adventure to come here with Grammy. They'd explored every inch of the mountain, played in the river, and climbed the trees like monkeys.

A little rain and cold wouldn't hurt. This was probably the last time she'd— . . .

A twig snapped behind her. The pencil jerked in her hand, leaving a jagged smear across the paper. Marnie froze. She looked at Duchess. The animal shifted impatiently on the front porch of the little cottage, brow furrowed, ears rotating like radar. Marnie's shoulders relaxed.

For half a second.

"This is private property."

Her head shot up, and she looked over her shoulder.

He stood slightly to the left and behind her, as big as a mountain and impossible to miss. Why hadn't Duchess raced up to protect her, as she usually did? And how had he walked up this close without her hearing him? And he *was* close. He stood with booted feet spread, a shotgun cradled casually in the crook of his arm.

Dark hair hung to his massive shoulders. A heavy, five o'clock shadow blurred his features. Tall and broad-shouldered, he was dressed in jeans and covered to midthigh by a thick down jacket similar to her own. He looked like something out of *Soldier of Fortune* magazine, only a great deal less friendly.

"Where'd you come from?" Marnie asked brightly, flipping the cardboard cover over the sketch pad in her lap. She gathered her wits and braced her feet in preparation for quick action if it became necessary.

"Who are you, and what are you doing here?"

"Marnie Wright. I'm visiting— I'm— I'm just here," she

finished in exasperation. *I'm here to rethink my life. I'm here to contemplate my future. I* wasn't *expecting the Incredible Hulk!*

"There isn't anyone else up here. Who are you supposed to be visiting?"

"I'm visiting my grandmother's old cottage. It's down there." Marnie pointed down the hill. "She—"

"Are you alone?"

She wasn't stupid. "I'm expecting company later. Soon."

"Meet your company across the bridge."

Instead of his rudeness putting her off, Marnie was intrigued. "Who are you?" she asked curiously. "And what are *you* doing here at this time of year?"

"Lady, this isn't a goddamn cocktail party. Forget the chitchat and get lost." His lips thinned to a hard line. "Take the dog and move out."

"Move out?" Marnie cocked her head and pulled the canvas bag into her lap. Military, for sure. She definitely knew the type. Her brother Michael was a navy SEAL.

Unfortunately for this guy, she was sick and tired of being told what to do, and when to do it, by bossy men. She was pretty sure he wouldn't shoot her. In the meantime she was perfectly happy where she was, thank you very much. She gave him a limpid look.

He repeated his words in French, then in German, just in case she didn't get the message. His deep baritone stroked across her imagination, shimmied through her bones. The quiet tone, deep and compelling, rough with impatience, made her shiver.

This was a man used to giving commands and receiving immediate obedience. His gaze slid downward over her open jacket, purple sweatshirt, well-worn jeans, and heavy hiking boots, then slowly back up again.

Marnie trembled as if he'd physically touched her. He had remarkable eyes—a mesmerizing, unfriendly dark blue. He scrutinized her with an intensity usually reserved for particularly dangerous reptiles. He held her gaze as he strode around the exposed roots of the tree until he stood before her.

Considerably more intimidating head on, he had a straight nose and heavy eyebrows, one of which was bisected by a thin white scar—a scar more recent than childhood. The man was a fighter. Beneath the blur of dark facial hair she detected a square, stubborn chin.

And the sexiest mouth . . .

His nearness unsettled her to the core. But that had nothing to do with his attitude. She had four brothers who could appear just as intimidating. She'd been raised around men, but she'd never had this sort of immediate reaction. Her knee-jerk response to him unnerved her.

He glared, then said, as well as signed, "Are you deaf, woman?"

Marnie's gaze flickered from the movement of his large, expressive hands back to his scowling face. She felt a leap of interest, a spark of excitement, a frisson of searing attraction as he stood there glaring down at her.

Lust at first sight.

She sighed.

Lust was a wholly inappropriate reaction considering the circumstances. She held his gaze, one eyebrow raised in query at his threatening stance. He was a huge man, taller than her five-six by almost a foot. A warning glittered from narrowed eyes; his hostility was meant to scare away even the most intrepid. The shotgun was overkill.

"I'd be able to hear you even if you weren't yelling."

"Then what part of 'get lost' don't you understand?"

"It's a big mountain. I'm not taking up much room, am I?"

Not taking her eyes off him, she rested her hand lightly on her day pack. Besides her art supplies, she carried a can of Mace and a roll of quarters knotted in an old knee-high stocking. A girl could never be too prepared. Unfortunately, she had a feeling neither her makeshift weapon nor her yellow belt in Aikido would make a dent in this guy. Part of her wondered at her temerity baiting this angry stranger. The part that was fascinated made her stay put.

In her peripheral vision, she saw Duchess directly behind

him. The dog stood four square, staring at his back, a sappy, slobbery grin on her canine face.

"This might be a big mountain, but this is *my* little chunk, and I like it just fine without you on it. Move, lady."

"Sorry, I'm not ready to move yet."

She tried the fluttering-eyelash thing that worked with her brothers, knowing she was playing with fire, and enjoying it immensely.

"Honest, I'm harmless. All I'm doing is drawing the cottage for a book I'm illus—"

"Lady, I don't give a damn if you're Picasso. The cabin belongs to me. The tree you're sitting on belongs to me, and the damn land you're on belongs to me. Haul your butt and your dog off my property."

"Well, since you put it so nicely . . ."

More amused by his annoyance than afraid, she smiled up at him. There wasn't a trace of indulgent humor in those dark, glacial eyes. He obviously didn't find her as cute and adorable as her brothers did.

He scowled. "Are you as stupid as you look?"

"That's kind of like asking the man if he's stopped beating his wife, isn't it?" Marnie stood, dusting moss and bits of bark off her behind. Her butt was damp. "Are you always this rude to strangers?"

Duchess walked daintily around him, coming to her side and leaning her enormous head against Marnie's arm.

"Lady." Obviously exasperated, he clicked the safety off the gun. Her shoulders stiffened. "What the hell do I have to do to get you off this mountain? Shoot you?"

"Jeez, keep your shirt on. I'm going already!" She picked up the pencils that had rolled to the ground when she'd stood, then slipped icy fingers beneath Duchess's collar.

"Come on, sweetheart." She managed to take two steps before she realized that Duchess wasn't moving. "Come *on*, girl."

Duchess shook off her restraint. For a moment Marnie hoped her dog wasn't going for Mountain Man's throat. She had to choke back a laugh as Duchess wagged her tail, stuffed her head under his free hand, and gazed up at him adoringly.

By his expression she could tell he was not a happy camper. She bit her lip; this was no time to smile. Duchess gave her mistress a soulful look, Marnie made a subtle "stay" hand gesture. And her dog leaned against a very large masculine thigh, and heaved an enormous sigh.

"What the hell is this animal doing?"

Marnie's feet scuffed up damp leaves as she strolled away without looking back. "She likes you." She had to raise her voice to be heard as she put some distance between them.

"Damn it, I told you to—stop that, dog!—take your dog."

"Oh, Duchess goes exactly where she wants. Never have been able to make her come when she wants to stay." She glanced over her shoulder. Duchess was looking up at him as if he were God's gift.

Marnie started to laugh.

"Come back here, woman. What the hell's so funny?"

"She's crazy about you." She stuffed her hands into the warmth of her pockets and hunched her shoulders to keep her ears warm.

"Damn it," he yelled again. "Call her off."

"Don't worry, she'll come home when she's ready."

As she strolled down the hillside through the trees, she heard the man cursing a blue streak. Mingled with his deep baritone was Duchess's attempt at loverlike conversation. Marnie almost tripped over her own feet. It was hard to walk when she was laughing so hard.

The timpani of rain on the shake roof woke her. Marnie snuggled deeper into the warmth of the sleeping bag. Despite sleeping fully clothed, sharp, icy air filtered inside, giving her goose bumps. She felt as though she'd only slept a moment. Resigned, she opened gritty eyes.

Four feet away, her dog snored, dead to the world. Duchess had curled up as close to the fireplace as she could get. Marnie chuckled; the dog had loped home after a couple of hours visiting her new friend.

She wished Duchess spoke a more easily translatable language. Then she could have grilled her pet about their taciturn neighbor.

Strange man.

But interesting, very interesting.

She felt a little zing of guilt for pushing him so hard yesterday afternoon. He'd wanted her gone so badly, but she hadn't been able to resist teasing him. He hadn't been amused. Yet as annoyed as he'd been, she hadn't felt as though she was really in danger.

She sighed. She was lucky the guy hadn't shot her on the spot.

Marnie had promised her dad she'd be back at work on Monday. That meant she had today and Sunday to sort out her life.

She'd save the poor guy any more aggravation and keep out of his way for the next couple of days. Which was too bad; he was the most interesting man she'd met in years.

She scrunched deeper into the bag, the floor uncomfortably hard under her hip. Rain pounded steadily on the roof. She shivered, curled into a ball, and debated whether to get up and toss a few more logs on the fire or conserve what little warmth existed inside the bag.

It was barely six A.M., but she was awake and knew she wouldn't go back to sleep now. Grizzly light filtered through water-smeared, uncurtained windows. Branches snapped and whipped in the high wind, showering pine needles and leaves against the panes. Trees bent under the storm's onslaught.

The wind had picked up late last night after she'd finished the lukewarm coffee in her thermos, and she and Duchess had shared a solitary dinner of cold canned stew. Now the wind howled outside like a banshee, screamed through the trees surrounding the cottage, and sneaked through the crevices between the shingles and wood siding. It sounded lonely.

Grammy had adored bringing all the kids up here with her for weeks at a time. When Grandpa was alive, the two of them had lived in nearby Gray Feather. He'd built the cottage for weekend getaways. The half dozen small houses between the river and the ravine were used as summer vacation homes. No one lived here all year round. They were miles from civilization and help.

Marnie had consciously pushed aside years of warnings and cautions when she decided to come up here alone. Her family tended to be overprotective. But there was no need. She was as healthy and fit as a woman her age should be.

Another thing she wanted to change. That constant niggling worry on the edge of her subconscious. To hell with it. She wanted to live, to experience life to the fullest, to gorge herself at life's banquet.

And in the next couple of days she would decide just how she was going to do it.

Then she was going home to implement her plans.

By the flickering firelight, she looked around the small, empty room with a pang of nostalgia. Although her grandmother hadn't returned to the mountains for many years, the little house still held the warmth of memories that would keep Marnie wrapped in her love for the rest of her life. Her grandmother would have wholeheartedly approved of what she was doing.

The shrieking wind reminded her of vacations spent here with her family, telling ghost stories sprawled on the floor before a roaring fire, roasting marshmallows. Snuggled inside her sleeping bag, Marnie pictured the little cottage as it had been when she and the boys had come up here with Grammy for vacations.

The furniture, handcrafted by her grandfather, was gone. The quilts and framed needlework hung in Marnie's own house in Sunnyvale. Now Grammy's cottage was just a small, empty wood building tucked away under the trees in the mountains, filled only with happy memories.

Grandpa had passed away, and a year later her mother had died in a senseless car accident. Marnie had been six. Grammy had come down off her beloved mountain to take care of her and her brothers. Grammy was the only mother Marnie had known, and she ached with her loss. She would have given anything right now to have Grammy with her, just for a little while. She could have benefited from a little grandmotherly wisdom.

Martha Washburn had been a shining example. She'd been strong. Independent. Courageous.

She'd shaped who and what Marnie had become. She'd fought tooth and nail to free her granddaughter from her father and brothers' overprotectiveness and tight control. She'd tried to make Marnie's life normal.

They hadn't always agreed, but Marnie had loved her cantankerous grandmother fiercely and with all her heart.

Getting involved with some guy wasn't the solution to her problems. She'd proven that. Years ago she'd started looking for *someone*. Someone . . . tame. Someone who was the opposite of her macho brothers, who drove her nuts bossing her around. *They* weren't settling-down kind of men. As much as she adored them, she'd wanted something different. Someone housebroken. Someone with a normal job and a regular hobby. Yet in each case, the men she'd thought she could share some kind of life with had ended up being wrong for her. There'd been no spark. No electricity. No sizzle.

Thinking she needed a man to complete her life had been the problem. Maybe she was a slow learner. It wasn't a *man* she needed. It was the ability to say no to her family and yes to herself.

For years her grandmother had warned her she was looking for the wrong thing. Instead of looking around for someone to make her feel complete, she needed to examine herself. To know who she really was. To feel whole within herself.

Marnie had vehemently disagreed. Every woman her age was marrying. Having kids. It was what women *did*.

Twice she'd accepted engagement rings from nice men who were all the things she thought she wanted, only to find herself aching for something they didn't have. Couldn't give her.

And while she wasn't in a hurry to get married anymore, she wasn't getting any younger, either. She was only twenty-seven. Her biological clock would probably start to tick soon, but she had years before age became an issue.

Grammy had been dead right.

Marnie had to learn about herself before she could share her life with someone else. Whoever he might be.

Luckily that decision had come before she'd made it to the altar. One small step. Yet she hadn't moved from the safety of her dad's house until a year ago. And she still worked for him as a programmer when what she really wanted to do was something involving her art. Like the Cowardly Lion, she was still looking for courage.

Grammy's death five weeks ago had been a turning point in her life. She'd ridden on the current of taking the path of least resistance for too long. The times they were a-changing. She'd missed so much by letting others tell her what was best for her.

Now she wanted it all. Art school in Paris. Living in a sun-filled loft with the smell of paint and the Seine. Excitement. Challenge. Freedom.

Or perhaps she'd find a job with an advertising agency. Or a greeting card company. Or . . . The choices were limitless. All she had to do was decide which road to take. Which grand adventure to pursue.

Someday she'd want a husband. And children. And a house in the country, with a tire swing hanging from a tree, smoke curling from the chimney, and marigolds growing near the front door. But not yet.

She needed to learn to spread her wings and fly. And by God, when she left this mountain she'd know precisely how she was going to achieve that. Come hell or high water, as Grammy used to say.

Marnie smiled into the darkness. She didn't need to wonder what her grandmother would think of her antisocial mountain man. Her grandmother had always had a lively sense of adventure. *She* wouldn't have been scared off.

He didn't scare Marnie off, exactly, but in this case keeping out of his way would be wise. He was dangerously attractive, and she had far too much thinking to do this weekend.

Thinking that could become muddied getting mixed up with another macho man who thought he knew what was best for her.

Her smile grew. But there wasn't any harm in daydreaming about him.

She recalled his dark blue eyes as he'd glared at her. His sexy mouth. That rich, husky voice that made her bone marrow shimmy like Jell-O. She snuggled deeper into the sleeping bag and forced herself to rein in her thoughts about a man she didn't know. And probably shouldn't. The thoughts, however, kept her nice and warm. She wondered what he was doing right—

A *booooom*, similar to a volcano erupting, cut her off in midthought. The noise was deafening. And close.

With a howl of fright Duchess jerked awake and skittered across the plank floor to land quivering on her mistress's legs.

At the same time Marnie bolted upright, wide-eyed, heart pounding. "What the—"

The cottage shuddered, groaned, and creaked. The walls shook with a series of earsplitting screeches. Tangled in the sleeping bag and dog, adrenaline rushing, she kicked her legs free and jumped to her feet just as a huge tree crashed through the ceiling.

With a bloodcurdling yell, Marnie threw her arms over her head, and her body over Duchess, as chunks of roof and ceiling, branches, and rain showered down.

Duchess's frantic barking wasn't helping matters. "Shhh, girl. Shhh." The dog wriggled from beneath her but didn't stop her frantic barking.

After several moments, when no more horrendous sounds ripped through the night, Marnie straightened. Bits of debris drifted off her head and shoulders. She stared uncomprehendingly at the quivering branches of a ponderosa pine poking through a huge gaping hole in the shake roof. Broken branches littered the floor. Heavy raindrops slashed through the opening. Wet branches moaned under the sodden weight, then dripped puddles on the bare wooden floor at her feet.

The weight sprang the hinges on the front door, which now hung drunkenly, letting in a blast of wind and rain.

"Oh, wow!" she whispered in a gross understatement.

Duchess sniffed a branch, looking over her shoulder she let out a puzzled whine.

"No kidding, Sherlock."

A small whirlpool swirled pine needles and debris, stirring up the fire in the hearth into a shower of orange and blue sparks.

The tree dropped another few feet.

With a loud yelp, Duchess flew through the partially open front door and disappeared into the darkness.

"Hey," Marnie yelled. "Wait for me!"

She grabbed up her jacket and put it on, the sleeves of her sweatshirt bunched uncomfortably beneath it. She crammed sketch pad and pencils into her backpack, but there was no time to put on her boots.

Hurry. Hurry. Hurry.

The fire flared and sparked as more debris dropped into the room.

Marnie grabbed the bootlaces in one hand, dug in her backpack, pulled out a bottle of water, and hurriedly doused the fire in the hearth. She left yesterday's damp clothes where they had been drying before the fire. Her problems were more immediate than having only the clothes she stood up in.

Hurry. Hurry. Hurry.

The tree creaked ominously then dropped another four feet into the room, effectively blocking the door.

Nonplussed, she stared at the quaking branches for a second. The tree was huge, the branches thick and widespread.

She slung her backpack over her shoulders, draped the lightweight sleeping bag around her neck, then grasped the closest branch. With more speed than grace, she clambered partway up the thick branches until she reached the broken window on the far side of the room. The backpack kept snagging on branches, and she had to repeatedly pause to unhook herself, all the while chanting under her breath, "Hurry. Hurry. Hurry."

It wasn't easy to slide open the sash, which was partially blocked by foliage. By the time she was done, her hands were sticky with pitch from having to break off the small branches in her way, and she was breathing hard.

Mindful of broken glass, she eased herself gingerly out of the narrow opening. The moment Marnie's stockinged foot touched the ground outside the window, she felt a tug on the hem of her jacket.

"Gee, thanks for the help, you traitor." Duchess's cold nose nudged her knee, urging her to swing her other leg over the sill. "Yeah, yeah. I'm hurrying. Stop pulling."

The monster tree dipped farther into the house with a shriek that sounded eerily like a woman's scream. The sound of glass shattering on the other side of the house was followed by a series of pops. Sounding like the score to a chain-saw horror movie, bark scraped across wood in the tree's long, slow descent.

Duchess grabbed the sleeve of her mistress's jacket in her mouth and started pulling again. Hopping on one foot to regain her balance, Marnie was only too happy to follow. In seconds the rain plastered her hair against her face and pasted her clothing to her body. She managed to zip her jacket and push her hair out of her eyes before she felt far enough away to pause and tug on hiking boots over wet, muddy socks. "Ugh!"

Duchess nudged her arm, almost knocking her over into the mud. "You could have waited for me. I was right behind you, you know."

God, her heart was racing. She'd never been so happy to see her dog in her life.

"Please tell me the bridge is still there so we can sleep in the car, or tell me you found a warm, toasty dry, animal-free cave somewhere."

Talking to Duchess beat thinking about becoming a shish kebab in Grammy's little house, which was now a pancake. Tears stung her eyes, and she dashed them away. "Did you, huh, clever girl? 'Cause dollars to doughnuts the bridge is flood—"

Duchess barked a warning. A second too late.

"Don't you have enough sense to get out of the rain, woman?"

Oh, joy, Paul Bunyan, Marnie thought, reacting instinctively to his derisive tone. Nevertheless, she felt a leap of relief at his sudden appearance.

"I can take care of myself, thank you very much." She squinted through the slashing rain and the thick gray gloom of predawn. He was huge—and so welcome she wanted to hug him.

"So I've noticed," he said wryly, walking into the clearing. He wore blue jeans, a navy blue parka, and a black scowl. "By the way, there aren't any caves around here."

"I know that. I was just making conversation," Marnie said stiffly, hugging the sleeping bag, instead of him, to her wet, cold chest. Keeping the shiver out of her voice was difficult.

"With a dog?"

"Don't you have nails to chew or wings to rip off butterflies or something?"

"I came to save your ass."

She narrowed her eyes. "How did you know my ass needed saving?" Marnie shuddered as she realized just how long it had taken her to get out. Ten or fifteen minutes at least.

"Your dog here started whining and howling fit to wake the dead. She woke me up. I let her in. She whined. I let her out. She howled. In. Out. She kept coming back. Obviously she wanted me to follow her."

He looked Marnie up and down in a far from complimentary way. "I did. I'm here. We're wet. Let's go."

"How incredibly sweet and thoughtful of you to dash out here to rescue me. However, silly little me went and rescued herself. So while I'd love to say it's been delightful chatting with you, Duchess and I are going the other way."

She thumbed through the rain in the general direction of the path leading down to the footbridge and her car.

"First of all, it's *that* way." He pointed. "Which is immaterial at the moment. The bridge is flooded."

"Maybe not."

"Trust me on this. It's out," he snarled, as though it were her fault.

"I'd prefer to check that for myself. Come on, girl."

Duchess leaned against him, her big, square head resting on his arm. Marnie tried snapping her wet fingers. All she achieved was a spray of raindrops off her hand and an obstinate yip from her dog.

"You're going to walk three miles in this weather to prove me wrong?"

"It hasn't been raining that long!"

"Long enough. Just follow your dog." He strode off into the trees.

"To where?" Marnie watched his silhouette blend into the darkness of the trees up ahead. "To *where*?" she shouted.

She realized the sleeping bag clutched to her chest was trailing on the ground and now soaking wet. "Well?" she demanded, but Duchess ignored her and bounded off behind him.

"What have you done to my dog?" Marnie yelled into the slanting rain. With a muttered curse she dug a flashlight out of her backpack, tossed the soggy, useless sleeping bag onto the ground, and followed Romeo and Juliet up the hill.

Chapter Two

Jake heard her muttering as she stumbled along behind him. The dog, big as a horse and fifty times more intelligent than a number of human beings he knew, darted between them, tongue lolling.

At least *someone* was happy.

Damn. It was cold. And wet. Unfortunately he hadn't taken the time to light a fire in the cabin before he'd left.

The dog's obvious agitation had spurred him to hastily throw on his coat, grab a weapon, and run.

He'd had no idea what he'd been running *to*. God only knew a pretty blonde could get into trouble anywhere.

She'd been climbing out of the window when he and the dog had arrived at the demolished cabin. The downed tree had cut the small structure neatly in half. It had been a long time, years, since Jake had felt his heart stop as it had when he'd seen her. She was none of his business; still, he'd have hated seeing anything that soft crushed out of existence.

"That was my grandmother's cottage. Did I mention that?" Her voice sounded shaky. "My brothers are coming up in the spring to tear it down. They told me I couldn't put it off another year just because I'm sentimental about it. They said it was a fire hazard. Fat lot they knew."

She took a quivery breath, then said too brightly, "Well, it's obvious that it isn't habitable anymore. I mean, I *knew* that before I came. None of us has done any maintenance in years, so I expected the worst—but hoped for the best." She huffed and puffed for a few moments before continuing. "I just wanted . . . I just wanted to see it one more time before—"

"The tree saved them a trip."

She gave an indignant little gasp. "Sheesh! I can tell *you* aren't big on sentimentality. I have wonderful memories here. I adored my grandmother. My family came up here every year, usually in the summer. We'd hike and fish. . . ."

Christ. Is she going to tell me her whole life story? He turned to look at her and cut her off in midsentence. "Do you ever stop talking, woman?"

Even in the lousy visibility she gave a mean glare. "I stop when I'm not scared out of my wits, okay?"

"Trust me," he said with utmost sincerity. "You have nothing to be scared of. You're as safe as houses with me."

"*Not* a good analogy."

Trust her to be literal. He let out a put-upon sigh. "If I don't let any more trees fall on you, will you shut up?"

She stopped talking, but she wasn't quiet.

Jake became excruciatingly aware of her, there, right behind him. The small grunts and groans as she placed each foot carefully on the slick ground reverberated in his gut. He wanted to turn around and tell her to shut the hell up.

She sounded as though she was having sex.

Good sex.

Slow sex.

Everything-about-the-body-involved sex.

He didn't want to think about sex. He didn't want to think about *her*. And he sure as hell didn't want to think about sex and her at the same time.

But here she was. He was the only game in town at the moment. He didn't have a choice, did he? No, he didn't. Jake trudged on.

Belligerent. Resentful. Horny.

He gritted his teeth as she made a sweet moaning sound behind him as she stumbled. "How many brothers do you have?" he asked grimly. He'd rather hear her babble than listen to those damn sighs and moans. He had some serious questions to ask, but he wanted to see her eyes when she answered.

"I thought you wanted me to be quiet."

"I changed my mind. How many?"

"Four."

"And you used to come up here every summer to vacation with your grandmother?" He had to practically shout. The wind blew straight into his mouth, freezing his teeth. Which annoyed the hell out of him.

"Yes."

The golden cone from her flashlight screwed up his night vision. First she talked too much. Now the woman was a clam. Go figure. To hell with it, he didn't want to hear her life story anyway.

Under the tree canopy it was still the anticipatory gray before dawn. The air smelled of wet leaves, overlaid by the sharp tang of pine and the musty scent of wet dog. And it was cold.

The rain was going to turn to snow any minute. The trail wasn't particularly steep, but in this kind of weather and with such poor visibility, it was dangerous. Mud, wet pine needles, and decaying leaves made footing unstable. He leaned against the insistent push of the wind, his muscles pulling against the back draft. It howled through the trees, whipping the hem of his thick jacket about his thighs and slashing his hair across his face. He forged on grimly.

Behind him Jake heard a splash. A small, impatient moan. A sigh.

It took everything in him not to stop, pick her up, and carry her the rest of the way up to the cabin before she started bitching and moaning. But he wasn't going to touch her. She and her lovesick dog had disrupted his peace and quiet. He couldn't leave her down there in a cabin of toothpicks, but by the same token, he didn't have to make her feel welcome, either.

He didn't know who or what she was, and until he did, he didn't intend trusting her farther than he could spit.

She started humming under her breath—something perky and totally inappropriate to the occasion, which Jake thought warranted a dirge. The woman was irritating as hell.

"What are their names?" he asked desperately.

"Michael—"

"Can't hear you," he yelled. Let her work for it. Maybe she'd be hoarse by the time they reached the cabin.

"Michael," she shouted, "Kyle, Derek, and Kane."

Rain continued coming down in torrents. Hot on his heels, she came abreast, and slipped on the muddy runoff. Jake grabbed her arm before she went down.

"Thanks," she panted, her breath a white drift as she paused to center herself. Through the sleeve of her jacket he felt her muscles quiver with her fight against the elements. He let go but kept one large hand open and inches from her back in case she needed steadying.

Thank God she didn't, and he didn't have to touch her again.

The second her boots found purchase she was off. He dropped his arm and overtook her, then positioned himself as a windbreak. Oh yeah, he was the original immovable object.

She kept pace surprisingly well. He wasn't slowing to accommodate her shorter legs. Obviously she didn't want to have to shout.

"They're a little overprotective. Okay, a *lot* overprotective," she chatted as they climbed.

Lord, did she ever run out of juice?

"But I'm the only girl, so I guess it was automatic for them to spoil me. Although it gets old after a while, you know?" She huffed and puffed but kept pace with his long strides.

The woman had two speeds; on, at sixty miles per hour, and off.

"I've been able to keep up with them for years." She laughed, and the sound grabbed a seldom-used part of his chest. *Oh, man.*

"The boys are big on bets. Always daring each other to do some crazy thing or other. I wouldn't let them exclude me, so I—"

"Ever been married?" Jake interrupted, desperate for a break from the chirpy familial story. Besides, she didn't need to tell him she'd been spoiled rotten.

That was why cute, delicate blondes had been put on the

earth. To be pampered and spoiled and doted on by thick-headed males.

Been there, done that. Got the scar to prove it.

He ruthlessly dredged up the memory of another "chance" meeting, another sweet-faced, helplessly appealing blonde—and felt better for it. Nothing like a quick refresher course to remind a man of his priorities.

Jake quickened his pace, feeling the pull of his muscles and dragging in a large breath of chilly air. The tree canopy sheltered them from the continuing torrent, and the wide trunks deflected some of the wind. She kept up, close enough for him to smell. Cute, delicate. Delicious. Off-limits.

"Nope. Never married. But engaged a couple of times."

"Can't commit?"

"Apparently not."

Don't ask, he instructed himself. "Why the hell not?"

She breathed through her mouth a couple of gut-wrenching times. "Maybe I'm picky."

"Then you should have thought of that before you got those schmucks to fork over big bucks for engagement rings, shouldn't you?"

"I gave them back." She was starting to breathe hard from the climb, but it wasn't slowing her down any. "And it wasn't like I broke their hearts or anything. They weren't in love with me."

"Why'd they ask you to marry them, then?" Besides wanting to get her into the closest bed to hear those little noises she made. Between crisp sheets, instead of climbing up a mountain in the frigging rain. He didn't want to know any of this. He shouldn't have asked. He should have let her take her chances on the bridge.

She sighed. "My family has a bit of money."

Jake glanced down. It was hard to see in this light, but he discerned enough to know that whatever the light, whatever the circumstances, the last thing a man would think about when he looked at her was money.

He snorted.

"Okay, a *lot* of money."

"Does your family own a liquor store?" he asked dryly.

"A liquor store? No, why?"

"Just an old joke." The one about the rich blonde and the liquor store required her to be mute.

"Look, we're almost there. Conserve your energy." *And give me a few moments of silence.*

She managed not to talk for a while, and he managed to block out the infernal noises she made. Jake slowed as she trailed him past the felled tree near his cabin, the one she'd sat on yesterday. The slate-colored light was now tinged with a pale yellow as dawn struggled through the thick clouds overhead. The rain had slacked off slightly.

The dog danced around them, then raced to the front door and sat there, tongue lolling, tail thumping the wooden planks of the porch.

The beam of Miss-Engaged-a-Couple-of-Times's flashlight wavered on the ground as Jake stepped up onto the narrow porch and opened the door. He glanced down at her.

She looked like a drowned kitten as she lifted her eyes to his and pushed dripping strands of hair off her face. "What?"

"After you." Jake indicated the battered front door.

"Oh, yeah, thanks."

She pushed it open, standing so close he could smell her evening fire on her skin. And a subtle, soft female fragrance he didn't want to notice. With her blond hair, dark with rain, molded against her skull, he could see the tips of her small pink ears through the wet strands. The green of her jacket was black with moisture, her jeans were soaked, and she was shivering.

He prepared for her litany of complaints once they got inside. So far she hadn't bitched once, but that didn't mean she wasn't going to.

"Nice security system you have." She glanced around as she stepped inside. "No lock?"

"Anyone who comes up here and needs to use the cabin would break in. This way I get to keep my front door." If it looked like a cabin and smelled like a cabin . . .

"Be it ever so crumble, there's no place like home?"

He stepped around her and struck a match, lighting an old-fashioned hurricane lamp on the dusty table behind the couch. Duchess dashed behind the counter separating kitchen from living area, making herself right at home. Her nails clicked on the bare pine floor. Marnie saw her ears swivel as she nosed a cupboard in the kitchen.

"Well, apparently she knows where the food is." Marnie slid the straps of her backpack off her shoulders but hung on to it while debating whether to remove her soaked jacket. The cottage was frigid. She gave a massive shudder as she glanced around.

"This is . . . nice."

The large single room was almost bare, just the essentials, and none too clean. A large, grimy, maybe-green tweed couch, a few sooty hurricane lamps, an empty fireplace, and a couple of scarred, banged-up tables. Roller shades, no drapes. No carpet. No pictures. A few leaves and pine needles. A lot of spiderwebs, dust, and mud.

In the far corner a swaybacked single bed pushed up against the wood-paneled wall was spread with an old army blanket and a pillow with no slip. Just looking at the place made her itch.

She sneezed, clutching her wet backpack to her chest. "I appreciate your coming to get me," she said politely. He hadn't done it graciously, but he *had* done it. It wasn't the Hilton. But it was shelter.

She wasn't a crier, but a good weep might relieve some of this pressure she felt right now. It had been an emotional month, culminating in a hellish night. She hadn't shed a tear since Grammy had died. The loss had been too great, the sadness too deep. But now she felt the pressure of those gallons of tears like a tightening tourniquet in her chest.

"If you could spare a couple of towels so I can dry off, I'd be happy to borrow the couch and get a couple of hours' sleep. As soon as it stops raining I'll be out of your hair."

He narrowed his eyes. "You should take a hot shower first. I'll find you something dry to put on and then we'll talk."

"A shower? Oh, *yes*. God, I'd kiss your feet for a hot shower."

His boot heels snapped across the floor toward the bed. The doors of the closet almost ripped off in his massive hand as he yanked them open. "I don't want you kissing anything," he mumbled under his breath. Doors slammed.

He marched back to her side. "Here." He shoved an armful of threadbare, musty-smelling towels into her arms.

Ookay. "Thanks."

"I'll turn the shower on. Takes a while for the water to heat." He yanked off his own wet jacket, revealing a black T-shirt stretched over an impressive chest, and tossed the coat onto the counter. Pulling open another door at the back of the room, he disappeared inside. The door slammed behind him.

"Nice boyfriend you have there, girl," she told Duchess. Marnie threw the towels and pack on the couch, removed her own waterlogged jacket, and laid it beside his. She heard water running, then a muffled male oath.

Marnie bit back a grin. "What a guy. He's showering first and using up all that nasty cold water. Hey." she rubbed Duchess's ears. "Maybe your prince isn't a frog after all. Whadyaknow?"

Taking off her shoes, she examined her wet, muddy socks, then stripped them off and set everything outside the bathroom door to clean after she'd showered. Barefoot and shivering, she inspected the stone fireplace. Wood? "Check."

Spiders? "Ugh. Check."

Newspaper? "Check."

Matches? "Check."

"Flue open? Check." With a steady blaze in the grate to start warming up the room, her thoughts turned to food. Lots of it.

Marnie walked around the end of the counter and reached over her dog, who lay with her nose to the crack of what Marnie presumed was the pantry door.

"You have to move, Your Majesty. I can't open the . . . Thank you." She opened the narrow doors. "Bingo."

Four feet wide and only about eight inches deep, it had

ceiling-to-floor shelves and was fully stocked with canned goods—about a hundred cans of chicken noodle soup and what looked like two hundred cans of chili. "Bet he likes chicken noodle and chili, huh?" Marnie said dryly.

The shower turned off.

Her bare toes curled against the dusty pine floor.

He was naked in there.

Oh, my God. She was alone in a mountain cabin, miles from anywhere, with a naked stranger.

She wasn't sure she was ready for quite this much adventure. "And I don't even know his name," she finished aloud as he stepped into the room wearing dry jeans and a black sweatshirt, his long hair slicked back. Steam surrounded him like the smoke from Dante's furnace. Her heart did a double thump. He'd shaved. He was gorgeous.

Apparently it wasn't necessary for her to be ready.

"Jake Dolan." He glanced down at the cans she held. "Calisthenics or weapons?"

"Breakfast." She hefted the cans. "You seem to be out of bacon and eggs."

"You're turning an interesting shade of blue." He lifted a massive hand. "Here. I'll take care of the food."

Marnie tossed the cans. He caught both in one hand.

"Water's hot. Clothes on the sink."

"Terrific, thanks."

She walked into the bathroom and was about to close the door when she remembered she'd forgotten the towels and turned back—just in time to see her host rummaging through her backpack.

In three strides Marnie was at his side. He gave her a mild look as she snatched the canvas bag out of his hands.

"Excuse me," she said with exaggerated politeness, "but I believe this is mine."

"Ownership wasn't in dispute. Just who the owner *is*."

"You must run in very strange circles," Marnie told him, clutching the bag to her chest like a Victorian maiden. "Once I'm introduced to someone, I usually tend to believe they are who they say they are. What were you looking for? Picture ID?"

"Driver's license or social security card."

"Since I don't have either in here, you'll just have to take my word for it that I am who I say I am."

"I never take anyone's word about anything," he told her flatly, stuffing his hands deep into his pockets.

What a strange guy. "That must get old in a hurry. You need a better quality of friends."

He had no comment to that one.

"If you shiver any harder, you're going to break in half. Go shower." He jerked his chin toward the open bathroom door.

She stared wide-eyed at his clean-shaven neck a second too long before bolting.

Someone had tried to cut Jake Dolan's throat.

And done a lousy job of it.

The bathroom was steamy, hot, and smelled of pine soap. Marnie leaned against the door, eyes closed, the backpack dangling from her limp fingers.

Oh, my God.

The thin white scar on his throat loomed to gigantic proportions in her mind's eye. If the light hadn't caught the shiny sliver of a curved line at the base of his throat just so, she probably wouldn't have seen it. But now she had.

She slid to the floor, sick to her stomach, and buried her face on her knees. Who would do such a thing? Why? How dare they?

The race of indignation and fury she felt on his behalf shocked her. Marnie snorted back a laugh of mockery. If someone had gotten that close to Jake Dolan and Jake was alive to show off the scar, then the other guy was probably stone dead.

"Hey! You alive in there?"

She got to her feet. "I'm taking a while to defrost."

"Turn on the water and lock the door," he told her irritably.

It bugged her that she had to be reminded. She snicked the old-fashioned key in the lock. Cranking on the shower, she stripped quickly, then stepped into the narrow, rust-stained metal stall. She groaned as the hot water hit her cold skin. Heaven.

Adrenaline leaked out of her as she leaned her head against the cool wall. The water poured over her head and shoulders, taking away the outer chill but leaving her still with a gaping hole of loss inside. She stayed as she was, eyes tightly closed, as the events of the last few hours replayed in her mind.

Marnie pressed her fist against her mouth. She'd wanted more time in Grammy's cottage. More time to feel close to her grandmother before she was forced to acknowledge that she was gone forever.

Tears fought for release in her throat, and her chest ached with the desperate need to cry. She wanted to cry, *needed* to cry, but her eyes remained stubbornly dry and the pressure in her chest expanded painfully. She wanted to lay her head in Grammy's lap, as she had done so many times in her life. She yearned unbearably to feel her grandmother's gentle hand stroking her hair. The pain was like a physical entity. A black hole of sorrow too deep to traverse alone.

Yet here she was, really on her own for the first time in her life. Marnie lifted her head and rubbed the hollow ache behind her breastbone. Alone and doing a crummy job of it so far.

The water had gone from hot to warm, and she hurriedly washed and shampooed. There was no comfort to be found in the small shower stall.

By the time she got out, she was warm all the way through to her bones. And she remembered she'd again forgotten to bring in the towels. Darn.

She grimaced and looked around. Should she call out to him? Let in cold air? Have him see her naked?

The idea was dangerously appealing.

Marnie looked longingly at the bundle of clothing he'd left for her on the counter next to the rusted sink. Then at the damp navy blue towel hanging over the towel rack beside the metal shower stall.

He couldn't have cooties after showering, could he? If she stood around thinking about it much longer, the hot shower would have been a waste of time. She dried off with his towel. It smelled of fresh air and pine soap and wasn't too damp. She closed her eyes, imagining that the rasp of the Jake-scented towel was his callused hands skimming her damp skin.

Perhaps the shock of having a tree almost kill her had turned her last few brain cells to mush, she thought wryly, opening her eyes and hastily drying off. He was only a man. And a belligerent, nosy one at that.

He'd left black fleece sweatpants and a red fleece top, which was a good thing, as there was nothing to wear in her pack. His top came to her knees, and the pants bagged around her ankles. She stared at herself in the fly-speckled mirror over the sink.

What a fashion statement. Her hair sprang up around her face in curlicue tendrils. Her face was I'm-terrified-my-grandmother's-house-almost-crushed-me-to-death pale, but at least she was warm.

She looked around. What was wrong with this picture?

The bathroom was small, utilitarian, no frills. A toilet, a pedestal sink, and the shower stall. No cabinets, no closets, no drawers. She looked down at the clothes she wore.

While the clothing and his towel had all been here when she'd entered the bathroom, Jake Dolan had *not* taken them in with him.

He'd entered empty-handed.

Where had they come from?

She looked like an angel.

Or the devil in disguise.

Jake dragged his gaze away from rosy cheeks and big blue eyes and focused instead on the unopened bottle of hundred-year-old Scotch sitting on the counter. Same difference. Both screwed with his head and tested his willpower.

"Thanks for the clothes."

"No problem."

It wasn't too bad with the breakfast bar between them, though he could still smell her. His soap, surely to God, didn't smell like that on him.

"Chili or soup? I made both."

"Either. You choose what you want. I'll have the other." Her face was dewy from the steam.

"I ate earlier." *Judas, I sounded like a—* Jake couldn't think what the hell he sounded like. Either she had to go or he was going to crack open the Scotch. But right now neither was a viable option. His molars ground together.

"Okay, then I'll eat both. I'm starving." She slid onto a stool on the other side of the counter and pushed up the sleeves of his sweatshirt. She looked good in red. An understatement—she looked dynamite in red. Jake realized he was fondling the Scotch bottle and pulled his hand away.

He poured the hot soup from the pan into a chipped coffee mug, the chili into a measuring cup, stuck a spoon in each, and set both in front of her. "Didn't you eat dinner?"

She looked up at him, the spoon up to her mouth. "Sure. But that was hours ago. Besides, this is breakfast. Mmmm. This smells wonderful. Thanks."

Jake watched her lips part and take in the spoon. She closed her eyes in ecstasy. It was only soup. Soup! The spoon slid out, leaving her lips sheened with grease. The spoon dipped back into the hot soup. Man, he'd be dead of petrifaction if she didn't hurry the hell up and finish eating.

"Tell me again what you're doing here at this time of year."

She glanced up with a frown. "I told you. My grammy died about a month ago, and I wanted to see her cottage before my brothers smashed it to pieces. I needed a quiet place to think. I thought I could do two things at once." She spooned soup into her mouth, her eyes misty.

"Think about what?"

"My life."

"Why?"

"Why what? Think about my life? Because I need to make some changes. Instead of jumping in feet first, as I have a tendency to do, I want to give it some serious deliberation. What are *you* doing up here?"

"What's your social security number?"

He was dead serious.

She laughed. "You must be a hoot at parties."

"I don't go to parties. Number?"

Still smiling, she shook her head and ladled more soup into her mouth.

"I'm less than amused at your intrusion, Miss Wright. Give me your social security number, or go back outside and fend for yourself."

"Get real. I'm not giving some strange guy my social security number, even if he *does* let me use his shower and feeds me. I told you who I am. I'll leave you a couple of bucks for the food Duchess and I have eaten, and then get going. You can growl at yourself for the rest of the weekend."

She sounded confident until Jake noticed the rapid, nervous throb at the base of her throat.

Crap.

"You might as well stick around until the weather lets up." He gave her a baleful glance. "I put clean sheets on the bed while you showered."

He could hear the woman *breathing*. She swallowed. Jake watched her throat move, his fingers flexed around the base of the bottle.

"Oh. Thanks." She eyed him a little more warily than she had before. "But I'll be just fine on the couch for a couple of hours. It's much too short for you."

He had no intention of sleeping. She was bad enough with his eyes open. "Suit yourself. I'll get you some blankets."

He wasn't going to fight over the damn bed. It was a single, sagged on the left, and hadn't been slept in since before he'd bought it in a thrift shop five years ago. He thought of the wide, firm, California king twenty feet below the soles of his boots and bit back an oath imagining her on it. Naked. Willing.

The dog nudged his arm and gazed up at him with soulful puppy eyes. *Damn.*

"You hungry again?" he demanded gruffly. The dog had shared a four-pound steak and french fries, then polished off almost a whole bag of frozen oatmeal-raisin cookies last night before Jake had managed to get rid of her.

Marnie pushed the empty mug aside and started on the chili. "Don't give her the chili," she warned.

"She doesn't like chili?" Jake asked, opening the pantry door and looking at his guest over his shoulder. He knew damn well the hound would eat anything put in front of her.

Duchess protested, eyes going hopefully from Jake to Marnie and back to Jake.

"I know you do." Marnie gave Duchess a reproving glance. She looked back at Jake. "She loves chili. I'm just not sleeping in the same room if she eats it."

"Chicken soup for the beast, then." Jake removed two cans, looked at the dog, then removed two more.

"I can do that." Marnie came around the counter. Jake backed up a step. She advanced, hands outstretched for the cans. He retreated two more steps.

She frowned. "Are you okay?"

"Fine. Here." He thrust the cans at her and maneuvered himself around her and out of the narrow kitchen. "I'll find you a couple of blank—"

A phone rang.

They looked at each other. "Must be yours," he said shortly. His was on another level and couldn't be heard up here.

The phone continued ringing. "Could you hand me my— Thanks."

She took the phone out of the backpack and flipped it open. "Hi." She looked at him and mouthed, "Sorry. It's—" She pointed to her bare wrist and looked at him.

"Seven-fifteen," he said quietly.

"Dad. It's only seven-fifteen. Why are you calling m— Yes. Of course you can. No, I'm wide awake." She rolled her eyes. Jake tried to make his feet move to find those blankets. He stood rooted to the spot. The love she had for her father was brilliantly obvious. Even her exasperation at being called so early couldn't disguise that this was an often-repeated conversation.

"Really? The sun's been shining, and it's beautiful up here." Rain drummed its steady beat on the windows. "Well, I'll keep a close watch in case those clouds come this way. But it doesn't look like— Yes, I know the bridge goes out if it r— No, I'm not, actually. There's a nice family staying in another cottage close by." Pause. "A mom. A dad. Three little kids. . . . No, no cold air comes in. . . . Yes, it is surprising after all these years. They knew how to build things to last in those days."

She listened, a faraway look in her eyes. "I promise, I'm just fine. I'll call you when I get home on Monday, okay?" She closed her eyes tightly, listening to what her father was saying on the other end of the phone. The tip of her nose turned pink.

Hell. Is she going to cry?

"Love you, too, Daddy. Bye."

"So." Jake rested his hip on the counter as she turned off the phone and set it down on the counter. "Who am I? The mom, the dad, or one of the three kids?"

"He worries."

"Good thing the sun's shining so brightly then, isn't it?" He looked out the window. The rain was still coming down in torrents.

Shit.

He might as well get started on the damn ark now.

Chapter Three

"And for your information," Jake told her, "this is a *cabin*, not a *cottage*."

Ookay.

Marnie rolled her eyes and followed his line of sight. Rain ad infinitum. "You know, it doesn't look like it's going to stop soon. There doesn't seem like much point in waiting." His dark blue eyes narrowed on her face. Why did she feel as though he could read her mind?

"There's another bridge a little farther upriver," she offered. "That one doesn't usually flood. I know the way. I think if I left now I could—"

"I've already rescued you once today," he said tautly. "I'm not going out again. Stay put. Sleep. Don't sleep. Do whatever you want."

"I want to—" She broke off and shook her head, "—stop being ridiculous," she finished with a sigh. "You're right. I'll wait it out." Although he was standing at least six feet from her, she felt crowded. Marnie grabbed up the wet backpack. "I'll put my things in front of the fire to dry, then."

Draping her jeans, sweatshirt, and wet socks over one of the bar stools, she dragged it closer to the leaping fire. That took all of seven seconds. The wet underwear she left in the bottom of the bag. She dusted off her hands. "I'd kill for a cup of coffee." She turned around to find him still leaning against the counter watching her.

"It's probably stale."

Wonderful. Stuck in the Great Flood with Mr. Tall-and-Not-So-Sweet.

"No problem, as long as it's hot."

Marnie walked past him to get into the kitchen. He didn't move, other than his mouth tightening, as she brushed past. The little hairs on her arm tingled. It was a good thing she was leaving soon. She was far too physically attracted to him. Erk! Talk about bad timing. "Do we have a coffeepot?"

"Under the sink."

Absolutely, why hadn't she thought of that?

She found the Mr. Coffee where normal people kept their trash and cleaning supplies. It was full of cobwebs and dead brown things. She grimaced, wrestled the top off, spritzed dishwashing liquid into it, then filled it with scalding hot water and dropped the grungy lid into the pot to soak.

"You've got some kind of power for your appliances. How come you don't have real lights? And heat?"

"Because I don't. That's why."

She shot him a glance, then continued opening and closing cabinets, looking for the coffee. Soup and chili—that was it.

After he'd watched her go through every single cabinet and drawer, he said flatly, "In the freezer."

Marnie tugged open the small upper door to the freezer. Even the air in there smelled stale. She took out a large can of coffee, leaving several foil-wrapped packages of mystery meat behind. "How long have you been up here?" she asked curiously.

"Why?"

"Because unless you've figured out how to get take-out delivered, I'm curious what you've been eating."

"Why?"

He obviously didn't want her here. Even more obvious, the man was used to being alone. The men she'd briefly been engaged to had both been sociable. They had also been handsome. While Jake Dolan had an interesting face, he wasn't handsome by any stretch of the imagination. His face showed character, the physical and psychological scars of life. He was, in fact, exactly the kind of man a smart woman avoided at all cost. Bossy. Opinionated. A misogynist.

With that scowl he looked downright intimidating. Yet his

appearance accelerated her heartbeat, which was rather baffling. What on earth were the gods thinking to toss a man like this at her now of all times? There was some weird kind of chemistry going on between them, something she'd never encountered with any other man. Marnie cocked her head. Why him? Why now?

When he looked at her, her skin tingled, and she felt giddy. Her heart beat faster. The room was icy, yet her skin felt warm. Colors seemed brighter, and his raspy voice seemed to stroke her skin, making the little hairs on her arms stand up.

Oh, boy. I've lost it for sure. Get a grip, she told herself sternly. *Think about something else. Anything else.*

"So," she asked in desperation, "are you on vacation?"

"Do you have an off button?"

Unoffended, she shrugged. "How do you get to know someone if you don't ask questions?"

The attraction between them must be a pheromone thing, she decided. Something chemical. *Something that better quit it before I make a complete fool of myself.*

"Want to hear what I know about you without asking questions?"

"Sure." She found a large, green plastic ashtray under the sink and washed it. Then opened the four cans of soup and used the ashtray as a bowl for Duchess.

"You're a natural blonde. Your hair gets lighter in the summer. You have a trust fund you don't use. You manage, barely, on your income, and run out of money before the end of the month because you're always giving handouts. You live in a house, not an apartment. Bold colors. Clean lines. Original art. No clutter."

"I'm impressed." And delighted he'd been thinking about her.

"You're spoiled rotten. Used to getting your own way. Can't cook worth a damn—"

"Beep. Wrong. I'm a superior chef." She smiled at him sweetly, then tilted her head. "Now I'll give it a try. Hmmm. Let's see, you're a loner. Only child?" He nodded. "See, I'm good at this, too. Let's see . . . What do you do for a living? I bet it has something to do with radio."

He looked blank. "Radio?"

"You have an incredibly sexy voice." She gazed into his eyes.

He looked back steadily. Inscrutably. "I had a little trouble with my vocal cords a while back. My voice is ruined."

Her stomach flipped, and she kept her eyes away from the scar on his neck with difficulty. She swallowed a lump in her own throat and said huskily, "I like it. It makes me—"

One dark brow rose. "Makes you what?"

Hot. Shivery. Turned on.

"Nothing."

Although it wasn't a character trait of which she was particularly proud, she often spoke without thinking. At the rate she was going, he'd toss her back out in the rain.

"That's if you *do* work, of course," she continued blithely. "You could be a career criminal, on the lam from the law, hiding out up here in the mountains waiting for the heat to die down. Am I getting warm?"

"I thought this was a monologue."

"Funny man. Knowing what someone does for a living can tell you quite a lot about the person, that's all."

"Want to see a credit report?"

She gave him a snotty look. "Do you *like* what you do? Whatever that might be," she added under her breath.

"Haven't thought about it one way or the other."

"Why don't you quit, then?"

"I'm thinking about it. You work?"

"I worked all the way through high school. My dad insisted I learn the value of a dollar." She was used to people thinking that since she was a rich Wright, she didn't need gainful employment. "I've worked for the same computer company for almost eight years."

"I thought you were an artist." He sounded suspicious.

"Yes, well, at the moment, one pays my rent and the other doesn't. Admittedly it's nepotism. I work for my father—Wright Computers? But I assure you I *do* work. He's real big on sowing before one reaps. I started sowing as a programmer before I was out of college. One of these days I'm going to reap and do illustrating full time. That's one of the things I'm here to think about." Go to Paris, wear black, and look mysterious. She smiled.

"Fiancé number three?"

Marnie frowned. "What does that— Oh. Nope. One doesn't have anything to do with the other. No more engagements. I'll see, I'll conquer, eventually I'll marry."

"Set your sights on the poor sap yet?"

She scanned his face and gave a noncommittal shrug.

For years she'd convinced herself that what she'd wanted was too ephemeral, too storybook to be real. She'd analyzed all her relationships to death and found both the men and herself lacking.

She'd never been remotely aggressive. Never pursued a man. Never wanted to. Probably because, until now, she'd just never felt strongly enough.

Whatever the reason, she certainly felt strongly enough now.

When she'd come here to make life-altering decisions, she hadn't thought that her grand adventure was already under way.

She'd never been this physically attracted to any man.

Never. Not even close.

What was it about this abrasive man that made her heart speed up and her breasts ache with longing? What was it about him that made her hungry for sensations she hadn't known she was missing? What was it about him that made her want to cast caution to the winds and explore all that he was?

He was a puzzle. An enigma. She shouldn't be so intrigued, but she was. Everything about Jake Dolan intrigued and, heaven help her, turned her on. The way he looked. The way he talked. The way he smelled, and walked, and scowled. The whole package intrigued and tantalized her.

Marnie stared at his mouth and ached to taste him. She looked at his long hair and longed to bury her fingers in the silken strands. She wanted to touch his broad chest and feel his arms around her. She wanted to—

He scowled. "Why are you looking at me like that?"

"Like what?" she asked innocently.

"Like I'm a food product."

Oh, Marnie wanted to taste him, all right. "Hmmm."

His scowl deepened. "That's not an answer. That's a . . ."

"A what?"

"An irritant."

"What else do you think you know about me?" Marnie challenged softly, wanting to touch him so badly she ached. She stayed where she was, but it was as though a magnetic force field drew them closer and closer.

She felt bold, daring, and giddy with want.

Poor Jake was struggling like the fish on the end of a hook. But he was in the force field, too.

"Are you really who you say you are?" he asked, so roughly she barely understood the words.

She nodded. "Marnie Christine Wright. Twenty-seven-year-old computer geek." She felt like a butterfly emerging from her chrysalis. Perhaps too fast. Perhaps too close to a flame for safety. But she felt her wings begin to unfurl as he watched her with hot eyes.

"You like the outdoors," he continued, sounding strained as he assiduously watched her mouth. Thank God he couldn't read her mind.

"Music." His voice got hoarser.

She wondered what his skin felt like. "I sleep naked," she blurted out, for reasons she didn't bother contemplating.

His eyes glazed. "Naked?"

She nodded, her mouth too dry to speak. She wondered what he would do if she went up to him, stood on tiptoe, and planted a long wet one on him. Her heart beat faster. For several moments they stared at each other. Blindly she placed the frozen coffee can down on the counter beside her.

Her eyes moved from his dark hair, drying now against his neck, to his razor-sharp blue eyes and down to his mouth. And locked there. She couldn't help it. Jake Dolan had the most succulent, inviting mouth she'd ever laid eyes on.

Duchess rose from her spot near the pantry and came to

lean against her hip. She braced herself for the animal's weight but remained immobile, watching Jake watch her.

Mouth dry, palms damp, heart pounding, she licked her lower lip, then sucked it between her teeth. And knew exactly what it did to him by the way a muscle tightened in his lean jaw and his pupils dilated.

Duchess ambled back to her place of observation on the floor.

Marnie's pulse skittered as Jake's eyes heated. He felt it, too. "I think," she whispered, "we're in big trouble here."

It took him a lifetime to say roughly, "You aren't my type."

"Yes, I am."

"No." It was barely a croak. "You are not."

Marnie stepped forward. He crossed his arms over his massive chest. She could *feel* his eyes moving over her mouth. Her lips tingled. She held his gaze as she moved closer.

"Can't stand blondes."

"I'll dye my hair."

"You're too short."

Not when we're both lying down. "I'll wear heels."

He squeezed his eyes shut as if in pain. "Dirty pool."

Marnie reached out and touched his forearm, her desire for this man vast and unfathomable. She didn't try to understand. It just was.

Electricity shot up through her fingertips into her chest. Her heart thumped into a heavier, harder rhythm. Hot blood coursed through her veins with the urgency of a pounding, rushing river. Current arced to every extremity, then pooled hot and thick, low in her belly.

He opened smoky, unreadable eyes, his expression closed. Arms folded, Jake Dolan stood absolutely rigid under her tactile exploration. Color darkened his high cheekbones. A small muscle jerked in his jaw.

Stubborn man.

Feeling bold and reckless, Marnie ran her hands over the taut muscle of his forearms. Crisp dark hair tantalized her fingertips. His skin felt sizzling hot to her touch; his life force pulsed beneath the surface.

She stood on her tiptoes and slid her arms around his neck. With his arms folded, his elbows jabbed into her chest. For a moment she thought he was going to push her away.

She stiffened, tightening her fingers instinctively in his long hair. "One kiss," she begged, her voice husky, heated, hungry. "If it's lousy, we'll call it quits."

There was a long pause. "This is a cosmic joke," he managed grimly. "It *won't* be lousy."

With agonizing slowness Jake unfolded his arms. His massive hands moved with reluctance to palm her shoulders, then gingerly slid down her back to cup her behind. Marnie closed her eyes in relief as he pressed her body against his. His groan vibrated through her bones.

Oh, God. Liquid heat shimmered through her veins. She wrapped one leg around his to pull him even closer. His thigh muscle flexed and bunched against her, and she almost climbed his body to get their mouths and body parts aligned correctly. She wanted his sexy mouth on her.

All over her.

She wanted his big hands on her.

All over her.

She wanted his large body pinning her to the thin mattress across the room, moving with intensity and heat until neither of them could move.

Dizziness rocked her as strong hands lifted her in one easy movement. She clung to his neck, then found herself perched on the edge of the breakfast bar, her knees straddling his hips. The Formica felt cold under her behind. His erection pressed hot and eager against the juncture of her thighs through the soft fleece sweatpants. She wrapped her legs around his waist and pulled him closer.

Without giving her time to think, Jake captured her mouth in a kiss so deep, so carnal, she forgot to breathe. She made a sound, a soft murmur of surrender, and slid her tongue against his, pushing him for more, terrified he'd refuse, scared out of her wits that he'd accept.

The pounding of the rain on the roof became the thick, syrupy throb of her heartbeat. The scent of the fire became the rich scent of Jake's skin. She tasted his need on her tongue, his desire in the fierce grip of his fingers on her bottom.

Her skin was on fire. Her lips tingled. She couldn't seem to get close enough. She *had* to feel his bare skin, and yanked up the hem of his sweatshirt with determined hands.

She ran her palms over his chest. Hot satin, overlaid with crisp dark hair. Pebble-hard nipples. Rigid stomach muscles jerked in response as her exploration slid lower.

One large hand shifted from her behind to her breast. Her nipples ached. She pressed her chest against his, trapping his hand, making the pressure harder. Unbearable.

He nudged her back a little, just enough. His fingers found her nipple through the fleece. He squeezed to just this side of pain, then captured her cry against his damp neck. Marnie panted. She managed to get the top button of his fly undone and blindly sought the tiny zipper tab.

He shifted. For a few seconds they were separated—just enough time for Marnie to suddenly think: *What on earth am I doing?*

Their eyes met.

For a split second she caught a glimpse of heat in his eyes. Then Jake banked the flame and broke out of her embrace.

Marnie felt a hot blush rise from her toes to her nose.

It took a moment for her eyes to focus and her brain to function. Bewildered, she looked up to find him watching her. His heavy-lidded eyes held a strange desperation as he reached back and unhooked the vice of her ankles from around his waist.

Her legs dropped. Her heels thumped against the cabinet.

Beneath his hawklike gaze she felt stripped bare and vulnerable. He studied her face, seeming to see more than her features. He seemed to delve into her mind, to touch things deep and frightening—parts of herself Marnie was still exploring.

The muscles in his jaw knotted and unknotted. After a moment he stepped back and casually, but with difficulty, adjusted his jeans.

Heat flooded her cheeks. Legs splayed, nipples peaked to

his clinical gaze, she'd never experienced such acute embarrassment in her life. Her breath hitched as she jumped off the counter, tugging her top down and her pants up.

At a loss for words, she half laughed. "I have absolutely no idea what to say." Which was a reasonable start, she guessed. It was rare for her to be speechless. But then, this was a day of firsts.

"I told you you weren't my type." The brass button on his jeans closed like the clasp of a miser's purse. Other than a faint flush on the ridge of his cheekbones and what looked like a painful erection, he seemed totally unaffected by what had just happened.

She stared at him. "Not your t— What do you call what just happened?" Marnie was confused. It was out of character for her to be sexually aggressive. But now that she'd done it, she wasn't sorry.

"What part of 'I don't want you' didn't you understand?"

He'd wanted her. He might lie about it, but his body had been honest. He was as hard as petrified wood.

"Then what"—she pointed—"is *that*?"

He ignored the bulge in his jeans. "Just because I have it doesn't mean I intend to use it."

Marnie stepped forward and touched his arm. He jerked away from her as if she'd used a cattle prod.

"Was it something I said?" she asked quietly, dropping her hand to her side. "Look, I have a tendency to sort of speak without running the words through my brain first. But I know I didn't give out mixed signals just now. I *wanted* to make love with you. It was very good. No, darn it, it was *excellent*. So if you have some sort of medical condition, let's talk about i—"

He moved backward, almost tripping over Duchess sprawled on the floor. The dog rose to hover anxiously between them. Jake's eyes turned as he said, "I do *not* have a medical condition."

Marnie backed up—mentally as well as physically. Her hip bumped the counter. "Good."

He scowled and swore under his breath.

"That *is* good, isn't it?" she asked tentatively.

He had a cowlick in his hair. Right in front. It was noticeable only when he repeatedly raked his fingers through the long strands, as he was doing now. It made him look like a disgruntled little boy. And so sexy, she wanted to lick him all over.

"I don't see anything good about it. Do you always make a habit of screwing guys you've just met?" he asked coldly.

"Actually, no," Marnie said just as coolly. "I don't. But in this instance I thought the attraction was mutual. And we didn't screw, so your virtue is safe." *For the moment.*

"Since you arrived," he said grimly, stabbing his fingertips into the front pocket of his jeans, "my weekend has gone from bad to worse. I don't see it improving anytime soon."

"I wasn't expecting a lifetime commitment, you know." She refused to squirm under his scowling scrutiny. How could she so desperately want a man she didn't even know? A man who refused to acknowledge he wanted her right back?

There was this weird chemical thing going on that she had never experienced in her life. Her chemicals wanted his chemicals, and there was no denying it. Pheromones still floated thick in the air between them. She touched her swollen mouth, still tasting him on her tongue.

"I'm very attracted to you. I thought— Well, never mind. Why is it men can have sex whenever they like, but a woman has to wait to be asked?"

She'd wanted to make some life-changing decisions, Marnie though wryly. Never in her wildest imagination would she have imagined she'd be taking a skydive without a parachute.

Jake opened his mouth. Closed it. Combed back his hair with ten stiff fingers and glared at her. "You're probably a screamer."

"Hmmm." She planned on doing plenty more than a little yelling—as soon as she figured out just what his problem was. She knew she had a tendency to take bigger bites than she could chew. It came from having missed out on so much as a kid.

She was greedy. She wanted to experience everything. *Now.* But this time she'd shocked herself.

Casually she rolled up her sleeves and tested the temperature of the water in the sink with one finger.

Duchess moved out of Jake's way as he backed up.

Hmmm, backing away some more. She'd once tamed a horse the same way. A little advance. A little retreat.

From the corner of her eye she observed his boots shift again slightly. "Man, you have big feet," she said without thinking.

She met his glare and blushed, then closed her eyes briefly before plunging her hands into the water in the sink and swishing a cloth inside the carafe.

"The rain's let up some. I'll take you farther upriver. You might still be able to cross there."

Marnie glanced out the window. If anything, it was raining harder than it had earlier. The air looked wet enough to swim through. She emptied the water from the coffeepot and set it carefully on the counter beside the sink, then dried her hands on her pants for lack of a towel and faced him.

"Look, I'm a great believer in discussing things to clear the air. As kids, we weren't allowed to go to bed on an argument. Not that you and I argued, but—never mind. Okay, I'll go first. I *wanted* you to—"

"I've got some rain gear somewhere. I'd better—"

"—make love to me."

"—find it. It'll take a couple of hours to climb up there and I want to get start—"

"You wanted me, too," Marnie interrupted again, militant now. "So what happened?"

He turned to face her fully. Eyes cold, mouth grim. "Nothing *happened*. Haven't you ever met a man who wasn't turned on by you?"

Marnie fisted her hands on her hips, eyes narrowed. "Yes, of course. There have been a zillion men not turned on by me. You, however, were not one of them."

"For all your experience, you have a thing or two to learn about men."

"Teach me, then."

He paled. "Not in this lifetime." His flinty gaze locked on her mouth.

"Chicken," she taunted softly.

His lips thinned. "The last time someone like you tried to seduce me I was in a hospital bed. She wore something soft and seductive and smelled like sin. The difference was, *she* was sophisticated and experienced and knew the score." He gave her a hard look. "She learned, to her regret, that I'm not a man to play games with."

"So what are you saying?" Marnie asked, resisting telling him she wasn't playing games at all. "You won't seduce me unless I wear something slinky and pour on the French perfume and you're in a hospital bed? It can be arranged."

"Men don't get turned on by aggressive women."

"Hmmm." Marnie bit the inside of her lip. "Is that so?"

"Yes."

"Okay. I'll try to remember not to be so aggressive next time. Is that it?"

He came up to the other side of the counter, a large, threatening, intimidating male. He rested enormous hands on the Formica and leaned forward to glare at her.

"No. That's *not* it. I hardly see the point in enlightening you, but here it is. First, there won't *be* a next time. Second, we don't know each other. Third, you'll be gone soon. Get it? Good."

"Ah."

"What does *that* mean?"

She looked at him innocently, eyes wide, and shrugged.

He closed his eyes as if in pain. Her dad and brothers frequently wore the same expression. She kept her features guileless.

"Do you think I could have some coffee before you throw me out into the cold, rainy night?"

"It's morning."

Grouch. She started to fill the basket with stale grounds and glanced at him over her shoulder. "And you don't need to go with me. I've been roaming this side of the mountain for years. I know the way to the other bridge perfectly well. There's no point in both of us getting cold and wet again, is there?"

His eyes were slits of annoyance. "I *said* I'd take you."

She poured water into the well, then set the carafe in its slot and turned the coffeemaker on. "No, thanks. I seem to do better when you're not around."

He scowled. The skin over his cheekbones stretched taut. "What does that mean?"

"I'm still hungry. Want some chili?"

"No." Frustration ate at him like a canker.

Her dog rose and ambled over to her side. The dog got its ears fondled. Jake bit back a nasty crack. He was jealous of her pet. Unfortunately he was now intimately acquainted with the feel of those slender fingers. On him. All over him. He wanted more. He wanted it all.

He was a fool.

It wasn't her fault she was desirable. It wasn't her concern he couldn't have her. Would never have her. He'd made the rules years ago. No more blondes.

For a few glorious, earth-shattering minutes, he'd forgotten and allowed his hunger for her to eclipse reason. She'd been perfect in his arms, everything he dreamed a woman could be.

His dream and his nightmare.

Almost too late he'd remembered Dolan's First Law of Survival.

He'd remembered about a second before he would have plunged himself into the hot wet center of her. He'd had to use considerable willpower and tooth-grinding control to refuse her offer.

Which was why he stayed the hell away from her type. Far away. He had a negative history with fluffy blondes. Six years ago one had put paid to that craving. The ingredients had been a South American jungle, an out-of-place blond "journalist," and a sharp knife. He'd found out too late that the fragile blonde belonged to the leader of the particular little band of terrorists Jake was attempting to round up.

She'd been sent to distract him.

She'd been good. Damn good.

He'd fallen for the bait like a rank amateur. The terrorists had covered their tracks and split while he nursed his bruised balls and sliced trachea. His best friend had died saving his life.

Jake had never stopped looking for the son of a bitch responsible. Every insertion, every operation, Jake kept his eyes and ears open for news of Dancer or information of a sighting.

He hadn't believed much in love before Soledad.

His belief in it after her was nonexistent.

The memory had put him off soft, delicate little blondes for life. It had done a number on his general trust indicator, too. To hell with logic—in his mind, blondes had become synonymous with pain, mayhem, and death.

And while Jake liked sex as much as the next man, he could control his urges until the appropriate time and place with the appropriate woman. Someone a hell of a lot less dangerous to his equilibrium than this deliciously scented time bomb.

"You sure?" Marnie asked, blue eyes heavy-lidded and sexy as sin. Her sweet little nipples peaked seductively under red fleece.

"Damn straight I'm sure," he bit out a second before he realized she was referring to the chili she'd offered, not listening in on his mental trip down memory lane. Her skin looked as soft as it felt. Petal soft and silky, scented with the aphrodisiac fragrance of her arousal. He could still smell it.

Sexual frustration clawed at his gut. He had several choices: use the booze to interrupt the circuit from his brain to his groin, take care of the problem himself, or get the hell away from her as fast as possible.

"I'm going out."

"Ookay."

Duchess danced around the counter, tail wagging. She sat before him, head cocked, eyes alert. She whined, seeming to be saying, *Poor sap*. Which was a fitting end to the last few miserable hours. Jake leaned down to snag his jacket from the floor. They'd pushed it off the counter when they'd been grappling.

He shook his head. *Dumb bastard.*

"Make yourself at home," he said sourly, dragging on his damp jacket, trying not to trip over her dog. There wasn't anything Marnie could find while he was gone that he didn't want any stranger to discover. He was a careful and methodical man. There was no margin for error in his line of work.

Of any kind.

Skeptical eyes grazed the cottage. "Yeah, right." She poured coffee into another chipped cup, took a sip, and shuddered in distaste. Then she glanced back at him. "See ya."

Jake slammed the door behind him and strode into the deluge, her dog prancing at his heels.

Great. Just great.

Chapter Four

It was a good thing Marnie rarely got bored. She set her sketch pad down beside her on the couch and stretched cramped muscles. There was nothing of interest in the cabin. She'd wandered around aimlessly after Jake stormed out. There was no point sleeping now.

How on earth anyone lived without creature comforts, even for an odd weekend, baffled her. Her little house in Sunnyvale was filled with *things*. Mementos of her life. Photos of her family, friends, and places she'd been. The stuff one collected without realizing it.

Jake Dolan's cabin was the clean slate of a man with no past and no future. Despite the dirt, everything about the cabin seemed sterile, scrubbed of character. Sanitized. It looked, Marnie decided, choreographed, like a stage set. Abandoned cabin in the woods. The play was obviously *not* a romance, she thought wryly, glancing at the narrow single bed against the far wall.

During his absence she'd done several intricate, detailed sketches of Jake. Most of them were conjured more from imagination than based on reality. She'd had to do some serious imagining to sketch Jake smiling, laughing, looking out of the pages with love, not just heat, in his eyes. She had a great imagination.

And while this attraction for a dangerous stranger hadn't exactly been in the cards, she wondered at the timing. Marnie pictured Grammy on a fluffy white cloud, chuckling as she manipulated her granddaughter's fate.

It didn't matter how unlikely and illogical her heated response to him had been. The fact of the matter was that she felt *something*. Something she'd never experienced before.

It was more than physical, although God help her, there had been that. Something greater than physical allure called to a part of herself she was still discovering. It was as though by seeing herself through his eyes, she would come to learn who the real Marnie Wright was.

The least the dratted man could have done was stand still and cooperate so she could fully explore the possibilities.

The rain had stopped an hour ago. Jake had been gone for almost three. She didn't need to be hit over the head with a two-by-four to know he didn't want her anywhere near him. And it made no difference that she knew her feelings were irrational. She'd known him for less than twenty-four hours. It was inconceivable she felt so strongly while he felt nothing in return. His lengthy absence made it pretty obvious he wouldn't return to the cabin until she'd left.

Was he out there somewhere, watching, waiting for her to leave? She stood in the middle of his dusty, inhospitable cabin and weighed her choices. Foolishly, her heart wanted her to stay and see what would happen in the next round. Eventually he'd have to come back.

Her brain told her to pack up, put on her coat, and go upriver in the hope the other bridge was passable.

But what about Duchess? Marnie suddenly smiled. Unless Jake planned on kidnapping her dog, he'd be back. They'd have to see each other at least once more.

Her coat had dried in front of the fire. She put it on, wrote a brief note on a page from her sketchbook, and left it propped up on the breakfast bar where he couldn't miss it.

A frigid breeze ruffled Marnie's hair and stung her cheeks. She dug into her pocket for her red knit cap, then pulled it on to cover her cold ears. Leaves and branches swayed and mingled their music with the sound of her Timberlines swooshing through leaves. There'd been no sign of Jake and Duchess along the way.

It didn't take long to walk down to her grandmother's

cottage. Or what was left of it. A hard knot of sadness welled within her chest. She sat on a mossy rock nearby, chin cupped in her hands, and took in the devastation.

The tree didn't look nearly as large by daylight as it had in the dark. Nevertheless, it had crushed the little one-room house. Vision blurred, Marnie bit her lip.

Her grandmother's death in her sleep at the age of eighty-eight had hit her hard, forcing her to question her lifestyle and the choices she'd made.

Grammy's death had been a turning point.

There had been nothing the old woman had been afraid of. Nothing she hadn't dared. Nothing she hadn't ventured. And while Marnie had always considered them kindred spirits, after Grammy's death she'd suddenly had the rude awakening that they weren't alike at all.

She didn't take chances. *She* never risked anything. Her life had fallen into a rut without her being aware of it. She'd always taken the path of least resistance because it was easy and trouble free.

She worked for her father because he'd wanted her close and she didn't want to hurt him. And although her love of drawing and painting fulfilled her, she'd always considered it a hobby.

It was painfully ironic that Grammy had to die before Marnie could at last hear what her grandmother had been trying to tell her.

Live life to the fullest.

The tightness in her chest threatened to double her over. She bent over her knees to press her fists tight against her chest. It hurt to breathe.

"I'm going to do it, Gram. I'm going to do it."

Marnie didn't know how, when, or even what. But God help her, she was going to make her life a life Grammy would have been proud of. Not just for her adored grandmother, but for herself. Because twenty-seven wasn't too old to change.

There was enough of Martha Washburn in her to know there was hope. She wanted life with a capital *L*. She wanted to paint and draw; she wanted to taste excitement and grab life with both hands.

She wanted to *live*, not just exist.

A sob ripped through her.

She wanted it all, everything she'd missed by allowing herself to follow the path of least resistance. By taking the easy way out. By allowing herself to believe other people's reality of who and what she was.

Another choked sob tore through her.

She missed her grandmother. She needed her grandmother. She *wanted* her grandmother.

She and Grammy had shared their love of the outdoors, family, and all things traditional. Maybe they shared the same dash of daring, too.

The landscape blurred as the tears came—heavy and painful, and from so deep the well seemed bottomless.

She didn't try to stop them.

Grammy had been mother and best friend to her all her life. Marnie couldn't imagine life without her. She swallowed a sob, then let them come, one after the other. The tears, falling unchecked, felt hot on her icy cheeks. This was the first time in five weeks she'd been able to cry. The loss had just been too great, too deep. She made up for it now.

She'd always cried easily. A sappy commercial, a baby, or a beautiful sunset could make her misty-eyed. But when she cried for real, it wasn't pretty. She sobbed and hiccuped and blubbered; her nose ran and her face got red and puffy. She was thankful only a squirrel was witness to her outpouring of grief.

She cried long enough to give herself a stuffy nose and swollen eyelids. Feeling slightly better when she finished, she rose and walked around the crushed walls, trailing her fingertips along the wood siding, remembering the laughter, the words of wisdom, the lessons she'd learned inside these four walls. It was almost impossible to continue being sad when the memories were so happy. She said her final goodbye—but just to the place. Grammy would be in her heart forever.

Feeling as though she'd been through some sort of rebirth, Marnie trudged back up the hill.

Returning to Jake's, she considered what her grandmother would have thought about him. Grammy had a soft spot for strays. She would have pulled him into the circle of their home and treated him like one of her boys. Grammy also had a connoisseur's eye for a good-looking male. She would have liked the way Jake's dark hair brushed his broad shoulders; she would have appreciated the wariness of his blue eyes and the length of his legs. She would have liked his gentleness and his strength. She, too, would have seen in his determination to be unfriendly the need to have a friend.

And what would Grammy have thought of me trying to jump his bones? Marnie grimaced at her lack of finesse. Admittedly that had been a little bold for the first time out of the gate. But the physical attraction was there. Even he couldn't deny it.

The reality was Jake Dolan was a little too much man for her right now. She didn't have time to add a sexy male into her equation. Not just yet. She had to figure out who she was to herself before she tried to figure out what she was to a man.

She sighed. Trust her to start her quest with the most difficult challenge of all.

Her breath misted as she trudged back up through the trees. The soft sounds of breeze and leaves soothed her, as they always did. The crisp, piney mountain air filled her lungs. Her muscles pulled pleasantly as she retraced her steps to Jake's cabin.

If he had his way, she'd be gone by nightfall. Probably the best thing for both of them.

But her heart leaped at the thought of seeing him again.

It took only a second to open the front door and look inside to see he and Duchess hadn't returned. Disappointed, she updated her note and closed the front door, then headed in the opposite direction.

A few hours without rain and the river might have subsided enough to cross. She'd check it out, then come back to wait for Duchess. She wasn't leaving the mountain without her.

Marnie grinned. That sounded as good as any other excuse she might come up with. And it was valid.

The rain might have stopped, but by the look of the clouds it was about to return, or maybe snow. She hunched inside her coat, pulling the collar up. Regardless of the weather, she'd rather be outdoors than in, any day. She'd spent enough passive hours indoors to last a lifetime.

The undergrowth was thicker beneath the trees, and snow from several weeks ago had turned into patches of ice in the shady pockets. She scrambled down into the wide, shallow ravine, where the going was considerably easier.

The expanse of water-smooth stones was dry except for the narrow shimmer of water meandering down the center. The snowmelt and rain had collected behind the main dam about a mile upstream. The overflow raced furiously down the parallel tributary about two miles up the mountain. Two footbridges provided access to this side of the mountain.

For the next mile it would be easier to keep to the riverbed, but soon she'd have to climb the bank again and take the route through the trees. The higher she went, the steeper the sides became. Before she got to the towering wall of the lower dam, six stories of vertical cement, she'd cut off into the trees to reach the tributary and the upper bridge.

A thin trickle of water cascaded in a silver ribbon over the sixty-foot drop of the cement retaining wall, fed from a bigger dam higher up the mountain. It had been an unseasonably dry winter, and the upper lake had not been full enough this year to be opened. The lower dam was empty, the ravine dry but for this narrow trickle of water down the middle.

The two rivers ran parallel to the logging road, but that had been closed for more than thirty years, right after the lumber and mining had played out.

Forty minutes later Marnie clambered up onto the half-mile-wide spit of land between the two rivers. It wasn't far to the narrow cement footbridge; she could hear the rushing water.

A strange noise cut off her thoughts. The sound was so out

of place in the pristine outdoors that it took her a moment to identify.

It was the metallic action of a gun being cocked, and was followed immediately by the low rumble of men's voices. They were close. Extremely close.

Instinctively she dropped to the ground. Flat on her stomach, she snaked slowly backward into the thick brush, then ruffled the greenery so she couldn't be seen. She hoped.

Moments later five men dressed in black from head to toe strode past her hiding place. Their clothing was a loose version of a wetsuit, their heads covered with a drape of the same rubbery matte black fabric, making them all appear identical—right down to the long, lethal, matte black knives strapped to their calves, the automatic weapons slung over their shoulders, and the small, snub-nosed pistols in their gloved hands. One man spoke briefly and quietly in a foreign language. Another answered. Then they were eerily quiet.

Was one of them Jake Dolan? Was that why he was in such a hurry to get rid of her?

Either way this did not look good. Not good at all.

Marnie's mouth went dry and her heart started to beat faster as they passed within feet of her hiding place.

The wet leaves and earth soaked the front of her jacket and jeans, but she dared not move. Her eyes burned from trying not to blink. Who were these guys? Survivalists? No. They reminded her of ninjas or something out of a James Bond movie.

They looked like professionals. But professional what?

They moved so stealthily, so quietly, that if she hadn't known exactly where to look, she wouldn't have seen them at all.

Heart pounding in her ears, Marnie waited for the men to disappear from view. But no sooner had the trees swallowed them than another small group followed. Too frightened to breathe, she stayed frozen in place.

Whoever these men were, she was dead certain they had something to do with antisocial Jake Dolan.

* * *

It started to snow. So far just a light dusting, but by the look of the clouds they were in for one mother of a storm. Jake reluctantly headed back. There was a strange hush in the air. No animal sounds, no birds. Even the leaves seemed unnaturally still. He paused to listen. Nothing but the distant whisper of the river. Beside him Duchess stopped as well, ears swiveling.

Jake rested his hand on her large head, his gut sending up a warning flare. "What is it, girl?" he asked softly. "What do you hear?"

Duchess laid her ears back and growled deep in her throat.

"Yeah," Jake agreed grimly, trusting his instincts. "I feel it, too. Go to Marnie, girl. Make sure she's okay." The dog cocked her head, looking at him.

"Yeah, yeah. I'll be right behind you. Go!"

Her boobs were frozen. Marnie grimaced. Her entire front felt numb. It had been, she estimated, a good hour since she'd seen the last man. She flexed her fingers and contemplated the wisdom of standing up. A light dusting of snow coated her clothing and had melted into the knit cap, soaking her hair.

She decided to get up. If she didn't, she'd freeze to death.

She'd just shifted her feet under her when a large, icy hand clamped over her mouth.

Her heart ping-ponged in her chest. *Damn. Too soon.*

She definitely didn't plan on screaming and alerting the guy's friends, but she didn't have four big brothers for nothing. Using both hands, she pressed her captor's hand in place over her mouth and bit down on his palm. He muttered a vicious curse. At the same time she twisted around, gave his forearm a hard chop with her elbow, and rose to an upright crouch.

His arm dropped away. They came eye to eye.

He scowled.

Jake.

She grinned. She couldn't help it. "There are a bunch of bad guys around," she whispered. "Why'd you have to grab *me*?"

"None of *them* look like screamers," Jake said dryly, his voice as soft as hers. "Watch out," he warned as Duchess nudged her from behind. He braced Marnie's shoulder, letting go the moment she regained her balance.

They sat on their haunches facing each other. Duchess looked from one to the other, then turned her back to watch the path, ears swiveling, eyes sharp.

Jake scanned Marnie up and down. "You okay?"

"Cold, wet, hungry. Fine," she said, using his brand of shorthand. His face ruddy with the cold, his dark hair tousled by the wind, he looked good enough to eat. "You?"

"Apparently batting a thousand this weekend." He gave her a penetrating look. "Who are your friends?"

"You saw them?" she whispered back, relieved.

Jake shook his head. "Felt them. Me and the dog."

"Yeah, well, they aren't *my* friends. They're the type my brothers warned me to avoid like the plague. And for once I'm inclined to listen. I think they've crashed our party and come calling on *you*."

He gave her an odd look. "How many?"

"I saw five. But there were more. I'm not certain how many."

"Physical description?"

"Black clothing, strange headdress. Professionals for sure. They all had Uzis slung over their shoulders, and small pistols. Their language was unfamiliar. I mean totally unfamiliar. I'm good with languages, but I didn't get a cl—"

"Don't ramble." He reached out and touched her frozen cheek. His warm breath fanned her face. He dropped his hand and draped it over his knee. "What else did you notice?"

"That's it."

"Close your eyes. Tell me what you saw."

"I told you, noth—" She closed her eyes. "Oh, wait. Each of them had a knife strapped to his leg. Right calf. No scabbard. The blades were about twelve inches long." She opened her eyes to look at him. "They were made out of some weird metal. Matte. Black. Sharp. Nasty-looking."

"Good. Anything else?" he asked grimly, his eyes scanning her face for God only knew what. "You were unusually observant," he said roughly. "Sure you didn't recognize any of them?"

"I'm an artist. Of course I notice details. But I can't recognize people I don't know, especially if their faces are covered. And trust me, Jake Dolan, those guys aren't in my little black book."

She sounded indignant enough to be convincing. But then, so had good old Soledad—just before she kneed him in the balls and tried to give him a Colombian necktie.

Marnie would have fought to the death, Jake realized, rubbing his smarting palm where she'd bitten him. But for which side?

The woman was a mass of contradictions. She should have fainted the second he clamped his hand over her mouth. Hell, she should have freaked out when she saw the men. But she hadn't.

Bravery or conspiracy?

She wasn't going to cooperate with his stereotypical notion of a delicate blonde. Nevertheless, he wasn't about to be taken in again. The timing of her presence couldn't have been worse. And the similarities to the journalist six years ago were too obvious to be coincidence. Yet he couldn't believe the enemy would think him fool enough to be conned the same way twice.

"What do they want?"

Lord, her mouth looks like sin when she whispers.

"My ass, sweet cheeks. My ass. You're in the wrong place at the wrong time."

By her description of the assassins he had a damn good idea who they were. But Judas, he didn't want to believe what his gut was telling him. Believe it or not, he had to be prepared. And he would be, once he could get rid of the girl. ASAP. She was a complication he couldn't afford.

So his enemies were upping the ante, were they? How the hell had they tracked him here?

"You could be wrong." She shivered, and he knew it wasn't

just from the frigid cold. "They could be here to . . . to . . . something!" She sounded panicky.

"I'm going to get you across the river," *Out of my hair one way or the other.*

"Good. You'll come with me?"

"And look over my shoulder for the rest of my life? No, thanks. They started this. I'll finish it. Here. Now."

She grabbed his wrist and held on, her fingers cold. "Who *are* you?"

He hesitated. "A security expert."

"Bull."

"The information is on a need-to-know basis. You don't need to know. We'll wait another fifteen minutes. If there's no more activity, we'll head for the bridge."

"What about Duchess?" The edge of fear crept back into her voice. The dog's ears swiveled, either at the sound of her name, or the tone in her mistress's voice.

"I'll try to get her over, too. If not, she's not stupid. She'll head for the cabin and keep out of sight. I'll make sure she's returned to you."

"Promise?"

"Yes."

"How, if you're dead?" She looked him straight in the eye without flinching. "Tell me how you think you can fight all those men by yourself!"

"You'll get your dog back. On my word."

"You'll see her personally to my front door in Sunnyvale."

"You'll get the dog back."

"You," she insisted roughly, "personally. To my front door."

Snow, like bits of lint, drifted around them. Her cheeks were pink with the cold, her eyes hot, her mouth— He jerked his gaze to the soft strands of wind-ruffled fair hair framing her face.

Without thinking, Jake tucked a strand back under her damp knit cap. It felt like the finest Chinese silk. A few filaments caught on the calluses on his thumb. He absently rubbed the silky length between his fingers, getting more pleasure than he deserved from the small tactile treat.

His eyes met hers, and he saw they held a gleam of fear, anger, and anticipation. He let his gaze skim down and linger on her mouth.

Plump, soft, arousing. *Don't go there, buddy.* His blood pounded, a compelling primal beat.

Marnie narrowed her eyes at that look. "Don't change the subject!"

Jake dipped his head. He just wanted a taste. A refresher, to see if their last kiss could possibly have been as profound as he remembered.

He didn't want to talk about hand-delivering her dog. He didn't want to think about all the wet work he had to do in the next few hours. He didn't want to contemplate what he would have to do to her if the visitors were her allies.

They had another fifteen minutes together, tops.

The last kiss they shared was to be quick. Quick, he promised himself, touching his mouth to hers.

God, he tastes good. Desire shot through her. Shocking and intense. How could a mere kiss affect every nerve ending in her body? She could have gone on kissing him forever.

The second he stopped kissing her, Marnie opened her eyes and gave him a mild look, as if the kiss had been no big deal. But her heart was going a million miles an hour.

He gave her a quirky look back, then picked up a goopy handful of mud. Resigned, she closed her eyes again, knowing what he was about to do.

"You're sure this is absolutely necessary?"

"I'm not taking any chances." He smoothed it over her cheeks and chin. Icy mud. Warm hands. "Okay, open."

She opened her eyes.

Duchess stood watching them, head tilted, eyes puzzled at this new game. The dog whined hopefully.

Marnie could just imagine what she looked like. "This isn't a game, girl. Shhh."

Jake was busy smearing his own face. Marnie grimaced, then dug a handful of the dark sludge and covered her hands.

"You look like you know what you're doing." Jake followed suit, then wiped his right palm down the leg of his jeans.

"War games. Ninth grade. Kane had a friend I had a crush on that summer. It was either blend in with the boys or have Grammy teach me how to make ribbon roses."

They stood at the same time. Jake drew his gun, then held it loosely in his right hand. The weapon was big, black, and menacing. He indicated their direction. She and Duchess led the way through the trees, Jake close behind them.

The river was a good mile away. It had been years since Marnie had explored this part of the mountain. The terrain was steep and slippery. The trees grew closer together here, and the sparse undergrowth made the going easier, despite the fact that they were heading uphill. Oppressive clouds added to the wind chill. Pockets of snow shone white on the ground.

Every noise spooked her, although she managed not to jump each time a branch snapped or a rabbit raced through the undergrowth. Not that she didn't have every valid reason in the world to be incontinent right now. Her gaze darted from tree to tree, waiting for one of the ninjas to pop out.

Well, she'd wanted a grand adventure. *Be careful what you wish for,* Marnie thought with grim amusement as a sharp breeze zipped through the trees and filtered through her damp jacket. She tugged her woolen cap over her ears and ignored the cold.

The sound of the river got louder. Duchess danced ahead, disappearing through the trees. Jake gave a soft whistle and she loped back, tongue lolling as if she were grinning and delighted with the game.

But this wasn't a game. A chill washed through Marnie as they came to the bank and she got an up-close-and-personal look at the river.

There wasn't a snowball's hope in hell of getting her across. The noise of the water rushing over the rocks was thunderous. They stood side by side, watching the boiling brown mess flip logs like matchsticks in its race to the Pacific.

Marnie nudged Jake's shoulder with hers to get his attention. "How did they get across?"

"Must have done a helo jump. Probably beyond the ridge. I didn't hear it."

"Where's the bridge?" Hands stuffed into the pockets of her jacket, shoulders hunched, she looked up at him. "It washed out completely, didn't it?"

"Looks like." Jake glanced away from those clear blue eyes peering out at him from a muddy face. "Probably with a little help from your pals back there."

"Oh, yeah. My pals. Happy, Grumpy, and Snoopy. Give me a break, okay? Unless you plan on tossing me in there, let's make other plans before we freeze to death."

She walked around him so they were face-to-face. The mud was drying and starting to crack on her skin. Jake knew what it felt like, but she hadn't complained. So far.

"Look, I hate to tell you this, but I'm so scared I can't decide which to do first, throw up or wet my pants. Could we *please* find a nice warm place to defrost while we figure out what to do about those guys?"

"We?"

"Fine, macho man. You. Personally, I don't care who comes up with the best escape plan. Just as long as someone does." She turned on her heel and walked away. The dog looked back at Jake reproachfully before bounding after her mistress.

Jake stared at Marnie's back for a moment and scowled. She was unpredictable as hell. Between them and any sort of decent cover was a pod of determined men. Resigned, Jake caught up.

"Not so fast, Red Riding Hood." He caught her arm, leaving a muddy handprint on her wet sleeve. He was surprised to feel muscle beneath the padding of her jacket. Even so, her bones were as delicate and breakable as a cat's. He let go.

"Just where do you think you're going?"

Her breath came in little white puffs. She gave him a blank look. "Nowhere." After a moment a smile lit her eyes. "Fast, apparently. Got any brilliant plans, Mr. Big Bad Wolf?"

Jake bit back a smile. "Like your fairy tales, do you?"

"Most of the time. Right now I'd appreciate the arrival of Superman rather than wussy Prince Charming in his dumb white pantyhose, wouldn't you?"

She was trying hard not to look terrified, Jake thought, watching the irregular movement of her chest as she struggled to maintain her flip attitude. Not that she didn't have every reason to be scared shitless. "You don't think they'd send all those guys to get me if I wasn't hard to kill, do you?"

"Are you faster than a speeding bullet?"

"You bet."

She looked at him. "Yeah, I believe you are."

It was snowing harder now, making visibility poor. It was midafternoon but looked like dusk. Which gave him the advantage.

"Look, you can't go off half cocked here. I know this mountain like the back of my hand. Those guys don't. What we're going to do is get to a cave about two miles downriver from the dam. It's our best shot. Stay close and alert."

"What cave? I've been coming up here all my life, I've never seen a cave."

"Want to stand around and chat about it? Or should we get going before they pick us off?"

"Good point. Lead on, Macduff."

Chapter Five

Marnie didn't know what Jake Dolan did for a living. It was moot at this point. An undisclosed number of men were searching for them with an impressive arsenal of weapons.

Jake had one gun. A plus.

And her. A minus.

She didn't much like the odds.

She wasn't an idiot. Right now she was a liability to him. She'd seen spy movies. The dumb blonde always got killed first because she was a . . . dumb blonde.

Jake knew what he was doing. At least he behaved as though he knew what he was doing. Marnie wasn't going to argue.

The cloud-thick sky hung directly over their heads as they made their cautious way through the trees. There were several places, Marnie knew, where they'd be sitting ducks. The small clearing up ahead was one. Her heart had lodged in her throat half an hour ago and stayed there. She walked as close to Jake's left side as she could get without ducking under his arm and hugging his ribs.

Which would have been nice and cozy. Unfortunately they weren't in a cozy situation. As the trees thinned, it became evident the snow wasn't about to stop, not anytime soon. The flakes drifted in slow motion as a continuous fall of white, blanketed the branches, and drifted silently to the frozen ground.

The forest was quiet. Eerily quiet. Icy wind sliced right through her damp clothing and chilled her to the bone. The mud on her face and hands had dried like a cement face pack, making her skin itch and burn.

Ahead, Duchess paused, ears pricked, hackles raised. Jake put his arm across Marnie's chest.

They stopped. Alert. Listening.

Tension, sudden and electric, arced between them. Someone was waiting for them in the clearing.

Jake pulled her behind a broad tree trunk, his weapon drawn and raised to fire.

Marnie hunched her shoulders to make a smaller target and held her breath. A branch snapped. Something small scurried across the ground behind them. Her eyes burned as she searched the surrounding area for movement.

"Stay here," Jake breathed in her ear.

She wanted to grab the front of his jacket and close her eyes tight. Instead she nodded and watched him slip from one patch of deep shadow to the next. He paused a beat to make a hand motion to Duchess. The dog shot from sentry duty to her side.

Jake melted into the trees.

Marnie welcomed the familiar weight leaning against her hip. She and Duchess waited, ears and eyes strained for the slightest movement. Moments later she heard a soft pop, quickly followed by another.

She sucked in a shaky breath, then held it.

After what seemed like an eternity, Jake emerged through the trees.

She released the breath she'd been holding as he came closer. Her gaze checked him for bullet holes. He looked hale and hearty. Covered with mud, but big and strong and dangerous.

"Two down." His voice barely carried the few inches between them. She shivered at the cold tundra in his eyes.

"You killed them?"

He gave her a droll look. "What did you think I was going to do? Tell them not to play on my mountain?"

Marnie narrowed her eyes and summoned her defenses. "Cute. I'd feel way happier if you'd given them a group discount so they were *all* gone."

"Bloodthirsty wench, aren't you?"

"As long as the blood isn't ours."

"Yeah, well, so far the home team is ahead. This is the plan." Jake took her chin in his hand and stared coldly into her eyes. "Don't deviate, don't improvise, don't slow down. Scared is good; it'll keep you sharp. Terrified is bad; it could get us both killed. Understand?"

Marnie nodded. She was scared *and* terrified, and hoped it didn't show too terribly much. Although Jake must surely have heard her heart *flub-dub*bing, he didn't mention it.

"We get through the clearing. Fast. Know where the old logging road is?" He waited for her nod. "Go up there to the left. As soon as you're above the dam, take the fork. Keep as close to the trees as you can, and haul ass." He narrowed his eyes. "Any questions?"

"Where will *you* be?"

"Right on your tail, sweetheart. Right on your tail. Let's go."

Adrenaline had an interesting way of heating the body, Marnie decided, moving quickly through the trees, Jake on one side, Duchess on the other.

They came to the clearing, a serene glade, surrounded by Douglas fir and enormous ponderosa pine. The ground was slippery with needles and cones over muddy, half-frozen earth.

Other than the tail end of a deer on the far side, there was nothing but grass, small piñon shrubs, and sparse clumps of snow in the deep shadows.

She paused, gathered herself, and started to run. She aimed for the center, where three large rock outcroppings formed a halfway point. Duchess panted as she loped alongside her. Peripherally, she saw Jake moving up beside her.

She was almost there when she heard a high-pitched whine.

"Down!" Jake hissed behind her, sharp and urgent.

She turned to see him flying at her. They fell in a tangle of arms and legs, Marnie flat on her back, Jake on top of her. Their rolling bodies thumped into the base of the rocks. She saw stars and comets as her head bounced on the hard surface.

"Ow!"

His mouth was close to her ear. "Lie still."

Considering he had her spread-eagled and flat on her back, with his body covering hers like a two-hundred-pound X-ray blanket, it was impossible to do anything else.

A round of whines.

Bits of rock ricocheted off the boulder directly above them.

Jake pressed her harder into the damp earth as more gunfire came from the fringe of trees beyond the meadow.

"I don't like this," he muttered roughly against her jaw.

"No kidding? Darn, and here I thought you were loving it."

"How close are the strikes?" he asked against her ear.

"So?" His warm breath puffing in her ear was extremely distracting. "None of them is a great marksman. What's your point?"

"They wouldn't be here if they weren't the best. If they wanted to take us out, they *would* have."

Marnie inhaled a shaky breath, her face smothered by his chest. She smelled the damp wool of his sweater, the sharp scent of pine on his jacket and the strangely comforting and familiar smell of the man himself.

"Want me to go and ask them why they haven't shot us yet?" she demanded, blinking snow out of her eyes and glaring at his ear.

"If you know them well enough, feel free."

"Maybe I'll just stroll over there and ask them to knock some sense into your thick skull," Marnie said, exasperated now as well as frightened. "I told you I didn't invite them. Either believe it or get off me. You're mashing me into the ground."

"Just following Dolan's law of Survival number two. Never trust anyone."

"What's rule number one?" she asked, although she thought she probably knew that one.

"Never believe a cute blonde."

"You think I'm cute?"

She felt his hot breath against her neck, but he didn't answer. Exasperating man.

Pressed intimately from head to toe, she was dynamically aware of how solid and strong his body felt. His heart beat a tattoo against her crushed breasts, and one of his long, muscled legs was wedged dangerously in the apex of her thighs. His hot breath seared her forehead as he held her down with his body, his arms wrapped around her so nothing was exposed.

"If we die today, you'll be sorry we didn't make love," she whispered directly into his ear.

"Where the hell is your off switch?"

"I told you, I talk when I'm n—" He put a large, muddy hand over her mouth. Her voice muffled, she said, "They've stopped shooting. Where's Duchess?"

"Behind the rocks. Don't move."

He took his hand away and shifted against her. The heat of his body and the musky scent of his skin overwhelmed her. Marnie was aware of every move he made.

From the other side of the rock Duchess gave a low, quick bark to indicate she was in one piece.

"Okay?" he asked, his voice strained as he shifted down her body a little more. Now his narrow hips were nestled between her thighs. Their jigsaw puzzle pieces matched perfectly.

His chest pressed her breasts flat, making breathing difficult. Eyes riveted to his, she said breathlessly, "Can we get up and run? Or are we going to lie here and wait for them to come right up and shoot you in the back of the head?"

Jake's chest shifted. "Give me a second, then we're going to get up and run." A bullet whizzed over their heads. "When I say go, head for the upper dam. Keep as close to the trees as you can."

"What about the logging road?" Marnie whispered desperately. Going up the mountain would take them even farther away from civilization.

"Our hotshot's between us and that road." Nose to nose, Jake looked down at her, his eyes dark, his mouth a breath away from hers. "Ready? Let's go."

He grabbed her hand and yanked her up beside him and

into a full, low-crouched run before she even drew a complete breath.

There were several more volleys of shots, this time coming from where they'd entered the clearing. A divot of grass and dirt jumped near their feet.

"Damn." Jake squeezed off a shot, then jerked her the other way, changing direction to head straight for the ravine.

When Marnie realized which way they were going, her feet slowed, trying to pull back. Duchess wasn't with them. She wanted to whistle but didn't have the air to do so.

Jake almost yanked her arm out of its socket as he hauled her in his wake. Once down this slight slope they would be perched on the edge of a sharp drop. "We can't—"

"No choice. Move it!"

Branches and pine needles hooked their clothing as they dashed madly through the trees, making it impossible to hear what was happening behind them. Marnie didn't think she could have heard anything over her own heartbeat and the breath sawing from her lungs anyway.

They reached the drop-off, a dangerous slope down to the dry riverbed between the upper and lower dams. Behind them, a spray of automatic-weapon fire decided their direction.

Jake pulled her with him, bracing her so that she wouldn't tumble to the rocky bottom. With his help, and holding on to small saplings or handfuls of grass, Marnie slid down the bank onto the snow-dusted, water-smoothed rocks.

The shooting stopped.

Her hands throbbed. Sweat stung her eyes. Her breath heaved from her burning lungs. Dropping her hands to her knees, she dragged in a deep, steadying gasp of air.

Above them came shouts, then the loud report of gunfire. A flock of birds rose noisily from the treetops. Another rapid round of shots followed closely behind the first.

Jake threw her up against the bank, pressing against her back, again protecting her with his body.

He was heavy, and she felt his hot, moist breath on the back of her neck. She tasted gritty sand on her tongue as he pushed her face into the dirt. She didn't move so much as an eyelash as they waited for the voices above them to fade.

He kept her pinned to the bank until the voices receded, and then he stepped away from her and grabbed her hand.

"Stay ahead of me." He waited half a beat while she swiped her wrist over her sandy mouth. "Go like a bat outta hell. And don't look back."

He pulled the zipper of her jacket up to her chin. "I'm right behind you."

A sharp crack split the air. Louder. Closer. Scarier.

Marnie ran.

Sweat ran down her face. Behind her she heard the rapid steady crunch of Jake's boots as he moved easily across the rocks. He moved fast, but so did she. Marnie knew he was purposely staying behind her, covering her back.

She was fit; even so, she was breathing hard. Exertion and the warm coat made her sweat uncomfortably. She stepped on a rock that rolled underfoot and did a hop, skip, and jump to keep her balance.

Suddenly there was a shower of gunfire off to their right. The noise echoed in the ravine. Bullets ricocheted off rocks with enough force to shatter them to dust.

Behind her Jake yelled, "Go, go, go!"

She sensed rather than felt his hand under her elbow, and found an extra burst of speed.

The ravine was deep, the walls on either side steep. Despite the intermittent gunfire, they hadn't been hit. Either these guys were lousy shots or Jake was right—they didn't *intend* to hit them. It took Marnie a while to realize what was happening.

They were being herded down the narrow gorge like animals to the slaughter.

Rock became slippery mud as they charged around a bend in the riverbed, vision hampered by the gauzy veil of falling snow. Their labored breath echoed back from the dirt walls, leaving a vapor trail behind them.

Marnie listened for more shots, sensing the menace behind them as they ran.

Under the sound of Jake's steady breathing was layered another sound she couldn't quite identify. Her legs pistoned, her heart pumped at the speed of a train. She glanced up, somehow expecting lightning to accompany the low, rolling sound.

"Is that thunder?" she panted, not slowing. The trees and ground blurred, she swiped her hand across the sweat stinging her eyes. "Or an earthquake?"

One moment she could hear Jake behind her, the next he'd run alongside and wrapped one strong arm around her waist, lifting her off her feet. His momentum carried her a dozen feet before he yelled, "The bastards have opened the upper dam."

It took Marnie a split second to digest what he'd just said. They were going to try to outrun a tidal wave? *Yeah, right!*

There was no point keeping to the deep shadow of the bank now. The terrain was easier to traverse closer to the center. Her left foot splashed in the meandering trickle of water, but Jake kept her moving so fast she practically flew.

Behind them came an ominous thundering rumble as millions of gallons of released water rushed toward them with the speed of a freight train. Marnie concentrated on where she was going, trying not to calculate how fast a wall of water could travel downhill.

They were now boxed into the canyon that made up the lower dam. There were only two ways to go: back toward the water, or forward.

She saw what was ahead and faltered. That way lay certain death. She shot him a helpless look, sweat sharp in the small lacerations on her face.

Marnie hoped to hell Jake had a plan.

Or could fly.

Jake had a death grip around Marnie's waist. She felt light as a feather as he urged her to run flat out. Ahead was the wide lip of the cement spillway, a dizzying drop six stories to the rocks below.

"Trust me," Jake shouted. The mountain of water was right

behind them, out of sight behind the last curve, but on its way. He could imagine what it carried with it—tons of sand and rock and trees, turbulent and lethal.

There wasn't a second to lose. Before Marnie could so much as scream, he grabbed her by the arm and swung her over the ledge, sensing when her feet hit the narrow metal ladder fastened to the face of the wall just below the lip.

In seconds he'd scrambled down after her. He pointed, urging her to descend to the narrow cement ledge spanning the width of the wall. As soon as she'd reached it Jake urged her behind the ladder, and she wedged herself between the metal bars and the face of the dam.

Ignoring her white face, he held on to the ladder with one hand for balance and inspected the narrow, rusted metal door imbedded in the wall beside her. It probably housed maintenance equipment and the controls for regulating the water flow, and Jake wanted in.

Marnie clutched the neck of his jacket as he crouched down beside her. The roar of the rapidly approaching water urged him to make quick work of opening the door. He ran his fingers along the seams. The cement walkway vibrated beneath the heavy soles of his boots. Her cold fingers brushed his neck as she gripped his collar and held on to him for dear life.

He yanked at the handle. It refused to budge.

The force of the coming deluge caused his teeth to chatter in time with the structure's oscillation. Using both hands, he pulled again, teeth gritted, the cords in his neck straining. But disuse and neglect had rusted the metal fast.

Precariously balanced, his expression grim, Jake stood. He shook his head to her querying look.

She briefly squeezed her eyes shut, then gave him a look filled with confidence. Somewhere her cap had fallen off, and pale hair frothed around her shoulders and face. Strands stuck to the sweat and mud on her face.

He scanned the rusted bolts that held the ladder to the cement. They looked none too secure. With his and Marnie's combined weights and the water pounding down on them, there was a damn good chance the ladder would rip free and plummet them both to the rocks below.

Mission accomplished for the hit team.

He felt the vibration under his hands as the wall of water surged closer and closer, the ground shaking under the onslaught.

Jake checked to be sure Marnie was as safely anchored as possible, then shouted over the din, with no hope of being heard, "Hold on tight."

The ledge was too narrow for them to stand abreast, and he started to swing himself around the ladder. One hand, covered with rust particles and black slime from the door, lost its purchase on the rung as he swung out at an awkward angle. For several seconds his heart hung as suspended as his body.

"No!" Marnie shouted, eyes wide with horror. In a flash, she lunged forward to grab the front of his jacket through the rungs with both hands. She hung on to him for dear life. The only thing supporting her was her own body weight against the ladder. Fierce concentration painted her features as Jake automatically grabbed her with one powerful hand and swung his body securely onto the ladder.

He was quick and would eventually have managed to gain a grip on his own. But he'd never seen anything like the tenacity on the face of this woman as she held on to him. The strain of his weight on her shoulders and arms had to be tremendous.

She gave him a worried look. "Are you okay?" she mouthed, brow wrinkled.

His heart beat an extra time or two. He nodded, then grabbed her fisted hand off the front of his jacket and placed it on the frame. Next he did the same with her other hand and made sure her fingers were curled tightly. He shifted her booted feet with his own to more evenly balance her body weight and made sure she was braced.

Hell, yes. He was fine and dandy.

They were face-to-face, the rusted metal rungs between them. He placed his large hands over her smaller ones with a punishing grip.

She shuddered, her knuckles white in a death grip on the bars on either side of her face. Sweat gave her skin a pearly sheen, but her fingers were like ice. He held her gaze.

Above, the ominous roar of millions of gallons of raging water thundered inexorably toward them as they clung precariously to the sheer face of the wall. The metal rungs of the ladder shuddered and vibrated beneath their feet, dusting the air with flecks of rust.

Jake braced himself, adrenaline giving him a rush. With the cement wall at her back and his own body covering her front, this was the best he could do.

He hoped the water wouldn't decide to rush straight down instead of shooting out.

He hoped the rusty ladder retained its tenuous hold on the thirty-year-old wall.

And he hoped the bastards hadn't let out every frigging drop of water in the bigger dam upriver.

That was one hell of a lot to hope for.

Marnie's body trembled. He wasn't feeling too chipper himself. There was absolutely nothing more he could do. The ladder vibrated and the rusted bolts shimmied against the equally rusted braces as the rushing water pounded the spillway.

The shit was about to hit the fan.

He braced his body protectively in front of her, gave her white fingers a reassuring squeeze, and looked at her . . . chin.

Marnie was looking straight up.

The water shot out, twenty feet away from the wall and them, before plummeting to the river below.

She looked back at him and grinned.

"Judas Priest! You're enjoying this!" Jake shouted incredulously. The cacophony made speech unintelligible and jarred every bone in his body. But he could read her lips.

"Exhilarating!"

She tilted back her head with a laugh, in seconds her hair was plastered to her skull from the spray.

"Put your head down before you drown, for godsake!"

Jake took the brunt of icy spray on his back. Her fingers

flexed under his, and she looked straight at him. Their faces were three inches apart. Between streaks of mud, Marnie's skin looked luminous. Her impossibly blue eyes were filled with wicked mirth.

Jake shook his head. The woman was nuts!

Crystalline drops misted the air in a thundering, tumultuous spray, the sound deafening. Droplets as fine as diamond dust sparkled on her spiky lashes. Marnie grinned. Most of the mud had washed away, and her cheeks were flushed; her eyes shone with wonder. Jake's throat locked as heat exploded through him. He could almost hear the cold water sizzle to steam around him.

Between the rigid metal bars of the ladder he imagined feeling the answering heat of Marnie's body through the layers of their soaked clothing. His fingers tightened over hers.

Six stories below, muddy water frothed and boiled, violently churning in on itself. The driving force of the torrent drowned out every other sound.

Cocooned behind an opaque curtain of coffee-colored water, amazingly safe on their precarious perch, Jake leaned forward.

He bent his head and touched his mouth to hers. Her tongue greeted his descending lips. He could taste the smile still curving her soft mouth.

His lips were cold and wet, the kiss brief and hard.

Marnie felt his warm breath enter her mouth, mingling with her own, and a furnace of heat shot through her, making her forget they were hazardously balanced over a six-story drop. Her lips burned as Jake slanted his mouth to taste more, sliding his tongue deep into her mouth.

Her fingers flexed against the metal bars on either side of her face. She wanted to touch him, feel his wet skin. Jake's hands tightened over hers to lock her in place, reminding her where they were. Wet cloth abraded icily against wet cloth as their bodies strained against the barrier of the ladder between them.

Boldly her tongue dueled with his. She forgot to breathe;

she couldn't think as her heartbeat accelerated and made her dizzy.

Jake felt the roar of water deep in his gut. Marnie's hot mouth welcomed him, and everything in him tightened one more notch. He wanted her soft and pliant against him. He groaned deep into her mouth. Her breath sighed against his tongue. He felt like Superman. He could fly, he could leap tall buildings, he could—

What in the hell was he doing?

Jake disengaged their mouths.

Concentrate, you idiot. There's a time and place for everything, and this is neither.

Marnie slowly opened her eyes. She looked dazed, amazed, and unbelievably gorgeous.

Water poured more slowly over the spillway, and somewhere in the distance a bird resumed singing. Snow drifted lazily from the ever-darkening sky.

"Still having fun?" Jake asked dryly.

Marnie glanced down at the rushing water below, then looked straight into his eyes. "Yeah, as a matter of fact, I am. Now what?"

"Now we walk, very carefully, along this nice little ledge back to terra firma."

The going was tricky. The ledge was barely wide enough to traverse single file. In several places the cement had crumbled, and in others it was wet and dangerously slimy. Marnie used the narrow electrical pipe running overhead as a handhold. Knowing Jake was right behind her made her feel marginally safer.

Clothing and hair soaked, Marnie shivered in earnest. She had a real good reason to bitch and complain now. Behind her Jake had a brief, irritating flash of Soledad, snuggling inside the blue fox fur she'd begged for so prettily because she was cold in the New York spring. He snorted. Hell, he must be a magnet for the type.

"Careful!" He made a grab for Marnie's wrist on the

overhead pipe as her foot slipped in the green gunk on the walkway.

Her breath plumed white as she muttered, "Thanks," and kept going. Jake kept his hand right behind hers as they inched across to the other side.

It seemed to take hours before they reached the rocky outcrop at the end of the dam.

Senses alert, he checked the woods on either side as he helped her down the rocks and boulders alongside the spillway.

After scrambling the last few steps down to flat land, Marnie turned to glance up at the wall where they'd clung like spiders moments ago.

As they watched, an enormous sheared-off tree shot to the edge, tangled with other debris, and did a free fall over the lip. Jake's gaze followed the descent of the ladder as it was ripped away from the old and crumbling cement. The whole mess crashed and splintered into the raging waters below.

He turned and gave her a pointed look.

She grinned, wiped her brow, then flicked off imaginary sweat. "My hero!"

Her eyes sparkled. Her cheeks and the tip of her nose bloomed bright pink from the cold. Water trickled down her face from her saturated hair.

Jake pushed his hands into the wet pockets of his down jacket. It was a ridiculous time to be charmed.

"Judas! We could be dead right now. In case you haven't noticed, they're trying to kill us."

"Yeah, but they *didn't*. You saved us from the baddies." Marnie flung herself into his arms and kissed him, hard.

With his hands in his pockets, he was trapped for a moment. Jake pulled away, freeing his hands to hold her firmly by her upper arms. He made sure there was not a glimmer of warmth in his eyes. She was either one damn fine actress or she was for real. He didn't have time right now to figure out which.

"Own a fur coat?"

"What?" She gave him a blank look. "No, ugh. I'd never

wear fur. But if there was a nice woolly bear around I'd be ecstatic to snuggle up to him to get warm."

"And get eaten for your pains."

"Why'd you ask me, then?" She gave him a puzzled look. "You'd have gotten cranky no matter what my answer was, wouldn't you?"

He kept his tone sleety. "If the idea is to distract me so your pals have another easy shot at me, forget it."

"Huh? You're the one who asked the dumb question." She stared at him for a moment, then shook her head. "You're a real jerk, you know that?" She didn't sound particularly bothered by the fact, which annoyed him for some reason.

"So I've been told."

He took her arm roughly, and she winced.

"Now what?"

As the words left his mouth he remembered the moment when she'd put her own life on the line by holding him until he could regain his balance. "That was a damn foolish thing you did, grabbing me like that. You could have fallen yourself."

"Too bad I wasn't thinking that way. I just figured it would be tough for you to swim with broken bones."

She hadn't taken a breath for that one. Jake stared at her. She couldn't work for the bad guys—unless she was their secret weapon, he thought morosely. "Let's go."

"I'm quite capable of walking by myself, thank you."

Jake felt as though he'd kicked a puppy for bringing him his slippers. *Shit.*

"Fine. Let's see you do it, then. Those guys aren't going to wait forever before they try again."

"They think we drowned. Why would they still come after us?"

"They'll keep coming until they see my body. I don't plan on hanging around for a sighting, do you?" he bit out. "And just in case it slipped your notice, my weapon is floating somewhere downstream on its way to Sacramento."

"Maybe you could just look at them and freeze them to

death." She turned around smartly and marched ahead—dignity personified in saturated clothing, remnants of mud still streaking her face.

Obviously danger was a turn-on for her. He understood only too well what she was experiencing. He got a high from the adrenaline rush, too. He also knew without a doubt this situation wasn't going to be a pleasant rush for him. Not this time. Because his wasn't the life he was playing chicken with.

The burning question of the moment was which side these guys were on.

Who had given the order to off him?

The bad guys?

Or, as he was starting to suspect, his own team?

Chapter Six

Jake pulled himself up a rise using the same small fir tree for leverage as Marnie had. She was several paces ahead, back stiff, eyes straight ahead. Under her breath, very, very softly, she called for her dog.

Jake came alongside her. "No talking. Sound carries."

"You promised you'd keep my dog safe." She narrowed her eyes at him but kept her voice below a whisper. "I want her back. Now."

"Too damn bad. Right now I'm trying to save our *human* asses. Keep walking."

She gave a smart salute, spun on her booted heel, and trudged forward.

Jake sensed no one around them as they scrambled for handholds on the steep, rocky incline. Not the dog, not the bad guys. The bastards were probably congratulating themselves on an easy job.

Behind them the river, now swollen with the unexpected flood, rushed over boulders and swept trees and shrubs in its muddy wake. Soon it would be back to normal, but for now it was impossible to cross. Another barrier between them and civilization.

Snow continued to fall as the sky darkened. The air was crisp and icy with the sharp scent of pine stinging his nostrils. Marnie's breath plumed as she grabbed at bushes to keep her balance. Jake worried about her wet clothes. They had to get to shelter before hypothermia set in. He had to get her safe and out of the line of fire before he could retaliate. Being *re*-active wasn't his style.

Jake's skin burned with the cold. He hastened his steps, urging Marnie to a faster pace. The shadows lay long and cold on the ground now. It got dark fast in the mountains—faster with this snowstorm brewing. In fifteen minutes it would be blacker than pitch.

The terrain varied extremely. One moment the going was soft and steeply inclined, the soil slippery with mud, moss, and pine needles; the next, stone broke through in outcrops or buried boulders. Both were treacherous.

Jake closed the gap between them, ready to give her a hand if she needed it.

He could see her hunched shoulders under her wet green parka. She had her hands jammed into her sodden pockets. And she was still frantically whispering for the damn dog.

The bad guys might have failed to drown them, but if they didn't get to shelter soon, the mountain would take their lives in the darkness with silent snow. The air seemed to freeze his lungs. He pulled up the collar of his coat just as Marnie did the same, not that that would do much good.

At least ten men, maybe more.

Overkill.

Jake pushed ahead with a frown. Why so many? It wasn't practical or logical. He was only one man. And it had been purely by chance that he'd had advance warning of their arrival at all. Whoever they were, they would have no way of knowing what his resources were up here.

If he'd been safely in his lair, they wouldn't have known where to find him at all. Which led him to another question: How had they found him on this mountain in the first place? Only a handful of people had even known he owned property up here. The few that had were all dead now. And he would have staked his life that none of them would have divulged his whereabouts to anyone.

Which brought him right back to the delectable Miss Marnie Wright and *her* unlikely presence.

* * *

Marnie had forgotten how dark it got in the mountains. And cold. God, she was cold. The moon played coyly between the clouds, but at least it had stopped snowing.

At the best of times she had an abysmal sense of direction. Up here, where every tree looked pretty much the same as the last, she was hopelessly lost. It didn't help her sense of direction much when she kept anticipating a bullet slamming into her spine.

There'd been no sign of the bad guys. No shots, no voices. They'd walked for what seemed like hours.

When she ran smack bang into a boulder, she stayed where she was, cheek resting against the cold stony face, arms limp at her sides.

"I'd love you forever if you got us somewhere warm and dry, PDQ," she mumbled under her breath.

"You're in luck," Jake said quietly, so close he barely had to raise his voice above a thought. "We're here."

Here was an enormous outcrop of rocks, similar to the ones in the clearing where they'd been shot at earlier.

Marnie dragged her cheek from the cold stone pillow to glance around. In the sharp moonlight she could see the little hairs on the back of his hand as he indicated the beginning of the formation.

She frowned. "What am I looking *at*?" All she could see were the usual shrubs and a narrow wedge-shaped gap between the boulders. The opening was too narrow to squeeze through. Not that she had any desire to do so.

"There's shelter back there. Come on." He extended his hand. "We have to climb a bit. You stopped shivering a while back—we've got to get dry and warm."

"Didn't I just say that?" Marnie took his hand. His strong fingers closed securely around hers.

Jake set one large foot in the crevice and pulled her up. She clambered after him. He turned, saw she was steady, and dropped her hand. She flattened her palms on the frigid surface, parallel to her shoulders, and imitated Jake as he braced a foot on either side and straddled the gap.

It was slow going, but eventually the vee widened sufficiently for them to drop to the ground and walk normally. To the right and left loomed black, menacing rock faces, towering high above their heads. The scene gave the word *claustrophobia* new meaning.

Ahead Marnie saw a narrow split in the mountainside. She gave it a dubious look. "What was this? A mine?"

"Yeah, silver, back in the late eighteen hundreds. It was played out before this slide covered the entrance."

"*I'm* not going down a hundred-year-old mine shaft."

"Okay."

"I'm serious, wh—" Marnie stepped on a hard object in the sand and paused to regain her balance. She looked down and felt herself pale. "Ah, Jake?"

He didn't turn around, just kept walking. "What now?"

"I just stepped on a bone," she said in as reasonable a tone as she could muster.

Keeping her gaze fixed to the ground, she saw a trail of bones between Jake's boots and her own. Large bones. Bones that had been picked clean.

Human bones?

"Woman, do you want to freeze to death, or what? Move."

"Jake, there's something in your cave."

"He'll move. Get the lead out, will you? I'm freezing my ass off."

Marnie stepped over a single bone. "Do bears eat humans?" She sidestepped a small pile of bones gleaming white in the moonlight. A chill that had nothing to do with cold raced down her spine.

"Only if provoked." At the mouth of the cave Jake turned to wait for her. She swore his lips twitched.

"What about wolves?" Whatever animal had dined here had a voracious appetite. She flexed icy fingers. "Do you think they like their meat frozen?"

Jake snorted. "The second any animal hears *you* coming, he'll be long gone." He gave her a look she couldn't fail to interpret. "Want to stand out here all night chatting about the haute cuisine of the animal kingdom, or do you want to get warm?"

With a great deal of trepidation, Marnie followed him into

the mine. The darkness swallowed her whole, and she grabbed the back of his jacket with both hands.

"Steady there." Jake sounded amused, darn his hide, but he didn't slow down. Marnie had to keep up with his pace or lose her grip on the back of his jacket.

Between the railroad tracks imbedded in the dirt floor were several more piles of bones. Marnie stepped over them quickly. She could have sworn she spotted two unblinking red eyes glaring at her from the distance.

Her voice came out a wispy croak. "Jake. Jake? There's *something* in here with u—"

A low, throaty growl rumbled through the cave.

She shrieked, almost pulling Jake over backward as she clutched his jacket like a shield.

The growls became louder. Deeper. Scarier.

All the blood drained from Marnie's head. She'd worry about shrieking like a sissy later. Right now all she could manage was a small moan. The snarls changed pitch. While less amplified, they now sounded considerably more menacing.

And a lot closer.

"Jake . . . ?"

"Relax," he said, sounding amused. "There's nothing in here but us. The sound effects are noise-activated. The second we stepped inside, the show started. Something I was fooling around with in my spare time." The amusement left his voice. "I never intended to have to actually use it."

It was hard to talk with her heart still lodged in her throat. "There's no animal?"

"Nopc."

The "no animal" growled low and long.

Marnie mentally strung together several of her brothers' favorite curse words, then said reasonably. "Would you mind terribly much unplugging your imaginary pet? He's giving me the willies."

"The growls were a nice touch, don't you think?"

"I was thinking that whatever was in here would take ages gnawing on your tough hide, so I would have had plenty of time to get the hell out of Dodge."

Jake shifted. The next minute he turned on a powerful flashlight.

Marnie squinted against the sudden glare. "Where did that come from?" she demanded, leaning weakly against the jagged rock wall because her legs had turned to water.

Still smiling, Jake held up a nasty-looking gun. "Same place as this."

"Wipe that smile off your face this instant," she snarled, her hand covering her still frantically palpitating heart, "or I'll use that thing on you. What's going on? How did a flashlight and a gun suddenly appear out of thin air?"

Jake shone the powerful beam on a control panel faux painted to look like rock and all but invisible against the wall. He opened the housing and deactivated his pet. Silence echoed down the tunnel.

"I didn't want anyone in here but me. I figured the audio, coupled with the bones outside, would make an effective deterrent."

"Trust me, Jake, it's *very* effective. Even knowing it's pretend, I *still* don't like being in here."

Jake closed the control panel and resumed walking, the flashlight illuminating the narrow, roughly hewn corridor.

She didn't grab the back of his jacket again, despite the urge to do so. Apparently the most dangerous animal in this tunnel was Jake Dolan.

At a fork Jake turned right without slowing. The ceiling, a couple of feet above his head, looked solid enough. It was repulsively softened by cobwebs, which, by the size of them, housed Godzilla-sized spiders. There was no sign of the occupants, thank heavens.

"What kind of spiders make such huge webs?" she asked, trying to sound casual as she came up beside him.

"*I* made them."

"You are one strange man, you know that?" Marnie ignored the webs to shoot a skeptical glance at the heavy wood beams, which presumably supported the entire mountain resting above the mineshaft. The image of an elephant sitting on upright toothpicks didn't instill her with confidence.

"So this creepy mine shaft is just for effect? You have nice strong steel supports holding everything up?"

"Nope, the beams are the originals."

"I'm sure the historical society would be thrilled to know that." A few of the cross struts they passed looked to be in fairly reasonable shape. Insects, animals, or time, however, had chomped on the rest. The air, while considerably warmer than outside, was stale and damp.

Jake walked so fast Marnie almost had to run to keep up. "They won't find this place, will they?"

"In the unlikely event they do, I have a few more tricks up my sleeve."

"Duchess couldn't find her way inside here, either."

"Your dog's a whole hell of a lot smarter than a lot of humans I know. She'll find us."

When the light illuminated a sturdy metal door, Marnie wasn't surprised. Dully she watched Jake flatten his hand on a pad embedded in the rock. Seconds later the door slid open without a sound.

Marnie followed into another long passage that sloped steeply downhill. As the door whooshed closed behind them, small, dim bulbs every ten feet or so lit up to illuminate their way.

Jake deposited both gun and flashlight on a shoulder-high ledge beside the door. He gave her a searching glance before striding off again.

Wet boots dragging, Marnie followed. The air seemed fresher, not as cold, and the rock walls were smoother, too. Exhaustion dragged at her like a drug.

She'd had a tree fall on her cabin, hiked a zillion mountain miles, been shot at, survived a perilous near-death experience under a tsunami, and braved a woman-eating, computer-generated wild beast. It was enough.

Other than the crunch of their footsteps, there was nothing but throbbing silence. Marnie found it unnerving. Her boots weighed a ton. Her eyelids felt scritchy, and she wanted to lie down so badly, she was prepared to do so on the sandy floor.

"This is a nightmare, isn't it? It's that canned chili I ate for breakfast."

"Almost there." Jake turned to get a good look at her. It wasn't surprising that she was about to keel over. She was crashing from the adrenaline high. He couldn't believe she'd made it this far. Her hair had dried into a wild tangle around her parchment-pale, mud-streaked face. Her shoulders were hunched; her eyes were glazed, and bruised by fatigue.

Despite the bulk of her jacket, she looked fragile. He remembered vividly why that should totally nullify any arousal he might feel for her. Might? Hell, he imagined what she'd look like naked. Warm and naked. Under him naked. Satiated and naked.

Damn it. I'd better get a grip here. He cleared his throat.

She frowned. "Are you all right?"

He craved his bottle of Crown Royal. The whole bottle. No glass. No ice. "Couldn't be better. You?"

She didn't answer.

He strode back to her. She just stood there, her eyes heavy-lidded and sleepy, her arms hanging limply at her side.

"Want me to carry you?" he asked gruffly.

"Yes."

Surprised by her easy acquiescence, Jake picked her up. She wasn't as light as she looked. Marnie wrapped her arms about his neck, and her head flopped onto his chest.

"Run out of juice?" Impossible. She'd still be chatting if she were fast asleep.

"Yeah, somewhere between extinction by drowning and termination by your imaginary friend."

He grunted and continued walking. Her hair tickled his nose. Her heavy hiking boots thumped his thigh with each step he took, and despite the bulk of her jacket, he could feel the underside of her breast.

"Mmmm, this is nice."

Yeah. It's great. Just freaking great.

She stroked a light finger along the ridge of scar tissue at the base of his throat. The fairy-light touch shot like a rocket to his groin.

"Who did this to you?" Marnie whispered, her breath warm, and annoying, on his neck. "Someone like those guys out there?"

"No." *Thank you, God, for the reminder.* "Someone a lot more dangerous. A sweet-faced blonde with big, innocent blue eyes and a wicked knife with her initials engraved on the hilt." Long after the physical wound had healed he'd felt the sharp bite of betrayal.

"A *woman* did this to you?"

I did this to me, Jake reminded himself. "Oh, she wielded the knife. But I was the dumb bastard who let her get close enough to use it."

"That's terrible."

"That's freaking terminally stupid."

"No, I mean that it was—"

"No talking." Jake cut her off as they came to a dead end. In the unlikely event anyone got this far, they'd find it the end of the line. The door before them contained an impenetrable titanium shield.

It was fortunate the elevator utilized a retinal scan, as his hands were full of woman. Jake paused just long enough for the device to recognize him. The door slid open soundlessly, then just as silently closed behind them.

He thought she'd fallen asleep, but she said quietly against his throat, "We aren't moving."

"We're going down."

"Is that a Bond, James Bond thing?" she asked, voice slurred by exhaustion, eyes closed. "Like in the movies?" She deepened her voice. "We're going down, Guido, and there's not a damn thing we can do about it."

Jake couldn't help the chuckle. Damn. She never ran out of juice. "We're in an elevator."

"Ah. How far dow—"

"Phoenix two-two-one-two-zero clear." Jake waited a beat for the door to glide open, then stepped into his lair.

He'd never brought anyone down here. No one even knew of its existence. Too late now for second thoughts.

He was taking a risk. A huge risk. If it was the wrong choice, one of them would end up dead.

He welcomed the immediate sense of sanctuary, the dry warmth, the smell of home.

"We're here," he said unnecessarily.

She opened her eyes. "Holy cow! Put me down."

Marnie wriggled out of his arms like a 120-pound blue marlin, eyes wide, curiosity on full alert.

"Oh, wow. This is *amazing*."

Jake's underground lair consisted of an enormous living space, with a vaulted ceiling, pale gray walls, and tile the same color on the floor. The indirect lighting, as natural as outdoors, had an undetectable source, yet was bright enough to read by. The room reminded Marnie of the bridge of the starship *Enterprise* with its countless monitors, state-of-the-art equipment, and the backdrop of a low, electrical hum.

The elevator door whispered shut behind them.

"Guess we're not in Kansas anymore, Toto."

While she spun around to take it all in, Jake walked over to a wall unit and turned on the stereo. Something smooth and bluesy filled the room. The rich sound was loud enough to eliminate the buzz but soft enough to remind her of the attraction she felt for him. In the process of removing her jacket, she raised a brow.

Jake caught her eye and scowled slightly, then changed the music selection to something heartier, with lots of drums. He ignored her grin and strode across the room, shedding his own jacket as he went. He tossed it over the back of a worn brown corduroy couch.

One end of the couch was piled with multicolored pillows, none of which reflected the colors in what looked to be an extremely old and very valuable Persian carpet. A paperback cowboy book lay facedown beside a coffee mug and half a package of Oreo cookies on the battered seaman's trunk he used as a coffee table.

"Get out of those wet clothes," Jake said without turning around.

* * *

"In a second." Marnie snagged a couple of cookies while she checked out the rest of Jake's personality via his domain. The place had an efficient, comfortably lived-in feel. The temperature in the room was comfortably warm, and her adrenaline rush was subsiding. She didn't, however, feel like getting naked in front of Jake Dolan just at the moment. "Did you do all this?"

"Yeah." He walked over to adjust something on a panel above a long white counter across the room.

On the left, an unmade king-sized bed trailed a brilliant yellow-and-red Chinese silk throw. She scanned the orderly bookcases, filled with everything from Asimov to Zane Grey. His CDs, many of which Marnie had in her own collection, ranged from classical to jazz. A man with catholic tastes.

She ate another cookie; the sugar helped sweep away some of her exhaustion. Then she walked up behind Jake as he scanned the bank of monitors on the wall above an L-shaped, futuristic workstation. Twelve three-foot-by-two-foot flat-screen monitors embedded strategically in the walls around the room gave the appearance of windows.

Jake looked tired and frustrated, his expression intent. The temptation to run her hand over his hair in a gesture of comfort was nearly overwhelming. Instead she curled her fingers into her palm. She had a lot of things to worry about right now; Jake didn't need to be one of them. She rested her fingers on the pulse at her wrist. Fast. But fine. Just fine.

"Infrared?" she asked rhetorically, trying to make out what they were looking at. Each screen showed a different aspect of the surrounding woods in a dim, murky red glow.

She hoped to see Duchess, but there was no movement other than the wind in the trees and the steady fall of snow. Trying to identify each view, she moved down the length of the workstation to face the monitors head on.

"At night, infrared. During the day, normal view."

"Hmmm. You don't, by any chance, have any aspirin around, do you?"

"No." He gave her a piercing look. "Shoulder hurt?"

"Oh, my shoulder's fi— Yeah, it hurts a little."

"Can't hurt too badly if you can't figure out what hurts." Jake turned back to the screen.

Marnie stuck her tongue out at the back of his head. "What do you do if you get a headache? Bite down on a bullet?"

"I didn't used to *have* headaches."

One of the monitors showed the interior of Jake's cabin.

"Hmmm," she tried to keep the eagerness out of her voice. Moonlight through the window in the kitchen illuminated the edges of her sketch pad with its message to Jake. It was still propped up on the kitchen counter, where she'd left it this morning. It seemed a million years ago.

"How far away is that?"

Jake moved closer to see what she was looking at. "The cabin's directly above us."

Beneath the screen was a panel consisting of a series of flat buttons. As he punched out instructions the camera slowly panned the interior of the cabin. "Doesn't look like they've been in yet." He glanced at her. "With any luck the dog will get there first."

"But the entrance is miles away."

"The way we came isn't as far as you think. But she won't have to go that far. As long as she returns to the cabin, she'll be fine. There's another elevator behind the pantry."

She closed her eyes, thankful that the cabin and her things were this close. *There,* she told herself. *You were starting to get panicky for nothing.*

"Can I go up and get my backpack?" Marnie asked, casually, trying to keep the eagerness out of her voice with difficulty. "There are a couple of things in there I need."

Jake narrowed his eyes. "You don't need your lotions and potions. I'm not risking that they've already inventoried your cra— Yes! I see you, you son of a bitch," he said under his breath, gaze intent on the screen.

A blurred shape moved in a crouch toward the cabin twenty feet above their heads. "Come on in," Jake snarled as the figure was joined by another. He manipulated the camera.

The zoom motion didn't produce a clearer image, he zoomed back out again.

The men paused several hundred feet away from the front door.

"What are we going to do?" Marnie whispered, leaning close enough to feel the brush of his hair on her cheek and smell the damp fabric of his shirt. Knowing those men were up there, so close, looking for him, gave her the willies.

Jake shifted, eyes still fixed on the two men. "You don't have to whisper. They can't hear us."

"Good, 'cause I want to scream. Since I'm here, whether you like it or not, I think you'd better tell me just what I'm in the middle of."

He stared at her as if he had X-ray eyes. After a moment he said briskly, "I thought I told you to change. Get warm and dry first. Then we'll talk."

He strode across the room to the triangular black shower angled in the far corner and turned on both jets. There was no curtain around it, no door, no concealing walls. The hard spray fell in well-disciplined streams into a center drain.

Marnie crouched to untie the wet knots in the laces of her boots. She did need that hot shower. She could wait another ten minutes for answers.

"There's a magic screen that covers that, right?"

No matter how cold and damp she was, she had no intention of stripping off and hopping into that shower with Jake Dolan's eyes on her.

Well, not *this* time, anyway.

"I wasn't expecting company." Jake took several folded navy towels out of a cabinet and tossed them on the closed toilet seat. "There're some things I have to do. I'll be back in twenty minutes."

"Jake, wait. Those men aren't going anywhere. If you have to go out, at least warm up in a hot shower first, and put on dry clothes."

"I've been colder and wetter."

He strode to a narrow closet and removed a bundle of fleece. After he'd tossed the clothes on his bed, he went to the elevator they'd just exited.

"While you're out, would you mind grabbing my backp—my things?"

"I'm not going that way. Take a hot shower."

He placed his palm on a panel on the wall and the door slid open. He stepped inside, and the door closed silently behind him.

On the monitor above the sleek metal door, she could see him inside the elevator. He looked directly into a camera.

"Make use of the facilities, don't use all the hot water, and don't touch anything. I'll be back in twenty."

The cold kept him sharp. Jake moved quickly down the tunnel, checking his firepower and booby traps as he went. When he'd constructed his fortress from the old mine shafts years ago, he'd been playing mental war games. Worst-case scenario. He had never intended it for his own protection.

He came to the mountain to rejuvenate. To remember his own humanity. To remember his friends. The lair had become a laboratory to test his products, to see which of his inventions worked, which would hold up under attack. He was trying to achieve the dreams of the Musketeers.

Face it—he'd built it to fill the gaping hole in his life. Five years of hard labor and sweat equity building something he had never thought he'd need.

Well, now he needed it.

He'd spent a hell of a lot of time alone as a kid. Isolated by circumstances and his age, there'd been nowhere to go but his imagination. He'd dreamed big. At first his thoughts had been consumed with family and friends. Warmth. Security. Stability. He hadn't found anything close until after he'd done his stint in the navy and then joined T-FLAC.

He'd loved the danger, the thrill, the adrenaline rush, the fight for right. But more than having found his niche, Jake had found the three best friends a man could have.

His boots crunched on the gravel as he rounded the corner. He hit the off switch before his beast could growl at him, and returned the flashlight and weapon to their original spot.

And now here he was. Back to square one. Isolated. Without

the comfort of imagination to sustain him. Because the days of false illusion were over. He faced cold reality every day. It was a given, like drawing the next goddamn breath. Once again he'd learned how fatal it was to trust. It was considerably easier to know he had only himself to depend on. His friends were gone. T-FLAC had turned its back on him. He was on his own.

No illusions there.

Back to the business at hand.

Who *were* these bastards?

Just because they wore the same protective gear as T-FLAC operatives didn't mean they *were* T-FLAC. Just because Marnie didn't understand the language they'd spoken didn't mean they spoke the shorthand he'd learned sixteen years ago in T-FLAC boot camp.

Hell. He didn't want to believe they'd send his own people to erase him.

He welcomed the cold air blasting through his damp clothing as he got closer to the entrance of the tunnel.

Was all this somehow tied into the fiasco his professional life had become in the last year? The reason for his suspension? The reason he was taking an enforced leave of absence up here in the first place?

It pissed him off anew that his superiors believed Jake Dolan was a traitor. They hadn't said it outright. But that was the consensus when they'd suggested he take a vacation. Vacation, hell. He was suspended. Indefinitely.

There was a mole at T-FLAC, all right. But *he* wasn't it.

His priority in coming up here was to track down who was screwing with his impeccable record. Now this crap with the assassins. It seemed unlikely the two were connected. But anything was possible.

Shit. Back to square one.

Who and why?

And how the hell had anyone tracked him here? No one knew about this place. No one. Not anymore.

Four of them had bought the land with the old cabin on it, dirt cheap, more than ten years ago. They used to come up here to drink beer and swap wild stories about the women they'd encountered on various assignments. The lair had been a pipe dream.

He, Lurch, Brit, and Skully had toyed with the concept of building similar structures for the protection of heads of state or anyone else threatened by terrorists.

Save the world. Make a million bucks.

The Four Musketeers.

Except three had died in the line of duty before any of it could become a reality.

He missed them the same way an amputee missed a limb. Missed knowing that no matter what they'd be there for him, as he'd been there for them. Missed knowing he didn't have to look over his shoulder to know one of them was covering his back.

Four young men, high on the adrenaline and idealism. The good guys, making the world safe. They'd felt invincible, cocky, and so damn sure of their rightful place in the scheme of things.

And then there was one.

And he wasn't so damn cocky and sure of anything anymore.

The adrenaline rush, the thrill, had lost its shine. There was a never-ending supply of terrorists. It was harder than hell to fight the good fight when the bad guys kept on going like the Energizer bunny.

Hell, he was only thirty-six, though sometimes he felt older than dirt. But trying to save the world from terrorist threats was all he knew. Maybe it was time to train the next batch of gung-ho young operatives to fight the good fight.

He owned a decent chunk of Wyoming cow country he seldom visited. Maybe he'd go there. Fix up the house. Buy some cattle . . .

Not anytime soon. He wasn't ready to retire.

He'd clear his name and get back to business.

His prime directive was to track down a tango named Dancer and make him pay for Lurch's death.

All he had to do was get rid of a bunch of determined assassins, an equally determined woman, and a missing dog.

Piece of cake.

Snagging a pair of hidden night vision goggles, Jake put them on, then clambered up the rocky vee until he was outside.

The snow fell in large, wet flakes. The NVGs showed no movement, nothing out of the ordinary. He checked for signs of his and Marnie's earlier passage, then, satisfied the snowfall had covered their tracks, clambered back into the cave.

What the hell was he going to do with her?

He double-checked that the Walther had a full clip, repositioned the NVGs, and made sure the flashlight faced the rear of the cave, in case someone entered and saw a reflection on the glass. That done, he stared at the blackness leading back to his lair.

Dammit. She was down there. In the shower. Naked but for translucent wisps of steam. He imagined her lifting her arms to the spray, turning her slick, soapy body, running her hands over her skin.

She'd be making those damn noises deep in her throat.

He tried to remember what it had taken to build that shower. He'd lugged cement, tile, and a frigging water heater three miles up the mountainside just so he could have hot water whenever he wanted it.

Her skin would be soft. Smooth. Warm.

Pale against the black tile.

Jake stopped midstride, tempted as hell to do an about-face and go back outside. The way he felt right now, he could off four or five guys with his eyes closed and one hand tied behind his back.

It would beat going back and smelling his soap on her skin.

Hell.

Chapter Seven

Marnie figured she'd been less exposed pooping in the woods on camping trips than she was here, showering in Jake's basement. She used the facilities with her eyes glued to the monitors, feeling vulnerable and self-conscious even though she was completely alone. She didn't consider herself particularly modest, but she'd taken the fastest shower on record.

As she hurriedly dried off with a thick navy towel, she realized how ingenious the underground room actually was. Nobody could approach without being seen. Wherever one stood, a monitor could be observed.

The second Jake exited the elevator into the tunnel on ground level, she had stripped and stepped into the shower. While she washed and defrosted, she'd watched him travel down the corridor. Cameras picked up each bend in the tunnel.

By the time she'd showered, she was both warm and invigorated. And starving.

With a towel wrapped around her, she snatched a cookie to sustain her while she dressed. She glanced at Jake's unmade bed. This was the bed he'd left to come and get her at the crack of dawn this morning. It seemed like days ago instead of only twelve hours.

A little shiver raced up her spine. She'd never run so far or so fast in her life. Abject terror was a great motivator.

Thank God she'd been jogging around the local high school track for the last few years and was in decent shape.

She'd never been quite so terrified in her life as when she'd heard those bullets whizzing over their heads or the inexorable thunder of the water racing down on them.

She glanced around the cozy lair. Unreal. But if she wanted a reality check, it was there on the monitor near the bed. A bulky, blurred red shape moved through the trees.

She had about a zillion questions. One of which was, would she be home on Monday before her dad freaked out?

He expected to hear from her when she got into the office on Monday morning. He and the boys hadn't approved of her impromptu trip in the first place. They were already worried about her. If her brothers knew what was going on up here, they'd arrive like the cavalry, guns blazing.

The first person they'd shoot would be Jake.

It was unlikely this would all be over by tomorrow night so that she could go home. She might as well make the best of the situation.

The best of the situation was her attraction to the mysterious Jake Dolan.

She thought of his mouth on hers. The feel of his arms tight around her. The heat in his eyes, despite his insistence that he was immune to her. With a wicked grin, she wondered how he'd react if he came back and found her waiting for him in his bed, stark naked under his exotic silk throw. How immune would he be then?

She relished a bite of cookie, then almost bit off her tongue as the sound of a buzzer split the air.

"Which one?"

She scanned the monitors frantically, trying to figure out what had triggered the alarm. The half-eaten cookie in one hand, the top of the towel clutched between her breasts in the other, Marnie dashed from one screen to the next.

The buzzer sounded again.

"Damn it, what does that *mean*? Jake, get back here!" She glared at the tunnel monitor. "Thank God."

He was on his way back.

"Get the lead out, big guy. Things are happening. *What,* I have no idea. But something."

Jake stepped into the elevator. He looked right at her. *Well,* Marnie amended, *right at the camera.*

The buzzer continued, overshadowing the sound of crashing cymbals and bongo drums from the CD.

Out of the corner of her eye she suddenly noticed a movement on one of the other screens. Feeling as though she were watching a particularly engrossing tennis match, she rested her behind on the back of the couch.

On the right, in the red glow, she could just see Duchess, crouched low. Three men stood talking, mere feet away from her dog.

On the left screen, Jake stripped off his wet jacket, hair damp, face ruddy from the cold. His lips were pressed into a grim line.

"Come on, Jake. Move it," she whispered urgently, switching to watch the motionless dog almost hidden by the shrubs. So close and yet so far.

Marnie figured Duchess had been on her way to Jake's cabin when the men had intercepted her. They didn't seem in any hurry to leave. Fortunately, it didn't look as though they'd seen Duchess. Yet.

"Good girl, you stay put." Her voice was a soft entreaty, but her heart pounded.

"Find a good channel?" Jake asked, coming up beside her before she even realized he'd entered the room.

Marnie dropped the cookie, stifled a scream, then dragged in a shaky breath. "Holy cow, Jake! You scared *another* ten years off my life. Next time, cough or whistle or something when you come in." She nodded at the monitor. "Duchess was almost here, and those creeps aren't moving."

Damn. I might have known.

She was wearing a towel.

Just a towel, by the looks of it. Unwillingly Jake's gaze followed the naked curve of her shoulder. Her skin was pale. And smooth-looking. And smelled, God help him, sexy as sin. He wanted to bend down and lick those droplets off the curve of her throat.

"Jake? What can we do?"

She had a faint dusting of freckles across her shoulders, well-defined biceps, and about a mile of silky, slender leg showing beneath the dark towel. She looked soft, feminine, and sultry.

A deadly combination.

"Nothing," he managed around the growing thickness in his throat. "I left clothes for you over there. Put them on."

"Sure."

She didn't move.

He looked at her mouth. It made him want to do things. Hot things. Wild things. Things that had nothing to do with what he *should* be doing.

His flannel shirt clung to his damp skin like a shroud. His boots felt too hot. His chest was too constricted and his pants too damn tight.

"I should have tossed you in the river and made you swim to the other side." His voice sounded like ground chuck.

Her eyes, with their long, spiky, childlike lashes, sparkled as she gave him an angelic look. "I would have drowned, then come back to haunt you."

She was haunting him *now*.

"Get some clothes on. We need to talk."

She held his gaze. "What about Duchess?"

"I don't think she can add anything to the conversation," Jake said dryly.

"Funny man."

"We aren't going to do anything." Which answered both their questions rather succinctly, Jake thought.

"But she—"

"When the men move, I'll get her." It came out more harshly than he intended. "Just because you're used to getting your own sweet way doesn't mean I'm going up there to rescue your dog and take the chance of getting shot."

"All I w—"

"I'm not going up there."

Marnie slipped her hand over his mouth. "I didn't *ask* you to."

Her hand felt soft and warm against his lips. This close he could see a darker ring around the clear blue of her irises, exhaustion smudged her eyes, damp hair clung to her creamy neck and shoulders. The smell of his soap on her skin gave him a hard-on. *Ah, Judas.*

Very gently he put his fingers around her wrist and removed her hand, then let go of her as if he'd been electrically charged.

"For now we stay put. They can't see the dog. And they don't know we're down here watching them. Relax. The dog's smart enough to stay hidden, and nobody can get to us in here."

"Hmmm." She held his gaze a moment longer. "Is that why you built a fortress? So nobody can get to you?"

"I never expected visitors. It was constructed as an exercise. A testing ground for my inventions, far away from prying eyes. The place is perfect. People rarely come up here, especially at this time of the year. I do most of the work in spring and winter. Nobody knows about its existence."

"I don't understand." Marnie gave him a puzzled look. "If you aren't hiding and you didn't expect anyone to come up here, why do you *have* all this?" Her sweeping hand indicated the monitors, the computer, the entire setup. She frowned. "And people *do* know about it and *are* up here."

"So I've noticed." He was freezing his ass off and wanted a hot shower almost more than he wanted her. He knew she had trouble controlling her breathing when she looked at him, as she was doing right now. Her cornflower blue eyes couldn't hide the fact that she wanted him right back. Luckily for him, he was a master at disguising the few feelings he still had.

He returned her heated gaze with cool detachment. Without actually looking, he noticed the bead of water that trembled on her collarbone, and then saw it trail, with excruciating slowness, down the soft plumpness of her right breast. "This gadgetry is a hobby."

"You mean you *invented* all this cool stuff?" She gave him a droll look. "A hobby would be something like building model airplanes, Jake. This is more than a hobby."

"Some of the things I've come up with have sold. The money has come in handy for making more espionage detection and deterrent hardware."

She was incredibly appealing when she grinned like this. Hell, she was incredibly appealing anytime. *Damn it. Why her? Why now?*

"You mean spy toys. Lord, it must have taken you years to build all this."

"Five. Get dressed, for godsake." If he looked at her in the skimpy towel much longer . . .

Marnie spun on one bare foot and walked to the bed. "What you need is a life, Jake." She picked up the clothing he'd left for her and said over her shoulder, "There's a lot more going on here than a hobby, and I want to know what that is. Close your eyes."

She dropped the towel.

Close his eyes? Judas Priest. A two-by-four applied directly to his forehead couldn't close his eyes right now.

His gaze riveted on the sweet curve of her backside, on a mile of curvaceous leg and thigh, on—

He took a step forward. Something crunched underfoot.

Saved by a cookie.

While Jake took a hot shower, Marnie fixed roast beef sandwiches. Unlike the cupboards in the cabin, Jake's stronghold revealed all sorts of goodies. The fridge was filled with fresh fruits and vegetables, the freezer jam-packed with a wide assortment of meats, chicken, and gallon containers of ice cream. A man after her own heart.

Marnie managed to keep her eyes fixed on sandwich making. Most of the time.

She'd felt his gaze on her like a brand when she dropped her towel, so she figured she was entitled to a couple of sneak peeks at Jake Dolan naked. It was only fair. There didn't appear to be an ounce of fat on him, and he was tanned all over. He had a runner's legs dusted with dark hair, a tight, sexy behind, a narrow waist, and broad shoulders. The picture of him soaping his lean flanks was indelibly imprinted on her synapses. She ached inside with the need to touch him. Biting her lip, she turned back to the mundane task of sandwich making before she lost all reason and attacked him in the shower.

She almost amputated a finger with the sharp knife in her hand when he came up behind her and interrupted her mental fantasy.

"Cough, remember?" she reminded him, blushing as she handed him a plate with a sandwich on it.

"That looks good. Thanks."

He wore black jeans and a black sweatshirt with the sleeves pushed up his muscular arms. Like her, he was barefoot.

Jake glanced down her bare legs. "Didn't I give you sweatpants to wear?"

She rolled her eyes. "There's a ten-foot difference in our heights. I almost killed myself tripping over the legs. Don't worry, I'm decently covered. I have a pair of your boxers on underneath, see?"

She lifted the hem of the thigh-length sweatshirt to show him the navy cotton shorts she wore underneath. "I know it's kinda personal wearing your underwear, but necessity is the mother of invention, right?"

"You didn't *invent* my underwear, you took it out of the drawer." He dragged his eyes away from her legs with great reluctance. Or so it seemed to Marnie.

She gave him a curious look. "Unlike your cabin, this place could handle a year-long siege. How on earth did you haul all this stuff up here? Not just the food, but all these machines, and those huge monitors. Someone must have helped you."

"No, just a hell of a lot of trips over the years. Most of the components were brought up, then constructed here. What I didn't haul in on my back, I brought by chopper."

"How long have you—"

"Enough cocktail chitchat." Jake cut her off. "Let's sit down. We need to cover some things before this gets hairy. Then I want to get some shut-eye."

"Fine. You take the plates, I'll bring the coffee." She added milk to her mug, then followed him to the couch. "Okay. Fill me in." She set the mugs down on the trunk and sat down, wrapping her arms around her drawn-up knees. "Who's who and what's what?"

His eyes on her mouth, Jake growled low in his throat, then pressed his fingers into his eye sockets.

About to reach for her mug, she shot him a startled glance. "Are you okay?"

"I'm starting to believe in mercy killing," he said in a strangled voice.

She gave him a puzzled look, then tossed some of the pillows off the couch and onto the floor to make more room. She picked up her mug. She'd made the coffee strong, and it was too hot to drink. She cradled it between her hands and waited.

The Dave Sanborn CD she'd put on while Jake showered played softly in the background.

On the monitor, Duchess remained hidden while the three men conferred, or took shelter from the snow. No one was going anywhere tonight.

Jake ran his fingers through his wet hair. "You should get some rest."

"You said we needed to talk. So let's do it. I have a right to know what I'm in the middle of. And since my need to know who the bad guys are exceeds my need to sleep, and I can talk with my mouth full, let's talk. First of all, Jake Dolan, who are you really? You live in a basement like a techno mole."

"Basement?" He gave a short, sardonic laugh. "Okay, why the hell not? At this rate I'll atrophy in my two-million-dollar *basement* anyway."

He rubbed a hand across his chin, obviously reluctant to tell her anything, but torn due to the circumstances.

"Those guys are here to erase me. The question is, whose people are they?"

A chill raced across Marnie's skin at his casual use of the word *erase*.

"Whose do you think?" Her fingers tightened around the warmth of the mug. "Come on, Jake, *talk* to me. I'm trapped here just like you are. And I'm not embarrassed to say the situation scares me to death. I'm not used to assassins chasing me up and down a mountain and shooting at me. The least you could do is tell me what I've landed myself in the middle of."

"You do realize," he said flatly, "if you're *not* who you say you are, and I debrief you, I'll have to kill you?"

She wasn't a hundred percent sure he was joking.

"I am who I say I am. Debrief me. Please." She had a quick irreverent flash of his hands skimming her hips as he "debriefed" her out of his underwear.

"I work for a covert, black-ops organization called T-FLAC. Terrorist Force Logistical Assault Command. We're the ones who go in when there's a problem with terrorists."

"You work for the government? Thank God, call—"

"Not officially, and not only ours," he said flatly, shutting her up with a dark glance. He drank his coffee in silence for a moment before he spoke again, his voice grim. "Terrorists are global and, unfortunately, prolific. We go where we're needed."

"You must be very good at your job."

"Why?"

"They wouldn't have sent a whole army to bump off one guy if you weren't."

He was good at what he did because, as she'd quickly learned, he was a man who could control his emotions. Just as she was no more than a nuisance to him, those men out there were a job, no matter who sent them.

"Killing me wouldn't make much of an impact in the scheme of things. *All* T-FLAC operatives are good." He rubbed his jaw. "All indications point to the assassins *being* T-FLAC, and that—"

"Your own team is trying to kill you?" Marnie asked indignantly.

"Judas, I don't know. I suspect—yeah. Something's been going down for several years. It escalated last month.

"T-FLAC's been around a lot of years. Good rep. Top people. Two months ago I was hauled off an important assignment in the Midwest and sent on garbage detail to a small no-name cesspool in the Middle East. It wasn't a big deal. Just a favor. I wasn't happy about it—the Omaha operation was about to pay off. I took a junior guy with me to the cleanup site.

"When we got there, the shit hit the fan. The tangos were expecting me. They killed my man. The garbage wasn't ready for pickup. It was a hell of a mess. I cleaned up what I could, and split."

Marnie looked up at him. "Did they ever find out who warned them?"

Jake looked grim. "Every indication pointed to me being the mole."

"How *dare* they think that!"

"The evidence was strong. No one knew where I was or what I was doing."

"Nonsense! The man who was killed knew where you were and what you were doing. The person who sent you there knew what you were doing and where you were."

"The guy I took with me had a low security clearance. He didn't know where or what until we were there. The man who sent me in is the head of T-FLAC. No way, nohow would he put two of his operatives in that kind of danger. The only one it could have been was me."

"*What* evidence?" she asked indignantly. Then, without waiting for him to answer, she said crossly, "I don't care if they found you pushing up marigolds with soil on top of your head and the roots in your teeth. You're no mole!"

She might not know much about Jake Dolan, but the little she did know indicated that he was an honorable man. And an honorable man wouldn't sell out his own team no matter what anyone thought. She was irrationally furious on his behalf and narrowed her eyes when he chuckled.

"Don't laugh. You know what I meant. And what kind of organization doubts you when you're their best spy guy and have worked there for— How long?"

"Sixteen years," Jake muttered. "There's more. A hell of a lot more. Before I was pulled out to go overseas, I'd been control for an ongoing assignment in Omaha. When I hit stateside it was to discover that all our people on the inside had been massacred. They'd worked for two years undercover, and a month before the bust, every last one of them died. And I was conveniently out of the country at the time."

"But they *sent* you."

"Men and women killed. Good people." His tone didn't change, but his body stiffened as taut as a violin string.

"Too many screwups, too close together. The price tag was too damn steep. Our organization isn't huge, but we sure as hell are the best at what we do. If our people believe I was responsible for the screwups and the deaths, you bet they'd off me in a heartbeat."

"I don't get it. Why would they believe the worst of you?"

He paused for a long time. "They know I've become single-minded in my need to pursue one man." Jake looked at her, his eyes dark and dangerously flat. "Revenge can make a man sloppy."

"Against whom?"

"A terrorist named Dancer. I've been after the son of a bitch for six years. Everyone knows I won't stop until I find him. They think I've been distracted, careless, because my efforts to find the rock he's hiding under have been relentless."

"Have you been?"

"Careless?"

"Relentless."

"Dancer is the driving force behind the Shining Path of America in Omaha, where my people were murdered last month. He was the reason I was selected to do the Middle East cleanup. Because *I'm* the one who knows Dancer best. I didn't give a damn about his disciples, his army, or his chemical plant," Jake said bitterly. "I wanted *Dancer*. And Dancer had fled to the Middle East. He was the only thing that could have gotten me to leave so close to the end. So my single-mindedness *did* kill my people in Omaha, and the kid who went with me to the Middle East."

Jake raked his fingers through his hair, his face gaunt, his eyes haunted. "Dancer was responsible for the death of one of my closest friends six years ago."

Obviously exhausted, he was also frustrated and majorly ticked off. Marnie wished there was something she could do to help Jake.

He leaned forward with his elbows on his knees and stared at the intricate patterns on the area rug at his feet. His dark hair fell forward, so she couldn't see his face.

"People tend to think of terrorists as a handful of Middle Eastern or leftist fanatics, bent on achieving ideological goals through death and intimidation. The reality is terrorists are more obscure. Groups of fanatics pursuing sometimes hard-to-understand agendas, with random violence as their common denominator. Some of them are doing it for money, some for political gain, others because of ethnic conflicts.

"We have no damn idea *what* the hell Dancer's agenda is. He's number three on the U.S. State Department's 'dirty thirty' list.

Jake's dark blue eyes met hers. A shiver of fear climbed Marnie's spine at the look in his.

"He's number one on *mine*," he finished flatly. "And everyone knows it. Things have escalated. We caught Dancer's people with eighty pounds of typhoid bacteria cultures they planned to dump into the water of midwestern cities two years ago. We stopped them. That time. But we don't know where he'll hit next.

"After the massacre in Omaha, he disappeared like smoke. Again. In the meantime, I've been suspended awaiting a full inquiry. And while I'm pinned down here by the guys topside, God only knows what the son of a bitch is doing. Or where he's doing it."

Marnie drained her cup, needing more coffee but not wanting to get up. The story was riveting. She would have preferred reading it to actually living it, but she had wanted a grand adventure. And this was certainly that and more.

"I guess the bad guys up there are a more immediate problem, right? How can you find out who they are?"

Jake picked up his sandwich and brought it to his mouth, looking through her. "The last one will talk."

Which meant he planned on getting them before they got

him. "I definitely like a guy who's so sure of himself. In the meantime, since I'm here and a captive audience, why don't you tell me what I can do to help?"

His eyes refocused as he looked at her. "I can't think of a thing. Don't freak out. Don't *chat*, and stay put."

Ookay. "Not what I had in mind."

"Know how to shoot?" When she shook her head Jake said flatly, "Then you can't help. Do what you do best—lie around and look pretty."

Been there, Marnie thought, unoffended, *done that.*

She smiled and nudged his hip with her bare toes. "You're a chauvinist, Jake Dolan. I *do* have a functional brain, you know." She kept her foot against his hip.

"Don't," he snapped, shifting impatiently. A muscle ticked in his jaw. "I'm not a chauvinist. If you could shoot what you aimed at, I'd consider taking you topside with me."

Marnie brought both feet together next to his thigh and leaned back comfortably against the pillows, watching him over her knees. "Liar. You wouldn't let me shoot at someone. You might not like me, but you'd never risk me taking a bullet you thought was meant for you."

He turned his head and gave her the strangest look. "Oh, yeah?" he almost snarled. "Where the hell did you get that idea?" He didn't contradict her statement that he didn't like her, however.

"You must have a hundred cowboy books in here. It's the code of the West." Her feet were still cold. She wriggled them a little deeper between the cushion and Jake's butt. "Come on, admittedly I've never even held a gun, and frankly I don't particularly want to start now. But I don't want to lie around doing nothing, either."

"Fine. Watch the monitors for me."

"Where will you be?"

"Taking care of business."

His body heat warmed her cold bare toes. Her eyes felt gritty, as though the sandman had sprinkled sleepy dust in them. Marnie blinked, trying to stay awake. "Who else knows about this place?"

"No one."

She slid a little lower, nestling her head into the cushions. She liked looking at him and let her gaze move over his face as he concentrated on the monitors across the room. She wished she had her sketch pad and pencils so she could catch his brooding, pensive expression. His mouth was made to kiss a woman, yet right now it was a tight, grim line. Although he sat absolutely still, an air of unleashed electricity crackled. She wondered if she was a good enough artist to capture the suppressed energy in a man who sat so still.

He was analyzing the situation in his head. When he reached a conclusion, he'd be gone. Up there in the icy snow and dead of night. One man against . . . too many.

Her eyelids drooped, and she closed them for a moment to relieve the burning sensation. Opening them, she found Jake watching her. She wished she had the right to slide her arms around his narrow waist and rest her head on his shoulder.

"Anyone interested in finding you could check with the county offices and do a title search." She was talking to stay awake, but yawned anyway.

"Nope. I've buried this so far down, there's no way. My name isn't on anything. Are you going to finish that?" He indicated the other half of her sandwich.

"I'm not really hungry. Go ahead." Other than a few cookies, she hadn't eaten since the chili and soup this morning, but her stomach warned her not to add to the churning acid.

The muscles in his back shifted under the black cotton sweatshirt as he reached over and picked up her sandwich, demolishing half of it in one bite.

"Someone could have followed you," she suggested, snuggling her head on the soft sofa back.

"No."

"Maybe not this visit, but some other time?"

"I never come here using the same mode of travel. My routes are so convoluted not even I could have followed me, and I knew where I was going." He polished off the sandwich.

"What about family?"

He shook his head.

"Friends?"

"We don't exchange chatty letters."

"Now, why doesn't that surprise me? Come on, Jake, *someone* has to know about this place."

"Other than me, and now you, anyone who knew about the lair is long dead. Four of us pooled our resources more than ten years ago to buy the land and the cabin. Now I'm the only one left, and there's no maybe about it. I saw them die. Long before this 'basement' was started."

"But they knew about it?" She closed her eyes for a moment to relieve the dryness. Hmmm. That felt good. She left them closed for a while longer.

"Sure they knew. We planned it together," he said impatiently. "But they didn't tell anyone. Just like I didn't. Subject closed."

"Do you have a phone?" She squinted up at him. Jake nodded. "Secure line? On roam mode?"

He scrutinized her. "For an artist, you seem awfully knowledgeable about computers and secure lines."

Ridiculously pleased he'd remembered, Marnie smiled. "I'm a programmer, Jake. Wright Computers, my dad's company in Silicon Valley, remember? I know something about tracing crackers, the more sinister form of hackers. These guys are good, but I've caught quite a few of them. We do work for several high-profile companies who have the best possible security. If you were traced through this computer, I'll be able to tell you how and probably who as well. Is the computer on a secure line, too?"

"Yeah."

She couldn't help it—she yawned again. "Have you sent any messages out while you've been here?"

"A couple to my headquarters. But I changed the signature file. No one could have traced me that way."

"Yes," she told him grimly, "they could." A small quirk curved her lips. "See? There *is* something I can do. I'm good at what I do, too. I can figure out who traced your E-mail. And once you have that info, maybe you can figure out who those men work for and why they're after you.

"Either way, it sounds as though the only way you could have been traced was through your computer. And if I know anything, Jake, I know computers. You deal with the bad guys up there. I'll figure out who they are from down here."

Chapter Eight

Jake didn't want her doing *anything*.

The fact of the matter was he didn't want her within a hundred miles of this mountain. He didn't want her on his computer doing God knew what and talking to God knew who. He didn't want her close enough to smell her unique fragrance. And he damn sure didn't want her to watch him with sleepy, heavy-lidded eyes filled with a warmth he hadn't known he was missing until she came along.

He hated like hell that he'd brought up the guys. Even after all this time the loss of three of the Musketeers, the best damn friends a man could ever have, was still a spike in his chest.

"I don't think that's a good idea," he told her impatiently. At his words those baby blues narrowed. "While I appreciate the offer, you won't be here that long. As soon as the river goes down I'll get you across the upper bridge. It'll take you a while to get to your vehicle, but you'll probably be home by tomorrow night."

She burrowed her toes under his thigh. The woman loved to *touch*.

"I'll be here long enough to—" The light dawned. "You don't trust me enough to *let* me help you, do you?" She paused and gave him a calculating look, then said conversationally, "Do you have a sharp knife?"

He shifted his hip but couldn't get out of her reach. "In the kitchen. Why?"

"Because if some blonde tried to slice your throat, and you lump all blondes together, then I might as well get it over with. It must be hell waiting for the other shoe to drop." Her pretty blue eyes looked quite serious.

"Although I ought to warn you," she added, "the sight of blood has a tendency to make me faint. And frankly, I'm too tired to move. So why don't you go over there and pick out one you think would do the job? Then come back here, lay your head on my lap, and indicate which way you want me to cut your carotid artery, right to left or left to right."

"You want me to get you a knife so you can cut my throat?"

"Isn't that what you're waiting for?"

Jake stared at her; he'd never met anyone like her in his life. "Do you always just blurt out what's on your mind?"

"It's a waste of time to dance around the issue. Why not cut to the chase? It eliminates misunderstan— Hey," she said brightly. "Those guys are gone."

He'd noticed several minutes ago. She jumped from one subject to the next like a dragonfly. It was disconcerting.

He levered himself off the couch, away from her scent, her guileless eyes, and her pale bare feet.

"I'll go get the dog."

"Terrific. Could you bring my backpack while you're at it? And Jake? Be careful."

He'd rather face a hundred assassins than stay down here with her and her screwy logic. "I always am."

Despite her physical and mental exhaustion, the second Jake left, Marnie found herself too wired to sleep. Standing between two monitors, she watched Jake take the short trip topside in the elevator. From her vantage point she could observe both the cabin and Jake. She wanted to be alert in case the men came back.

Seconds later they did.

"Oh, shoot."

Three of them entered the front door of the cabin. Her imagination filled in color and detail. Black clothing, headgear, knives, Uzis. The infrared images diverged on entering.

"Oh, my God. *Jake!*"

Her eyes shot to the screen showing Jake, still in the

narrow confines of the elevator. If he had spoken, she knew, she would be able to hear him. But there was no way he would be able to hear her.

Frantically she scanned the walls on either side of the metal door across the room, half hoping for a call button. She rolled her eyes. "Yeah, right." Naturally Jake had some high-tech gizmo that read his palm print. It wasn't going to help *her* any. There was no way to let him know that within seconds he'd be walking in on three of the bad guys.

The iffy moonlight sliced into the cabin, bisecting it into light and dark. It also messed up the infrared of the camera, making it hard to see. The men looked like fuzzy red blurs—though somehow their weapons seemed much clearer. Perhaps it was her imagination working overtime.

One man spoke, and the other two spread out. The words, while perfectly clear, were totally unrecognizable to Marnie. She scowled.

Powerless, she observed one of the men cross to the counter separating the kitchen from the rest of the room.

"Nuh-uh, you don't need to look at tha— Darn it."

He picked up her sketch pad, still propped on the counter. The sketch pad filled with her drawings of Jake. Her heart sank.

It was possible, *possible,* they weren't sure Jake was here. But one look at those sketches and there would be no doubt. Although she wasn't sure anyone would recognize the mellow-looking Jake Dolan in her drawings. The guy said something to the other two, indicating a page in the large sketchbook.

They answered in the same unintelligible language. The base didn't sound Latin, it sounded like . . .

Language was the least of Jake's problems, Marnie reminded herself, pulse thumping in her throat. There was no way to stop the confrontation about to take place.

Her head swiveled the other way. Jake, trapped inside the elevator, hadn't moved. "Good, you stay right where you are," she urged, dry-mouthed, waiting for the door to slide open, for the three men to ambush him. For the inevitable conclusion.

The phone in the cabin rang. *Her* phone.

Paralyzed, she stared at the screen. "Oh, hell, it's Dad."

One of the men picked up her cell phone from where she'd left it on the kitchen counter.

"No. No. No."

The phone continued ringing as the men conferred. The shrill *tring-tring-tring* sounded like fingernails on a blackboard as she waited. Marnie couldn't drag her gaze away to see how Jake was reacting to this latest development.

The ringing stopped abruptly.

The man handed the phone off to one of the others. They continued searching the cabin.

In the elevator Jake glared at the camera.

"Come down here and say that, darn it." She found herself standing a foot away from the sleek elevator door in Jake's high-tech basement. As if she could will the door to open, and him to step back inside the room where she waited, practically biting her nails.

Her attention shifted from one view to the other. One monitor showed the progress of the men systematically going through drawers and cabinets.

The other showed Jake, still as a statue.

Marnie shook her head. He'd never leave himself in a position to be trapped. Somewhere in that small box where he stood was a warning device.

"There'd *better* be," she muttered grimly, head turning to see what the baddies were up to now.

"Hey!" she yelled at the screen as one of them found her backpack and roughly went through the contents. "Don't you know it's rude to go through a lady's purse?"

He took something out of the side flap of the pack, called to one of his friends, and showed him the small brown plastic prescription pill bottle.

Her heart literally stopped, and she felt the blood drain from her head. "Oh, damn, don't take that."

After a brief dialogue the bottle disappeared into his pocket.

Marnie closed her eyes.

A thought occurred to her, and she groaned. Taking her pills was bad enough, but now the bad guys knew she was here, too.

Jake was going to kill her for not telling him about her need for medication.

"If I tell him. Which I won't," Marnie decided. It served no purpose. Jake had enough problems on his plate. One of them worrying about it was enough.

But oh, God. What if she had an attack?

She had to tell Jake.

She *had* to. There was no choice now.

Since Jake was immobile in his fancy silver box, and the men in black continued going through both the sketchbook and her backpack, Marnie went to retrieve the Oreos.

It was that or panic big time.

She was suddenly aware of each beat of her heart as she hadn't been in years. "Damn, damn, damn."

Pushing aside, for the moment, thoughts of impending doom, she took the half-empty package and perched on the very edge of the foot of Jake's bed.

She felt as she did when she watched a ball game. If she didn't root for the home team, they invariably lost. No matter how tired she was, she had to stay alert in case Jake needed her.

Time crawled. It seemed like forever, but it was only four cookies later that the men left the cabin. Marnie watched their progress from monitor to monitor until they disappeared into the trees.

"Okay, Jake, they've left. Be careful. And would you *please* speed this up? I'm having excessive heart palps here."

One cookie after they'd disappeared, Jake exited through the pantry.

No wonder the shelves appeared so shallow.

He moved silently through the shadows to the window. After checking outside, he went to the counter, where he quickly flipped the pages of her sketch pad. He glared directly into the camera and quirked a brow. Marnie gave him a little wave, knowing he couldn't see her.

He slipped inconspicuously across the room to check her backpack, as the bad guys had done. Then left both objects exactly where he'd found them. She sighed and bit into another cookie.

There wasn't much point having her backpack now, anyway.

She should have realized the moment the baddies had seen her stuff that Jake would leave everything as they had found it. Obviously he didn't want them to know he'd returned to his cabin.

She tamped down a shudder of panic.

She'd be fine without her medication.

Just fine.

There was no point getting herself into a knot when there was nothing she could do about it.

She allowed her gaze to slip from Jake to the reddish glow outside where Duchess still lay low, almost hidden by the foliage.

"Come on, big guy, she's waiting for the all-clear."

Jake's broad back came into view as he cracked the front door. He whistled softly. She imagined Duchess's ears swiveling at the sound. Marnie perked up. Yes!

He whistled again.

Head low, Duchess crawled cautiously from her hiding place, then became a swiftly moving red ghost as she shot like a bat out of hell across the clearing. The large dog took the fallen tree in front of the cabin in one long, low, graceful leap.

Jake opened the door a little wider. Duchess darted into the room. He pushed the door shut behind her.

Marnie punched the air with her fist. "Yes!"

Duchess was one happy dog. Her nails clicked ecstatically on the wood flooring as she danced around Jake, tongue lolling as she told him in doggie-speak just how grateful she was he'd saved her. It was frustrating to be able to hear them up there and not be able to join in.

Marnie had to grin. She wished she could see the expression on Jake's face at such lavish gratitude.

A movement from one of the other monitors caught her eye. Still smiling, she turned to get a good look at the red image.

The smile slipped. "No, no, no, no, *no!*"

An assassin stood silently, half hidden by the corner of the building. "How long have *you* been there, you turkey?"

Had he seen Duchess? Had he seen Jake open the door?

Her heart lodged in her throat and stayed there.

His movements illuminated by uncertain moonlight, Jake moved around inside the cabin. What in heaven's name was he doing now?

The man moved stealthily around outside the cabin. Marnie could observe every inch of the front of the small structure in one or the other of the monitors. She watched him pause three feet from a window and realized she'd been holding her breath. She exhaled shakily and leaned forward.

In the cabin, Jake lay his hand on Duchess's large head in a clear warning.

The assassin slid another foot, his back to the wall. His right hand lifted, holding what was obviously a weapon.

"Comeoncomeoncomeon."

Jake crouched, then stood, holding a hundred and five pounds of dog in his arms. With movements as slow and graceful as a choreographed ballet dancer's, Jake, carrying Duchess, moved to the back of the cabin.

He'd heard the guy. "Right, Jake? You know he's out there?"

A board creaked beneath Jake's boots.

Marnie bit her lower lip and froze.

Outside, the man shifted but didn't take a step.

Inside the cabin the enormous bulk of Jake and dog slipped into the bathroom. The door glided closed behind them.

The bad guy took the two steps necessary to stare in the window. Marnie could see his back in one monitor, his head and chest in another. Like the others, he was mummy-wrapped, his features well concealed by his black garb.

Jake and Duchess were now trapped in the bathroom.

"Jeez, Jake—" Marnie shook her head "—what the heck are you doing?"

It almost seemed anticlimactic when he finally entered the small elevator. Clever Jake—there were entrances and exits galore.

Seconds later the door into the basement slid open. Duchess bounded out ahead of him. Marnie hopped off the bed and braced herself. "Hi, pretty girl," she crooned in relief to the dog, but her eyes were on the man.

The dog's nails clicked ecstatically on the floor as she raced toward her mistress.

Duchess leaped, and her front paws slammed into Marnie's chest. If Marnie hadn't been ready, she would have fallen. The dog slathered her face with kisses, whimpering and wagging her tail before abandoning her to do the same to her hero.

Eyes still locked with hers, Jake stopped the dog's antics with a hand gesture. Duchess turned and gave her mistress a happy grin, then darted off to sniff and explore.

Still maintaining eye contact, Marnie walked over and punched Jake in the solar plexus, not hard enough to hurt, just hard enough for him to blink in surprise.

"You—you *jerk!* You scared me half to death! There were three, *three,* of those creepy guys right there in the cabin, just waiting to . . . to do *whatever* they planned on doing to you. Then, no sooner had they slunk off into the trees than that other one came—he was right outside. If he'd moved a little faster, he would have seen you. And if he'd seen you, he would have shot you. I saw the gun. And I was stuck down here, with no way to warn you."

"Take a breath," Jake said dryly.

She socked him again, this time leaving her balled fist on his chest. "You have to give me a way to help you. A way to warn you. Damn it, Jake, you could have been killed, or hurt, or something."

"So you punched me?"

Marnie flattened her palm on his chest, feeling the steady thud of his heart through his jacket. "Yeah, so I punched you.

You're lucky that's all I did. I hate feeling helpless. Don't make me go through that again."

"Or what?" Jake asked, stepping forward and crowding her against the foot of the bed.

Marnie gave him a blank look. "Oh. I'm supposed to have an answer to the 'or what' question, right?"

Jake's mouth quirked. "It makes it more effective, yes."

The last bit of adrenaline leaked out of her, Marnie let her head flop on his chest. He didn't exactly stiffen, but she felt him go dead still. What *was* it with this guy? How could he be so impervious?

"Just out of curiosity," Jake said over her head, "why the hell would you give a damn, one way or the other, if they got me?"

She squeezed her eyes shut, wrapped her arms about his waist inside his damp jacket, and pressed her cheek against his chest. *Oh, Jake.* "I told you, I hate the sight of blood."

"You really do chatter when you're scared, don't you?"

She could have sworn she felt his mouth against her hair. She swallowed the thickness in her throat. "Even the Man of Steel was vulnerable if the bad guys had kryptonite."

"There's a silent alarm in the elevator," he said calmly. "I knew they were there."

He laid his cheek against her temple and locked his left arm around her waist. Her calves were flush against the bed. If she leaned back just a little . . .

"If they'd got me, you would never have been able to exit the lair. Did you think of that?"

"No, frankly I didn't. I was worried about *you*. And I got whiplash while I was at it," she added, nose buried against the heavy beat at the base of his throat. He smelled of the outdoors, of pine and snow, and man. So vital, yet not indestructible. *Oh, God, what if . . .*

"Is this how it works?" he asked roughly, his arms tightening around her. "The tear-filled eyes?" He kissed the outside corner of her eye.

"The sincerity in your voice?"

His large, callused hand stroked her throat. A shiver racked her frame. Ripples of desire started in her belly, then fanned out in concentric circles to engulf her body.

"Is this where I start to believe you could possibly give a damn?" he whispered, his mouth a breath away from hers.

"Is this where we take our clothes off and you show me how badly you want to make love to me?" He nibbled an agonizingly slow path to her lips. Marnie turned her head slightly, catching his mouth with hers.

For half a heartbeat he sank into the kiss. Then he jerked his head away sharply and looked down at her with a detached coldness that made blood pound in her ears.

"Is that how this works for you, Marnie?" he repeated, voice and eyes hard.

She had been listening to his tone. Not what he was saying. She'd been anticipating what came next. And the answer with him was, of course, nothing. *Lover talk,* she'd idiotically thought. She shook her head, more at herself than at Jake, and adroitly sidestepped him.

"Are you speaking to me?" she asked tiredly. "Or the woman who betrayed you and tried to cut your throat?" She held her arms out at her sides. "Take a good look, Jake. She and I aren't the same person. It'll be your loss if you keep comparing apples and oranges."

"It's all fruit to me."

"Oh, Jake." Her gaze skimmed his features. "Are you in or out again?"

His eyes met hers. "Why? Got plans?"

"I thought you might like something hot to drink if you were going out again."

Jake walked over to the monitors and sat down in the chair before the console. Duchess looked back and forth between them as if trying to decide which one to go to. Marnie indicated with a subtle hand gesture to go to Jake. He was the one in need of comfort right now. If he wouldn't take it from her, perhaps he'd take it from Duchess.

The dog ambled over, resting her large head against Jake's thigh as he manipulated the cameras. He absently fondled her ears, as he scanned each screen.

Marnie smiled and went to the kitchen area to make a fresh pot of coffee. "Where will they sleep?"

He glanced over at her, his mouth a hard, grim line. "Who? The bad guys? What are you? A bleeding heart? The elements won't bother them. Those outfits will keep them warm and dry."

"I don't care if they freeze their collective butts off," she informed him, cutting thick slices of roast beef for Duchess. She arranged the slices on a plate and put it on the floor, then cut several more. One she bit into, leaning a hip against the counter.

Duchess gobbled down the treats, then, catching the tension in the room, retreated with a sigh to lie down on the area rug, chin on her paws, eyes alert.

Marnie poured a mug of coffee for Jake, then walked over to give it to him. "I was just thinking that if they came back to the cabin for shelter, you could get them all in one place."

His laugh was rusty. "Yeah, right. Why don't you go topside and call them in for coffee?"

It was screwy, but then her logic usually was. Still, it wasn't a bad idea. The cabin could be practically hermetically sealed from down here.

There was a movement on camera seven. Jake zoomed. Just the wind in the trees. He zoomed out again. She was close. Too close. How the *hell* could she smell like spring flowers?

He drained half the mug of coffee and enjoyed the painful burn all the way down.

She perched on the workstation beside the control panel, bare legs swinging, head tilted to look at him. They were eye to eye.

"You know who they are, don't you?"

"Their MO was telling, but hearing them cinched it. We learn that 'language' at T-FLAC. It's complex and damn hard to decode. It's useful in the field when there's a chance we might be overheard. I heard enough to know they're closing in."

She put her hand on his arm. The sensation shot up through bone and muscle like an electrical current.

"I'm so sorry, Jake."

He moved away. The sizzle stayed with him. "It makes no damn difference which side kills me. I'll still be dead."

"Still," she said gently, "it's got to hurt to know people you thought you could trust are trying to hurt you."

"They aren't trying to hurt me. They plan to *kill* me. And I haven't trusted a damn soul since Lurch, Skully, and Brit died. It makes no damn difference to me who the hell they are."

She hopped off the counter and came around behind him. Jake froze as she wrapped her arms about his neck from behind and rested her chin on his hair.

What the hell was it with this woman? She just loved to *touch*. He stiffened, ready to break her hold. But, damn, it felt okay to have her touch him like this. Just for a second, of course. He didn't like it, wasn't used to being cuddled. He wasn't the warm, fuzzy type. Never had been.

No.

He couldn't like her. He *wouldn't.*

Jake squeezed his eyes shut, and felt the strength of her slender arms wrap about him like a cashmere blanket on a cold winter's night. Like spring water to a parched throat. Like balm on an open wound.

Judas Priest.

He could deal with the lust. Lust was controllable.

It was tenderness he couldn't handle.

Sex with her was out of the question. She tangled things. Made logic illogical. Made things he knew to be right seem wrong. Made nonsense out of sense.

A good night's sleep was all he needed, Jake assured himself, not shaking her off just yet. By tomorrow he'd have her across the river. If he had to *toss* her across, he'd have her safe. In the meantime all he had to do was keep distance between them.

He carefully untangled her arms from about his neck. A chill swept over him like nothing he'd felt before. Jake ignored it and leaned over to adjust a camera angle from the console.

"Just in case they get lucky, I'll show you how to exit in an emergency."

He put her through the procedure and encoded her fingerprints and her retina into the scanners via the computer. It was fortunate he'd trained in deep-sea diving and could hold his breath for long periods. Right now that was the only way he had of not inhaling her fragrance.

He showed her how to exit, told her when to exit, and did everything in his power not to brush against her.

It was peculiar she hadn't freaked out about being stuck down here if he was offed. What kind of woman was she that she cared more for the dog than her own safety?

"Get some rest. I have to go out and take care of business."

"I'll be in a coma in about thirty seconds," Marnie assured him around a jaw-cracking yawn that made her look like a sleepy cat. "What about you?"

"I'll rest while they run around looking for me tomorrow."

"Jake?" She followed him to the tunnel elevator.

He half turned. "What now?"

She came right up to him, showing no fear at his obvious impatience and irritation. She stood on tiptoe and fiddled with the collar of his jacket until it lay the way she wanted it. Her eyes met his. "Thank you for bringing Duchess home safely."

"This isn't *home*," he informed her in the tone of voice that had terrorists backing away if they were smart.

She gave him a solemn look. "Kiss me good-bye."

"Don't you ever give up?"

She had very pretty eyes. Hypnotic eyes, Jake decided, mesmerized by the heat and the sweet clarity he saw there. He tried to shift out of her reach. He tried to drag his gaze away from the bewitching appeal of her.

Somehow his arms wrapped about her slender waist. Her arms looped around his neck. Her mouth touched his.

Soft.

Smooth.

Sweet.

The embers in his gut, which had been glowing for hours, days, a lifetime, roared into an inferno.

Jake didn't give a damn if it was witchcraft or insanity. With a groan of pure agony, he crushed his mouth onto hers and felt the slick heat of her tongue meet his.

Judas Priest. The woman took prisoners.

One more second, he promised himself, and he'd pull away.

One more lick. One more nibble.

Two minutes later, he tore himself away from her arms. Band-Aid quick.

"Lights. Off. Ninety-five percent." His voice sounded ridiculously hoarse.

He strode into the waiting elevator, turned, and saw her standing where he'd left her in the gloom.

"Be careful out there," she said softly.

The door slid shut.

Jake closed his eyes, then leaned forward to thump his head *hard* on the metal panel.

She was hunched over the computer when he returned hours later, the dog snoring at her feet.

"What the hell do you think you're doing?" Jake demanded, striding across to her. His hands and face tingled in the warmth of the room. She'd turned up the heat.

"Heat," he said tersely. "Sixty-four degrees."

Dumb ass. He was the one who'd given her the keys to the castle. He shouldn't be surprised she'd burglarized him.

The dog opened her eyes. She grinned a doggy grin, then slumped her chin back on her paws and with a contented sigh closed her eyes again.

"That was hello," Marnie told him unnecessarily, head down as she concentrated on the computer monitor. "I made some vegetable soup. It's on the stove. And corn bread," she muttered without looking up.

"You did a good job covering your trail. All I'm doing is coming up with dead ends. I've got one . . . last—" her fingers skimmed the keys "—thing to try."

The savory smell of the soup made his mouth water. The sight of *her* made his heart stop.

She'd turned up the heat and then, obviously too warm, changed from his sweatshirt into the old tank top he used when he went running. Soft from a hundred washings, the fabric hung from her slender body, accentuating her curves and making her skin look like silk. Paired with his blue boxer shorts, it was a formidable outfit.

She embraced the rules of engagement. *As long as it works, anything goes.*

He watched as she ran her fingers through hair that had dried to soft, springy curls the color of honey. One step and he could touch her. He stayed where he was.

Oblivious to the impact her state of undress had on him, Marnie turned back to the computer. "I coded a package trace program to see if I could get an echo back from the satellite using your encryption algorithm. Let's see if the baddies came in through the back door." Her fingers flew across the keyboard. "Now for the satellite coordinates . . . Okay, let's see what happens." She pressed a key, then folded her arms and sat back.

Her blue eyes twinkled as she looked at him over her shoulder. "How was work, honey?"

Jake snorted.

Beside her, numbers flashed across the monitor almost faster than the eye could see. Marnie whirled around and leaned forward to avidly scan the screen. She tapped out a few more rapid keystrokes.

Jake strode up behind her.

"Damn." She nibbled her lower lip.

"What is it?"

"Nothing. Not a blasted thing." She pushed a curl out of her eyes and scowled. "I don't know how they did it, but a cracker didn't trace you through the computer, Jake. I've tried every trick in the book and then some. I've found zippity-do-dah. Maybe if I called my dad—"

"No, no calls," Jake said sharply. "It doesn't matter. Besides, I told you, I don't need your help. It's one-thirty in the morning, and you've been up since six. Why aren't you sleeping?"

"It's not like I have to get up early," she said dryly, with a final glare at the screen. "Thanks to the coffee and cookies I ate, I got a second wind after you left. Besides, I needed to wait for you."

Jake stripped off his jacket and tossed it on the coffee table. He strode toward the stove to poke at the soup with the spoon she'd left beside it. "Why?"

"To make sure you're in one piece."

"I'm in one piece."

The soup was thick with vegetables and savory with spices. He found a mug and used it to ladle out a serving. Wiping the drips off the side with a finger, he sampled the taste. It was great. "Go to bed."

She busied herself turning off the computer, then swiveled on his chair to face him. Her bare legs looked pale and vulnerable wrapped around the base of the chair. "You need rest even more than I do."

Jake closed his eyes on a long-forgotten prayer. "You're not my mother. Sleep, don't sleep, I don't give a damn. Just give me some space."

"You're mad because I kissed you and you liked it."

Jake found the warm, butter-saturated squares of corn bread. He drank soup from the mug. "Kisses are a dime a dozen. Yours are good but nothing special. I told you. I'm immune."

She untwined herself from the chair. Eyes narrow, she came toward him like a sniper stalking her kill.

"You may be the spy king of the universe, Jake Dolan, but you are one big fat liar. You want me. You want me bad. You're just being disbuggerable about it."

"There's no such word as *disbuggerable*." Reluctantly Jake put the mug and slice of corn bread down. Just in case he had to defend himself.

"Don't change the subject."

"It was either kiss you or kill you," Jake told her, his hip striking the counter behind him. "I hope I didn't make the wrong choice."

She giggled.

Jake closed his eyes. *Oh, man. This isn't goddamned fair.*

"Don't you have a lick of sense, woman? I scare most people."

She tried to straighten her face and ended up biting her smile in half by sinking her teeth into her lower lip. "I'm sure you do."

"Is this what you did to those fiancés of yours, Marnie? Pestered them until they gave in?"

She stopped a few feet away and said quietly, "If you want to know if I've had any previous lovers, all you have to do is ask."

Jake picked up his soup mug and took a slug. It was good soup. She could cook. BFD. Who the hell cared? "I don't give a damn if you were the featured date du jour of the sultan of Brunei. Get it through your head: You're here under duress, *my* duress, and the second I can get you across the river, the better I'll like it."

"Even if Winkie wants me?"

"Who the hell is Winkie?"

In answer, her gaze traveled to his crotch.

"Woman," Jake roared, beyond insane, "do you have a death wish? Get in that bed, pull the covers over your head, and go to sleep before I do something we'll both regret."

She went.

"Lights. Off. One hundred percent."

Except for the illumination of the infrared on the multiple screens around the perimeter, the room immediately plunged into darkness.

A second later she was a motionless lump under the silk throw he'd brought back from China last year.

Jake wished he had a cellar where he could chain her for the next few days. He wished he'd left her in her grandmother's cottage with the tree through the roof. He wished he'd urged her to swim across the flooded river and left her to be swept downstream.

Most of all, he wished she didn't tempt him so much.

Lurch used to call him the Man of Steel for his phenomenal willpower. Jake wondered morosely if his pal was watching him from some pearly cloud in heaven and having the last laugh right now.

Chapter Nine

Marnie slept the way she did everything else, with one hundred percent commitment. Jake woke beside her after a solid six hours' rest. Refreshed and alert, he turned to look at her sprawled out beside him.

He should have sacked out on the couch—it was comfortable, and he'd done it before. But there was something dangerously appealing about crawling beneath the covers with her, even though he'd left a wide space between them. It was a form of insanity, but he couldn't resist. Within minutes she'd closed the three feet of space and gravitated to his side as if she belonged there.

He'd gone out like a light within seconds.

It didn't surprise him that during the night she'd flung one leg across his, or that her head was sharing his pillow.

Jake glowered at her.

He wished she'd stop telling him to be careful. Acting like she gave a damn.

She had hot pants, that was all. But she embodied a lethal siren song of uninhibited sexuality and genuine naïveté he found hard to resist.

The woman even had a pet name for his body parts. Judas, He got an erection every time he so much as looked at her. Biological. Nothing more. That didn't mean he had to act on it.

Especially now.

He glanced away from her sleeping face to check the flat-screen monitors. *Knock yourselves out,* he thought as the gray early morning light showed four men skulking through the trees near camera nine, a good half mile away.

He could easily remain where he was, twenty feet under the earth and undetectable. He had enough supplies to last through the coming winter and beyond. After a few weeks the men topside would leave, convinced they'd been fed disinformation or that he'd died when they'd opened the dam.

The woman beside him made the idea of staying put dangerously appealing. Tempting as it was, he wasn't going to do it.

For one thing, he needed to know who the hell had instigated the hit. There was no doubt it was the same person, or persons, who had been doing a fine job framing him as a T-FLAC mole for the past several months.

For another, while infinitely patient, he was damned if he'd remain hidden while a bunch of goons ruined his reputation and tromped over his mountain trying to find and kill him.

He had the home field advantage. They were on his turf now.

There was no rush. Time was on his side.

With uncanny perception, Marnie had mocked him last night about waiting for the other shoe to drop. As it always did when he thought of it, the scar at the base of his neck began to itch.

Of course, he was no longer gullible enough to be blindsided by a woman, even one as clear-eyed and innocent as Marnie. For the first time in years a woman mentally entertained him. She was unique.

He'd been content living by himself and worrying about nothing but his own hide. The thought of being stuck down here with her for weeks on end was dangerously appealing.

Hell, what am I thinking? He had to get her off the mountain so he could concentrate on the job at hand.

It had been years since he'd needed to concern himself with someone else's welfare. After Soledad, he'd relished the deadening effect of having no emotion. It simplified life. He didn't give a shit if he came out at the end of an assignment in one piece or in a body bag. It was all the same to him.

He'd been a damn good operative before Soledad. A.S.,

after Soledad, he'd become one of T-FLAC's most feared operatives. Immune to emotion, he'd become lethal.

Good for him. Bad for the tangos.

He took pride knowing he was called a cold, heartless bastard.

He didn't need emotion, didn't want the trouble and baggage that went with it.

He was happy with his life. Happy with himself. And perfectly content to maintain the status quo.

He had no desire to get all het up about a woman. And since Soledad, he'd never been tempted.

He glared at the woman sleeping beside him.

Her eyelashes made intriguing fringed shadows on her creamy cheeks as she slept the sleep of the innocent. A good night's rest had brought a flush to her cheeks, and her lips were slightly parted, making her look sensual and vulnerable at the same time. He put a tentative hand out and moved a spiraled curl off her cheek. Fingering the silky filaments, Jake experienced a bemusing wash of emotion. It was an odd and vastly annoying sensation.

He had to look away from her for a moment to control the hunger that exploded through him.

He'd forgotten what it was like to want a woman this badly. He wanted to trail his tongue over her warm, ripe breasts. He wanted to explore her with his hands, his mouth, and his teeth. He wanted to taste her, test her, and tease her. He wanted to evoke those same responses in her. *Damn it all to hell.*

He felt eyes on him and looked up to see the dog watching with brown-eyed reproach from the other side of the bed.

"Wanna go outside, girl?" he asked softly, grateful for the diversion.

"Not particularly," Marnie said around a yawn, her eyes twinkling. "But Duchess does." She stretched luxuriously. "Wow, I feel terrific. How about you?"

Hell, yes, you feel terrific, Jake thought as she dragged the silky smoothness of her bare leg across his. It was like being stroked by a satin-covered live wire. He came to immediate attention. Her voice, morning-husky, sexy as hell, did strange things to his entire nervous system.

"I'll take the dog out," he said shortly, not moving.

She looked breathlessly irresistible with her hair tangled, her pretty eyes bright, her body warm from sleep.

From sleeping nestled against *him* all night.

Her eyes glowed. "You know what would be fabulous?"

God, yes.

"Pancakes."

Pancakes?

The only pancake he could imagine was her, flattened between his body and the mattress while he pumped into her again and again.

She rolled onto her side, as if they'd shared a bed their entire lives, and braced herself on an elbow to gaze down at him. Totally discounting the fact that her leg had slithered over both of his. That her hair tickled his face as she shifted. That a week ago she hadn't known he existed.

"Yep, pancakes. With lots of syrup. What do you say?"

"Sure. Pancakes." He flung the silk throw aside. "I'll take the dog outside now." Duchess, butt wagging, came around the bed to escort him.

"Oh, wow. You have gorgeous legs."

Jake, in the process of pulling his jeans up over his boxers, stiffened. He felt the tips of his ears get hot, and he glared at her over his shoulder. "I have what?"

She propped herself up on both elbows—which then threw her unfettered breasts into relief under the tank top. "Gorgeous legs. Hasn't anyone ever told you that?"

They'd told him he was a son of a bitch. They'd told him he had no heart. They'd told him his eyes alone could scare the crap out of a person from twenty paces. They'd never mentioned his legs. "No."

The dog nudged him not so subtly with her head. He dragged his gaze away from the adorable fruitcake in his bed to her horse of a dog, then back again. "I'll be back."

"Can I go with you?"

"No."

Marnie flopped onto her back. "I'll be here."

"Tell me about these guys you were engaged to."

"You need a dishwasher, you know that?" Marnie grumbled, washing the few dishes they'd used.

"I have one. You." Jake stacked his hands behind his head as he stretched out on the couch. He wore jeans, a black-and-red flannel shirt, and no shoes. While he and Duchess had gone for a walk, she'd commandeered another pair of his boxers and changed into her own flannel shirt. She could feel the heat of Jake's gaze on her bare legs.

"Your fiancés?"

She picked up a plate, dunked it in the sink, and swished the dishrag around.

She would have bet good money that Jake would have slept on the couch last night. Instead she'd woken briefly sometime during the night to find her nose mashed on his chest, his fingers tangled in her hair, his legs twined with hers.

Too bad she had merely surfaced, then slipped back deep into sleep. She would have enjoyed having Jake's arms around her when they were both not only horizontal but conscious. She wondered what he'd do if she went over there right now and stretched out over his body like a blanket. She bit back a smile.

Problem was, she was starting to get stir crazy, and when that happened she tended to get into trouble. Add that tendency to being fatally attracted to him, and she was already in big, *big* trouble.

She had to admire his self-control.

Was that why she found Jake so intriguing? Because he blatantly *didn't* want her?

Marnie had been giving that some serious consideration for the past twenty-four hours. Yes, she admitted with her usual self-honesty, that was part of it. But not the biggest part.

Fascination and curiosity were to be expected, considering their circumstances. But it wasn't simple proximity.

Jake Dolan intrigued her, fascinated her.

She liked the way he moved. For such a large man he was very graceful. He did everything with quiet efficiency and assurance. He didn't accept help, because he was obviously used to being alone.

The constant shadow in his eyes reminded Marnie of a wildlife documentary she'd seen once. A jaguar had been found in a trap, its paw mangled by the cruel metal jaws. Its yellow eyes acknowledged impending death. It had almost ripped out the throat of one of its rescuers before it was tranquilized and the light of battle had died.

Marnie had never forgotten that jaguar's eyes.

Jake had that same look: a man betrayed. A man who wouldn't trust easily, if at all.

She liked the way he talked tough yet was gentle when he touched her. She liked the way he'd protected her back when they'd been running, and the way he cared for Duchess. She liked the way his eyes crinkled at the corners, indicating amusement, even when his stern mouth refused to smile.

She liked the way he fought himself.

It made her more determined.

She thought of the hundreds of cowboy books filling his shelves. The code of the West. Jake Dolan had a white-hat, superhero attitude that was sexy as hell.

He was a man with ethics. A man with integrity.

He wouldn't be an easy man to love.

But if she wasn't careful, he was a man she could easily fall in love with.

"I never realized washing a few dishes by hand took so much concentration," Jake said from his reclining position. "Or are you avoiding the subject?"

She sighed. "It's a long story."

"Can't wait to hear it."

"Don't you have to go chase baddies or something?"

"There's a storm warning. It's still snowing. The bridge is impassable."

Jake propped his large bare feet on the opposite arm of the couch, then reached for his mug, which he balanced on his flat stomach. "While those guys are running themselves ragged in the freezing cold looking for me, I'm down here, full of pancakes, syrup, and hot coffee. Let's hear your story."

Marnie folded the towel and left it to dry next to the small sink. There was only so much a woman could do in a one-room lair.

She gave Jake's long body, taking up the entire couch, an assessing look, then searched for a pencil, grabbed a small stack of paper from the printer, and wheeled the desk chair closer. She sat with her bare feet propped on the trunk and started doodling, the papers balanced on her lap.

"Do you have any siblings?" she asked absently. She'd never drawn a man's feet before.

"No."

"How about parents?"

"Yeah, I have a set of those."

She glanced up. "Where are they?"

"Last I knew, Chicago."

"I take it you weren't close?"

"We weren't. We were talking about you, and *your* family, and your lack of commitment."

"Hey! I can too commit. It's no big whoop. The relationships didn't work. End of story." She shaded in his big toe.

"That's a short story. Let's hear the unabridged version."

"Jaaake."

"Got something better to do?"

"We could bake the frozen cookie dough in the freezer."

Duchess's ears perked eagerly.

"We just ate breakfast," Jake said to both of them. Duchess subsided on the area rug, head on her paws, eyes reproachful.

Marnie didn't particularly want to be the entertainment for the morning. Having all of Jake Dolan's attention focused exclusively on her was a little overwhelming. She reached over, plucked the mug out of his hand, and gulped the last two inches of coffee.

"There was nothing wrong with the men I was engaged to. I liked them just fine. The thing is . . ." She dragged the chair forward until she could wrap her arms around her bent knees, and stared at his toes. She wished she had her favorite pencils.

Jake had sexy feet. Actually, she decided, letting her eyes do a nice slow perusal, *all* of him was sexy. And there was a lot of him. She wondered how she could wangle a kiss out of him. He looked so damn tempting lying there. . . .

"You were in the middle of a sentence," Jake prodded. "Mind completing the thought?"

"My brothers thought I'd be better off with someone . . . someone . . ."

"Someone what? Like a lion tamer?"

"Low-key," she said sweetly. "And for sure, someone that at least one of them knew. The boys wanted to protect me from men who might want me for my money." *And my life insurance policy,* she added silently.

"Not," Marnie told him wryly, resting her chin on the rather good sketch of half his left foot, "that I'm incapable of taking care of myself, but *they* needed to do it. And to tell the truth, I have a bad habit of taking the route that's the least hassle. It was easy to let them do my looking for me. Lord," she said wryly. "What a twit I was.

"Nevertheless, I do trust my brothers, and I'd always liked their friends. And at the time I wanted to get married—shoot, I thought I was *supposed* to be married. Happily ever after, you know?

"There was nothing wrong with any of them. My brothers know me—they wouldn't drag some dork to the altar by the hair just to prove a point. Well, Michael might. Be that as it may, neither of the engagements worked out."

Her legs itched. "Got any lotion?"

"No. What were they trying to do? Get rid of you?" Jake didn't have the usual edge of exasperation in his tone. In fact, he was starting to look . . . She had no idea how to interpret his expression. Sort of a combination of resignation and fear, which was obviously a misinterpretation.

"Nope. They love me. *Too* much, sometimes, but my brothers do love me. I guess it was because I was such a late bloomer, and they were trying to help in their own way. It's pretty funny." She rubbed her hands up her calf, then noticed, and was fascinated by, the way Jake's eyes followed the movement.

Up. Down. Up. Down. *Hmmm.*

"They thought it was time. I was of marriageable age, and malleable, and willing, to say the least. I just couldn't find the One—that's with a capital letter. Anyway, the boys got together and decided I was taking too long—which is amusing, since *they're* in their thirties and still single—but that's a whole other subject. They decided I needed someone nice and steady. No humongous ups and downs. No huge upheavals."

In fact, just the opposite of themselves.

"They figured you were enough excitement for any one couple, right?"

"Me?" She stared at him. Was he nuts? "Jake, I'm the most boring person I know! I'm a wanna-be artist working as a programmer at my dad's company. You can't get geekier than that. I've worked for him since high school, and all through college. Then nine to five. Time off for good behavior. That's one of the reasons I came up here. To decide just what I'm going to do to change things."

"What things?"

"My life. I want to be an artist. I *am* an artist." She picked up the top sheet of paper and showed him her sketch. "Look at this foot! It's a *fabulous* foot. I can draw. I'm good at it. I *love* it. What am I doing working nine to five for my dad?"

"What *are* you doing working for your dad?" Jake asked obediently.

"Taking the path of least resistance, that's what. Not making waves. Being a good girl . . . Get that look off your face. I can't help myself, I behave strangely around you. After this weekend I'm going to know where I'm bound. Like the Cowardly Lion, I'll find my courage and act accordingly."

Jake frowned. "The Cowardly Lion?"

The poor man was having a hard time following the conversation. She picked up her drawing and shaded his crooked baby toe. It was very cute. She wondered if his children would have crooked baby toes.

"*The Wizard of Oz.* Remember? The Cowardly Lion was searching for courage, the Tin Man was searching for his heart, the straw guy was looking for his brain."

His lips twitched, and he got a funny glint in his eye. "Ah. And what do you need more courage for? You seem to have it in spades."

"*Not.* I am one major cluck. Ask my dad. Ask my brothers. No, on second thought, don't. They'd tell you my life story, and you'd be bored to tears, I assure you."

Duchess trotted over and laid her head on Marnie's shoulder. She reached up and stroked the dog between her eyes. "While I adore them, the Four Musketeers have always treated me—"

His eyes narrowed. "The *who*?"

"My brothers. That's what we call them. Why? What's the matter?"

"I had a bunch of fr—guys. We were known as the Four Musketeers."

"Wow. How cool is *that* for a coincidence? Where are—"

"You were saying?"

Marnie shook her head, then put down her papers and dislodged Duchess's head to get up and refill Jake's mug from the pot on the counter. "You and my brothers would get on great. Or kill each other," she muttered under her breath. She came back and sat down again, cradling the steaming mug. "They t—"

"Is that my coffee?"

She took a quick sip, then another, before stretching out to hand it to him. Their fingers brushed, and her heart gave a crazy thump. "Would you . . ."

His gaze fell to her mouth, then seemed to lock on for eternity. Very slowly he dragged his gaze back to meet hers.

"Would you like another refill?" she asked absently, watching his pupils dilate. Her heart leapt, then started to speed up. Intimate body parts started to tingle. Wow. This man was potent.

"The question is moot, since you're the one who keeps drinking it," he said tightly, putting the mug on the trunk coffee table. A muscle twitched in his jaw. "Finish the story."

The princess had been asleep for a hundred years, and the prince kissed her. . . . "They treat me like spun glass." She leaned back in a vain attempt to escape his force field. *Faint hope.* "Like some dinky, fragile little kid. I love them madly, but it drives me bonkers."

His focus was on her lips as he said raggedly, "So you had to kiss a few frogs to find a prince?"

She wanted his mouth on hers so badly her lips itched. She rubbed the back of her hand over her mouth and shifted in her seat. If this wasn't the most ridiculous situation she'd ever encountered . . .

She felt like a fly at a window. *Thump. Thump. Thump.*

Was she destined to want a man who didn't want her? How ridiculous was this? Perhaps it was some sort of weird cosmic joke. Now that she knew she didn't *need* a man, she'd suddenly met a man she wanted?

Get a clue, girl. This guy is made of steel, she reminded herself. Her heart felt like a runaway train in her chest. He might have a will of iron, but right now his eyes were as hot and sharp as lasers. Her throat felt extraordinarily dry. "It's getting warm in here."

"The temperature's a steady sixty-four degrees. It hasn't changed. Get on with the story."

"Yeah, well, I like fairy tales just fine, but the reality was, most guys are attracted to Daddy's money, and my brothers made them *very* nervous. I dated what I hoped were princes—some were nice guys, others were frogs. My brothers brought me their version of prince look-alikes. But they still looked green and warty to me."

"You appear to be pretty damn self-sufficient to me. Why are your brothers so protective of you?"

Oops. He was the last person on the planet she wanted to tell. Too late, she realized she'd talked herself into a blind alley.

"Um . . . I had this heart thing when I was a kid."

Jake sat up. "*Heart* thing?"

"A little heart thing. No biggie. But I was sort of puny until I was about fifteen."

Jake swung his long legs off the couch. "And this 'little heart thing,' it's fixed now?"

Marnie waved a hand. "Oh, sure. I was all done with the surgeries by my fifteenth birthday."

"Surgeries?"

"I had stenosis and had a couple of valve replacements."

He went pale, and she was sorry she'd told him. Very sorry. People *always* reacted that way. She dredged up a grin. "Wanna see my scars?"

"Yeah," he said softly. "Show me."

Marnie made a face. "I was joking, Jake." *Sort of.* "But of course the Four Mutineers have never gotten over all the time I spent in the hosp—" She felt a little leap, part fear, part anticipation, as he rose from the couch and stalked toward her. "What are you doing?"

"Have to check something out."

"What?" The wheels screeched as she scooted back. She looked up at him suspiciously. "Are you going to kiss me?" *And if so, could you hurry up? The anticipation is killing me.*

"Hmmm," Jake said softly, walking around the trunk toward her, his eyes so dark they appeared black. "This could go either way."

Grammy used to tell her to be careful what she wished for, because she might get it. She swallowed. "If you had a mustache, you'd be twirling it."

"I don't."

She closed her eyes. "Yeah, I know, but—"

He snagged her foot as the chair bumped into the long console behind her. She let out a huff of air.

"We were talking about you." His fingers slipped up to wrap around her ankle, effectively stopping her retreat. "So they protected you?" His hand skimmed from her ankle up her leg.

"Yes."

"You used my razor last night."

She felt a flutter zing up her spine. "Yeah, that's why my skin's so dr- Jake, what are you doing?"

His smile was slow, dangerous, and heart-stoppingly sexy. "I wanna see that scar."

"It's on my chest."

"I'm getting there." He slipped his hands under her arms and swung her off the chair as if she were a doll.

Marnie clutched at his shoulders as he carried her over to the couch. He laid her down as carefully as if she were a land mine ready to detonate. And by the way her heart pounded off the seconds like a timer, perhaps she was.

The soft fabric was still warm from his body. Her head found the indentation his head had made in the cushion. She licked dry lips and watched his eyes smolder as he followed the movement.

He sat down beside her and started unbuttoning her shirt. Very, very slowly, his eyes never leaving her face.

"They insist on taking care of you now, and don't particularly like the men you keep choosing for yourself?"

"That a-about sums it up."

Cool air bathed her chest as he used both hands to slide open her shirt. Inch by inch. Marnie felt a ridiculously Victorian urge to grasp the fabric closed over her bare boobs and closed her eyes. Instead she lay back, muscles twitching, lungs aching for a breath, body thrumming with need, as Jake took his sweet time.

Her blood became a slow fire as he parted the shirt, his hands brushed against her skin with maddening slowness. Her breasts tightened and ached as the path of his gaze seared her skin everywhere it touched.

She didn't stifle the moan of pleasure when his fingers brushed her tight nipple.

Her hands slid up the satin, heated skin of his upper arms. Solid muscle. Tensile strength. Her fingers kneaded with restless, hungry urgency.

He was a large man. Well muscled, strong. Yet she felt completely safe in his hands. He savored her with his eyes, making her senses simmer and churn with pleasure. The musky maleness of his skin filled her senses as he leaned over her. She closed her eyes on a whimper. Just the scent of him turned her on.

"Jaaake," she moaned, her voice shaking with urgency.

He arranged the edges of her shirt so he had a nice full view of her chest. She had a beautiful chest, small plump breasts, creamy pale skin. The scar was a pearl-white streak on smooth satin.

"Is there a metal valve operating under this soft flesh?"

"Metal? Oh." She tried to refocus. "Yeah, metal. They tried the other. Didn't w-work."

"Your heart was stopped." Judas Priest. They'd stopped this heart he felt under his fingertips. Stopped it, and inserted an obscene, life-giving piece of metal.

"Can we change the subject, please?"

"Sure."

Hell, yeah. Let's have something life-affirming to take away the taste of her lying on a table in a sterile room. "Judas, woman. I had you running all over God's creation, to hell and beyond. Why the hell didn't you— I should have— damn it!"

"Calm down, Jake. I've been exercising and running for years. I'm fit as a fiddle, really."

He traced the path up her sternum with one finger. He wanted her so badly he thought he'd explode, but he couldn't get enough of touching her. He *needed* to touch her. Absorb her. To feel the throb of her heart, the ebb and flow of her lifeblood.

It had been a long time since he'd had a woman. Suddenly fiercely glad the woman he was with was Marnie, Jake opened his hand flat between her breasts. Finger and thumb practically spanned her chest.

Her pupils dilated as she stared up at him, lips parted. Her fingers flexed on his arms.

Light from the monitors bathed her as a weak noonday sun made a brief appearance, turning her skin pale gold. Her nipples puckered. She breathed a sound somewhere between a sigh and a vibration of pleasure.

She was as responsive as he'd known she'd be. Jake focused his mind down to a pinpoint. Marnie. Soft, passionate flesh and bone. He stroked his hand up over the gentle inner swell of her breasts until he could put two fingers on the unsteady pulse at the base of her throat.

Vibrantly alive.

"The gospel according to Michael, Derek, Kane, and Kyle," she said breathlessly. "Thou shalt not touch their baby sister until they have folded, stapled, spindled, or mutilated you f-first."

"Is that so?" Jake drawled. Motor mouth was at it again.

"Yeah, that's so," she echoed, eyes glazed. She licked her lips. "My life story to date. Let's hear yours."

Her nipples were the same pale pink as her lips. He lowered his head and touched the tip of his tongue to one hard peak. She jerked and gasped his name. Heat spiraled through him in a shocking burst.

Jake felt her fingers on the back of his head tunnel through his hair.

"Thirty-six years old."

He skimmed his other hand up her narrow rib cage, feeling the goose bumps on her skin.

"Born, Chicago. Navy at sixteen."

God, yes, Jake thought on a curse and a prayer. She *did* make those sexy little noises. He filled his palm with the sweet plumpness of one breast while his mouth laved the other, and she moaned and whimpered.

"T-FLAC from twenty-one." Her body vibrated under his mouth. "Never been engaged or married. That's it."

Her fingers tightened in his hair. "No!"

He chuckled. He'd meant, *That's it. I'm done talking.* He skimmed his knuckles down her hot cheek. She made a noise somewhere between a sob and a whimper.

His heart skittered crazily. "You don't want me to stop?"

"Can a mermaid do the splits?" she asked unsteadily.

The sound he made was part moan, part laugh. He bent his head and brushed his mouth over hers.

A thought streaked through his mind. *Ah, hell.*

"I don't have protection."

"It doesn't matter. I don't care. Oh," she said softly, closing her eyes, fingers tightened in his hair as he stroked her breast. "It feels so *good* having you touch me like this."

He bent the last half inch and kissed her hungrily. The only truly effective way he'd found of shutting her up.

When the time came, he'd pull out. It wasn't perfect, but right now it was that or abstinence. And abstaining would be like trying to hold the dam back with his tongue.

She rose to meet him, wound her arms tightly about his neck, and opened her mouth to greet him.

Her tongue was scorching, insatiable. A blatant simulation of the more intimate act. She kissed him with hot, sweet abandon, a low hum in the back of her throat. Nothing held back, no artifice. Her tongue active, insistent, ravenous. Frantic hands brailled his back and shoulders. She managed to get his shirt pulled from his waistband.

He felt her hands on his back, on his sides, on his scalp, gripping his hair. Wherever she touched, flames licked and spread. Her hand clenched in his hair as his mouth left hers to blaze a trail down the sweet, silky valley between her breasts.

When he took her nipple in his mouth again her back arched and she cried out, her breath strangling in her throat.

His stomach contracted as she started to unbutton his shirt. She stroked his chest. Touched his nipples. Made him shudder.

Another button sprang free. Her hand skimmed down his midriff.

Another button. Fingers brushed across his belly button.

The last button.

Two fingers dipped into the waistband of his jeans. He dragged in a breath, and they slipped down farther, fingertips brushing his sex.

His hand slid between her thighs. Through the shorts he felt her wet heat, slick with desire. She whimpered and her hips curved up off the couch at his touch. Her scent surrounded him, made him hotter. Harder. He couldn't get enough of her.

Wanted to taste, to touch, to devour everything before him like a man presented with a banquet.

His hands moved over her body, demanding, seeking, pressing. Frantic, bruising caresses—hers were no more gentle.

She gripped the waistband of his jeans so tightly he thought his penis might tear free through cotton and denim.

"Jake. Jake. Jake."

While kissing her he managed to get his jeans unzipped. He sprang free, pulsing, ready. Pleasure, pain.

Her hand found him, her fingers curling, cool around his hot flesh.

Judas.

His eyes closed and his stomach muscles clenched as she stroked and teased with just the right pressure to make him even harder. His stomach muscles clenched convulsively.

"Enough . . ." He sucked in air as her fingertip found the head of his sex, rubbed at the bead of moisture there.

He wanted to touch all of her, to feel her nipples pressed against his chest, feel the moist heat of her pressed intimately against him, open to him. He wanted it all. The couch was wide enough, the bed six feet too far away.

He found where she was most responsive, most sensitive, and brought her close to the brink. She was vocal in her pleasure, making inarticulate sounds that went through him like the sweet notes of a violin. He played his fingers over her, in her, until she begged for release.

"Please, Jake . . ."

Half standing, he dragged the cotton boxers down her legs.

"Hmmm. I knew I was gonna enjoy being debriefed." She opened slumberous eyes, level with his groin. "Mmmm-mmmm-mmmm." She licked her lips. Suggestive, sexy, eager. "Is that for me?"

"Think you can handle it?" He came down into the cradle of her thighs.

"After." It was a promise. "I don't want to rush you. But could you *please* hurry? Oh, god. Jake."

With his jeans around his ankles, Jake slipped into her wet

heat, entering her on one long, deep, gut-wrenching thrust. He watched as her eyes lost focus, felt her breath snag, felt the internal throbbing of her muscles clamp him like a fist.

Her heels dug into his flanks as he reaffirmed life with every pump of his hips, every flex of his muscles, every thrust.

"That's it," he said through clenched teeth, in near agony as he thrust powerfully again. "Take. More. Take it all."

He watched her climb closer and closer until he just couldn't focus on her features anymore.

Her breath tore on a strangled sob as she peaked. With a wordless cry, Jake followed a few seconds later.

Chapter Ten

They finally made it to the bed. Jake had stripped her in seconds flat. And as erotic as it was making love with his jeans about his ankles, Marnie wanted to try it bare skin to bare skin. She'd made short work of his clothes.

After making love again, she could barely move. Yet she sensed within Jake a restlessness, despite the seemingly relaxed sprawl of his body.

Both times they'd made love he'd withdrawn at the last moment, spilling himself outside her. Despite knowing she should be grateful, Marnie felt somehow cheated. Having Jake's child didn't seem such a terrible thing. In fact, the idea was extremely appealing.

Not that she'd terrify him by saying so.

"I wish I smoked." She smiled down at him as she sprawled on his large, hard body. Arms folded across his chest, she enjoyed the tickle of his chest hair against her sensitized breasts. "It always looks so sexy in the movies."

Jake pushed a dangling curl out of her eyes. "It doesn't *smell* sexy." He nuzzled her throat, his breath warm and damp on her skin. "You smell like—"

She traced the curve of his ear with a fingertip. "Like?" she asked softly, feeling the shift as the muscles in his chest flexed against her breasts. His eyes were hooded when he looked up.

"Like promises. You smell like promises." He frowned.

Clearly the perfume of promises was like stinkweed to Jake. The very mention of the word made him acutely uncomfortable. Her heart skipped a beat as he morphed back into the Jake who'd threatened her off his property. Had that been only the day before yesterday?

Short, dark lashes closed for an instant, covering the blueness of his eyes. Then his gaze flickered to the monitors across the room, where clouds scudded to cover the sun again, and wind whipped through the trees hiding the bad guys.

Although he wasn't making any overt movements, Marnie felt the unleashed energy seething and snarling beneath his skin.

Promises? Oh, God. I want to make you promises, Jake Dolan. A whole raft of them. But they wouldn't mean a thing to you, would they?

Her hand trailed lightly down his side, over his lean flank, and cupped a hard cheek. She wanted to savor this moment of closeness as long as possible. Any second now he was going to roll over and say he had to leave—before promises and lies became interchangeable.

"I'd rather smell like silk sheets and candlelight." She lowered her voice to a purr and fluttered her lashes like a vamp. "Of Paris nights." She stroked his hair back and wiggled her hips suggestively. She felt him stir against her delta and felt a wild surge of power. Of hope. "Or tropical breezes." She lowered her mouth to an inch above his and whispered. "How about a sex slave in a hundred and one Arabian nights? Will you slay dragons for me?"

"You don't need a knight to slay your dragons." He traced his knuckles down her cheek, his eyes flat and hard. "You'd be out there carving them up yourself. Making them your slaves, cutting their hearts out before they even knew it."

The force of his conviction sent a shiver down her spine. She pretended to scowl. "Hmmm."

He groaned; she felt the vibration low in her belly.

"What?"

"If someone bottled those damn sexy noises you make, they could sell them and become millionaires."

He smelled so darn good she could have eaten him with a spoon. And she wouldn't sell one mouthful for any price. It was part soap, part outdoors, part sex, and wholly Jake's own unique scent. Blindfolded, she could pick him out of a lineup.

This man would make no promises.

She ran her hands up his hip and kissed him gently, nibbling at his stern mouth, at the taut muscles that held his smile in check.

She'd heard of chemistry. She'd read about attraction. But she'd never experienced anything like this in her life. It was as though her body wanted to absorb his. As if she could close her eyes and melt into him. Marnie wanted to taste him, learn him, and know everything there was to know about him.

But she wasn't stupid enough to say so right at this moment. She searched her brain for something to say, some words that would keep him in this bed with her a little while longer.

"Tell me about your friends. The other Musketeers. What were their names?"

He took so long to answer, she was afraid he was going to spring out of bed and leave.

"Paul Britton, we called him Brit. Your tall, blond, and handsome type." Marnie shivered as Jake ran his hand lightly down her back. "Had more women after him than a movie star. Embarrassed the hell out of him. We used to rag him all the time about his looks."

"And the other two?"

"Ross. Ross Lerma." Jake's eyes did that internal smile she was becoming familiar with. "Lurch. Hell of a partner. Looked a little like Gene Kelly. Moved like him, too. Judas, he got in and out of the direst situations. Saved my butt a time or two. We knew each other so damn well, how the other guy's mind worked. It was magic when we paired on assignments. Perfect synchronicity, you know?" Jake got a strange look on his face. Part sad, part angry.

"What about the other one?" she asked softly, resting her hand on his chest and rubbing lightly over the springy hair she found there.

"Joe Skullestad. Skully. Big. Black. Bad." Jake smiled. "The kind of guy you'd want at your back in a dark alley. And

Skully and I were in a few. He's the one that saved my ass when this happened." Jake touched his throat.

Marnie gently moved his hand out of her way.

"What happened to them?"

"Brit was killed six years ago while defusing a bomb on a commercial flight stuck at Orly. He was a valuable T-FLAC agent. They knew of him. The tangos took him in exchange for the passengers. Saved three hundred people. They took him out with them.

"Lurch, almost a month to the day after Brit. South America." Jake's jaw tightened as he looked right through her. "Lurch offed the woman who gave me this scar necklace as a memento. She shot him before she went room temperature. He died in my arms. Skully hauled my ass out, got me home. *He* died five years ago. Embassy bombing, Beirut."

"And what did they call you?"

"Anything they wanted."

"Come on, Jake. You must have had a nickname, too."

"Tin Man. They called me the Tin Man."

"Why?" Marnie already knew the answer.

"Haven't you figured it out yet?" Jake said flatly. "They called me the Tin Man because I don't have a heart."

Oh, Jake. Marnie slid over his body and wrapped her arms around his neck, burying her face against his throat.

"Yes, you do," she told him softly. "You wouldn't care so passionately about finding this Dancer guy to avenge your friend's death if you didn't." *You wouldn't make love to me so sweetly if you didn't have a heart,* she thought, the ache in her own heart sharp and sweet.

In a way she wished she'd never tried to find a subject to hold him in bed. In another she was grateful for this small bit of insight into what had shaped him. No matter what Jake said, he was a hero with heart.

The true meaning of a hero was not his willingness to fight, but his unwavering determination to defend good against evil, weak against strong, right against wrong, no matter how unpopular his choices might be. A heartless man couldn't be all that.

He shifted restlessly, and she gave him space, moving to lie beside him. A shadow flickered across his suddenly taut features. He was sorry he'd revealed so much; Marnie could tell.

She wanted to comfort him, to tell him everything would be alright. But she couldn't do so with either knowledge or truth. She had no idea what demons drove him. And the chances of her ever knowing were slim to none.

The best she could do was to make her presence here easier for him.

"Thank you for telling me about your Musketeers. They must have been special men. And they were lucky to have you as their friend."

"Yeah, right."

With studied casualness, Marnie rolled off his body to sit on the edge of the bed. "I'm going to take a quick shower." She tried for a friendly glance over her shoulder. "Unless you want one before you leave?"

His eyes darkened and his lips became a hard line. He rolled to the other side of the bed and stood. She got her first good look at him in all his naked glory.

He felt incredible, and he looked spectacular. Jake was a big man, and everything was magnificently proportioned. She could attest to that, but *seeing* him . . .

Marnie resisted clutching her heart or fanning herself. *Gorgeous legs, a fabulous chest* . . . Her eyes skimmed down. *And other stupendous parts.* Even in repose.

It wasn't easy to hold a casual smile, but she did it. It never occurred to her to cover her body. The body he'd loved, licked, and fondled for the past hour. His eyes took a leisurely journey from her nose to her toes and back again. Her nipples peaked.

She knew he'd seen her response by the flare in his eyes before he carefully hooded his expression.

"That's it?" Jake asked, voice flat. "You sure you don't want to roll over and take a nap?"

Uh-oh. Another wrong choice.

Keep it light. Keep it casual. "We had mind-blowing sex.

You're an incredible lover. Is it politically incorrect to want to shower?"

A muscle ticked in his cheek. "Perhaps we could have showered together."

She didn't miss the past tense of that. "If you weren't in such a hurry to get outside. Right?"

His lips tightened. "Yeah, right."

On an impulse Marnie rose and walked around the bed. She took Jake's face in her hands. His jaw was tight and bristly with five o'clock shadow. She didn't want the best afternoon of her life to deteriorate into one of the worst. She had to give him a graceful and easy way out.

"I thoroughly enjoyed our lovemaking, Jake. I've never experienced anything like it, and I probably won't again." Her throat burned, but she dredged up a bright smile. She'd rather he thought her flaky than know she was halfway in love with him. "We didn't make a lifetime commitment, you know. It was only sex."

"Was it?" he snarled, eyes dark and flinty. "Had a lot of experience, have you?"

"Actually, no." *Are you jealous?* She looked at him. *Nah!* "There was only the time Tommy Bishop rented a hotel room when we were nineteen. Quite frankly, it wasn't so hot then. One of those insert-tab-A-into-slot-B sort of things. Not terribly romantic, but we were both tired of being virgins, so we decided to see what the fuss was about. It turned out it was no big whoop after all."

"And how was it with the fiancés?"

"Oh, I didn't sleep with them," she said honestly, then cocked her head. "Are you going to tell me about all *your* lovers? Or would that take too long?"

"We're not talking about me."

"Ah."

He scrunched his eyes shut, then opened them to glare at her. "I *hate* when you make those noises."

The same noises he'd wanted to bottle not two minutes ago? Marnie stood on tiptoe and kissed his mouth. "We had great sex, Jake," she murmured against his lips. "I hope we can do it again soon."

"How about right now?" he said flatly, holding her upper arms. "We're both naked, and the mood's still right. How about I just screw you out of my system? Bury myself deep inside you again until you scream and I pass out?"

"Uh, sure," she whispered uncertainly, incapable of reading the lightning fast emotions flashing through his eyes. Tension radiated from him as he searched her face.

Damn, Marnie thought, panicked. *Now what?* She thought it was only women who had morning-after syndrome.

He backed her up to the bed. "A little recreational sex to relieve the tension, is that what you think, Marnie?" He was practically snarling now as he tipped her over onto the rumpled, sex-scented sheets.

A gurgle of laughter bloomed. She nipped it in the bud and grabbed two handfuls of his hair, tugging him down on top of her. "You find me resistible, remember?"

Jake's smile was raw and humorless as he dug both hands under her hips and jerked her toward him. "You might have noticed I'm not immune. You're beautiful and soft, and I'd have given up a lung to make love to you the second I saw you."

"Then isn't it lucky," Marnie said, feet braced firmly on the floor as she opened her thighs for him to slide home, "that you can have me without giving up any of your stupendous parts?"

Their open mouths met, as hungry now as they had been an hour ago. She sucked his tongue. He surged into her. She bit his shoulder. He nipped her hard on the side of her neck, his arms extended beside her head, fingers laced with hers on the mattress, tendons and muscles taut, bulging as he pumped his hips.

This was primitive and basic, with none of the finesse and gentleness he'd used before.

Mine. Mine. Mine. Mine, Marnie thought with each piston stroke. Feet braced on the floor, she met him thrust for thrust.

She took savage delight in hearing his inarticulate groans,

seeing sweat sheen his face and chest, watching his muscles flex and strain. She brought her arms down and her short nails dug into the clenched muscles of his butt, urging him to a faster pace. He hammered into her, teeth bared, holding her gaze with a fierce wildness in his eyes.

War. *Oh, Jake.*

Marnie couldn't help the smile tugging at her mouth as the pressure inside her built. She wrapped her arms around him and held on tightly.

Jake scowled, then nipped the smile from her lips with his teeth.

Her smile widened into a grin.

She felt laughter bubble alongside her climax. Every nerve and pore shimmered with delight as Jake staked his claim.

"Crazy," Jake breathed hard, "woman."

For you.

She wrapped her legs around his hips, pressing down with her heels, driving him insane, and knowing it.

He took no prisoners.

But then neither did she.

"Okay, tell me what they took out of your backpack."

"My backpack?" Marnie yawned, stalling for time.

Jake, braced on his elbow, traced a path with his finger from the damp nest of curls at the apex of her thighs to her throat.

"That tickles."

He cupped her chin and turned her to face him. He looked far too serious for a man who'd just had fabulous sex. Sweat glued them at the hip. It felt wonderful.

"Did they take your medication, Marnie? What're you on? A blood thinner?"

"Coumadin." She sighed. "I'll be okay without it for a few da—for a while. Don't worry, Jake. I've forgotten to take it a couple of times," she lied. "I'll be fine."

"Until the blood clot hits."

"It won't. Sheesh, did you *have* to talk about it? Here, feel this." She pressed his open hand over her breast. "Ninety-nine percent of the time I forget I even have that little piece of metal in there."

His fingers flexed on her breast. He bent his head and touched his mouth to her skin in a gentle tribute. The kiss he pressed to her heart made that organ speed up and do somersaults.

He lifted his head, looking grim. "I have to get you over that damn river."

Marnie ran her fingers through his long dark hair. "Until you do, I'll be fine."

Jake swung his legs off the bed and looked down at her. "I'll make sure you are."

Marnie leaned over the back of the couch. She'd slept for a couple of hours and felt refreshed and full of energy and high spirits. By the time she'd blinked awake, Jake had showered without her. She was sorry to have missed the show. But she planned a little audience participation for next time.

She'd showered and dressed in another pair of his boxers and one of his flannel shirts while he sat at the computer. She'd watched him. He hadn't turned around once. *Darn him.*

She'd finished several drawings of him, his feet, his hands, and secretly some of his more interesting body parts. Now she was bored, bored, bored.

"Can I go with you when you take Duchess out? I'm going stir crazy in here. I need fresh air and light."

"It's starting to get dark out, the air in here is fresh, and there's plenty of light. Hang tough—you'll have your freedom the second the river subsides. Read a book or something to keep yourself occupied."

"Got any good romances?" she asked dryly as Jake leaned over the console to manipulate a camera. He had great buns. *Very* nicely displayed in those worn jeans.

"All those books have romance in them," Jake told her, opening a closet to pull out a handful of black fabric.

"I didn't mean a cowboy kissing his horse, Jake."

He walked away from the console and started stripping off his shirt. He pulled a scrap of skin-tight black spandex or something over his head and tugged it down to cover his chest. It accentuated every contour of his shoulders and chest and covered him from neck to wrist. He looked exactly like the assassins. A chill of foreboding raced down her spine. She tamped it down. *This* was Jake Dolan.

He undid the top button on his jeans. Her eyes followed the movement avidly.

Jake shot her an amused look. "You're staring."

Without taking her focus away, she grinned. "It's a good show."

Jake shook his head and finished undoing the zipper on his jeans.

Storming down the mine shaft tunnel, boots crunching on the gravel, he rechecked his weapons as he walked and swore silently under his breath. The woman muddied his thinking.

"Only sex." Jake repeated out loud what he'd been churning over since they'd made love. Only sex? Judas Priest. For some inexplicable reason he felt cheated.

He didn't know what or how, but he felt gypped nevertheless. It didn't matter how many times he had her, he was insatiable around her.

Only sex. Judas.

He was a man who liked things neat. Compartmentalized.

It *was* only sex. Of course it was. They were two healthy animals with a damn good chemical thing going. Why deny it?

He felt slightly mollified. He'd only been ticked because she'd taken the words right out of his mouth and said them first.

He'd made her a promise. The only kind of promise a man like him made to a woman like her. And he would keep that promise if it killed him. If he had to swim across the swollen river with Marnie strapped to his back, that's what he'd do. He swore again. He'd thought he had all the goddamn time in the world to play with these goons topside.

Marnie had upped the ante with her need for medication.

He was no doctor, but he knew that putting a patient on a blood thinner for life was done for good reason. A blood clot would kill her.

How long did he have? Hours? Days? Jake didn't know. But he could hear the ticking clock, like a time bomb, resonate inside his head with each step he took.

It was Sunday night. She'd been without her medication since sometime on Friday. How much longer?

One bridge was washed out. The other, as he'd seen on the monitor, still flooded.

Fury and frustration seethed in Jake's gut.

Who the hell could he trust?

Who could he call to medevac her out? Who in their right mind would chance landing in this terrain and in this kind of weather?

There was a clearing a couple of miles upstream. He'd used it several times airlifting stuff in for the lair. A good chopper pilot could navigate the mountains, trees, and weather to land and take off in relative safety.

And he'd have to be satisfied with "relative." He didn't have a choice. He thought of Skully with a pang. His daredevil friend would have flown in despite the odds.

He didn't know who the assassins were. But he had to find out, and fast. Playtime had run out, he thought grimly. Not for the first time in the past several years, he missed his three friends fiercely.

Now he preferred to work alone, although he had been on assignments involving a full nine-man T-FLAC team. At those times, while scrupulously backing up anyone he worked with, he found it almost impossible to trust his life to someone else.

It was a matter of trust. And there was no one left to trust.

He wished to hell the assassins *were* tangos. But by every indication they were T-FLAC. Which meant he couldn't risk calling in the cavalry to extract Marnie.

He wondered if these were men who'd worked side by side with him. Men whose butts he'd covered in some war-torn armpit of the world. Men who'd faced him, and called him friend, while they sold him out.

For what?

He shook his head. Did the logic matter?

Whoever these guys were, they'd been exposed to the elements and he hadn't. Jake emerged from the mine shaft opening and started climbing through the canyon of rocks blocking the entrance. Icy snow pelted him from a charcoal sky, the clouds so low, so dark and heavy, they felt oppressive.

He'd been on countless missions where he and his team had had to make do with what they could carry. It was doable but not comfortable.

He counted on his enemy's inactivity and frustration to make them careless. Throughout last night and the better part of today, he'd watched their progress as they'd crisscrossed this section of the mountain.

Jake lightly jumped down from the rocks, scanned the area, and slipped silently into the trees. He slid from shadow to shadow, boots barely making a sound on the soft, wet, pine-needle-strewn ground. The storm front had fulfilled its promise, dumping inches of rain onto the already sodden landscape. Jake could feel the turbulence of the storm on his head and shoulders even as he walked beneath the sheltering trees.

The fact that the men knew to search for him here, this close to the lair, indicated they knew *where* he was, just not how to get their hands on him.

He didn't give a continental fig for himself, but without him, Marnie didn't stand a chance.

He'd just have to show the bad guys that their timetable had been seriously compromised.

A couple of hours later he found two assassins at the cabin. After securing the area, he returned to watch their systematic search. Not a board went uninspected. Jake stood in the shadows. Rain sluiced unnoticed off his head and shoulders as he watched each man move carefully over the entire face of the small structure. So they knew exactly *where*, just not *how* to open the can.

There was some danger of them discovering the elevator entrances from the cabin, but even if they did, they couldn't activate the retinal scan without his cooperation. And in that event there was a contingency plan.

Jake adjusted the black headpiece over his head and the

lower half of his face. Only his eyes were visible when he strode into the clearing.

One man turned, his hand going to the weapon strapped to his thigh, the other man continued searching.

Jake took a chance and gave a hand signal as identification. The man stepped down, relaxed.

Jake said quietly in the T-FLAC shorthand, "I've come to relieve one of you. Go back to camp."

"We've only been on three hours."

"Fine." Jake allowed impatience to creep into his voice. "You do what you want. I'll go back and get some of that coffee myself." He turned to go.

"No. I'll take the break." The shorter of the two men came toward Jake, nodding as he passed. The garb made him unrecognizable. There was nothing familiar about him. Jake watched him disappear into the trees, then strolled up to the cabin through the long, wet weeds.

His glance flickered to what could be misconstrued as a sparkling raindrop trembling on the edge of the roof. He'd forgotten Marnie could see every inch of the cabin. For half a second he considered disabling the camera craftily hidden on the eaves. Then deliberately put her out of his mind and went to work.

The second man was now on the right-hand corner of the house, tapping each board, checking every window. Jake passed the open front door. Quick glance. No one inside.

Jake seized the split-second advantage. He came up alongside his prey, put his arm around his throat, and efficiently snapped his neck.

Seconds later he dragged the body away from the cabin and hid it beneath a dense clump of deadfall.

He looped up the mountainside until he was behind the soldier he'd relieved.

The man was good.

Jake was better.

When he found the camp and calculated the size of the cell, he'd know how to handle the situation. All he had to do was follow this guy to the end of the line.

They looked, smelled, and talked T-FLAC, but something about them didn't quite ring true. It made no difference. An assassin was an assassin was an assassin.

Jake let the guy ahead of him move a little distance before he moved again.

Suddenly he found himself face-to-face with another man coming the opposite way. If the guy could count, Jake was in deep shit.

The man was cautious but not careful enough. Before he was aware of Jake's presence, it was over. It took seconds for Jake to secure, search, and hide the body. Two more down. How many to go?

He had to find their camp, but the guy he'd been following was now lost up ahead in the trees. *Shit.*

The strike team had used choppers to reach this side of the river. The bridges had been down when they'd arrived. He had to find their extraction point, secure the rest of them, and radio in for pickup.

If he could figure out who to call.

Jake headed in the direction he'd been going before he'd been sidetracked. Careful this time to watch where he was going. That had been an amateur stunt that could have cost him his life, and consequently Marnie's as well.

He couldn't afford to take those kind of risks anymore. Not until he got Marnie safely off the mountain.

Half an hour later he encountered another guy, busy re-arranging himself after taking a leak. He knew he was headed in the right direction. Jake paused. Get the goon to take him back to mama, or off him here? One less to worry about later.

Jake stepped out of the trees. The man looked up, startled, hands busy. Jake drew the knife from the scabbard on his ankle—it flew true. The man barely gasped as it imbedded in his throat. Surprise widened his eyes and his fingers tightened on his groin as he crumpled into a rock-hard snowbank beneath a ponderosa pine. Not that his final resting place made any difference at this point.

The ticking clock in Jake's mind echoed ominously as he worked. Where the hell were the rest of them? How many of the sons of bitches were there? The dead weight of the man pulled at his shoulder muscles as he dragged him away from the small clearing between the trees. Jake wasn't big on garbage detail, but it was part of the job.

There wasn't a sound, but the texture of the air changed. Jake whirled.

In the lair, Marnie stared at the flat-screen monitor across the room, a ham sandwich halfway to her mouth. "Damn it, Jake, there's another—Oh, you see him. No, wait, he's—"

Beside her Duchess added her own warning.

Marnie, who'd been propped up in bed with a snack and a cup of coffee, abandoned her food to crawl to the foot of the bed, not taking her eyes off the screen. The sandwich clung to the inside of her throat like wallpaper paste as she stared, appalled.

Jake and the bad guy circled each other. They were on a slight incline, and rivulets of water ran down small fissures in the packed snow, making the footing slippery and dangerous.

Marnie winced as Jake's foot slid. He grabbed his opponent by the arm to stop his momentum, or to drag the baddie down with him. The two went rolling and skidding down the slope and were stopped by the base of a huge tree.

In seconds they were up again. Circling, feinting.

"Doesn't the man use a gun?" Marnie demanded, jumping off the bed to race to the monitor, where she could see them better.

They looked like two well-choreographed dancers. Rain bounced off the apparently impervious fabric of their suits and beaded on the camera lens, making visibility a challenge. Which one was Jake?

"Ah. See, girl, our guy is bigger."

Jake punched the other guy, who doubled over.

"Good one, Jake!"

Duchess leaned against Marnie, growling low in her throat.

The bad guy let fly with a kick to Jake's thigh. Marnie winced. "Ow! Sock him one, big guy, yeah, like that! Take that, and that, and *that!*" Her heart jackhammered inside her chest. The two men were evenly matched. For several minutes they were lost to view between the trees.

"Damn it!" Marnie snarled. She looked at Duchess, who was whining and growling. "What, girl?"

Duchess raced across the room, nails skittering on the floor, tail wagging. At the door to the elevator into the mine shaft, she stopped and looked back at her mistress.

"He's busy right now, goofus. He'll be back after work," she finished wryly, searching the gray murk for a sighting of the two men.

Duchess growled low and rough and came racing back to Marnie's side. She nudged her mistress with her head.

"Come? Come where?" There was no sign of them. She moved to another view with no luck.

The dog insisted, frantic now as she paced and nudged, nudged and paced.

Marnie dragged her eyes away from the bleak trees for a second to glare at the dog. "You don't mean out there? Are you *nuts*? I wouldn't be able to— Listen to me, damn it! I wouldn't be able to help him, I wouldn't!"

She spun back to the monitors. She didn't have time to argue with a dog. A man emerged from behind the trees, back into view on monitor seven. Marnie, palms sweating, braced her hands on the cool surface of the workstation and tried to see who the man was. The sky opened up like an upended watering can, and it was getting too dark to see who was who out there.

Anxiety laid a blanket of goose bumps over her naked body. "Jake . . . ?"

Duchess barked a warning as a man came flying from out of camera range and took the first man down. Marnie had no idea which man was which. This was a fight to the death. Blood drained from her head as the two combatants fought beneath the driving force of rain. Fists and feet flew in a flurry of lethal strikes that left her breathless and shaking, as if she were the one fighting.

She flinched and grunted as an elbow met a chin. With each

blow her own muscles tightened a notch and her stomach churned.

One of the men reached to the small of his back and withdrew a ridiculously small gun. The other guy picked himself up off the ground and didn't see it. "Did Jake have a gun there, girl? Did he? Oh, God, Jake—"

Duchess howled. The sound sent a chill of dread right down Marnie's spine.

A shot rang out.

The first man staggered. He fell against the trunk of a nearby tree.

Marnie dug her fingernails into her palm as her eyes darted from one man to the other. She couldn't tell. Her terrified heart beat so fast she could barely breathe.

Duchess's nails clicked frantically across the floor to the elevator. Back. To the elevator. Back. Urging Marnie to go topside and save her hero.

Torn, Marnie stared at the screen until the two men blurred. Who had been shot?

Another shot rang out.

The second man stumbled, fell to a knee, rose, and fired off a third shot. The first man stood for a moment as if paralyzed, then in slow motion slid down the tree trunk until he sat, legs extended and head lolling to the side. In seconds a pink stain spread in the snow beneath him.

A scream of denial rose in her throat. She gripped each side of the monitor in white-knuckled hands, squinting, trying desperately to see through the snow and identify which man was which.

"Damn it, Jake! If you're dead, I'm going to *kill* you!"

For several seconds Marnie stared at the tableau before her, then, galvanized into action, raced to find her clothes.

Chapter Eleven

Marnie tied her bootlaces in the elevator, hopping from foot to foot. Fear made her clumsy; her fingers refused to cooperate.

"Come on. Come on."

She burst through the elevator door. Lights popped on as she raced through the tunnel, her breath huffing in harsh, desperate pants. She tried to control her panic.

"He's going to be fine," she told herself. *"Fine."*

While she jogged down the tunnel she buttoned one of Jake's oversized shirts, zipped her jacket, zipped her pants. "Jake knows what he's doing, he'll be okay." *Please be okay.*

Jake. Jake. Jake.

Duchess raced ahead. Came back. Raced ahead. Came back. *Hurry. Hurry. Hurry.*

"Please be alive."

The next door blocked her.

Palm print.

She slapped her hand on the scanner as Jake had shown her.

"Open. Open." Open . . . ed.

She almost fell through the doorway into the long corridor leading outside. The air was colder here. Fresher. Her breath led the way.

She couldn't just go dashing around out there without a plan. But her brain refused to wrap around anything beyond seeing a man bleeding into the snow.

Dying in the snow.

Even if the dead man wasn't Jake, please God, both men had been shot. "Make it a flesh wound, a scratch, okay?"

She knew where the two men had fought. It wasn't far from the opening to the mine shaft. Although, as she'd seen on the monitors, it had started to get dark and the snow sifted in ever-increasing drifts on the rocks and trees.

She had to hurry.

Think. Make a plan. Go.

She wouldn't be any good to him if the bad guys killed *her*. The thought made her shudder. Suddenly this was all terrifyingly real. Watching Jake and the assassins on the monitors had given her the illusion of safety. It kept her at a distance, almost as if she were watching TV. But this wasn't a movie. It was pee-in-your-pants real, and men were dying.

"But not Jake. Please, God, not Jake."

The tunnel seemed to go on forever. Was this the way Jake had brought her? Had she taken a wrong turn somewhere? No, she recognized the ledge where he'd picked up the gun and flashlight.

Around the next corner. A low, fierce growl. She shrieked, then remembered. "The darn animatronic guard dog."

Hurry. Hurry. Hurry.

Not far now.

Another two hundred yards. A hundred. Fifty.

Wet, icy air blasted her as she and Duchess burst outside. Shudders of terror rippled across her muscles. Panting, she pressed her hand to the stitch in her side and leaned against a wood beam to catch her breath.

"Damn you, Jake, I wanted to work my way up to telling you I love you. I'm going to be so mad if—" She couldn't bear to complete the sentence.

Find Jake, she thought grimly. *Drag him back. By the hair if necessary. To hell with the bad guys.* She was pissed off and terrified enough to *want* to tackle them.

Duchess stopped beside her. "If one of the bad guys comes, you rip his throat out, you hear me, girl?" Marnie whispered fiercely, grateful for the heat and weight of her pet against her side. She wrapped one arm around Duchess's neck, putting off the moment when they would be outside the protection of the rocks. Out in the open . . .

"We'll find hi— Oh, God, Jake!" Marnie breathed, relieved beyond anything as he came through the narrow canyon of rocks toward her. The skin-tight black outfit he wore looked like a seal-sleek wetsuit. He pushed back the head covering as he walked, leaving his hair flattened damply to his skull and faint pink marks on his face.

She rushed toward him, then put her hands in the air as he aimed his gun at her.

"Whoa. I'm not armed!"

He lowered the weapon. His face appeared paler than normal. The lines on either side of his mouth seemed more pronounced. He was the best thing Marnie had ever seen.

"Judas, woman, what the hell kind of stupid move is that to make? I could have shot you. What are you doing out here?"

"I saw that man shoot you. I came to help you get back inside." *He isn't dead. Thank you, God, he isn't dead.*

"It's a scratch."

Marnie rushed to his side and glared up at him. She wanted to sock him for scaring her to death. She wanted to kill him. She wanted to fling herself into his strong arms and sob like a baby. She took a deep, cleansing breath and released the tension in her shoulders.

"Hmmm? Really? A scratch? Well, let's get you home and see, okay, big guy? Go on the other side, goofus," she told Duchess, who seemed unsure if being out here with the two of them was a fun thing or an in-trouble thing. She finally went on the other side of Jake and looked up at him hopefully. Marnie came around to his uninjured side and carefully pulled his left arm over her shoulder.

"I watched the whole thing. I can't *tell* you how *insane* it makes me not to be able to yell and warn you when I see you out there," she said through her teeth. Jake's hand, hanging over her chest, felt like ice. Crazy fool. She cupped his fingers firmly in her own warm hand and felt his chill.

"Planning on carrying me?" Jake's voice held a thread of amusement as they turned back inside.

"If I have to, I will." She concentrated on setting each foot as they walked. As macho as Jake was, he didn't take his arm from her shoulder. The sweet-metallic smell of blood made her swallow convulsively.

"How bad do you think it is?"

"I told you, a scratch. I've got everything I need to patch it up. Don't worry."

"Oh, I'm not worried," Marnie told him blithely, heart in her throat as she took a little more of his weight on her shoulder. If he passed out here in the tunnel, how was she going to get him down to the medical supplies? She pushed the thought away. Jake was upright and walking. She wasn't going to borrow trouble.

He let her do the palm print and the retinal scan. By the time the door to the elevators opened below into the lair, they were both bathed with sweat. Jake, followed by Duchess, headed for the couch and sank into it, eyes closed, head back. Duchess sat as close as she dared, eyes fixed on Jake's face.

From the CD, Blood, Sweat, and Tears belted out, "And When I Die." It was eerie. Marnie blocked out the music.

"Tell me where to find what I'll need."

Jake opened dark, enigmatic eyes. "There's a first-aid box in that drawer over there—no, the next one, yeah. Bring it over here. Let's see what we have to deal with first."

She found the first-aid kit, then poured a mug of coffee. Spilling crystals all over the counter, she spooned sugar into the inky liquid with shaking hands. Sugar for shock.

She needed it herself. She gave it to Jake. "Here—you have to get warm."

She set the large first-aid box on the table in front of him, saw he had something pressed to the wound, then raced over, grabbed the silk throw off the floor at the foot of the bed, and settled it over his lap. Jake quirked a brow but didn't comment.

She went back to the kitchen area for a bowl of hot water. Dreading what had to come. Hating that he was hurt. Scared because she was the only one who could do anything about it. And unsure of her ability.

He'd been holding her flannel shirt against his shoulder. Marnie took the damp clump of fabric and tossed it on the table. It left a smear of blood on the surface of the wood. She swallowed roughly and removed her jacket, dropping it on the floor behind her.

Jake tried to pull the skin-tight fabric up his body. His face contorted.

Every drop of blood drained from her brain, leaving her light-headed and pukey.

"Here, for godsake Jake, let me do it." She climbed over his leg and sat on the trunk coffee table between his knees.

Duchess shifted. Brow wrinkled, she rested her chin on a sofa cushion and watched the proceedings with worried puppy eyes.

Very carefully Marnie started to peel the fabric up Jake's chest. The material felt slick, slippery.

Blood.

Little black dots flittered in her vision. She ignored them.

"You're bleeding pretty badly," she said calmly, keeping her gaze steady, the rusty tang of fear sharp in her mouth.

"I've bled worse."

She pushed his hands away as he tried to help her. "Let me do it. Hang on, let's see if—" Rummaging around in the metal box, she found a pair of scissors. "Perfect. I hope this isn't one of your favorite spy outfits!" The tight fabric sprang away from his body as she cut into it. His skin felt warm beneath her icy hands.

"What is this stuff, anyway?" The fabric wasn't silk; it was almost rubbery, cold and damp on the outside, but dry and warm inside.

"I call it LockOut."

"Why do you—" She stared at him. "Did you *invent* this?"

His cheeks darkened. "I told you I played around with stuff. Yeah, this was one of the better ideas. It's like a second skin. Traps in the body's heat. It also acts as a shield."

Marnie snorted. "That part didn't work so well."

"If I hadn't been wearing it, I'd be dead right now. It's not impervious. It did what it was designed to do—deflect the strike."

She shuddered. "It didn't deflect it enough for me. I'd demand a refund. And how did the bad guys get your invention, anyway? Aren't they wearing this same stuff?"

"Yeah, they are. But that's no mystery. Any special-forces operations have access to it. It's sold all over the world now."

"Great. In spy shops?" Marnie said under her breath.

She'd put off looking at the gory hole in his shoulder as long as possible. What was she supposed to do next? There was so much blood. Red. Thick. Pulsing. It blipped out of the jagged tear in his skin and ran in rivulets down his bare arm and chest.

For several seconds she thought she might just keel over. Considering her position between Jake's knees, she'd land nose first on his chest. His painful, *bleeding* chest.

"Tell me what to do!" How could her mouth be this dry when she was swallowing convulsively?

He leaned forward with a grunt. "Check out the back." He paused while she looked at the blood smeared over his hard muscles and tanned skin. "How's it look?"

Like cat food. She swallowed and said mildly, "Awful." It wasn't a hole. But it *was* a deep, nasty-looking canyon of a gash across the top of his shoulder.

"Yeah? Well, it can't look any worse than it feels, but it's just a graze."

Vertigo swamped her; she gripped the edge of the table with clammy hands. "That's good."

"Hell, yes. You won't have to dig a bullet out."

Thank you, Jesus. "Now what?"

"Get that brown bottle over there . . . yeah, that one. It's an antiseptic. Use a couple of those sterile gauze pads and clean it as best you can. Back and front."

Jake calmly gave her instructions and she followed them blindly.

"Talk to me."

Marnie dabbed carefully around the wound. "What about?"

"Tell me about your family."

She glanced up, the bloody cloth clutched in her hand. "Not now. I have to concentrate."

"Do that like you mean it, Marnie. I'm not going to break." He guided her hand more efficiently. "You can talk and do this at the same time." Jake gulped half the coffee and cradled the mug in one hand. "Come on, I need the distraction. Tell me about your grandmother."

Marnie suspected Jake wanted *her* to have the distraction while she worked. She swallowed the metallic taste in her mouth and dabbed more thoroughly at his wound.

Front.

Don't gag.

Grammy, guide my hands.

"I adored her. Bless her heart. Grammy was all of four foot eight, with a backbone like a steel rod and a heart big enough to shelter the world."

Don't cry. Clean. Disinfect.

How much blood does he have in his body? Fifty gallons? she wondered frantically as it kept seeping and she kept blotting. It seemed most of it was on the cloths she kept exchanging. Marnie ran her tongue over her dry lips.

"As—As far back as I can remember, her hair was white," she went on, her throat raw with tension. "She always smelled of Pond's face cream and Yardley's lavender eau de cologne, and she had the softest, most gentle hands in the world. Whenever I was sad I'd lay my head in her lap, and she'd stroke my hair."

Marnie worked to stanch the blood and felt it crust beneath her fingernails. She swallowed bile and doggedly kept going. *Breathe.*

"Put more antiseptic on the . . . Yeah, good. Okay. Keep talking."

"I'll remind you that you said that one day." Marnie forced a smile. "Grammy was a benign despot. She ruled the house with a hard stare and chocolate chip cookies. Every kid in the neighborhood wanted to hang out at our house."

"Hold that there a little longer. Up a bit." He shifted her

fingers. "Yeah, here. That where you learned to cook? At Grammy's knee?"

"Hang on I have to concentrate—Yes, I did." Marnie paused to smile at the memories, then resumed what she'd been doing. "She was an inspired teacher. I had to spend so much time indoors, and she made cooking lessons fun. Even though I would've much preferred being outside with the boys, finally I did learn what she was trying to teach me. Along with how to cook a roast and how to crush the bejesus out of a clove of garlic, she had a great deal of advice to impart."

"Like what?"

"Like 'Never run after a man or a bus, there's always another one in five minutes.' " Marnie smiled without glancing up. "Like 'Live out loud.' Grammy was full of helpful little homilies for every occasion."

"How about, 'No good deed goes unpunished'?"

Marnie *tsk*ed. "Cynic."

"Pollyanna," he replied without heat. "It goes without saying she spoiled you rotten."

"Actually, she was the only one who *didn't*. She made very few concessions for my illness and allowed me to do a lot of things with the Musketeers that my dad had a conniption about later. She was the one who taught me to ride a bike when the males of the family thought it too strenuous. She's also the one who encouraged me to climb trees. . . . How's this feel?"

"Fine. Did she spoil your brothers, too?"

"Of course." She glanced up to find him watching her intently, and gave him what she hoped to hell was a reassuring smile. Marnie swallowed the saliva pooling in her mouth and bent her head to see what she was doing.

"It was really hilarious when they got into trouble. There was this itty-bitty little old lady confronting one or more of my six-foot-tall brothers. You should have seen them blush and quake. She never had to raise her voice, either."

She wiped her sweaty cheek on her shoulder. "I miss her so

much." Dip. Twist. Wipe. "I wish I could cry for a week and get rid of this sore spot around my heart."

Jake frowned. "You haven't cried?"

"Not enough. It's there, a whole flood of tears just building up, waiting to explode."

"Did you cry when your mother passed away?"

"*Big* time. But I was six. She dropped me off on my first day of first grade and on the way home had an accident." She glanced up to find his eyes on her. "Drunk driver. She died instantly."

"Shit."

"I won't say it was easy not having a mom, but I never lacked for anything. Dad, Grammy, and the Musketeers made sure of that."

"No wonder your father and brothers are so protective of you. A bad heart, all those surgeries, no mother. Hell, it's understandable they'd want you to lead a stress-free life."

"I think having me to worry about helped them get over losing our mom. In a way, though, I let them keep on believing I needed them far longer than I really did. Oh, I didn't fake it. But I certainly went along with whatever they suggested when they suggested things, because I knew it made them happy. It became a habit. A bad habit. That's why I'm determined to change . . . to change . . . Never mind."

She was babbling like a fool. Talking about Grammy now, of all times. Knowing Jake could so easily have died out there made her voice thick and her throat ache.

The last thing she wanted to do was talk about death. *Anybody's.* The dam of grief hoarded behind her breastbone pressed for release. Her eyes burned, and her skin prickled, and moisture pooled in her mouth.

"Now what?" she asked roughly. The wound looked clean. Icky, but clean. She suppressed a shudder of empathy and felt no surprise when her tears refused to rip free. Now wasn't the appropriate time, anyway.

Jake explained patiently how to use the ninety-nine miles of bandage her nervous fingers had unraveled. With trembling hands she rerolled the bandage, then followed his direction.

She ducked her head and swallowed tears. "Your t-turn in the hot seat."

"I'm not in a chatty mood."

"I don't care. Do it anyway. Where'd you grow up?"

"Working-class neighborhood outside Chicago."

"Jeez, Jake, this is like dragging a kid to the dentist! What did your dad do?"

"To me? Nothing. Absolutely not a damn thing."

"No," Marnie said gently, "for a *living*."

"He was on social security. On permanent disability from some accident at the construction site where he'd worked. He was as healthy as a horse, despite chain-smoking and drinking himself into oblivion. But they paid him to sit home and watch game shows all day. And that's pretty much what he did."

It sounded like an awful B movie. Marnie's chest ache grew. "And your mom?" *Please tell me she adored you and protected you from your father's neglect.*

"She didn't get social security."

"I don't understand."

"She was exactly the same as he was. She just didn't get a check every week for it."

"That's child abuse."

"They never raised a hand to me."

"They *neglected* you. That's a form of abuse, Jake." She couldn't keep her palm from curling around his jaw. His cheek felt bristly and warm, and she wanted to lean forward and kiss him, but there was still bandaging and cleanup to be done. And Jake didn't look as though any show of sympathy would be welcome right now.

"So you ran away from home to join the navy. You said you were only sixteen?"

"Big for my age, and smart enough to fake ID— Pull that taut."

"Lift your arm. Does this hurt? Stupid question. Sorry. . . . What did your parents have to say when you joined?"

Jake shifted so she could pull the elastic bandage around his chest and up over his shoulder.

"Since I wasn't there at the time, I have no idea." He didn't so much as flinch as she worked. "It probably took them a couple of weeks to notice I wasn't around. And before you get all misty about it, both my parents were alcoholics. If they remembered they had a kid, it was to send me to the liquor store for more booze."

"Were they at least happy with one another?"

Jake snorted. "Not a damn thing made them happy, except for the booze. Unhappiness hung like smog over my folks. Hell, over the whole house. My mother was forced to marry at sixteen. And she never let either me or my old man forget that she had been forced to be where she didn't want to be. Stuck with a kid when she was a kid herself.

"My old man was silent, long-suffering, morose. He drank to block out the complaints of my mother. My pathetic discontented mother drank to block out how useless she'd let her life become. Neither, as far as I know, ever did one damn thing to change their lives for the better. They whined, complained, and drank.

"I can't remember any occasion they weren't irritated or downright angry with each other or with me if I was in the way. It was a blessing to get the hell out of there. I left and never looked back."

"That's awful. Wasn't there an adult you could go to for help?"

"No."

"Friends?"

"I was sick of trying to come up with new excuses for people who— It was easier to— No, no friends."

Marnie wondered about the bottle of Scotch on his kitchen counter in the cabin above them. The *sealed* bottle of Scotch. Another way for Jake to show himself just how inviolable, how strong, he was?

"And before you ask, I don't drink, for obvious reasons. Doesn't mean the propensity isn't there, though."

Another conversation she should have left well enough alone. He was already physically hurt; now she'd made him talk about another painful time in his past.

"Yet despite all that, you've made a wonderful life for yourself."

Jake laughed. "Yeah, haven't I, though? Kicked out of the organization I've worked for half my life, marooned on this damn mountain with assassins after my ass, nobody to give a shit what the hell happens to me one way or the other. Yeah, I've made a damn fine life for myself."

"*I* give a shit."

"Yeah? And how long would *that* last in the real world?"

"As long as you'd want it to."

"Not interested, cupcake. Okay, wrap this up."

"I'm sorry, Jake, you're right. Let's change the subject."

"Let's." His words were counterpointed by the music still soaring out of the CD across the room. "Spinning Wheel." Now *that* was appropriate.

Bandage. *Don't forget to breathe.*

How could he tell a story like that and not show any emotion? How could he keep his expression so impassive when he'd lived his childhood like a little ghost to the people who should have cared for him the most?

What would Jake Dolan have been like if he'd had someone like Grammy to shower him with love and make him feel special?

She finished bandaging the wound, biting the inside of her cheek until she tasted blood. "Okay. I think I have it. How does it feel?"

Jake moved his arm. "Perfect. Thanks."

Marnie dipped a rag into the warm water, wrung it out, and started to wash the smeared blood off his arm and chest.

She swallowed roughly. God, would this cleanup never end?

Dip. Twist.

Wipe at the bloody smear near his navel . . .

Dip. Twist. Wipe.

What if she'd made the wound worse? What if she hadn't cleaned it well enough? What if—

She'd done it.

It was the best she could do.

Giddy, she dropped the rag she'd been using into the red water in the bowl and dried her hands on her jeans.

Jake closed his eyes for a second.

She stood. She wanted to be outside. She wanted to run fast and far. She wanted to feel the wind on her face. She wanted to find a warm, dark place to hide so she could sob her heart out once and for all. For Jake, for Grammy, and for herself. A lava of grief bubbled too close to the surface, and nausea made her skin clammy.

"All done." *And I didn't even throw up.*

He looked up, and gave her a half smile. "Very efficient."

She picked up the bloody cloths, the bowl, and first-aid box and stepped over his leg. "I'd have asked Duchess, but she's not as dexterous as I am."

Duchess, who'd watched Marnie's every move with worried eyes, gave Jake a gentle nudge on the knee, He rubbed the dog between her ears, his gaze on his nurse. "How're *you* holding up, Florence?"

"Just peachy!"

And then everything went black.

Jake paused, listening to the rhetoric on the other end of the phone. "Look, Leon, if you're too chicken-shit to do it yourself, find me someone who— I don't care. I'll pay you a hundred grand. *Cash.*"

That got the guy's attention, he thought with satisfaction. Jake's heart pounded in his chest as he closed the deal, made the necessary arrangements, and gave the pilot the number to call back when he had a confirmed pickup time.

Tick-tock. Tick-tock. A time bomb waiting to go off.

He clicked off the phone and set it on the trunk. Beneath the fingers of his right hand, Marnie's pulse leapt. He gave her a penetrating look as she opened her eyes.

"How do you feel?"

"Stupid, thank you." Her eyes appeared extraordinarily blue in her pale face. She gave him an apologetic smile. "Told you I can't stand the sight of blood."

He couldn't help himself. He cupped her cheek and brushed his thumb across soft, smooth, delicate skin. He wanted to wrap her in cotton batting and put her away on a high shelf.

"You scared the crap outta me. I thought—hell—"

He'd thought she'd had a heart attack.

It was so sudden, so unexpected. Yeah, she'd looked pale, but that was to be expected. It was pretty unlikely she'd ever seen a gunshot wound before, let alone treated it. But she'd been chirpy, chatty, philosophical, her normal self. When she'd keeled over, he'd about had a heart attack himself.

Jake figured he'd never moved that fast in his life. Still, she'd hit the floor with a thud. Water had gone everywhere, the dog had gone ballistic, he'd used every creative swear word he knew, and she'd been out like a light.

To hell with the fact that he'd ripped open his wound. She was unconscious, damnit.

Her eyes flickered from his face to the seeping bandage on his shoulder and back to his face. She sighed and struggled to sit up. "Now look what you've done. It's bleeding again."

"It's fine," Jake said quickly. "Don't look at it."

Duchess, who'd been walking circles around the couch since Jake had picked up her mistress, leaned her head over the back of the couch.

Marnie pushed upright and rested her back on the arm of the couch. She fondled the dog's ear and looked at Jake.

"Sorry about that. Just for the record, don't bleed, throw up, or cry," she said wryly. "I'll either pass out or join you. I have this empathy thing going. Otherwise, I'm sure I'd be a terrific nurse."

"I'll keep that in mind." His fingers itched to push her hair off her face. To feel her soft, smooth skin. To check and recheck her pulse.

Despite her faint, Jake came to a startling realization: This woman had surprising strength beneath her softness.

"First you save me from taking a header off the dam, now you patch me up like a trouper. You're full of surprises, aren't you?"

Marnie gave him an odd look. "I could hardly let you fall, could I?" She glanced at the floor and wrinkled her nose. "I'd better clean up that m—"

"Stay where you are," he ordered. "I'll do it." He wanted to stay beside her. He wanted to rest his fingers on the pulse at her throat to make sure she was really all right.

He rose. "How about some coffee?"

"No, thanks. I'm okay, really. Who were you talking to?" She drew her knees up, circled them with her arms, and watched as he disposed of the bloody cloths.

"A helicopter service out of Sacramento. I've used them a couple of times—personal stuff. They're not affiliated with T-FLAC. As soon as there's a break in the weather someone will fly in and pick you up."

He searched for towels and started mopping up. Her jacket, tossed on the floor when they'd come in, was soaking wet, too. Jake laid it over the sink and went back to cleaning detail.

He'd never had anyone take care of him like that. It left him feeling edgy, unnerved. Needy.

He was a private man who prized his solitude. Not even the Musketeers, who'd known him for years, knew him like this small, feisty bundle of pure female. He'd never considered his aloneness an option. It just was. Yet Marnie compelled him to see inside himself to the person he could be under her healing touch.

He liked who he became when he was with her.

Of course a man *would* think that after he'd been shot. Nothing like a pretty woman oohing and ahhing over a guy to make him receptive.

"Didn't sound like the guy was too enthused about coming up here," she said, and rested her chin on her knees. She didn't look pale anymore. Her cheeks were a healthy pink, her eyes clear. She looked normal. Beautiful. Breakable.

Jake shuddered.

"Did I hear you right? Did you tell him you'd pay him a hundred thousand dollars?"

Jake shrugged, tossing the soiled towels and Marnie's jacket into the small built-in washing machine. "It's a dangerous landing, and the weather's unpredictable here in the mountains." He added soap and turned on the machine. Money was plentiful. His inventions made ridiculous amounts of the stuff. It was almost embarrassing.

He would have paid any amount to get her out of here ASAP.

"But Jake—"

He didn't want to hear what she had to say. "He'll contact me the second this front moves off."

She reached over, picked up his half-filled cup from the coffee table, and drained the cold contents with a shudder. "And you'll come with me, right?"

"Wrong." Jake walked over to change CDs. "Aerosmith or the Beatles?"

"Aerosmith. Why, Jake? You could let those baddies run around up here until hell freezes over."

"And I'd never know who they are or why they were here in the first place."

She got a mutinous expression on her lovely face. "I want you to come back with me."

"It's good to want things," Jake told her shortly, busying himself making a fresh pot of coffee. He'd never noticed how small and cramped the lair was. "In this case, it ain't gonna happen."

She shot him a glare, then got up and started remaking the bed. The bed they'd torn apart with their lovemaking. He didn't want to think about it. He had a permanent erection anyway. *Damn woman.*

She fluffed a pillow. "So you're going to stay here until either you kill all of them or they kill you?" She slammed the pillow down on the bed, the pillow slip half off. "Damn it,

Jake. Call someone to help you." Her cheeks were flushed, her eyes flinty.

There was no one to call. "No."

"Then I'll stay."

Ice replaced the blood in his veins. "You'll go when I tell you to go. No more discussion. Subject closed."

For several seconds she simply stared at him. "I'd better redo that bandage for you."

"It's fine the way it is." He felt so raw after that scare he didn't want her hands on him again. Everything about this infuriating woman affected him. It would be a blessing when she was gone.

"Fine." She glared at him for a moment, then her eyes skimmed down over his bare chest to the long-john-style pants he still wore. The fabric didn't hide a thing. "Put some clothes on before you freeze to death," she ordered.

Jake's lips twitched. "Yes, Mother."

She walked over the bed as a shortcut and came right up to him, snatching the mug he was about to fill out of his hand. He was surprised the ceramic didn't shatter on the counter as she slammed it down.

"Don't dink around with me, bub."

She stuck a finger in the middle of his chest and crowded him against the counter until there was nowhere else for him to go.

"You want to play macho spy king by yourself?" Poke. "Forget it." Poke. Poke. "I'm not—" She glared at him, tears standing bright in her eyes. Her mouth trembled. She bit her lower lip and pulled herself in tight. "I'm not going to let them kill you because you're too damn stubborn to ask for help. You got that?"

She was shaking. Delayed shock, Jake thought. He slid his arms around her. *Damn.* He hadn't meant to touch her right now. They were both raw. Frightened. On edge.

He had no instinct for this kind of simple tenderness. But Jake pressed her against him, striving for something beyond the wild sex they'd shared. Something he'd never had, yet suddenly found essential.

He pressed his lips to her forehead, her temple. He stroked her hair, her back, and the nape of her slender neck. It felt so damn good just holding her like this.

He ignored the clock ticking in his head. *Tick-tock. Tick-tock.*

Her breath whispered warm against his skin as she rested her head against his good shoulder. Pale, soft curls tickled his chin as he wrapped his arms about her slender body. She burrowed into him, her arms around his waist.

"Y-You scared me to death," she sobbed against his chest.

Her tears unnerved him, tearing through him like a well honed knife. He stroked her wet cheek. "Don't cry. I was scared, too." Scared she'd be here unprotected if they managed to kill him.

He kissed her temple.

"You had a right to be. They shot you!" Through her tears indignation burned.

Jake chuckled. "Not scared for me, scared for *you*."

She looked up at him without releasing her hold. "No one shot at me."

"And they won't," Jake vowed, lowering his mouth to the siren song of hers.

Marnie rose onto her toes to kiss him back. His mouth crushed down on hers, and she tasted anger mixed with the fear. She understood it, savored it, because it matched her own. What a frustrating man he was.

She met his almost violent demand. Her teeth raked his lip. His scraped her tongue. She heard a low, fierce growl and realized it had come from her.

The tears dried on her cheeks as he laved her mouth with his tongue, hungry, insatiable. His hands traveled up her back under the flannel shirt she wore. She loved the feel of those callused hands on her skin.

He was addictive, this Jake Dolan, spy king of the universe.

She sighed as he lifted her, swinging her up onto the counter behind him.

"You were too short." He stepped between her knees.

"Not anymore." Eye to eye, she traced his hard mouth with her finger. He nipped the tip. "If I'm very, very gentle with you, can we make love?"

Jake's eyes smiled. "Don't be gentle."

Chapter Twelve

Marnie's arms lifted to welcome him.

Jake framed her face with his hands and captured her eyes with his. Voice both rueful and amused, he said roughly, "You terrify me, you know that?"

Marnie traced his mouth with a fingertip. "I told you I'd be gentle." She caressed his face, combed her fingers through his hair to draw him closer, then leaned forward and brushed his mouth with a butterfly-light kiss, salty from her tears. "I won't hurt you, I promise."

Yes, he thought with terrifying insight, *you will.*

She kissed him, softly. Jake took her tenderness like a body blow.

The sensation of her soft mouth touching his with such exquisite care wasn't enough. Fierce hunger drove him; he couldn't handle the intimacy of gentleness.

He wanted to touch every part of her at once. He took her mouth the way a victor seized his spoils. His hands were everywhere: in her hair, stroking her breasts through her flannel shirt, caressing the arch of her throat. And all the while he devoured her with a fierce hunger that would not, could not be denied.

He'd never tasted anything as sweet as Marnie's avid mouth responding to his kiss. She sucked in a deep breath as he kneaded her breast, then gently pinched her nipple through the cloth of her shirt. Her breast fit his hand to perfection. Her mouth moved with heat and hunger beneath his, and her knees dug into his hips as she wiggled on the counter, trying to get closer.

For endless minutes kissing was enough as Jake laved her mouth with his tongue, nipped her lips with tender bites, and melted under her explorations. She was curious as a cat as she licked and nibbled back. A sound similar to a kitten's purr vibrated in the back of her throat, her arms tightened about his neck, and she kissed him as if there were no tomorrow.

Jake shifted closer, his hips nudging her thighs apart. His knee bumped the cabinet below. He didn't notice. Needing air, his mouth moved from her mouth to her cheek, to her eyes, to her cheek again. The soft fleshy part of her ear intrigued him. Her body shimmied with desire and her fingers tightened in his hair as he tested the taste and texture of her earlobe with an exploring tongue.

He traced the outer rim, and she moaned low in her throat. The low *hmmm* she made that drove him wild. Jake dampened deeper, letting his tongue imitate the love act until she arched and dug her nails into his scalp to pull his head up and away from her ear.

"Kiss me, damnit!" she demanded, then let out a little yelp when he did just that and crushed her mouth beneath his. She responded to his urgency with an instantaneous fierceness of her own. Sliding her hips to the very edge of the counter, she tightened her arms around his neck and gave him her tongue and teeth.

He felt the brush of her jean-clad legs as she encircled his waist. He sucked at the sweetness of her mouth. He'd never met a woman like her. Open, honest. Unafraid of her own sensuality. Unafraid to cry when her heart was full. Unafraid to show how she felt, even at the risk of being fatally wounded.

Mouth busy, Jake stroked his hands up along the elegant length of her thighs to the crease where her legs met her torso. Her breath came shallow and fast as he dipped his thumbs to explore her through her jeans.

He reached for her zipper, drawing it down slowly. She sucked in her breath as he brushed her soft curls.

She dragged her mouth from beneath his and looked straight at him with eyes heavy-lidded and filled with promise.

By a trick of the light, he saw himself reflected in her dark pupils.

He looked invincible. Whole. Complete.

A trick of the light, all right. A chimera. An optical illusion.

He had to protect her. Even if it was from herself.

But not now. Judas. Not now.

"Make love to me, Jake."

"I am." Words, unspoken, unthinkable, eddied through his brain like ground fog on a summer's day.

He lifted her off the counter. Her legs automatically tightened around his waist and her arms about his neck.

"Your shoulder—"

"Is fine."

He carried her around the foot of the bed and set her down beside the shower stall.

Holding her gaze, he slowly unbuttoned the remaining buttons on her shirt. His knuckles brushed the eager peaks of her bare breasts. She'd been in too much of a hurry to save his ass to put on a bra.

He sank to his knees in front of her and buried his face against the soft vee of flesh exposed by her open zipper. He traced a lazy line down from her navel with his tongue, and she buried her fingers in his hair, holding his head against her.

He tsked. "No underwear?"

"I was in a hurry."

Jake palmed her jeans down her hips, over her legs. She stepped out of them, leaving a puddle of fabric on the floor at her feet.

"So," he breathed against the pale curls exposed, "am I."

She was sweetly wet, musky-scented, irresistible. His thumb lightly brushed the sensitive nub between her legs, and he pressed his mouth intimately against her.

"Um . . . Jake? Wait. I've never . . . I'm not sure . . ."

"Want me to stop?" He nudged her legs a little farther apart. She wobbled, holding on to his hair for balance. He cupped her ass cheeks and buried his face against her soft belly.

"No . . . yes . . . noooo . . ."

He found the spot.

She fisted her hands in his hair and hummed the sexy sound that he loved deep in her throat. He tasted her, savored her, slowly, carefully drawing out her pleasure with painstaking care and attention to detail until she was gasping and breathing hard. He held her still and felt her body vibrate with pleasure.

Knowing that what he was doing was sweet torture, he used his thumb to drive her over the edge. Her body shuddered in fierce response as she came.

He held on to her, reveling in her release, aching and hard, but wanting this for her. All for her. She trembled, damp and weak against him.

Finally he rose to his feet, drawing his body up hers, sliding his arms around her as she collapsed in his arms and buried her face in the crook of his neck.

"Yeah?" he asked softly, smoothing a hand down her back.

She nuzzled her face against his chest, limp, satiated. "Mmmm."

Her breasts brushed against him as she lifted her arms up around his neck and stood on tiptoe to reach his mouth. "More," she demanded, licking his lower lip, tasting herself there, then nipping it gently with sharp white teeth.

"You're insatiable," he told her, backing her into the shower stall and reaching for the knob.

She yelped as temperature-controlled water sprayed her back. "You started it."

"Yes." He nudged her under the spray. "I did."

Her eyes glazed as he trailed a finger down her cleft. "What abo . . . ahh . . . the bandage?" Her lids fluttered as he inserted a finger deep inside her.

Jake didn't bother with an answer.

"You're still dressed. Let me . . . help . . . you."

Her palms slid down his chest. Using both hands, she tugged at the waistband of his pants. The fabric was tightly molded to his hips and thighs, and the bulge of his erection made her efforts harder. Her fingers slid between fabric and skin. Despite the tight fit, she wedged her hand down until she could curl her fingers around the hard jut of his penis.

Heaven. Hell.

He leaned against the cool tiled wall and bucked as she tormented him. Blue eyes wicked, she alternated feather-light caresses with firmer strokes until Jake had to squeeze his eyes shut with ecstasy and force himself to remain still before he came too soon.

"Open your eyes. Look at me," she demanded, voice husky as she cupped him with soft, clever fingers. "Know who I am."

How could he *not* look at her? Her pale skin gleamed with water. Rivulets trailed down the gentle slopes of her breasts, then quivered on the very tip of each nipple. A shimmering gleam as the water beaded, then slid around the plump underside, and trickled down her midriff sheening her skin.

Nimble fingers found the most sensitive, intimate nerves on his body and played them like a virtuoso. Her blue eyes were hazy with arousal and wickedly playful. Jake groaned as she intensified the pressure.

Afraid he'd lose control, he grasped her wrist, stilling the motion of her hand. "Trust me. I know who you are."

Even to his own ears his voice sounded rough enough to be unrecognizable. Unfamiliar words bubbled like the brew in a witches cauldron from deep in his soul. Hell, yes, he knew who she was.

His hope.

His salvation.

His every frigging wish and dream.

But she deserved better than a potential alcoholic. A man to whom violence was second nature. A man who had a long and ugly past and the promise of a short and futile future.

Hell, he had no business putting his hands anywhere near her soft white skin.

People he lo . . . cared about died.

"Jake?" Eyes suddenly shadowed, she searched his features.

Jake pushed aside reality and concentrated on the now.

His lips twitched. Her hand was still firmly down the front of his pants.

"You have my attention," he assured her, his smile widening even as he bent the scant few inches needed to crush her mouth beneath his again. The spray poured over them.

He wasn't going to waste one precious moment with her. He wasn't a fool.

Kissing Marnie was like setting a match to TNT. Fire surged through him. Her fingers tightened around him, her hand pressed tightly against his body by the elasticized pants.

He bent his head to settle his mouth against the hard point of her nipple. Her skin was slick and wet, and he wanted to absorb her until she was a part of him. He squeezed his eyes closed as a tremor speared through him.

Her fingers threaded in his hair, holding his head close as he laved the peak with his tongue, then raked it with his teeth. Moaning, she kissed his shoulder, his neck, anyplace she could reach, her short nails biting into his skin.

"Jake, please, oh, please, I'm going to explode. I want you inside me when I do." Her face was flushed and dewy, her mouth ripe and red from his. Her eyes glittered feverishly.

Her internal muscles clamped tight around his fingers as her juices sluiced his hand.

He'd wanted to make her wait. He'd wanted them *both* to wait. To draw it out. To savor every stroke, every touch. But it wasn't to be. Not this time.

Like hers, his breath came ragged and fast. In an ungainly move, Jake wrenched his pants down one-handed. He lifted her against the wall and, with her help, guided himself inside her.

In one thrust he buried deep, taking her strangled cry into his mouth as her nails gouged his back. Hot water sluiced down against his back as he kissed her mouth with a savage, primal passion.

He was starving for the taste of her. He could never get enough. He wanted to imprint her onto his cells, to sear the memory of himself into her brain so she'd never forget him.

It felt incredible to be buried deep inside her. Teeth gritted, attuned now to her body, Jake kept the rhythm steady, wanting to drive her wild. Her head dropped back, the muscles in her throat taut; her breasts rose and fell with her rapid breathing.

The satin of her thighs gripped his waist, and her fingers dug into his shoulders. She shuddered as he caressed her bare breasts with his chest hair, then cupped her breast firmly while flicking her distended nipple with his thumb.

"Beast," she gasped as he squeezed harder, maintaining his control, pushing her beyond pleasure. "I can't stand this." Her muscles tightened around him. Her skin glowed, rosy and damp, as she met him thrust for thrust. His fierce little warrior.

He wanted her stretched taut on the rack of passion. Wanted her mad with lust. Wanted her crying his name as she came. Judas, He wanted—

This. Only this.

Once, twice, again. Over and over, he drove deep and true, each thrust more powerful, a little faster than the last.

Yes. Yes. Yes.

Her orgasms came, one after the other, with such force she cried out his name and held on to him tightly, her body shaking with aftershocks, her damp face buried against his throat.

With a guttural groan, Jake followed suit, spasming as her internal muscles clenched to keep him inside her.

They remained as they were, water cascading over them, while their breath eased to normal.

"Hmmm." Marnie nibbled his shoulder, then looked up and gave him a sleepy smile. "You taste salty."

He handed her the soap with a wicked smile.

Her heels dug into his butt as she tightened her legs around his waist. "Can't we stay like this forever?"

Jake chuckled. "With you attached to me and beautifully naked, and me with my pants around my ankles?"

"You could always take your pants off," Marnie suggested, nibbling at his neck. "Hmmm. I love the feel of you growing inside me like this."

He thought of something else that could be growing inside her.

"I couldn't pull out in time." His voice sounded one hell of a lot calmer than he felt. God. The thought of her round with his child—

Then a knee-jerk reaction.

No.

Not just *no*, but *hell, no*.

His skin felt clammy as he looked at her. "What will you do if you're pregnant when this is over?"

She lifted her mouth from his throat to look at him. "I'll have a baby," she said calmly.

"Just like that?"

"Just like that." She smiled. "A baby who looks just like my spy king of the universe. I'd consider myself lucky."

"Judas, woman." Jake rested his forehead against hers. "You're a menace, you know that?"

Reluctantly he disengaged from her slick warmth. She clung to his arms for balance as her feet found purchase on the tile floor. She gave him a hot, sultry look. "Hand me that soap, Spy King, and let an artist show you a little finger painting."

He was going to have to protect her from himself.

But who the hell was going to protect him from her?

Too tired to move, Marnie rested her chin on her hand which lay flat on his still damp chest. "Lights off. Eighty percent." The lights immediately dimmed.

"You're getting good at this," Jake said lazily, stroking her back.

She smiled. "Having my wicked way with you?"

"That too." His lips quirked. Almost a smile.

She loved the steady thud of his heart beneath her fingertips and the way his long dark hair fell across his cheek.

His eyes appeared fathomless as he watched her. But they also looked achingly haunted. Jake never quite relaxed. Even after making love, despite lying absolutely still, she felt unleashed energy surging through him.

It was as if, even while in repose, his mind leapt from scenario to scenario. Problem to solution. Question to answer. Although his body lay beside her, his mind was up there, searching for the answers he needed so he could once again find the man responsible for his friend's death.

And even while her body felt limp and sated from their lovemaking, her soul yearned to heal his unseen wounds. The wounds and scars he carried on the inside like badges of honor.

She couldn't imagine living as he did. Never knowing who was friend or foe. Always having to be prepared to fight or die. Not trusting anyone. Not allowing people to get close to him after the deaths of his friends.

And his lover, Marnie thought bitterly.

The woman he'd taken a chance on loving. The woman who'd thrown that love back in his face and added another layer of mistrust to his wounded heart.

She pressed her cheek against his shoulder and tightened her arm across his taut belly, wishing to comfort him for things way out of her realm of understanding, but needing, *wanting* to heal him. She lightly ran her hand up his chest, to his neck.

He caught her hand and splayed his own beneath it. Dark to light. Large to small. Rough to smooth. He inspected her fingers and short nails and ran his thumb along a long faint scar on her wrist. "How'd you get this?" he asked lazily.

"When I was twelve I fell out of that big old tree, the one that crashed into Grammy's house. I broke my wrist." She grimaced. "When we got home my dad was furious. I cried. Not because it hurt, which it did. But because I'd done something really brave and daring, and I'd loved it, and by doing what I wanted I'd disappointed and frightened my family."

"It's understandable they'd be protective. You were a girl, the baby of the family, and sick."

"I wasn't bedridden. But I always had to be careful. Cautious, you know? Not too much activity, nothing to get me too excited. Stop that." She moved his hand. "It scared them when I rejected the first plastic valve—I scared myself.

"They love me. They wanted to protect me. And it was easy to let them. My dad and brothers tend to smother me with love. They take such good care of me that there was a time I wondered if I really had free will.

"I have to figure out what I'm going to do with the rest of my life. What *I* want to do. It's not so easy, you know? Suddenly trying to learn who I am at twenty-seven. The whole *world's* out there. I can have whatever I want. But I'm looking at the selection and the choices are so overwhelming, so diverse, so . . . confusing. It almost seems easier to sneak back into my nice protective little niche and leave it at that."

"And is that the decision you've made this weekend?" Jake asked. "You're not going back to work at your dad's computer company?"

"That's one thing I *know* I don't want to do anymore."

"Then what?"

"I don't know yet. Maybe go to Paris and study. Maybe . . . I don't know. *Something.*" Marnie smiled, sleepy, content to lie here with Jake, safe from the world for now.

"Why didn't you study in Paris instead of going to college here if that's what you wanted?"

"Because my dad was terrified something would happen to me, and I'd be too far away for him to get to me. And when he and the guys talked like that, I'd think, 'Well, maybe they're right. What if something *did* happen to me?' So I put it off, and put it off."

"You could have gone to art school in San Francisco."

"I know. I didn't do that, either. I told you, I had to find some spunk. I'm working on it. Okay, now you. What was the biggest thing that happened to you before you were a teenager?"

"A lot more *big* things happened to me *after* I was a teenager."

She heard the smile in his voice and socked him on the arm. "Not sex. Kid stuff."

"I wasn't a kid. Not really. I tried to keep my nose clean at school. But everyone knew about my folks. It was humiliating. I managed to get reasonable grades. I signed their names for any school stuff. My folks weren't big on education. Most of the time they forgot I was around. We weren't poor or anything. Nice house, fairly decent neighborhood. They just— I stole money from them to buy school clothes before they drank it."

"Oh, Jake. That's terrible. No wonder you ran away."

"It wasn't terrible. It wasn't great. It made me extremely cautious and distrustful around people. I didn't want them to feel sorry for me, and I didn't want Child Protective Services taking me away, either. The navy was one of the best things that happened to me. I got an education, and I wised up fast."

She stroked his chest. "I wish I'd known you then."

"You would have been a kid yourself. What would you have done?"

"Shared Grammy and my dad and brothers with you. Loved you. Shared my sprouts with you."

Jake chuckled and kissed her palm. "Don't like sprouts, huh?"

"Not much. Duchess won't eat them, either."

Jake grinned. "Bummer." His hand skated up her spine, then down to her bottom where he lingered. "What's going on in that mind of yours? I can practically hear your brain ticking."

With her fingertip she traced the sheened stripe, the obscene half smile, around the base of his throat. "Tell me how you got this scar," she said softly. *Tell me about the woman who spoiled you for me. The woman you loved.*

"Not important." He cupped one cheek of her behind in his hand and caressed her petal-soft skin.

She wiggled a little farther up his chest. "It *is* important. It's part of who you are. Part of what you are. Tell me."

Jake hesitated. Even after six years, the whole episode still stuck in his craw—part frustration, part red rage, part embarrassment.

Marnie's eyes were inches from his, clear, blue, languid from their lovemaking, and waiting for him to tell her things he'd rather leave unspoken until he could find some resolution.

She touched his face with her fingertips. "Start anywhere."

What the hell. The middle's as good a place as any.

"I told you about Dancer."

"Yes, but you haven't told me what he did to you."

"T-FLAC has been after him for years. Various operatives have tried, and failed, to catch the son of a bitch. No one has been able to ID him, he's a master at disguise, and he always seems to be a step or two ahead of us."

Jake saw images flash through his mind like an old-fashioned newsreel. A step behind Dancer in Turkey after the bombing of the U.S. embassy in Istanbul. Just missing him in Beirut. Following him to Johannesburg, only to realize he'd caught the wrong guy. Close, but no cigar.

"He's a crazy SOB. Unfortunately crazy like a fox. He's masterminded two attempted presidential assassinations, both of them too close for comfort. He's responsible for countless bombings here and in embassies abroad. He's the one responsible for flying that remote-control plane into the White House last year. We had to work fast on that one. The bomb it carried would have taken out a quarter of DC."

Watching him as if he were telling her the most fascinating story in the world, Marnie shifted against him to retrace the scar with her fingertip. "I thought a woman did this to you!"

"Physically, she did. I found out later she acted on Dancer's orders. I'd been after him for a couple of years by then. Getting close, only to find myself holding smoke. His acts of terrorism started escalating. He took his business outside the States and started stirring the pot overseas. Riling Israel. Pissing off Bosnia. Starting riots in South Africa. Hijacking planes. Planting bombs.

"Six years ago, while I was in a hospital in New York, I met a woman named Soledad O'Donnel."

Marnie snorted. "Soledad *O'Donnel*?"

"She claimed her mother was South American, her father Irish. Petite, blonde, pretty in a fey kind of way. I had nothing better to do, and she fascinated me."

Fascinated, beguiled, seduced. He'd fallen hard and fast. The delicate blonde with the dark, soulful eyes had made him feel ten feet tall, invincible. Lovable. Loved for the first time in his life. It was heady stuff. For two months while he recuperated from a bullet wound, courtesy of Dancer, Jake had basked in Soledad's warmth. The moment he'd been released, he'd moved from the sterile hospital to Soledad's Fifth Avenue apartment.

She'd told him she'd come from a poor family, where they'd had little to eat. She'd still been extremely slender, with dark circles under her eyes, and had an air of frailty about her that made Jake terrified to touch her. He'd wanted to take care of her.

He'd thought of quitting T-FLAC. He'd bought land, sight unseen, in Wyoming. Analyzed his retirement plan. Imagined a life away from violence and mayhem.

"Why were you in the hospital? What was wrong with you?"

"Lead poisoning. Do you want to hear this or not?"

Narrow-eyed, Marnie tweaked his chest hair. "She was beautiful, and you fell madly in love with her."

Jake rubbed his chest. "No I didn't. I fell in *lust* with her." Until this weekend he would have sworn he'd felt some form of love for the beautiful seductress. Now he knew better.

Marnie had a way of raising one pale brow as if to say *What do you take me for, bub? A fool?* "What color were her eyes?" she asked somewhat belligerently.

"Black. Why?"

"What was her favorite food?"

"What is this, Twenty Questions?"

"Just answer."

"Spaghetti."

"Did you ever watch her sleeping?"

"Yeah, so?"

"So, not a thing. Then what?"

"Soledad was a reporter. A stringer. She was an excellent journalist, and when I found out she too was on the trail of our mysterious friend, we pooled resources."

"How nice to share a hobby." She took a bite, not too gently, on his shoulder, then soothed it with her tongue.

"Three scientists from Livermore Labs were kidnapped.

No ransom asked. There was talk of a biological weapons factory. I had to act quickly. Through her sources, Soledad discovered Dancer had gathered a small radical group of mercenaries in San Cristóbal and was planning bigger and better things. Like chemical and/or biological warfare."

He felt a warm huff of air against his chest as Marnie rested her head there. "Lord, Jake, that's so scary. Is that what they were doing in South America? Making biological weapons?"

"Satellite photos showed new construction just outside the city of San Cristóbal. There were too many indicators. Viruses went missing from a lab in Canada. It was confirmed that Dancer supplied the sarin gas used in the Tokyo subway. Each act provided another jigsaw puzzle piece to what he intended. We dared not take the chance of waiting. We had to close in. Fast."

"What happened?"

"The clandestine ground assault was a culmination of years of intensive research into how his terrorist cell operated, where they were, and how many he had with him in South America. Soledad's information was the last piece needed."

Jake scrubbed a hand across his jaw as he stared into the middle distance. "By then we'd rounded up several of his small cells in Israel, Brazil, and Scotland, but we realized San Cristóbal was his new home base. We planned to get him and his factory before he could do any more harm. If it hadn't been for the information supplied by Soledad's source, they wouldn't have known about it.

"We knew someone in our organization was leaking information to Dancer. It was the only way he could possibly have kept a step ahead of us for all those years. Knowing that, I kept it on a need-to-know basis and took only a four-man team in with me.

"We scoped out where they were and got ready to take them out. All of them. We weren't taking any chances that time. Skully, Lurch, and Brit were with me. It was a small team, but hand-picked. Men I trusted implicitly. We knew

Dancer was coming in a couple of days; he'd left for Buenos Aires the morning we arrived.

"Taking turns keeping watch, we sacked out in a small hotel on the outskirts of town to wait. Soledad showed up."

He'd returned to his room after.his watch to find her naked on his bed. Like a horny high-school kid, he hadn't questioned how she'd found him or why the hell she was there.

Until this weekend, it was the last time he'd thought with his equipment instead of his brain. One would think he'd learn. . . .

"Jake?" Marnie brought him back softly. "If it's too painful for you to tell me, let's change the subject."

"Nothing painful about it," he told her shortly. Nothing other than having his heart ripped out twice in a matter of moments.

It was too goddamn late to change the subject anyhow.

He removed her hand from his chest and sat up, then, without looking at her, swung his legs over the side of the bed.

"Oh, damn it. Why do I always open my big mouth? Jake, I'm sorry. . . ."

He remembered the room. Dim. Hot. Muggy. The melodic sound of a guitar floated through the window from the cantina downstairs, accompanied by the fragrance of frying meat and cheap wine. A fly had buzzed around their sweating bodies.

He'd forgotten Dancer. Forgotten the mission. Judas. He'd forgotten to guard *himself*.

While they'd made love, Soledad told him of the child she carried. The moment stood out in Jake's mind, strobe-lit, crystal clear.

His joy. The marvel of it. The unexpected gift of renewal.

Then the ice-hot slice of the knife.

The paralyzing, unexpected betrayal.

"She was quick, I'll give her that," he said, grim as he remembered his shock. The stunned incredulity. The dumb-ass sensation of amazement. The disbelief that she was wielding that sharp, lethal knife in her delicate little hand. Laughing as she told him she was going to abort the baby the next day.

"While we were, ah, doing it, she sliced my throat. When I threw her off, she kneed me in the balls and tried to finish the job."

"Oh, please! Give me a break," Marnie snapped from behind him, where she'd been silent up till now.

The mattress shifted. Jake turned his head as Marnie sat up, reached to pull the silk throw up to cover her pretty breasts, and gave him a disgusted look. "You said Soledad was delicate. How could a woman like that take a trained professional like you?"

Because he'd taken his heart and soul into that bed and left his brain on the floor with his pants.

"A guy isn't *thinking* when he's *coming*. There are a few seconds there when a man can only think with his— What do you call it? Winkie?"

"I don't call it *anything* when you're doing it with another woman!"

"Jealous?"

"Is she dead?" Marnie demanded, jaw tight, blue eyes glittering.

"Lurch burst in and shot her."

"Good. I hope she died slowly."

"Not fast enough," Jake told her grimly. "She used my weapon to shoot Lurch. I was too busy trying to prevent Lurch and myself from bleeding to death to give a damn how she went. My best friend died before Skully arrived like the cavalry."

He rubbed his eyes. "If it hadn't been for Skully hauling my ass out of there and getting me to a hospital, we wouldn't be having this conversation."

"Oh, God, Jake." She pressed against his back, reaching down to splay both hands on his chest. He shuddered, but she didn't let go. "That's terrible. Horrifying! To discover in the space of seconds that the woman you loved was going to give you a child, and then to realize she'd betrayed you . . . And she tried to kill you. The bitch!"

Marnie pressed a kiss to the back of his bowed neck. Then,

keeping her arms lightly around his shoulders, she moved to rest her cheek against his. "And you didn't get Dancer?"

"By the time I went back, there was nothing *to* find. They'd effectively erased every trace of their presence there."

That had been his longest hospital stay to date. Lurch had died saving his life. Then his other two friends had been killed, and he was the last of the Musketeers. Jake hadn't been so sure at that stage of the game what the point was in living himself.

A year later Dancer had popped up again like a jack-in-the-box and moved his operation back to the States. Rumors of a new biological weapons facility in the Midwest started surfacing.

And Jake had come out of his pity party with a vengeance.

"I've been tracking Dancer ever since."

Marnie nuzzled his shoulder with her chin. "You're the best. You'll catch him."

Yes, Jake knew, he would. Eventually. Or die trying.

But before he went after Dancer again, he had to figure out who the hell had framed him and screwed up his career with the fiasco in Omaha. He had to get rid of the assassins topside. He had to get Marnie back to her family, who must be frantic with worry by now. And in his spare time he had to make sure he wasn't offed before he managed to get her out of danger.

Piece of cake.

Chapter Thirteen

At first Jake thought the noise that had awakened him was the dog whimpering in its sleep. But in the dim glow of the monitors he could see Duchess across the room, her ears perked and alert as she watched the bed.

Marnie slept snuggled to his side, her arm across his body, her hand over his heart. But instead of lying limp and satiated by their earlier lovemaking, she whimpered in her sleep.

"Ah, Judas." Jake curved his arm up to cup the back of her head in his palm. "Wake up, sweetheart, you're dreaming. Come on, wake up."

He stroked the curve of her back, then sifted his fingers through the silk of her hair in a helplessly male gesture of comfort as her eyes fluttered open.

"Jake?" She stared sightlessly up at him, eyes brimming.

"You were having a nightmare."

She turned her face into his bare chest and burst into tears, harsh, racking sobs that shook her body with such violence Jake thought they would tear her apart.

"Hey . . . hey. It'll be okay."

"I—I w-was in—in a b-black box. A-And I c-couldn't g-get out and it w-was so dark and c-cold . . . and I was s-so s-scared. . . ." The words were barely audible as she gasped and sobbed, her slender body heaving with the force of her tears.

"Lights twenty percent," Jake said softly, and a soft glow instantly permeated the room. He tightened his arms around her, knowing her grief was inconsolable. Raw. Anguished. Out of control. She needed this, God only knew.

Duchess trotted up beside the bed, her puppy eyes distressed as she looked from Jake to her mistress, then back again. She rested her head on the mattress beside Marnie's shoulder and kept watch, brow wrinkled, ears twitching.

Marnie continued to cry without restraint, her tears saturating Jake's chest, her breath hot on his skin as she burrowed as close as she could get.

Her arms tightened around his neck. "A-And then . . . then I was th-the one opening the box, a-and Grammy—"

Marnie buried her hot, wet face against his throat, and Jake felt the scalding pain of her tears run like acid across his skin. He tightened his arms around her fragile body, whispering soft reassurances as he would to a wounded child.

He'd never comforted a child. Never had a woman fall to pieces in his arms. Either would have been unthinkable a week ago. Now he was thankful he was here for Marnie. Grateful he was the one who got to hold her when her heart was breaking.

He was afraid she'd make herself sick with the ferocity of her weeping, but he didn't want her to stop until she'd cried herself out. He stroked her hair, her back, her hot cheeks.

"*G-Grammy* was in the coffin. But i-it wasn't—it wasn't *my* Grammy. Sh-She looked scary. L-Like in horror movies. Her f-face was melting and her m-mouth was o-open like she . . . she was terrified. I was screaming and screaming, because I wanted *my* Grammy back, not that—that thing. A-And then I opened my eyes, a-and *you* were in the coffin, Jake. You . . . you were covered with blood, and they made me th-throw dirt on youuu. You were d-dead, and I wanted to die, too. . . ."

He brushed her hair back off her forehead and pressed a kiss to the frown between her brows. "A dream, that's all. A scary nightmare. I'm alive and well and right here with you in the bed where we made love."

She burrowed closer, her leg over his to anchor him beneath her, and pressed her wet face against him with throat-tearing, gut-wrenching sobs.

The well of tears seemed bottomless. Utter despair, utter loneliness, utter, unadulterated grief.

"Let it out, sweetheart, let it out. I've got you."

"I m-miss her so m-much."

"I know you do," Jake crooned softly, feeling inadequate. He wrapped both arms around her, pulling her halfway across his body, and wished there was something he could do to help her. The weeping was necessary, but he hated to hear her gasping for every shuddering breath.

Her anguish didn't surprise him. God only knew, she'd been through hell and back this weekend.

It was enough to send anyone over the edge.

Jake caressed her smooth skin in a repetitive motion, his hands never still as he moved them over her slender, heaving body, letting her shuddering sobs and anguished cries find comfort against the wall of his chest.

Her throat must hurt like hell, he thought as he whispered silly nonsense. Words he'd never said to another living soul. The tears continued, rough and painful.

"That's my girl. Get it all out." She was ripping out his heart.

He remembered himself as a nine-year-old boy huddled in the dark of his bedroom closet as the war of the worlds was enacted in his parents' bedroom. He remembered the smell of the booze on the carpet outside his door—spilled, and cause for this particular fight. He remembered he hadn't gone to school that day because he'd been burning up with fever, throwing up. Some flu bug. Nobody had given a damn.

He remembered just what it felt like to sob uncontrollably, his mouth pressed to his knees as anguished cries rocked his body. He remembered the searing pain. The despair of helplessness. The utter futility of his life. And at that time he'd been able to see nothing in his future but more of the same.

Astoundingly, he felt the sting of tears now. He, the man with no heart, felt her sorrow and pain profoundly.

He cradled Marnie's wet cheek in his palm, stroking the tracks made by her tears with his thumb. "Ah, sweetheart, that's it. Cry as much as you want, I'm right here to hold you. I have you. I'll keep you safe," he whispered into the darkness.

Unfortunately while his brain had altruistic motives, his body had other ideas. His erection was rock hard and painful as Marnie's body almost straddled his.

Down boy, didn't seem to have much effect, Jake thought guiltily as he tried to shift a little out of temptation's way. His penis sought the hot, wet entrance of her, so tantalizingly near, so verboten right this moment. He wanted to bury himself hard and deep, to the very heart of her.

Her tears dwindled to a few shuddering hiccups and her leg skimmed his hip, her toes deftly tucked behind his left knee.

She lifted her head slightly. "Th-Thank you for letting me cry all over you."

"You're quite welcome," Jake said tenderly as he brushed away some of the wetness on her cheek with the edge of the silk throw. "Think we're done for a while?"

"God, I hope so," Marnie said feelingly. "It's like I've been turned inside out."

Her eyes were puffed almost shut. Her small, straight nose was pink and swollen. Her cheeks were blotchy, and her lips had lost definition as a result of her unrelenting bout of weeping. Yet Jake had never seen a more beautiful sight in his life. His heart did a double axel.

"You feel right side out to me." He lightly touched her bottom, and she slipped over him and took him inside her body as securely as a hot, wet glove.

"Judas, woman." He squeezed his eyes shut as Marnie slid to her knees, her body intimately a part of his.

She braced her hands on his chest, fingers splayed, and rode him with agonizing slowness.

Jake clasped her hips and let her set the pace. They came together. It wasn't the fireworks and rockets of earlier that evening. It was quiet, and peaceful, and achingly sweet. Like a misty morning sunrise.

Marnie's body wilted, and she flattened her breasts against his chest, still damp with her tears. Tucking her head beneath his chin, she was asleep in seconds.

"Lights off. One hundred percent." Jake stared into the darkness with burning eyes.

God help him. He was in trouble here.

When Marnie opened her eyes the next morning, Jake had already gone to work. It was still snowing. And Duchess needed to go outside. *Now.*

She felt wrung out and yet strangely buoyant. Jake had been wonderful last night; he'd comforted her without resorting to platitudes. Thank God it had been dark. She knew what she looked like after crying mildly. She had no desire to see what she looked like after a crying jag. She could tell by the tightness of her skin that she was puffy and probably pink. A shower would go a long way.

Duchess's nails clicked impatiently on the floor.

"I can't take you out there." Marnie yawned, squinting at the watery reflection on the walls cast by the various monitors. "Sorry, girl. You'll have to wait."

Duchess danced around the bed.

"I can *see* it's urgent." Marnie threw the silk throw off and got out of bed. Whew. Muscles she never knew she had, ached.

She went to look for a newspaper.

"Okay, plan B," she told the agitated dog when there was no newspaper to be found. "Plastic bag, paper towels?"

Indignant, Duchess ran to the elevator door and turned to indicate she was waaaaiting.

Marnie groaned. "Okay, okay. Your beloved Jake is *not* going to be pleased, but I'll take you up. Let's look to see where everybody is first, okay?"

She checked each of the screens while she dragged on some clothes. The last thing she needed was to bump into the bad guys, or Jake for that matter, while she was up there. "All clear. For now. Let's do it."

Within minutes she and the dog were pressed together like sardines in a can as they rode the small elevator up to the cabin.

Whichever route they took, Jake wasn't going to be happy.

At least this trip was considerably shorter than the fifteen or twenty minutes it took to get through the mine shaft tunnels. Jake wouldn't appreciate the dog using his labyrinth as a doggie bathroom.

Above the narrow door of the elevator, five hand-size monitors showed the cabin and surrounding area outside, clear of baddies.

"Which doesn't mean you can take forever to do your business. Got that, goofus?"

The door slid open; Marnie pushed at the back of the pantry door and stepped into the kitchen. She immediately crouched so as not to be seen by anyone walking by, and grabbed Duchess by the ear to get her attention.

"Be quick and don't let the bad guys see you. Got it?" She let go. Duchess skirted the kitchen counter, then sprinted through the partially open front door and disappeared.

Marnie took a deep breath of fresh, damp, pine-scented air. All she had on were her jeans, one of Jake's sweatshirts, and a pair of his socks. *She* wasn't going outside. But the cabin's frigid temperature made her shiver. "Hurry, girl."

She wanted her stuff. Her backpack, her sketch pad. Even her muddy socks, which still hung near the cold fireplace. Did she dare?

Still crouched behind the kitchen counter, she debated the wisdom of removing the items. If she did and the bad guys came back, they'd *know* she and Jake were nearby. She sighed and settled on her butt on the grimy floor, her back against the cabinets, to wait.

She wasn't wearing a watch, but it seemed as though the dog had been outside long enough to *build* a bathroom.

"Where are you, puppy girl?" Marnie grumbled under her breath. Jake was going to have a double fit if he got back to find them gone. She hadn't bothered with a note. This was supposed to be a quick trip.

She risked a peek over the windowsill. No sign of the pooch. But the snow looked as though it was letting up a little. Would the helicopter pilot come today?

For a second she stared at her sketchbook, still propped up on the counter. She wanted those sketches of Jake.

They'd probably notice if *all* the pages were gone. But surely a few . . . She popped up long enough to snatch the large sketch pad off the counter above her head. With it balanced on her knees, she chose five drawings to sustain her after she was home.

And without Jake.

Very carefully she tore the drawings out of the book, then returned it to exactly the position it had been in before. She slumped back down behind the cabinet, carefully folded the thick papers, and stuffed them down the front of her shirt.

Duchess had been gone forever. Marnie started to worry. Had they found her? *Shot* her? Was her dog lying somewhere bleeding?

"No. Don't think like that," she told herself fiercely. "She's hiding from them. That's what she's doing, she's hid—"

"I'm going to wring your neck," Jake snarled above her. "What the hell are you doing here—besides getting pneumonia with no jacket?"

Marnie knocked her head against the cabinet as she looked up at him. *Oops.* The part of Jake's face she could see was ruddy with the cold. His eyes, always expressive, spoke volumes.

"Duchess couldn't wait." Marnie spoke in the same barely-above-a-whisper tone he'd used, and rubbed the back of her head. "Did you see her out there?"

"No," Jake said shortly, coming around to crouch beside her. He looked enormous in the tight black clothing. Enormous and dangerous. "But *you* can't stay here. They know I'm close. This is the most logical place for them to look."

"What about Duchess?"

"We'll see her on the monitors in the lair when she returns."

Jake came down with her, showing her the alternative way, through the bathroom instead of the pantry, into the narrow elevator.

"The snow's letting up," he said against her hair. Since he'd used the same soap and shampoo only hours before, he couldn't fathom how she could smell so delicious. He scanned what he could see of her face at this angle. She was still a little swollen about the eyes, but all things considered, she looked damn good.

Physically, they couldn't have been any closer; the elevator had been built for one person, after all. He heard a shiver of noise from her, the sound similar to the soft *hmmm* of pleasure she made when he pushed inside her body. Jake knew she was as aware of his aroused state as he was. She made that humming sound again. Her noises drove him wild. And she knew it.

The second the door opened he strode out, almost breathing a sigh of relief. She gave him an innocent look, the one that made his heartbeat kamikaze, then raced to the monitors.

"Do you think—" She stopped midsentence and shook her head. "Why'm I asking you? You don't know that she's okay. Ignore the question. Are you hungry? Did you come home for lunch?"

"You make it sound as though I came home from the office."

"You came home from work, didn't you?" She searched the monitors for Duchess.

"That's one smart dog. She can take care of herself. Worrying isn't going to get her here any faster."

"I know." She walked into the kitchen area. "Do you want something to eat? I think there's a bit of h—"

"I came for more clips." He took several of the heavy boxes from the cabinet and set them on the workbench. "Better put on a dry shirt. That one's we—" He was cut off by the ringing telephone.

They looked at each other. They both knew who it was.

Jake strode to the counter and snatched up the phone and said into it without greeting, "This better be good news." The phone tucked under his ear, he continued rattling bullets and clips while he talked.

Marnie unbuttoned her jeans as she watched him reload

and check his arsenal as he talked to the pilot. She removed the pictures, still warm from her skin, and laid them carefully on the table. Then she slid the sweatshirt over her head and tossed it over the back of the couch. A wave of sadness threatened to swallow her. Her eyes stung.

This was it. The end. *Finito. Hasta la bye-bye.*

"Then why the hell did you ca— Fine," Jake said tautly. "I appreciate the weather forecast."

He ran his fingers through his hair in frustration, his back to her. When the rasp of her zipper being lowered broke the silence, Jake's only response was the slight tensing of his shoulders beneath the tight black fabric.

Sitting on the end of the bed, she stripped his large socks off her feet, then drew her jeans down her legs slowly. Jake didn't turn around, but his back was rigid. And she'd bet her last dollar that so were some other very interesting parts.

"The front's moved off." Pause. "Temporary? So? Plenty long enough to land a chopper. . . . If I *had* one here, I *would* fly her out myself." He bent to unlace a boot.

Marnie scooted back to lie on the bed, enjoying the view of his muscles flexing and shifting beneath the LockOut.

Jake jerked the boot off his foot and tossed it into the kitchen with a thud. He crouched to undo the laces of the second, then tossed it aside.

As if she'd called his name, he looked over his shoulder. Their eyes met.

Not breaking eye contact, he walked over and sat beside her, cupping her cheek with a cool hand, his tone at complete odds with his gentle touch. "Then find me a pilot who *will*."

Marnie's body immediately responded to his touch. Everything inside her turned to liquid heat. She nuzzled her face against his hand, then kissed his palm.

He continued speaking into the small cell phone, the pitch of his voice not changing one iota as his thumb brushed back and forth across her lower lip. The nerve endings in her lips tingled and transmitted a signal to her vital organs. His touch shimmied to her toes. She shifted restlessly, her breasts aching for the feel of his hands on her bare skin.

"I don't give a damn." His fingers glided up her cheek and combed through her hair. He cradled her head in his large palm, then drew her toward him, inch by slow inch, until she was sitting up. Cool air bathed her naked back. She touched his face with just the tips of her fingers. His jaw felt smooth. He'd shaved before they'd made love the second time last night.

"Hell, yeah. I'll do that. What the hell? *Two* hundred and fifty G's? You son of a bitch. Yesterday we agreed on a hundred thou—" Tense pause as the other man spoke. "Yeah," Jake said through gritted teeth, "she is. Half on pickup, the balance on her safe delivery in Sacramento."

The man was stupid enough to blackmail Jake Dolan? Marnie pitied the man when he and Jake met. A quarter of a million dollars was an incredible amount of money to pay for an hour-long helicopter ride.

A tiny, terrified part of her was relieved that she'd have access to her meds soon. The rest of her ached mournfully to be leaving.

Looking into his eyes, she traced the tender bottom curve of his lip. His strong white teeth nipped at her finger, and just a rim of blue showed around his black pupils as his gaze held hers.

"You have the coordinates? I'll expect you within the hour. Be prepared to lift off immediately."

Marnie closed her eyes at the exquisite sensation of Jake's cool hand on her superheated flesh. He measured her breasts, weighing each one in his cupped hand, and then tormented her by skimming each nipple with his thumb.

Her back arched as she leaned forward. In their last hour together she wanted Jake's undivided attention. She wanted to remember these last moments together. She wanted to imprint him into her DNA. She wanted to rub him with her scent so no matter what, he could never forget her.

Her lips found the pulse pounding at the base of his neck. Hers throbbed even faster. Her hands skimmed down his biceps and she looked up at him, knowing her heart was in her eyes.

Jake gave her a smoldering look, turning the phone so the mouthpiece was above his head, wrapped his free arm around her, and pulled her into his chest. He kissed her hard, his teeth sharp as he nibbled at her lower lip. His tongue laved away the small pain.

His large hand was on the back of her neck, under her hair. He squeezed once and tilted the phone back to his mouth. "We'll be waiting." Pause. "Bring your logbook with you." Jake's smile was slow, and she could hear the other voice spluttering through the phone. "For a quarter mil, I have *every* right to see it." With a flick of his finger he disconnected, then tossed the phone on the bedside table with a clatter.

"The forecast is for a mother of a storm," he whispered against her mouth.

"How do I get you out of this?" she demanded. He peeled his top off like a stripper on speed. "Oh, thank you. The river isn't going down," she whispered against his furred chest, inhaling the unique fragrance of his skin.

"Not for days." He tugged off his pants. "We don't have days. You need your medication. With you here, I'm on the defensive. They know that. This has to be over. And soon. The chopper's coming to lift you out."

"I heard you. Within the hour."

One hour. That was all they had left. Sixty miserable minutes. His naked weight slid over her body. Marnie parted her thighs in eager acceptance. She locked her ankles over his, fitting her curves to his hollows, her softness to his hardness, pelvises locked together as they rocked slowly.

"You feel so good, so good." Her breasts slid against his chest. Too sensitive. Too exquisite a sensation. She cried out softly, burying her face against his arched throat. Kissing the scar there. Praying for more, and satisfied with less.

This time their lovemaking was silent. Solemn. Heartbreaking.

They left via the mine shaft tunnel. The chopper would be landing in a small clearing north of the exit. Jake helped her across the rocks and down the other side. As soon as they cleared the obstacles, he dropped her hand, filling his instead with a nasty-looking gun.

It was broad daylight, and perversely the sun had decided to shine. Despite the afternoon brightness, it was icy cold and she hunched her ears into the collar of her jacket. In her right pocket she had one of Jake's athletic socks. She'd dropped a dozen bullets into the toe, then tied it off. A handy weapon. Jake hadn't even cracked a smile as she'd made it.

In her left pocket was a wad of bills in two separate bundles, one for pickup, one for delivery. She was a quarter-million-dollar air-freight package.

Marnie glanced back. "We're leaving footprints."

"I know." Jake forged ahead. "I want them to follow me. It'll save time."

She shivered and picked up her pace to keep up with him, and immediately slid on a patch of ice-frosted pine needles. She sucked in a gasp. Jake caught her elbow, keeping her upright.

"We've got plenty of time," Jake said quietly, not releasing her.

Plenty of time? "Yeah, like what? Eleven more minutes?"

"I don't hear the chopper. We'll be there long be— Quiet." He slapped his arm across her chest.

She hadn't heard a thing, but she stopped in midstride and held her breath. Other than the breeze stirring the high branches of the pines and the distant sound of rushing water, she heard nothing out of the ordinary.

Jake swiftly pulled her down and reversed them into the shelter of a clump of extremely wet, low-hanging pine branches. Before she could straighten from her contorted position, she heard two men talking quietly as they approached.

She didn't move. Half bent, half twisted, the muscles in her back screamed for her to straighten. She stayed as she was, breath frozen, heart in her throat as they came closer.

She glanced at Jake. He frowned, and she raised her eyebrows questioningly. He indicated her pretzel shape with a motion of his eyes, and she gave him a look back that said, *So? What can I do about it?*

For the longest time he crouched there staring at her as though she were some exotic animal in the zoo, until the sound of the men moving off drew his attention away.

She expected him to jump up and do something to the two men; instead he stayed as still as stone until they had passed. Long after Marnie could no longer hear their footsteps, Jake held her still.

"Okay?" he finally asked under his breath.

"Peachy." She could almost hear her muscles and tendons scream with relief as she straightened.

"Let's go."

It was uphill all the way. Marnie stumbled over a shadow. Jake reached out a hand to catch her. Tears pricked her eyes.

"Okay?" he asked as she dashed her fingers across her lids.

"Fine. The wind's making my eyes water."

Her mind was in turmoil. Each step they took carried her closer to saying good-bye to Jake. Would she ever see him again? The tightness in her chest made climbing harder, and tears felt icy on her cheeks.

And Duchess? She couldn't bear to think of the fate of her beloved pooch. *Where* are *you, girl?* She snapped a pine bough out of her way and got a handful of pitch and her face sprinkled with icy water. She set one squishy foot in front of the other as she climbed, her body on automatic pilot.

"How're you doing?" Jake turned to look at her, his face ruddy with the cold. She was starting to hate that damn black spy suit of his. Right now he didn't have it covering his hair or face, but it was still a symbol of the difference between them. This must be how the wives of police officers, firefighters, and soldiers felt every time their men left for work.

"I presume that's rhetorical?" She blew out a breath. "I'm worried about Duchess." Which was part of the whole truth. The other was the heartbreak she anticipated when she had to say good-bye. "I hate to leave you here by yourself. . . ."

"It's what I'm trained for," he said shortly. "That's the

chopper. Move it." Jake took her hand to help her move faster, traversing the muddy terrain in ground-eating strides.

She couldn't hear the helicopter, but if Jake said he could, then it was on the way. Panting, she gripped his hand tightly as they ran. The cold air ripped painfully at her lungs. "What about my car?"

"I'll make sure it's delivered to you." He held a branch aside, dragging her behind him when she reached for it herself. Water sprayed the back of her head when she released it.

She wanted to grab the front of his spy suit in both hands and beg him to at least find her dog before she left. She did nothing of the sort. Jake had enough on his plate without her going ballistic on him. "And Duchess?" she asked with what she thought was admirable restraint.

"She'll be in the car."

"You'll have to bring her. She can't drive."

Oh, God, I'm going to cry. She could feel the prickles behind her nose and the stinging of her lids. She bit her lip and tried to concentrate on where she was running. The last thing Jake needed now was a weepy female.

"I'll make sure there's a designated driver."

"You," Marnie huffed fiercely.

"I don't make promises. Don't believe in them."

"You can believe in *mine*." He ignored her assurance, which made her even sadder.

Oh, Jake.

She saw the trees ahead in a haze.

And now she could hear the faint *whop-whop-whop* of the helicopter as it came over the ridge toward them.

They stopped at the edge of the clearing. Heart pounding so hard she could barely hear the approaching aircraft, she looked at his shuttered expression. He was hawk-eyed as he watched for the bad guys.

"I'll pay back the money when you bring the car and Duchess, okay?" *In small installments, in person,* Marnie thought. *That should take about fifty years or so.*

He watched the helicopter's approach above them with a frown. "Don't worry about the money."

No, I'm worried about you, *Jake Dolan.* "I pay my debts." She touched his arm. "Can I ask you something before I go?"

His gaze flickered briefly to her face. "What now?"

She felt like a complete idiot for asking. "If there's anything you like about me other than incredible sex, could you tell me before I go?"

"It's hard to get over the incredible sex part." Jake's mouth quirked. He touched her cheek and used a thumb to brush away the tear she refused to acknowledge. "I admire the hell out of you."

It was hardly the declaration she longed for. She looked at his face. His stern mouth, his strong jaw. His unrelenting eyes, so hooded, so carefully unrevealing.

"I wish . . . ," she said softly, knowing she couldn't possibly be heard. The noise was deafening as the helicopter descended. Jake tugged at her hand. Leaves and debris swirled around them as, hunched over, they ran to meet it.

The pilot, bulky in a heavy jacket and wearing a belligerent expression on his red face, shouted over the sound of the rotors. "Money?" He rubbed his fingers together in the universal sign for cash.

Jake shouted back, "Papers?" He flicked the pages in an imaginary book.

The pilot tossed Jake his log. Jake did a quick glance at the man's logbook. She wondered what he would do if the records weren't satisfactory. Fly her into Sacramento himself?

She wished.

Jake threw the book back to the surly pilot, then indicated that Marnie should give the man one of the bundles in her pocket. She handed it over. The man did a quick count, his lips moving. The swirl of the blades above them made normal speech impossible. Probably a good thing, Marnie thought morosely. It wouldn't be hard to lip-read "good-bye." Her hair whipped around her head, stinging her cold cheeks, making her eyes water and her ears throb.

Jake motioned for Marnie to get into the helicopter. She knew she had to hurry. The bad guys must have heard the helicopter's approach and would be following their footprints.

Marnie framed his face with her hands, leaning into him, then wrapped her arms about his neck and held him as tightly as she could. Standing on her tippy-toes, she pressed herself against him from head to toe. *Oh, God, oh, God.* She couldn't *bear* leaving him. Their thick jackets made the embrace unsatisfactory and frustrating.

"Please be careful," she said against his scarred throat. "I . . . I don't want anything to happen to you." She knew he couldn't hear her. "I love you, Jake," she whispered achingly against his mouth. Then kissed him before he could set her aside.

His arms came around her, and he kissed her back. Hard, insistent. Meaningful.

Meaning what? Marnie asked herself as Jake released her. In the next heartbeat he lifted her into the open door of the helicopter and pounded on the Plexiglas for the pilot to take off.

His dark hair blew wildly about his face. He cupped his hands around his mouth and shouted, "Her life is in your hands, pal." He held up a scrap of paper, torn, Marnie presumed, from the pilot's logbook, although she hadn't seen him do it. He looked terrifying in his black spy suit with strategically strapped weapons and that ferocious glare.

The pilot, looking nervous, saluted Jake and fiddled with something on the lit-up control panel in front of him. The helicopter lifted from the ground.

Tears sharp in her eyes, Marnie watched as, without a backward glance, Jake melted into the trees and disappeared from view.

Out of sight under cover of the trees, Jake watched as the rotors accelerated, the nose dipped and the chopper lifted. He could see Marnie looking small and lost, face pale, eyes wounded, inside the bubble.

He withdrew his weapon from the shoulder holster and covered the chopper while remaining discreetly hidden amongst the trees.

The 9 mm Browning felt good and solid in his hand. The automatic had been custom-made for him, had an excellent sight, and could be fired in rapid succession. The Walther PPK would stay in his ankle holster unless needed. Tucked into the small of his back was the Daewoo DP-51. He wasn't taking any chances. He'd come loaded for bear. And intended finding it.

Stalking tangos always sharpened his senses. In this case the enemy wasn't tangos. It made no difference. They were still the bad guys.

The controls on his adrenaline opened several notches. This time it was going to take a lot more self-control to concentrate. While not impossible, it was going to be annoyingly difficult to shut Marnie out of his mind.

"Other than the incredible sex," she'd said. Jake felt a reluctant grin tug at his mouth. Other than the incredible sex? Judas, the woman had an unflagging way of blindsiding him.

He braced his back against a broad tree trunk, propping his foot on the gnarled bark. He scanned the clearing for movement, then refocused on the chopper.

The blades spun faster as the small chopper rose in a small tornado of wet leaves and pine needles. For a few seconds he watched the red strobe flashes of the chopper's flying lights blinking. Then flicked the safety on the Browning, kept the gun in his hand, and turned to start walking back down the mountain.

This time he didn't bother trying to hide his presence. He *wanted* the bastards to know where he was. Sending Marnie away had put him in a damn bad mood.

A slither of apprehension shimmied up his spine. Jake paused, head cocked, as he tuned his senses to the forest around him. Nothing seemed out of place, nothing appeared out of the ordinary. A mini whirlwind kicked up a circle of dead leaves. The tree branches creaked and swayed. The scent of crisp air mingled with the unmistakable pungent smell of fuel.

He turned slightly, listening, as the chopper lifted above the trees, a hundred feet above his head.

He had a bad feeling. A very bad feeling.

The familiar *whop-whop-whop* of the chopper overhead

sounded fine. Jake concentrated, separating the sounds beneath the noise of the rotors. The music of the forest, the rhythm of the river, the sibilant whisper of the breeze through the lacy pines.

Despite the normalcy of the sounds, his gut instinct warned him that something wasn't right.

He turned fully, heart already racing, ready to sprint up the hill and see if—

He looked up.

Just in time to hear the explosion and see the fireball in the sky as the chopper exploded in a burst of flame and blew to smithereens.

Chapter Fourteen

Jake hadn't heard the launch. Judas Priest. Despite his superior hearing, he'd been so damned busy thinking. He hadn't even heard it.

The ball flared like the sun. Bits of metal rained down on treetops, setting small bursts of flame dancing in the pines even as he started running toward it.

"Marnie!" Jake choked back the black terror that consumed him. *"Noooooooo!"*

He sprinted between the trees, slid on the slippery needles, and jumped over rocks and fallen logs in his race uphill. Breath sawing, lungs heaving, he kept his eyes glued to the horror ahead as he ran. Huge chunks of flaming debris fell from the sky like the wrath of God and lay smoldering on the sodden earth.

"You sons-of-bitches, I'll kill you for—"

The breath was knocked out of him as he was tackled from behind. The other man was up and at him before his momentum was arrested by a low rock. Jake rolled, swept his left foot out, and brought his attacker down. Locked together, they plunged ten feet down the steep slope.

Teeth bared, Jake slugged him in the gut. The man retaliated. Sweat and blood flew like confetti in the chill air. Jake used every trick learned in back alleys and dockside bars. Fists, elbows, knees. The fight wasn't equal. The other man didn't have his years of experience, nor his training. Most of all, he didn't have Jake's fury, pain, or guilt.

Jake was bigger, stronger, and deadlier. Motivated, and in a hurry. This skirmish didn't make a dent in his internal turmoil. Nothing would keep him from finding Marnie.

Jake grabbed his would-be assassin by the throat and hauled him upright to deliver the coup de grâce, a quick, efficient uppercut to the jaw. His attacker flew back, struck a knobby tree trunk with a satisfying *thwack*, then slid to the ground.

Jake staggered to his feet, adrenaline surging, heart pounding, mind reeling.

"Dolan, wait!" The man struggled to push the headpiece off his face so Jake could ID him.

Jake stared incomprehensibly at Sam Plunkett, a man he'd worked with several times at T-FLAC over the years. He didn't know the man well, but he had a decent rep in the agency. They weren't friends by any stretch of the imagination, but he'd held a grudging respect for the younger man. Until now. The last time they'd seen each other was two weeks ago, at the inquiry over the midwestern fiasco.

"You son of a bitch." Jake grabbed Plunkett by the loose fold of fabric at his throat and hauled him to his feet. Then he threw a punch that spun the guy around and onto his ass. Hauling him up, Jake punched him again. Plunkett fell to the dirt and doubled over, nose bleeding profusely.

Jake pulled the Daewoo from its holster in the small of his back. "You fire the rocket?" he demanded.

Plunkett looked up, eyes wild. "No!"

"Then who's pulling your chain?" Jake kept the pistol exactly where it was—between the traitor's eyes. Plunkett started to rise. "Stay the hell where you are."

Jake was ripped in two: stay and get the info he so desperately wanted, or search for Marnie's . . . his jaw clenched . . . body. Wishing he were an optimist, Jake prayed. Maybe she wasn't dead. Maybe she was alive. If so, he had to find her. *Now.*

The rank smell of burning jet A fuel filled the crisp mountain air. "Screw it," Jake said flatly as he stripped Plunkett of his weapons and tossed them into the brush. "I don't give a continental damn *what* you're doing here."

He lifted the business end of the gun a fraction of an inch. "I'll find out what's going on later."

"No, wait!" Plunkett unfolded his long legs and stood, hands in the air. "I'm one of the good guys, Dolan." His eyes darted nervously before coming back to Jake. "The others'll be here in less than two minutes. I'll talk fast."

"I'm not in the mood right now to chat." Jake withdrew a short length of clear plastic tucked beneath the harness of his shoulder holster. "Turn around. Don't even twitch, or so help me, I'll save myself the aggravation and waste you now."

Resigned, Plunkett lowered his arms and grimaced, one hand going to his midriff, where he rubbed at what looked like a small muddy footprint on the black fabric of his suit. He turned. Jake used the plastic handcuffs, pulling the end as tightly as possible.

"You're cutting off my circulation."

"Write a letter to Amnesty International." Jake prodded him in the back. "Move."

"There's no point in going to the wreckage," Plunkett said over his shoulder. "No one could've survived that."

Jake told him what he could do with himself anatomically. He should shoot the bastard. But a dozen unanswered questions buzzed in his head. He could kill him just as easily in five minutes as now.

"Keep moving," Jake shoved him in the shoulder.

The gruesome image of Marnie's body, charred beyond recognition, ripped out his heart. For the first time in his sixteen-year career, he felt emotion when confronting the bad guys. It boiled and churned in his gut like lava, and ran like a rat in a maze in his brain.

He wanted to rip out someone's heart while it was still beating. He wanted to wreak vengeance on a purely personal level. He craved a confrontation. Something violent. Something bloody. Something to the death.

Grimly Jake started up the steep incline to the crash site, pushing the younger man in front of him. He waited for the smell of death to reach them, borne on the stench of kerosene, listening as flames snapped in the clearing above them. His eyes stung. From the smoke. He pinched the bridge of his nose. Wind could be hell on a man's tear ducts.

He imagined a road not taken.

He allowed the pain to rip through him as he remembered the taste of her on his tongue. Her unique fragrance. The way her blue eyes often held a wicked glint, as if laughter hovered a second away from curving her sweet mouth.

Plunkett's steps lagged. "They'll be waiting up there for you to investigate."

"I'm looking forward to it."

Jake bent to pick up the Walther he'd dropped earlier, and checked it as he walked. The closer they got, the more profuse the smoke and the more powerful the reek of burnt fuel, burnt metal, and the sweet, nauseating stench of burnt flesh.

He swallowed bile. Dazed by the enormity of his despair, Jake stopped at the edge of the tree line. Black smoke and smoldering debris filled the small clearing. There were no large pieces of anything. Bright flames still licked at the edges of the scraps, soon to be smothered by the wet ground and inhospitable environment.

No one could have survived this.

There'd be nothing there but charred remains. He couldn't handle seeing them now.

His eyeballs felt scorched. The weight on his chest made breathing hard. He dragged in a lungful of toxic smoke.

"U.S. Army Red Eye?" he asked flatly, and Plunkett nodded. The same shoulder-fired, heat-seeking missile the U.S. of A. sold to anyone who had the price.

Jake ran his fingers through his hair and swallowed roughly, a lump the size of a barrel cactus lodged in his throat. What he felt was immaterial now. He dashed away the smoke-induced moisture in his eyes and let ice take over his organs. He'd done a piss-poor job of protecting the woman he . . .

He looked at Sam Plunkett, feeling savage, almost demented with the ripping rage and despair devouring him.

The rank smell turned his stomach. He'd smelled worse. Witnessed more carnage firsthand than this single aircraft carrying only two passengers. But it had never been this personal.

He *had* to put her firmly out of his mind. Jake couldn't bear even to think her name. Nothing must interfere with what he had to do. His ability to focus one-hundred percent was crucial now.

"All right." Jake's voice sounded flat and dead. About as flat and dead as he felt inside. "Talk."

He wanted Plunkett to make a break for it, to make a move that he could counter. Shooting him was too quick. He *wanted* hand-to-hand combat. Craved the physical release for his rage. Burned to hear bone crush and muscle tear. He wanted blood sport. To the death. May the best man win.

"Sure," Plunkett agreed nervously. He wiped his bloody nose on his shoulder and then looked around, skittish and twitchy. "But not *here*, man."

"I'm not walking all over this mountain so you can have a moment of privacy," Jake snarled. He backed against a broad, knobby trunk of a blue-tinged Douglas fir, the muscles in his entire body clenched for action, his stomach in a hard, unrelenting knot of anguish.

Push it aside, he commanded himself. *Focus on payback.*

Tendrils of pungent smoke drifted between the upper branches of the trees, ghostly and pale against the darkening sky.

There's not a damn thing you can do to help her now. Not one damn thing. You did it all when you lifted her sweet, fragile body into what ended up being her funeral pyre.

He looked away from the clearing. They were high enough to see over many of the treetops down into the dam below. The sky reflected pewter off the choppy water. Jake looked back at Plunkett. "Start talking, or spare the air."

"Know a tango called Dancer?"

"This is an SPA operation?" Jake asked incredulously. The Shining Path of America had been the militia group in the Midwest that was responsible for the massacre last month. *Dancer* was the group leader? This made no sense.

"What the hell does the SPA want with *me*?"

Plunkett shrugged.

Jake stared at him through narrowed eyes. God, he needed a drink. A kill. A moment without this gut wrenching . . . hole in his stomach. The adrenaline seemed to have been sucked out of his body. He suddenly didn't care who the hell was after him or why.

"Just tell me who ordered the hit on the chopper and who held the Red Eye."

"Dancer." Plunkett sank onto a nearby rock with a wince. His eyes flickered about—looking for his backup, Jake knew.

"Who the hell *is* Dancer? What's *your* involvement? You riding double?"

"Damn, I'd kill for a cigarette," the younger man said. A faint Texas accent emerged as he shifted nervously on his rock. "I'm true blue, one hundred percent T-FLAC," he said with a boyish grin that didn't impress Jake one iota. "Phantom called me in when we got back from that gig in Venezuela. Said you had someone riding your ass. He asked me to look into it."

"That right? Why didn't he let *me* know? That was two freaking years ago."

Plunkett shrugged. "Don't know. All I know is he told me to watch your back. I let it be known I could be bought. Someone approached me a couple of years ago, and I turned—" His eyes widened as Jake shifted the Daewoo. "Hey, hey, hey. Not for real, man. Not for *real*."

"So you rode double for T-FLAC and SPA, but your loyalties of course remained with T-FLAC?"

"Absolutely."

"Which lays the tab for the massacre entirely at your feet, doesn't it?" Jake said dangerously.

"*No!* No way, man. Dancer has people strategically positioned inside our organization who feed him data. I was just one of a whole bunch of—"

"And are you the traitorous son of a bitch who shared our language and signs with him, Plunkett?" Jake pushed away from the tree.

"Dancer knew all that *long* before I came on the scene. I swear."

"Are all the men up here with you current or former T-FLAC?"

"No. I'm the only one. The rest are SPA militia."

"How many?"

Plunkett managed a weak grin. "Thirteen of us were air-lifted in. You're good, man, the best. Dancer wasn't taking any chances."

"Thirteen," Jake repeated. "My lucky number. Which leads us back to the big question: Who's Dancer, and why is the son of a bitch after my ass in the first place?"

A man in black garb stepped into the clearing, a snub-nosed automatic in his hand and pointed at Jake. He pushed the headpiece off his face.

"Perhaps I'm the one you should ask."

Fear flashed across Plunkett's face. "Dancer!"

"Lurch," Jake said tonelessly at the same moment.

Shock. Joy. Anger. Betrayal. White-hot fury. A tumultuous barrage of emotions rushed at Jake with supersonic speed.

"Drop your piece." Lurch motioned to Jake with his weapon.

"Go to hell, you bastard."

"Aw." Lurch pouted. "Aren't you happy to see me, Tin Man?"

"I preferred you the way I last saw you. Dead."

"Funny. I believe at the time you almost cried."

Jake's gut twisted at the memory. "I got over it."

He stared at the man he'd thought he knew so well, and bile rose to choke him. A haze of red obscured his vision for a moment. "Why don't we save each other the trouble, and both shoot?"

"Oh, man, you don't think I came this far to play *fair,* do you, Jakie boy? Hell, no."

A shot rang out from the trees. The Walther flew from Jake's fingers leaving a stinging numbness all the way to his shoulder.

Lurch laughed. "Still have those scruples, I see. I just love how predictable you are. In fact, I'm banking on it. Nice guys finish last, Tin Man, haven't you heard?"

"I came loaded for bear," Jake said. "Too bad all I see is a weasel."

"Yeah? Well I'm the one with a gun in my hand, now, aren't I? Check him out," Lurch told Plunkett.

Jake stood still while the younger man stripped him of his weapons and secured his hands behind his back. What the hell did it matter at this point?

"Are you sure you have everything?"

"Yes, sir."

"Good." Lurch turned his weapon toward Plunkett. A pop, and it was done. The double agent looked startled, a neat hole in his temple, as he crumpled to the side and rolled to the ground.

Lurch stepped nimbly around the body and ambled over to Jake, who hadn't moved from his relaxed position against the tree. "How ya doin', Tin Man?"

Jake glanced at the body, then back to Ross Lerma without expression. "No honor amongst thieves, I see. You look pretty damn good for a corpse."

"Yeah." Lurch smiled his familiar, charming smile. "Being invisible is real good for me."

"Lucrative, too, I'm sure."

Lurch's smile got wider. "We used to talk about how damn unjust it was that the bad guys got all the dough, remember? Well, man, I got me a piece of that action. A *big* ol' piece."

It all suddenly made horrible sense to Jake. Too bad he didn't give a rat's ass anymore. "So you used Plunkett to work inside, keep you updated."

"Hell, there've been a dozen people at T-FLAC in the past six years who work for me," Lurch boasted as he kicked Plunkett's leg off the rock so he could sit down. His weapon was still trained almost casually on Jake's chest.

"Hey," he said conversationally, "remember Sylvia Cortez? Good operative, huh? You dated her a couple of times a while ago? Hoo-ee! Was *she* hot in the sack. What a babe. Too bad she got gree—"

"Lose the hardware." Jake cut him off. "Let's do this mano a mano. No holds barred."

Lurch laughed. "I'm not taking you hand to hand, pal. I know you too well." He looked behind Jake and nodded. Three men emerged through the trees.

Jake didn't bother moving; he kept his eyes on Ross Lerma. The friend he'd held in his arms for his big deathbed scene six years ago. He didn't need to know how. Several drugs could mimic death.

"Why?" he asked flatly.

A gross, gasoline-type, smell filled the air. Marnie coughed, opened her eyes, then wished she hadn't. The back of her head throbbed sharply. Blurred and fuzzy, her vision wavered as she tried to focus.

Flat on her back and spread-eagled, she could see the dark tree canopy against the purplish gray of the overcast sky above her. The moisture from the ground had soaked through the back of her coat and jeans. She shivered, both from the cold and from the aftereffects of her near-death experience.

Wiggling her toes experimentally inside her boots, she stayed sprawled where she was for a few moments, trying to orient herself and figure out what had happened. She hoped fervently that she didn't have any broken body parts and that she wasn't bleeding.

Seconds after she'd watched Jake turn away, a man had emerged from the trees on the opposite side of the clearing. Before she'd realized what was happening, he was inside the helicopter.

The pilot, busy with taking off, hadn't been able to help her as the man's intention to toss her out of the rising helicopter became clear.

Marnie had managed to get off an effective kick to the jerk's stomach before he'd backhanded her. That was the last thing she remembered.

No wonder she hurt. Looking up, she could make out the broken branches of the pine that had softened her fall all the way down. She was lucky she was still in one piece. She'd probably dropped twenty feet or more.

Although she wished her aching head belonged to someone else.

It had been midafternoon when she and the pilot had taken off. It was almost dark now.

Hours had gone by.

"Ow, ow, ow." Marnie cursed softly under her breath and sat up carefully. Every part of her body felt as if it had been tossed out of a helicopter onto the hard ground. She palmed her throbbing cheek; it felt hot and hurt like crazy. And by the obstructed vision in her left eye, she must have one heck of a shiner. It felt as huge as the state of California.

She was lucky. No blood.

She rested her head on her knees until the dizziness passed. Cautiously she staggered to her feet, leaning heavily on a nearby tree trunk for support while she found her equilibrium.

She eyed the debris of twisted black metal. The pilot dead, the helicopter destroyed. Jake must be worried sick about her. *Okay,* she amended, *maybe not worried sick. Concerned.*

But as she looked at the wreckage, she realized with a shudder that Jake would think she was dead.

Oh, Jake.

She couldn't very well go skipping down the mountainside calling his name to let him know she was okay. Logic dictated she return as quickly as possible to the lair, where she could wait for him in safety.

All she had to do was find her way back in the dark, avoid the who-knew-how-many bad guys, and not freeze to death in her wet clothing.

Despite the low clouds enough light reflected off the snow to at least allow her to see where she was going. In the darkness, the thick smell of smoke and burned pine resin was oppressive.

She started down the mountain. Though she felt dizzy and a little unfocused at first, the cold air cleared her head as she navigated the steep incline, and she made good time. Grabbing handfuls of needles as she used low branches to aid her, she used landmarks to guide her way, remembering the large icy patch under this tree, recalling Jake helping her over these rocks—or so she hoped. Her sense of direction wasn't too hot to begin with.

Ahead was the stand of ponderosa pine that marked the boundary of Jake's land. In about twenty minutes she'd be inside, out of the sharp wind. She narrowed her eyes, looking toward the hill sloping down to the lair and beyond it to the cabin. She was on the right track. With the smoke behind her, she could see the sunset, a spectacular, blazing, showy ball of orange and blood red. Tangerine rays reflected off water droplets like dancing fireflies.

Marnie didn't waste too much time admiring the scenery as she trudged down the slope. She tried to be as inconspicuous as possible, expecting one of the bad guys to pop out like a jack-in-the-box at any moment.

Wait a minute . . .

Something about that spectacular solar display niggled at the back of her mind. Then it hit her: It was already dark, and there was no way to see the sun's descent through a solid mountain anyway. She turned around.

Between the trees flames shot toward the sky, licking and eating at the surrounding pines. She could practically *hear* the snap and crackle as sap boiled and branches caught.

In the midst of the inferno sat Jake's cabin.

She stopped where she was, one arm against a wide tree trunk as she caught her breath. The cabin was ablaze. The helicopter gone. Her car inaccessible. Her dog lost. And somewhere on this mountain a bunch of radical maniacs were trying to kill Jake. "Damn, damn, damn."

There was little chance of the entire mountainside going up in flames. It had been raining or snowing hard for days. But the simple wood construction of the cabin would go up in minutes.

They hadn't been able to ferret out Jake's lair, so they'd burned the cabin down. Now the question was, had they managed to get inside his hi-tech basement?

The mine shaft entrance was fairly close. If they *were* inside the lair, they'd see her coming. She'd have no idea if they were down there or not. Not until that elevator door opened and it was too late.

The same fate awaited Jake.

Marnie bit her lip trying to decide the best course of action. She couldn't stay out here on the slope. The bad guys knew enough to blow up Jake's cabin. Chances were good they were close and crawling all over the area.

She almost fell over her own feet, and realized the laces on her boot were trailing in the mud like a kindergartner's. She crouched to tighten the laces, then froze.

Voices.

Close.

Heart in her throat, she instinctively dropped to her stomach and scooted backward until the heavy, low branches of a pungent juniper concealed her. *Here we go again,* she thought wryly.

She shivered as the voices got closer. Strawlike needles rained down on her hiding place, and tiny particles of frozen snow made small, hard pellets as they plopped from the branches and onto her head.

She could barely make out the two men. Their outlines were scarcely denser than the darkness around them. But they were no more than six feet away. Too bad she didn't understand a word they said, because they sounded agitated.

The red glow of a cigarette arced toward her hiding place. It landed a hair's breadth from her face. Marnie hoped to God the smoker didn't suddenly develop a conscience. All she needed now was for the man to come over and stomp it out.

She waited in vain for the damp earth to do its job, but the cigarette just lay there smoldering. *Damn.* She gathered up enough saliva and spat on the glowing butt. Just in case.

After what seemed like forever and was probably only minutes, they moved on. She stayed where she was until the sound of their voices disappeared, then slithered out from under the bushes. At the rate she was going, she'd probably get adrenaline poisoning, if such a thing was possible.

She sensed rather than felt the man standing between her spread legs. Without looking over her shoulder, she knew it wasn't Jake. *Uh-oh.*

Marnie twisted her body, sliced her legs, and caught the man off balance. Now they were both down on the spongy ground.

His curses masked her grunts and pants as he managed to stagger to his feet, grab her around the neck, and drag her upright. He pressed her back against his body, his elbow clamped around her throat, his other arm locked with hers between their bodies.

She fumbled in her pocket and managed to yank out the sock. With a whoop, she swung it in an arc over her head. The weight of the bullets struck his face.

He howled.

She swung again. *Thump. Whack.*

She tried to kick him, but he jerked his arm tighter, almost cutting off her air supply and pulling her off balance at the same time.

"I should warn you," Marnie managed in a raspy voice, rocking on her heels to throw him off, "when I'm not being held, I fight back." She said it more for herself than for him.

He spat out something rude. They did a bizarre dance as he teetered, almost ripping her arm from the socket. She swung her sock weapon again, this time striking his throat. He gagged but didn't let go.

Through eyes tearing with pain, Marnie struggled upright, her breath wheezing in and out in a thick white plume about her head.

The man asked a question. At least she presumed it was a question. She couldn't have answered even if she knew what he'd asked. He was cutting off her air. She tried twisting out of his grasp, but he was strong and determined.

She kicked backward. He grunted when her sturdy Timberline connected with his shin. He snatched the end of the sock as she let fly again. Marnie held on with all her might. Like a taffy pull, the sock stretched before he managed to yank it out of her grip, in the process pulling her inexorably closer. His arms wrapped around her.

Almost carrying her, he dragged her toward a wide-trunked ponderosa. What he had planned for her, Marnie had no idea. She wasn't hanging around to find out. As they got closer to the tree, she raised her bent leg waist high in front of her. He shoved her toward the tree. She used the leverage of her foot to push off the trunk and jettisoned them both backward.

They rolled down the hill, entwined like lovers. She used her fists and knees to good effect. She might fight like a girl, but she fought like a *tough* girl. She wasn't her brothers' sister for nothing.

He got in a few punches himself. Unlike the movies, these *hurt*. She managed to block a blow to her face with her arm, and felt the strike zing through the bone into her shoulder. She snarled instead of screaming, and clawed at his face.

They tumbled over a drop-off—only a few feet, but it felt like a mile. They rolled again, and shrubs and tangled weeds grabbed her hair.

They came to a breathless stop against a boulder, Marnie on top. She immediately pressed her knee strategically to his groin and sat up. He didn't move.

"Hey!" she whispered, trying to see his face. "Hey, you." She gave him a far from gentle slap. Nothing.

She didn't hang around. A quick search of his spy suit revealed several guns and a lethal-looking knife. Marnie took them all. The knife she tucked gingerly into the pocket of her jacket, as she did, she had a mental picture of Madame Butterfly falling on the sword. She shuddered.

The little-bitty gun she stuck in the back pocket of her jeans; one of the bigger guns went in her pocket, and the other she kept in her hand.

She'd never held a gun in her life. It was considerably heavier than it looked. She hefted it to get accustomed to the feel of it. She had no idea if the safety was on or off, or even if this particular one *had* a safety. It made no difference.

Point. Squeeze. That's all she knew how to do.

It would have to be enough. She felt better having the

weapons, although she prayed she wouldn't have to use them on anyone.

Marnie stumbled up the slight incline to find her sock. It glowed in the shadows, and she picked it up and stuffed it back in her pocket. *This* was a weapon she knew how to use.

She shivered as the wind picked up, sneaking under her jacket. Then she heard a sound that chilled her to the marrow, and her fingers tightened on the gun as she ran into the trees. Having traversed the open space, she'd just reached the shelter of an enormous ponderosa pine when she heard the unmistakable report of a gunshot.

Dropping like a stone, she rolled under the prickly shrubs. Her pubic bone landed forcefully on something hard. She screwed up her face and swallowed a yelp of pain. Her heart was beating with an irregular, painfully slow throb against her ribs; instinct warned her danger still lurked nearby.

Closer than that gunshot.

Chapter Fifteen

As still as a hunted animal, Marnie held her ground, not moving an eyelash as a man came within inches of her hand. He was alone as he melted into the trees.

The gun held between her knees, she took a moment to blow on her cupped hands. Plucking the weapon up again, she held on to it firmly. God, she was cold. The man was up ahead, barely visible through the trees. Marnie followed him.

She stopped when he stopped, taking every precaution to make as little noise as possible.

Okay, Jake Dolan, spy king of the universe, you can come and find me now.

The wind picked up, swirling shards of icy snow and soaking leaves around her feet as she moved from one concealing trunk to the next, her fingers numb around the grip of the gun.

Up ahead she could hear voices, too low to decipher what they were saying. The man sped up. Marnie was right behind him. It was much harder to keep hidden now that the moon shone through the scattered clouds. Everything looked faintly blue as patches of ground fog and smoke swirled, rising eerily around her legs.

The wet leaves that made her footsteps soundless also made the men up ahead harder to follow. Voices, pitched low, carried through the stillness of the forest.

Marnie sped up as the wind shifted, colder now. Something soft landed on her eyelash. Then another. She glanced up. It had started to snow again.

"This is a joke, right?" she whispered incredulously. All she needed now was a plague of locusts. She shook her head and aimed herself toward the lair.

The moon eventually peeked coyly around a cloud over the tips of the pines. She moved faster, keeping between the trees now that she could see where she was going. Through the branches she saw the rock formation to the lair up ahead. Every muscle and bone in her body had a complaint, some louder than others.

She wanted desperately to run, but restrained herself. About two hundred yards from the rocks she stopped dead as a noise alerted her that someone, or some*thing*, was close by. The same man she'd just avoided? Or another?

Heart pumping, mind racing, Marnie hefted the weight of the small gun in her hand and held her breath.

"Woof," came the soft inquiry from under a bush.

With a stifled cry Marnie dropped to her knees in the muddy earth. Duchess crawled out on her belly to greet her. She flung her arms around her dog's neck and buried her face in Duchess's short, wet fur.

"Oh, puppy!" Marnie whispered, "Are you all right? I missed you! I was so scared!" She half laughed, half cried. She hadn't wanted to imagine what could have happened to prevent the dog from returning.

She ran her hands over the dog's body, checking in the near darkness for obvious injuries. There didn't seem to be any. But her pup was cold and wet, and pathetically grateful to see her mistress.

Marnie wiped her cheeks with her palms and stood up. "Come on, goofus, let's go wait for Jake."

Duchess danced excitedly.

Marnie started walking. Duchess grabbed the flapping hem of her jacket in her mouth and tugged the opposite way. She stopped before the dog ripped her coat off her body.

"Now what?"

Duchess growled low in her throat.

Marnie looked down at the dog's agitated movements.

"Is this about Jake?" Her heart climbed higher in her

throat. "Jake, puppy girl? Jake? Okay, fine, I'll follow you. Please don't get us shot, that's all I ask."

"What are you going to do with me, Lurch? *Walk* me to death?" Jake asked, marching ahead of the men, the plastic cuffs tight on his wrists which were securely manacled behind his back. They'd stripped him of all his weapons none too gently. He could feel the warmth of blood as the wound on his shoulder reopened.

Jake had checked each man's face to see if any were T-FLAC operatives. None were. These three were a mix of corn-fed rednecks and paid killers with the flat, disinterested eyes of paid killers. Not bright enough to do more than act as Lurch's muscle.

Was this all of them? Were there more hidden somewhere along the route?

"Head back to our cabin." Lurch prodded him in the back with his knife. It nicked but didn't slice. Lurch had always been a man for petty revenge. Jake had overlooked it as a harmless weakness in his friend. Now he recognized it as a symptom of something far more malignant.

"Our cabin?" Jake repeated disdainfully. "Correct me if I'm wrong, but other than a six-pack the day we bought the place, what was *your* contribution to the property?"

"It always belonged to the four of us. Walk faster, it's freezing. That was all I could come up with at the time, so don't go accountant on me, Tin Man. The cabin is part mine."

"And what?" Jake asked. "Now you want it all?"

Lurch giggled. "Hell, yes, I want it all. Mostly I want the lair."

"What lair?" Jake asked mildly, narrowing his eyes as he suddenly noticed a fire twinkling between the trees up ahead. Not all the smoke in the air was from the crash site. The stupid bastard had torched the cabin.

"What lair?" Lurch mimicked. "The lair the four of us planned. The lair *you* built. The lair where you keep the patents for all those lucrative toys of yours. You've got plenty, and all those cool inventions will bring in *beaucoup* bucks," Lurch snapped. "I'm getting it all."

"Last I checked you weren't my next of kin."

"Because of your damned efficiency," Lurch continued furiously, as if Jake hadn't spoken, "my money's tied up, my best lieutenant's dead, and my Midwest camp is useless. You *owe* me, pal. You owe me this mountain."

"Take a breath and a reality check. Nobody owes you anything. You made your choices. Live with them."

"My choice is that the great and incorruptible Jake 'Tin Man' Dolan will retire in disgrace, never to be heard from again," Lurch told him with a pleased chuckle. "Except for when he has to deposit those nice fat checks, of course. And I've got your John Hancock down now."

Which explained how Lurch had obtained secret documents and authorized clandestine maneuvers supposedly authorized by Jake himself.

The stench of wood smoke hung low in the air. Without a glance, Jake walked parallel to the rocks hiding the entrance to the mineshaft. "You use that Red Eye?" he asked through teeth so tightly clenched his jaw ached.

"Aw," Lurch mocked. "Were you real attached to your Miss M. Wright?"

How the hell does the bastard know her name?

Lurch's face wore a smug expression as he recited, "Residing at nine-thirty-nine La Mesa Terrace, Sunnyvale, California?"

Her medication, Jake realized, his blood rising to a higher boil. Her name would have been on the bottle they'd taken from her backpack.

"You idiot, Lurch. You always were one to jump to conclusions. It still makes you sloppy. You wasted an expensive ordnance. The girl was a camper. Nothing to do with me."

No emotion, he warned himself, *no damned emotion*.

"You always did think I was a step behind, didn't you, Jake? Well, surprise, I'm not."

Lurch glanced back and snapped his fingers at one of the men trailing them. The man jogged up and handed him a wad of thick, textured white paper. Lurch unfolded it and showed Jake a charcoal sketch.

They'd passed the entrance to the lair and moved downhill.

It started to snow. Soft flakes drifted to the ground, backlit by ethereal, misty moonlight. *Marnie would have loved*—Jake ruthlessly cut off the thought.

Lurch shoved the papers forward so Jake could see them, angling them so the light of the cold, white moon could illuminate the pages.

"Now this just *doesn't* look like the face of a stranger to *me*. Your honey was hot for you when she drew this, old pal. Real hot. And by the look on your face right here"—he tapped the page with his knuckles—"I'd say you were about a step away from screwing her blind." Lurch roared with laughter.

Actually, Marnie thought, shivering from her hiding place behind a nearby rock, he'd been about a step away from killing her at the time. But that was moot at this point.

That Jake knew the man beside him was obvious. Another betrayal? *Oh, Jake.*

She and Duchess stayed hidden until the men moved out of sight among the trees and the sound of laughter drifted with the snowflakes.

"Now what, girl? *Now* what do we do?" She looked at the dog, hoping for an answer. The gun in her pocket weighed a ton, as did the one in her hand. Fine and dandy. She had three guns, a knife, and a sock full of bullets. And zero knowledge of how to use the first two. She couldn't very well sneak up behind the bad guys and shoot them like they did in the movies, and her mind shied away from anything as grisly as using the knife.

They were heading down to what was left of Jake's cabin. So they *didn't* know about the entrance to the lair up here . . . and they didn't know she was alive. They wouldn't be looking for her.

"Okay, puppy girl," Marnie whispered. "What we have to do is give these guns to Jake. *Somehow*."

Duchess agreed with a woof and, tail tucked, followed the men, Marnie right beside her.

The men talked in low voices. She couldn't discern what they said and could barely see Jake up ahead of them.

The four men stopped by the log in front of what had once been a four-sided building. She frowned. She could have sworn there'd been five men counting Jake. But maybe not. She hadn't had a clear view of them as they'd passed her.

From her hiding place amongst the bushes, she saw that the cabin had been reduced to kindling and ash. The chimney held up part of the roof, but the walls had collapsed and scattered on the ground. Damp wood smoldered, and every now and then a knothole produced a shower of sparks.

Her breath hitched as Jake moved into view. The moon lit the area like a spotlight on a stage.

A frisson of gut-wrenching fear paralyzed her for a moment. Somehow in all the hullabaloo, she'd almost forgotten that he wasn't invincible.

Jake stood with his back to her. His wrists were tied. His posture appeared perfectly relaxed, but he was carefully trying to free his hands as the other man spoke.

Move back about ten feet, would you, big guy? Marnie urged, frustrated and terrified.

A showy display of sparks and flame shot into the air. "You always were irresponsible with your possessions, Lurch. Now you don't have a cabin."

Lurch? Marnie frowned. One of Jake's Musketeers?

The man approached Jake. He was almost as tall, but of slighter build. And he moved as gracefully as a dancer. Marnie hated him on sight.

"Didn't *want* the damn cabin, wonder boy. I want the lair. And the land. This is gonna be SPA's new training facility."

"It's good to want things."

His friend hit Jake with his gun, right across the side of his face. Marnie winced and bit her lip so as not to cry out. Her heart pounded so hard she felt they must surely be able to hear it. Tears stung her eyes.

The fight-or-flight urge was overwhelming. Filled with a mix of fear and potent rage, she resisted with everything in her.

The man grabbed Jake by the throat, an expression of pure, unadulterated loathing on his narrow face. "How do I get into the lair?"

"I'm afraid that secret will have to die with me," Jake said calmly, his hands busy with whatever was holding his wrists together.

"Palm print?" Lurch demanded. "All I have to do is chop off your freakin' hand. Piece of cake."

Jake's muscles barely shifted as he tested the bonds and said flatly, "You have to find the panel first."

"I'll find it." Lurch started walking around him, chewing his lower lip like a child denied a favorite toy. "Bet you put in that retinal scanner we talked about."

"Bet you're right." Twist. Pull. Stretch.

That's not going to work, Jake. Marnie waited in an agony of suspense and felt sick. They were going to chop off Jake's hand and poke his eyes out any second, while she sat here in the shrubbery gnawing a hole in her lips and wetting her pants. *Think, damn it. Think.* She reached out carefully to touch Duchess, who lay beside her.

The dog was gone.

"I was trying to be civilized about this." Lurch motioned to his goons.

The scene unfolded before her eyes with the speed of a supersonic jet. Horrified, Marnie watched them race over to Jake, each grabbing an arm in a death lock. She dug her fingernails into her palms and bit her lip until she tasted blood.

Jake braced for the assault.

Lurch's fist shot out and ground into his chin. To the midriff, to the chest, to the face again. He felt the warmth of blood run from his nose as his wrist strained against the plastic handcuffs, drawing them tighter until they cut off the circulation in his hands.

Pain, like a hot knife, sliced into him as Lurch struck his wounded shoulder. The impact reverberated throughout his body, causing his stomach to heave. Lurch punched him in the stomach again. Several times. His fist landed on Jake's cheekbone with a dull crack that jerked his head back.

Lurch danced in front of him. Psyched. Manic. Enjoying the power.

Jake managed to dodge a pile-driver left to his face by quick footwork. Instead of retreating, Jake closed in, brought up his leg fast, and kneed Lurch in the groin. The other man spun aside as the goons pulled Jake out of range. But it was still a hit. Lurch doubled over, cursing a blue streak.

"You always were a miserable, sniveling coward," Jake taunted as Lurch slowly straightened, eyes watering and glittering wildly. "Need *two* men to hold me? What kind of man can't fight his own battles? Come on, you weaseling, two-faced bastard. Come and get me. Easy target, huh, Lurch? Cuffed, your muscle restraining me? Hell, even a kid could beat me up like this. Where's the sport?"

With a jerk of his head, Lurch called the goons off. Jake rolled his shoulders, not shifting his focus.

"You're not going to taunt me into losing control. I know how you operate."

Pain showed in the radiating lines beside Lurch's eyes. He clasped his groin in both hands, staying well back although no one was holding Jake any longer.

"No. You *knew* how I operated. A lot has changed in six years," Jake told him flatly.

Someone was behind him. Someone who didn't want to be seen or heard. While Lurch circled him, Jake casually took a step back, then another as Lurch paced, so filled with his own dramatics he didn't notice. Jake's gaze shot to the tangos who'd moved back and now stood closer to the fire. Their focus was on their boss while they warmed their asses.

Another gentle rustle behind the concealing bushes.

Who the hell was it? Lurch's man? The one who'd peeled off before they'd come into the clearing? Unlikely. The man wouldn't be skulking in the shrubbery. But where was he? Had he gone off to find the rest of the team? And who the hell was behind him?

Damn. Could it be the *dog*? He'd forgotten about Duchess.

Lurch stormed toward the smoking cabin, turned around, and glared at Jake. His two lieutenants flanked him and kept their weapons trained at Jake's heart. Neither had moved from his position.

"Thing is, Lurch, or rather Dancer," Jake said quietly while casually stepping another pace back toward the dense bushes behind him. An overhanging tree put him partially in shadow. "It's no biggie to take my eye. But you'd have what? Five minutes, tops, to use it to scan? Not great odds when you still don't know where the scanner device is, is it?"

"Shut up. Just shut up."

Jake backed up another step. Whoever was behind him stopped breathing.

Afraid of him? Or for him?

A man? Or the dog?

"The problem won't matter soon," Jake said loudly. "We're all going to freeze our asses off out here. In case you hadn't noticed, we're in for a mother of a snowstorm."

"I told you to shut the hell up!"

Lurch was losing his cool, Jake thought with satisfaction. He felt the sharp prick of a pine needle against his wrist as he came flush against the foliage.

"Why, Lurch? *Why'd* you do this? I thought we were friends." Jake almost flinched when something icy cold touched his wrist.

"I wanted to be on the winning side for a change." Lurch rubbed his hands together above a burning chunk of wood. He spoke as if they were chatting over a beer in front of a cozy fire instead of high on a snowy mountain in the dead of night with the embers of the cabin glowing in the darkness and two goons with Uzis trained on his heart.

"We couldn't win," Lurch said. "We never could win. The tangos had all the power. All the money. All the glory. There were a handful of us and a never-ending supply of them. I was sick of working for the losing team. And I was fucking sick of always being on *your* team. T-FLAC's golden boy. Jake Dolan, boy wonder.

"*You* got the accolades when we made a bust. *You* got the

pats on the back. *You* had everyone's admiration and respect. And when we had a piss-willy little bit of glory, when we *had* a victory, *you* were the one who stepped up to the plate and took it. Oh, yeah, you always made sure the powers that be knew who was on your team, but bottom line, *you* were the hero.

"Nobody saw that *I* was smarter than you could ever hope to be. *Me.* Not you. *I* was the one smart enough to be working for both sides. Nobody knew. Not even the brilliant Tin Man." Lurch giggled.

Whoever the hell was behind him was either too cold or too nervous to be efficient. *Come on, pal. Cut the damn thing.* Jake tried to spread his wrists a little to make the job easier. The knife nicked his wrist.

"You might invent stuff, but *I'm* the one on the winning team now. Me. Don't you know nice guys finish last? You played by the book, you stupid asshole, and look where you are now." Lurch laughed, eyes wild with delight at his own cleverness.

"*I* came up with half the stuff you invented. *You* have the money. It isn't fair. I want my share."

The knife finally sliced through the plastic handcuffs, and the pressure on Jake's wrists immediately released. Blood pounded through his hands in a welcome rush. With a flex of his wrists he was free.

"If you were instrumental in any of the inventions going to market, then of course you should have your share," Jake told him calmly, flexing his fingers. "However, you're going to have a hard time proving anything, since all my patents are filed and dated years after your death."

When Jake and Ross had been partners and friends there had been no down time. They'd been busy fighting the good fight. It had been two years after the Musketeers' deaths when Jake came up with a small device used in a weapon's laser sight. The part, invented out of necessity, had been patented and had netted Jake a nice chunk of change. He'd taken it from there. An amusing little hobby had turned into a lucrative business.

"Who the hell will believe that?" Lurch demanded, straightening from the burning embers at his feet. "I'll have proof. I'll make sure I do." Lurch shot him a smug look. "I've got people who'll mickey the paperwork to make it look like *I* was the inventor. I'll have all the money, and I didn't have to do a damn thing other than be smarter than you!"

Jake looked at his old friend dispassionately, keeping his hands behind his back. He stepped away from the bushes to give his rescuer time to move, and heard a muttered curse behind him.

"We were never in competition, Lurch. Never. We were best friends. The four of us." Jake watched him. "Did you have Britt and Skully killed?"

"Skully knew I was still alive. He saw me after I 'died.' Britt was expendable. You always told us to be sure we tied up loose ends. I tied up loose ends. Just like you told us. I did that. Tied up loose ends. I—" He cut himself off abruptly, realizing, Jake thought, that he was losing it.

"You always got the girl. Didn't you? Always got the girl." He stalked forward, his usually graceful gait jerky with unsuppressed anger.

"I'm *glad* she cut you. Glad. We laughed about your piss-poor technique in the sack, Soledad and me. We'd lie in bed and she'd tell me how much you *loooved* her. Stupid sap. She was mine first. *Mine.*"

Jake stared at him. "You were in love with Soledad, and yet you sent her to sleep with me?"

"I wanted you to trust her. I wanted you to fall for her. And you did, didn't you? I manipulated you through her. You were thinking with your dick, and I could control you like a pull toy." Lurch laughed, delighted with his cleverness.

He thumped his chest, then sneered. "I told you, remember? I told you after the bitch shot me that she was the tango's main squeeze. Remember? I told you. *I* was the tango, man. I was the tango!" Lurch roared with manic laughter.

"I was sent in to help you find *me*! Shit, that was funny. Skulking around, watching your back, when all along I was right there behind you. Oh, man. I *loved* that."

"And what did Soledad have to do with any of that? Were you in love with her? Is that it, Lurch, you were fighting for her cause?"

"Love had zip to do with it," Lurch snorted. "She was fighting for *my* cause. The almighty dollar. And the point, Jake, ol' pal of mine, was that *I* got her first. In love? Don't be ridiculous. I wasn't in *love* with her."

"Then what difference does it make?"

"Because"—Lurch came right up to him—"She. Was. Mine."

"You wasted her."

"She forgot who she belonged to. She didn't finish the job I sent her to do."

"To kill me." The scar on Jake's neck throbbed.

Beyond the circle of trees and the glow of the still smoldering cabin, the night was an impenetrable inky black as the moon shifted behind the clouds. The topmost branches of the tall trees danced in the icy wind. Bright sparks danced wildly in the current.

From the shrubbery came a violent rustle of branches and leaves. Then silence.

Run like hell, Jake thought.

Lurch jerked his head toward the trees, and one of the goons lumbered off to investigate.

Jake stared at the man he'd thought he knew so well. His gaze flickered to the muscle standing well back, weapon trained on him.

He calculated the odds of taking Lurch down before he was shot himself. Lurch was still pacing. Jake waited for him to close the distance. Move a little farther away from his—

A high-pitched scream. A gunshot. Another long screech.

God. For a moment he thought . . . Jake immediately reined in his leap of imagination but couldn't still the surge of blood that pumped through his heart and increased his rate of breathing. *No, of course it wasn't. Couldn't be.*

Men had been known to scream like a woman when terrified.

Another strangled shriek. The rustle of shrubbery being

pushed aside. Lurch's lieutenant staggered into the clearing, his arms in a stranglehold about a struggling woman. He had her around the waist like a sack of corn. Even with her back toward him, he wasn't having an easy time containing her. She screamed and flailed, fighting him for all she was worth, arms and legs thrashing wildly, and wielding a grubby white athletic sock.

Marnie.

She had a black eye. Her pale face was filthy, her hair spiked with pine needles and mud, her jacket ripped.

He'd never seen a more beautiful sight in his life.

Jake closed his eyes as a multitude of raw emotions swept through him. Blood rushed from his head, and he felt a leap of joy so intense, so profound, he almost forgot where the hell they were.

Lurch roared with laughter and clapped his hands as he strolled toward Marnie. "Well done, Price, well done."

He grabbed Marnie by her hair, pulling her head up. With his other hand he snatched her weapon out of her hand and tossed it aside. Still enraged, she couldn't cry out because of the unnatural arch of her throat. Her legs and arms struck out uselessly.

"Hello, darling," Lurch purred, then bent his head and kissed her hard on the mouth.

Jake locked his knees, gritted his teeth, and stayed exactly where he was. He ruthlessly kept his hands behind his back, even though all he wanted to do was rip out Lurch's heart. It was one of the hardest things he'd ever done. Rage rose in a blinding wave. He pushed it aside to center himself, focusing on the cold core deep inside.

Marnie jerked her head away, glared at Lurch, who still held her hair caveman style, and said in icy tones, "Your technique leaves a lot to be desired. Tell your goon to let me go, he's cutting off my circulation."

Grinning, Lurch asked the man behind her drolly, "Any weapons? Beside the sock?"

"No, sir. She had a gun. The little bitch tried to shoot me. I took it from her."

"Good. Let her go. Don't move, Miss Wright, or my men will shoot your boyfriend."

Marnie staggered as she was released. She rubbed her wrist and looked at each man with cool blue eyes. The hauteur of her expression was not diminished by either her black eye or the condition of her sodden, mud-stained clothing. Her gaze skimmed briefly over Jake and the other men, then back to Lurch.

"Which one of these Neanderthals is supposed to be my boyfriend?"

Lurch flung an arm about her shoulders and walked her toward Jake. "Here he is, darling, your sweetheart, Jake the Magnificent."

Jake's jaw ached from gritting his teeth. While Lurch was holding her casually, his fingers gripped her shoulder so tightly the fabric bunched beneath his hand. Despite the situation, she was as cool as a cucumber. His estimation of her climbed another dozen notches.

Good girl. Hang in there.

Jake watched them dispassionately as they came closer. He fixed his attention solely on Lurch, knowing that if he saw terror in Marnie's eyes, he'd lose it.

She didn't sound scared at all as she laughed a fake, brittle little laugh. "You must be joking. *This* guy? Oh, *please*. We don't even *know* each other. He let me spend the night in his cabin when a tree crushed mine to bits." She shot Jake a disdainful glance. "I don't associate with uncouth mountain men, even if they *are* the only game in town, thank you very much."

She stuffed her hand in her pocket and turned her head to look up at Lurch. "Look, I don't want to get involved in whatever you're doing. I don't even want to *know* what you guys are doing here. Just let me go."

"I'd never let a lady wander around alone in the dark," Lurch told her gallantly, giving her shoulder another squeeze. Then he grabbed her by her hair again and tilted her head back. "Let's see how my old pal the Tin Man likes it when *I* get the girl."

Jake choked back a snarl of fury, and Marnie's eyes narrowed as Lurch lowered his head to kiss her again.

Oh, shit, Jake thought, a second before she punched Lurch in the stomach with the full force of her weight behind it. Lurch staggered, looking stunned.

Her face was set, her eyes glittering. "Don't manhandle me. I don't like it." She forcibly pushed away from Lurch, and in doing so, bumped hard into Jake.

He almost put his hands out to catch her, then remembered he was supposed to be secured. Her clothing and hair were wet; she smelled like mud and wet dog. He wanted to wrap his arms about her and bury his face against her soft, sweet skin. He had to get her the hell away from these lunatics and—

"Fall *down*, damnit," she snarled under her breath, her body pressing hard against his.

Jake allowed her slight weight to tip him over. They fell to the ground. He heard the air rush from her lungs as she landed on top of him with a thud. She winced—and pushed a gun under his shoulder.

"The woman is nuts. Get her off me," he demanded when Lurch stood there laughing at the two of them.

Marnie rolled off him and glared at Lurch. "Well? Don't just stand there. Help me up." She stuck out her hand, expecting to be assisted.

While she made a production of getting up on her own, brushing at the clumps of mud and debris on her jacket and complaining bitterly, Jake rose, the weapon now in his hand behind his back.

"I don't know what you people are doing," Marnie said furiously. "But I want no part of it."

She walked toward the cabin and the men who stood there, still talking to Lurch over her shoulder, trying to get Lurch's attention away from Jake and on herself instead.

"If you persist in detaining me, I'm afraid I'll have to—to contact my congressman and complain. This is an outrage."

Oh, for goodness sake, Marnie thought desperately. Dancer would shoot her for being a blithering idiot. Beyond him she glimpsed Jake, utterly still, his attention focused on Lurch, ignoring her completely. He appeared deceptively calm, like a panther contemplating when to move in for the kill. Not a good sign for the bad guys, she thought with a frightened hitch in her breath. Unfortunately, there were three men just waiting for Jake to twitch.

She had to keep talking, distracting Lurch and his men until Jake made his move. *Come on big guy, do something. I'm running out of steam here.*

"My father is Geoffrey Wright. Of Wright Computers. You *do* know who he is, don't you?" She started finger-combing her wet hair, primping and fluffing as she talked. Out of the corner of her eye, she observed the soldiers avidly watching her every move. She fixed her gaze on Lurch. "Daddy's a millionaire. I know he'll pay a handsome reward for returning me home safely. The bridges are flooded. I presume you've figured how to get off this stupid mountain in this ridiculous weather?"

Lurch strode up to her and grabbed her by the collar. "Where is the lair?" he demanded furiously, not the least bit distracted by her nonsensical chatter.

She looked at him blankly for a second. "Oh, my God! You mean there are wild *animals* up here?"

She should have expected it, she really should, but the backhanded slap took her completely unaware. Her head snapped sharply, and the entire left side of her face went numb from the blow as she staggered several feet to keep her balance.

That's it! Fury, raw and powerful, surged through her like molten lava. With a shriek, she launched herself at Lurch with nails and teeth bared.

Chapter Sixteen

Jake brought his weapon up. In his peripheral vision he confirmed that Marnie was straddling Lurch as she attempted to pummel his head into the ground.

He got off a shot before the soldiers even knew what hit them. One fell where he stood. The second spun away from ogling the spectacle and fumbled his weapon in Jake's general direction.

No contest. Jake squeezed off another shot and dropped him before he could fire.

Where the hell was the third guy?

He spun around in time to see Lurch grab Marnie by the hair, roll, and come up in one fluid motion to haul her to her feet. She yelped, then bit her lower lip, her gaze flying to meet Jake's as Lurch wrapped an arm about her throat.

Judas Priest. Lurch had her in a headlock, his sharp, deadly knife at her pale throat. "I'll cut her if you come any closer." He laid the sharp edge against the frantic pounding at the base of her throat. "Drop your weapon. I'll slice her into ribbons so thin she'll look like a maypole. Back off."

Jake locked eyes with Lurch. He took a step and stopped. "Touch her with that, and you'll never be dead enough."

"Thought you didn't care about her?"

"That's the difference between us, Lurch. I don't have to care about someone not to want them dead," Jake said disdainfully. "First you have to have me held down so you could beat me up, and now you hide behind a woman?" He snorted in disgust, keeping his focus on Lurch's eyes for any sign of movement.

"All the money in the world didn't help you become any less a coward, did it? What are you going to do now?" Jake sneered. "The second she drops I'll have you. There's no backup."

Marnie didn't move. Jake managed another two steps before Lurch spoke again. "I could take you if I wanted to," he spat, his fist bunched tightly in Marnie's hair, pulling her off balance. "Tell you what. In the spirit of friendship I'll trade you the woman for the lair."

"Hardly a fair trade," Jake told him coldly, taking another step. "My life's work for a woman?" He raised the Walther another notch. "Let her go. This has nothing to do with the girl." For a second he allowed his gaze to drop to Marnie's face. There wasn't a vestige of color except for the blazing blue of her eyes.

"You two are doing a lot of talking," she said with barely a quiver in her voice. "Why don't you just shoot him, Jake, and get this over with?" With that, she let her knees buckle.

For a split second she hung by her hair alone, clutched in Lurch's fist. Surprise and her body weight threw him off balance.

Jake fired two shots so fast they sounded like one. Marnie dropped and rolled; the knife went one way, Lurch the other.

Jake closed the distance in four angry strides and grabbed Lurch around the throat. He hauled him upright. He'd aimed low. Shoulder, upper thigh. Blood oozed out of both entry and exit wounds. Lurch wouldn't be doing any running.

"Couldn't do it, could you?" Lurch sneered, holding a hand over his thigh. He grimaced. "Couldn't off a friend."

Out of the corner of his eye, Jake saw Marnie stagger to her feet. He felt beneath Lurch's shoulder holster for the strip of plastic handcuff and quickly secured his wrists behind his back.

Marnie came up beside him as he pulled the cuffs tight. "Now what?" he asked as she stepped right up to Lurch.

"Now I want to hit him some more!"

She rubbed her smarting scalp, then landed a satisfying punch to Lurch's nose before he could jerk his head out of the way. Blood spurted over her hand. She didn't seem to notice. She socked the man in the stomach.

"Get her off me. The bitch is crazy."

Jake stepped back. "Have at it, tiger."

She slammed Lurch's shin with her sturdy Timberlines. Lurch cringed, but there was nowhere for him to go. She kept up a nice steady rhythm: kick, punch, kick, kick.

For a few moments Jake enjoyed the sight of her working off her fear. The adrenaline was still surging through her. She needed to vent it. Her damp hair flew wildly about her shoulders as she danced around Lurch, jabbing, chopping. A fierce look of concentration tightened the skin on her cheekbones. But she was shivering so hard, her face so pale, Jake felt compelled to end it.

To expedite matters, Jake inserted, "May I?" and punched out the man who used to be his best friend. Lurch, who was doing his best to dodge the wild woman hopping and jabbing at him, didn't see it coming. His eyes widened for a second, then he dropped to Jake's feet like a rock.

Jake put a hand on Marnie's chest to halt her tirade. "That's enough."

She dropped her fists and shook her head like a terrier, staring at him blankly for a second.

"Don't," Jake told her, "*ever* do that to me again."

"Do what?" she panted, eyebrows winged. "Untie you and save your butt?"

Jake surprised himself with the intensity of his fury. He grabbed the front of her jacket. "Scare the crap out of me!"

Her eyes were huge in her white face as she looked up at him. Her lower lip trembled. She swayed on her feet.

Jake hauled her into his arms. "You're a damn good fighter. I'm glad I have you on my side. But Judas Priest, woman, I thought I'd lost you." He buried his face against her damp hair so she wouldn't know how choked his voice was. "I saw the chopper go up in flames. . . ."

"One of the bad guys wanted to go in my place, I think. He pushed me out of the helicopter." She wound her arms around his neck, pressing her face into his shoulder. She shook like a leaf in a high wind.

Jake held her lightweight body tightly against his, lifting her off the ground to kiss her hard and fast. She kissed him back feverishly, looking a little shell-shocked when he pulled back.

"There's still at least one more out there. Go stand near the fire and keep warm. I'm going to secure this piece of crap, then we need to contact someone to get us out of here."

She touched his lips with just the tips of her cold fingers and smiled. "You won't get any argument out of me on that one."

He loosened his grip a fraction until her toes touched the ground. She grinned up at him. He cupped her cold face between his hands. God, she was so soft, so sweet. So *alive*.

At knee level, Lurch groaned.

Jake snagged the front of Marnie's jacket in his fist, drawing her up against his body as he kissed her again, short and sweet. Then he bent to grab the other man by the neckline of his suit.

Marnie gave Lurch an evaluating glance. "I think he's choking."

"No, he isn't." Jake shook the man until he groaned again. "See? He can breathe just fine." He gave Lurch a good shake when the man twitched. "Go get warm. I'll be right with you."

Shaking her head, Marnie limped over to the ruin of Jake's cabin. The closer she got, the warmer the air felt against her cold cheeks and the more she shook.

Every last ounce of energy seemed to drain out of her, and she felt sick to her stomach. She sank to her knees on the wet ground and wheezed raggedly.

Jake's ex-friend screamed obscenities as Jake dragged him over to the tree stump and propped him up against it. Their voices blurred and droned as she dropped her head to her knees and took several deep, shuddering breaths. The last few hours hardly seemed real.

Jake shouted something in her direction. It sounded like,

"Are you all right?" She lifted a hand to show she was at least still breathing.

Marnie looked at her clenched hands curled on her knees, saw Lurch's blood there, and picked up a handful of soil. Like Lady Macbeth, she started scrubbing her hands like a madwoman. The soil was icy, not that muddy, and pretty ineffectual. She scrubbed harder, listening to the drone of the men's voices over the sound of her teeth chattering and the arrhythmic beat of her heart.

She desperately wanted Jake's arms around her. Preferably while they were lying in a steaming hot bath. She lifted dazed eyes to see what his ETA might be.

To her left moonlight glinted for just a second off metal. Her eyes shot from left to right. Goose bumps prickled the back of her neck, and she half stood, fumbling beneath her jacket to get to the back pocket of her jeans.

"Jake," she croaked.

He was bent over Lurch. He looked up at the sound of her voice and frowned.

The high ping of a bullet cut through the air. She heard Jake's shout of pain and pulled the little gun out of her pocket, firing it into the shadows under the tree without really aiming.

Jake started running toward her in slow motion. She kept her eyes fixed on the man who'd come out of the trees. The bad guy boldly stood, feet spread, weapon spitting bullets toward Jake.

Only Jake had his terrified gaze on her.

"Jake, eyes left—no, damn it, right!" Marnie screamed, already running to intercept. What the hell she hoped to do, she had no idea, but Jake was too busy running toward her to notice what was happening.

Something small slammed into her shoulder. Seconds later she felt something hook in her hair. She paused for a nanosecond, then started sprinting toward Jake again. The bad guy blasted off another round of bullets toward Jake, who was running flat out to come between Marnie and the weapon.

Before she had time to think, Marnie took a running jump,

knocking Jake over in a tangle of arms and legs. They fell hard, Marnie buried beneath the weight of Jake's huge body.

Dimly she heard another hail of fire, then someone yelling, "I got him." Jake's grip on her elbow was painful as he hauled her upright, his eyes midnight dark as they scanned her face.

"Jesus, Marnie! Are you all right?" He propped her back against his raised knee and searched her face, both visually and with his hands.

Terrible possibilities gripped her mind, including Jake being brave while he bled like a sieve from a million bullet holes. She tried to push his hands away, needing to do a tactile search of *his* body.

"Were you shot?" she demanded, out of breath and terrified. "Are you hit?"

Still holding her, Jake looked over his shoulder as four men wearing jeans and heavy jackets and carrying Uzis raced into the clearing. They pushed two sharpshooters ahead of them. Duchess was with them. She danced around the men before seeing Marnie and raced to her side. She circled Marnie and Jake, growling low in her throat, her tail waving.

Jake turned his head to look at the men as he helped Marnie to her feet. "What the hell is this? A frigging convention?"

"Brothers," she mumbled. Still woefully short of breath and feeling decidedly weird, she locked her spongy knees and managed to hobble upright.

"Derek, Michael, Kane, K-Kyle." It was a good thing Jake was still holding her upper arm.

"Your *brothers*? Well, hell. Saved by the cavalry. Truss the son of a bitch," he called to them, "and keep an eye on the other one. I'll be right there." He let go of her arm and peered into her face. "Sure you're okay?"

"Peach—ahhh—"

Pain.

There was suddenly no room for anything else. She staggered, and then her knees seemed to melt. A ball of fire ripped through her, taking her breath and constricting her muscles. She clenched her eyes shut, swaying until gravity made the decision and she collapsed against the frozen earth, rolling to her side and curling her knees up to the pain.

Oh, God, it hurts.

Through a haze, she heard a mishmash of her brothers' and Jake's voices. Felt Jake's hands on her, then heard his roar of rage. She wanted to tell him not to yell, but it took every ounce of strength she had not to scream herself.

The sound of gunshots reverberated in her head. She panted, panicking when she couldn't draw a deep breath. "I'm suff-o-ca-ting."

"No, you are not," Jake said with awful calm.

She felt his hands on her, but it was as if her body had been injected full of novocaine.

"Just calm down. I have you, Marnie. I have . . ."

His words became jumbled, distant, confusing.

"Jake?" She panicked. "Jake?"

She forced her eyes open. Something warm ran in a ticklish stream down her face. She put a shaking hand up and then looked at her red, sticky, mud-encrusted fingers. "I'm bleeding." Her voice sounded thready, indignant.

Jake knelt beside her, his arm cradling her head and upper body. He wiped her face with fingers that shook. She winced.

And the blood kept coming.

"Look at me. That's right, good girl, keep looking at me."

Her glassy eyes stared into his. He saw her focus go, and his heart sped up.

"Here, Marnie. Keep those gorgeous blue eyes open for me." He wanted to draw the sharpness of the pain into himself. Her face below him blurred, and she yelped as his hands involuntarily gripped her harder.

"Keep looking at me, darling. You'll be okay. You have a head wound."

A bullet had skimmed through her hair. Head wounds bled a lot. He *knew* that. *Oh, God . . .*

She lay heavily across his arm. A small smile curved her pillowy lower lip. "Hmmm . . . darling?"

"Yeah, darling, sweetheart, love."

"Hmmm. Like th . . ." Her eyes totally lost focus again.

"Jake?" she whispered in a panicky little voice that tore out his heart.

"Right here."

"Hmmm." Marnie squeezed her eyes shut.

"Don't lose consciousness." His voice sounded as scared as he felt.

"Bossy," Marnie slurred. "Just a little b . . . blood. 'M okay."

"Damnit, I told you not to close your eyes."

"Never been shot before," she said numbly, struggling for breath. "Hurts." She pressed her face against his arm.

Her breathing didn't sound right. Panic? Worse?

"I'm sorry, sweetheart. So damned sorry. I can't believe you'd pull such a damn dumb stunt. I meant to talk to you about this lousy habit you have of saving my life."

"Worth . . . it . . ."

Moonlight glinted for a moment off something dark and liquid oozing through her jacket. He put pressure on her shoulder, and she tried to withdraw from the pain. "Not . . . not your . . . f . . . fault."

Pain swamped her like a red tidal wave. She clamped her lips together so she wouldn't cry out. Her face lost every vestige of color. "Sorry."

Icy sweat bathed his body, and he was numb with terror. Blood soaked the shoulder of her jacket and trickled from the head wound down her temple and the side of her face.

"Brother doc . . ."

"Which one of you is the doctor?" Jake snarled at the four men who'd come running the second she'd collapsed, stripping off their jackets as they ran.

"Right here."

Jake looked up. He hadn't even noticed the man kneeling on her other side. The younger man was already systematically checking her.

"She's been off her Coumadin for four days," Jake said flatly, lifting her slightly as her brothers bundled her from head to toe in their jackets. He eased her back down. She felt as light and insubstantial as thistledown.

The doctor brother shot him a look, then went back to what he was doing. "Scalp wound, superficial. Here, Kane, press this right here—no, a little to the left—yeah. Hold that. Good thing you have such a hard head, little sis," he said in a completely different tone, then looked at his brothers.

"Her hard head deflected the bullet. It'll bleed, but other than some hair loss, no big deal. Derek, get something to elevate her legs."

Kyle felt her pulse, his lips thinned. "I'm going to open your jacket, poppet. It'll be cold for a minute while I check you out."

Jake squeezed her hand as her brother undid her jacket and checked her shoulder as she lay limp and unresisting. It worried the hell out of him. A second wound . . .

Terror wrapped icy tentacles around his heart. *Marnie. Marnie.*

"Decreased breathing sounds on this side." Kyle glanced up briefly. They all got it. Her lung was perforated. "Here's the point of entry. . . . Sorry, poppet, stay with me.

"Okay, pal," he told Jake, "you can put the pressure back. Yeah, nice steady pressure . . . right here. Good.

"There's deformity in her arm. The bullet must have ricocheted off the clavicle into the humerus. Thank God she has a radial pulse. Clavicle is broken. No, sis, put your hand down, you're all muddy. Why's she covered head to toe in mud? What the hell's going down here?"

The brother standing directly behind Jake spoke up quickly. "There'll be time later, Kyle. Cool it."

Kyle shot a quick, dangerous glance at Jake. "Keep that pressure steady." He carefully checked his sister's back. "No exit," he said grimly.

Jake closed his eyes on a prayer.

Marnie gasped for air like a goldfish out of its bowl.

The brothers paced, their voices a blurred drone. Lost in the terror of losing Marnie, he barely noticed them.

It should have been me. It should have been me.

She was going to die here. Before he could tell her . . .

"What are you doing here? How did you find us?" he asked as one of the brothers took up another cloth and applied pressure to the wound on her scalp.

"Our father contacted us when she didn't answer her phone," the tallest one said, not looking at Jake as he switched places with Kyle so his brother could check her hips and legs.

Kyle's eyes met those of his brothers and he gave a negative shake of his head.

"We knew the bridges were out." The taller brother hooked Jake's gaze, and Jake knew he was speaking slowly and calmly so as not to scare the shit out of his sister. Jake figured he was scared enough for both of them.

"The weather held us off yesterday. We did a helo drop five hours ago and came looking. The gunshots helped pinpoint your location. Jesus, it's freezing out here. Kane, get a fire going. Derek, radio for help."

"I have an underground setup beneath the cabin." Jake didn't take his eyes off her face. In the moonlight her skin looked almost transparent, her lashes ominously still against her cheeks. "If we can clear some of the rubble, the elevator should be working." He felt manic and frantic, but he wouldn't, by word or deed, let Marnie know that.

"Elevator?"

"Jake's the s-spy king of the universe, Mikey."

"Is he, little one?"

She felt Michael on her other side as he took her wrist in his warm hand again. "Fast and thready, Kyle, she's in shock. No surprise there. You better hope to hell you're a *good* guy, Mr. Spy King of the Universe, otherwise the universe won't be big enough for you to hide. What the hell were you thinking involving a woman in whatever the hell all this is about?"

"Don' shout, Mi . . . don' shout at him, please."

She wanted to tell them that she knew she'd be fine. But she didn't believe it herself. People died from gunshot wounds.

Only in the movies did people get up and walk away. "If I die, tell—"

"You are *not* going to die!" Jake ground out, his grip on her hand like a vise. It hurt, and she whimpered. Jake swore. Michael cursed as well. Out of her line of sight she heard the others tossing charred timbers away from the cabin, trying to get to the elevator shaft.

"I was having fun before." Marnie ran her tongue over her dry lips. Her brain buzzed, her mind whirled, her eyes were losing focus, and there didn't seem to be enough air. How could that be? They were outside. There must be plenty of air.

"This . . . isn't so fun anymore. It . . . hurts." She looked up with tremendous effort into Jake's face, dirt-streaked, gleaming with sweat, and grave with concern. "Can I . . . have some water?"

"No!" five voices shouted in unison.

"I know you're thirsty," Jake told her gently. "We can't take the chance of giving you anything to drink right now. Just keep your eyes open. We'll be down in the lair in a couple of minutes, so just hang in there with me, okay?" His face was chalky, his mouth grim.

She ran her tongue uselessly over her lips again. "Sure."

"Shit," Jake said bitterly. "I should have protected her better."

"Yeah, you should have, you son of a bitch," Michael snarled. "And your hour of reckoning is coming, don't think it isn't."

"Give it a rest, Michael," Kane said quietly. "He wasn't the one who shot her."

"Perhaps I didn't pull the trigger," Jake bit out, "but I should have made sure she was safe."

"You sure as hell should have."

Marnie struggled to grab Jake's hand. He turned his bleak eyes on her, and she managed a smile. "Not . . . m-my keeper."

He smoothed her hair. It felt nice.

"How are you feeling?" he asked softly. There was a faint tremor in his voice.

" 'Kay," she reassured him. "Sleepy. Hot. Kind of floaty."

Kane crouched down to look at her. "How's she doing?"

"Not good. Her blood pressure's dropped. She's lost too much blood. There's no exit wound." A long pause. "I've done all I can," Kyle said grimly. "Derek went off to radio for help."

"He told me," Kane said. "Chopper's ETA is nine minutes. Thank God we had it stand by."

"That's too damn long." Jake pulled at the coat covering her, tucking it under her chin. Her skin felt like ice.

"You look like you're about to pass out yourself," Kyle observed. "Want me to look at that hole in your side?"

"Later. I'm fine." He focused on another brother crouched nearby. "See if you can hail that chopper and tell them to get the lead out. There's another entrance to the lair, but it's too far to carry her, and it doesn't look as though this way in is feasible."

Duchess rested her head against Jake's shoulder.

"Marnie?" It took a few moments for her to surface. He stroked back her hair, careful of the bloody gash on her scalp.

"Mmmm. Grammy."

"What about your Grammy?"

"Did . . . that . . . stroky thing with m . . . my hair."

"Oh, God, sweetheart . . ."

"She smelled . . . so good. Flowers." Marnie thought she must be drunk. Her tongue felt thick. She wheezed when she tried to drag in more air. "*Where was I? Oh, yes.* Love . . ."

He had to keep her conscious until the chopper arrived. Her skin looked almost transparent, making her fair eyebrows and hair and the obscenely thick trail of blood oozing from her scalp stand out even more sharply. Coats covered her shoulder, where her skin was pale and soft and— He stopped his train of thought.

He shifted so he could pull the coats more snugly around her. Her lips were turning blue. Dawn was hours away on this hellish day and she was frozen to the marrow, bleeding like a frigging sieve and it was all his fault. Tears stung his lids as he rubbed a hand on his thigh to warm it, his eyes never leaving her face.

Cupping her cheeks in his warmed hand, he said in an achingly broken voice, "Marnie?" She didn't answer this time.

Desperately Jake searched the heavens for the rescue choppers. The sky was navy and empty. Minutes had come and gone.

"How's she doing?" Michael demanded, coming back from helping his brother try to shift debris to get inside the cabin.

Kyle looked grim. "Not good, not good at all. Where the frigging hell is the rescue team?"

"They'll be here."

"I hope to God it's not too late," Derek said in a low voice as he pulled off the black cashmere sweater he wore and tucked it around Marnie's head, unmindful of the fresh blood.

"Marnie? Open those beautiful eyes for me." Jake's voice sounded as panicked as he felt. "*Marnie.* Open your eyes. *Do it. Right now!*"

The last hurrah of the fire painted false color in her cheeks. She'd passed out. He pressed shaking fingertips on the weak pulse at the base of her throat. In the background he dimly heard the *whop-whop* of a chopper coming over the mountain, but his focus was on Marnie.

Her hand twitched and his eyes shot to her face, his heart leaping as her dry lips moved.

"Love y . . ." Her voice was low and raspy.

Jake rested his forehead against hers. Gritting his teeth, he dredged up the last minuscule drop of energy he possessed to stay conscious himself.

Chapter Seventeen

Jake had always thought himself infinitely patient. But then he'd never had to pace a hospital hallway desperate for a surgeon to come out and tell him if his life was worth living or not.

Marnie had required immediate surgery. The five and a half hours since they'd wheeled her into the OR seemed like decades.

They'd flown directly to Gray Feather. The fifteen-minute flight was the longest, most terror-filled journey of Jake's life. Just the memory of getting her inert body hoisted into the chopper was enough to make him break out in an icy sweat.

The chopper hadn't been able to land. Thank God it had been a military transport, commandeered by her navy SEAL brother, Michael. The exact details had been thankfully blurred. He'd been unconscious by the time his turn came to be lifted in the sling and dragged on board.

Some sixth sense had roused him enough to hold Marnie in his arms until they landed, and she was put on a gurney and taken away from him. That had been six hours ago.

The small mountain hospital's waiting room seemed filled to overflowing with raging testosterone—Jake on one side of the small room, Marnie's father and three of her brothers on the other. None of them sat in the molded orange plastic chairs.

There was barely room to move, let alone pace. Instead the men paced mentally, causing the heat in the room to rise with tempers and temperaments.

Besides having almost gotten their sister killed, Jake had

been at a distinct disadvantage in the skimpy hospital gown and drawstring cotton pants he'd been wearing. Luckily an obliging nurse had gone out and bought him some clothes. The jeans were stiffly new, the flannel shirt a size too small; still, he felt marginally better dressed.

"What the hell is taking them so long?" he demanded, sinking gingerly into one of the uncomfortable chairs before he fell over.

"She's still in surgery," Kyle said quietly as he entered the waiting room. "I just checked. They're closing now. It went well. Being off the Coumadin those few days helped her not bleed out. And the bullet didn't do as much damage as it could have.

"After piercing the lung, it lodged in the humerus. She required two and a half units of blood. With the cast on her arm, she'll be as good as new in no time."

He glanced at Jake. "I'm sure the doctor doesn't want you pacing."

"I don't give a rat's ass what he wants. I only had a few stitches. What the hell's taking so long?" Jake heard himself and scowled. He sounded like a petulant kid. He ran his fingers through his hair; the movement pulled at the stitches in his side. The bullet had passed through, leaving a gaping exit wound.

He rose. "Thanks for the update. I'm going for a walk."

"Don't bug the nurses again," Kyle warned. Jake nodded and strode out of the confining room and down the corridor to Marnie's empty room. They'd been damn decent, the father and brothers. Hell, if she'd been *his* sister . . .

Jake shook his head, at a loss to figure out why the other men had taken his explanation of the events at face value. Certainly Michael Wright knew of T-FLAC. They were in the same business, after all. But still, Jake was astounded they'd believed him and run interference with both the authorities and the press.

They'd also been remarkably calm in the face of his dementia when hospital personnel had taken Marnie away. Talk about behaving like a lunatic . . .

It figured that when he fell, he'd fall hard.

Jake wandered about the room. Sterile. White. Empty. Midmorning sunlight streamed through the open blinds. He strode the four paces to the window. The view from the second floor faced away from the mountains, looking down into the valley below.

He needed to see her. To touch her. To hold her.

His fingers curled on the windowsill as he stared sightlessly over the trees. How dare the damned sun shine now? How dare it come out as if nothing had happened? Where was the rain? The sleet? The promised snowstorm?

Standing here in this empty room, smelling the typical hospital smells, turned Jake's stomach. *What the hell is taking so long? How long could it possibly take to close her up?*

He paced back to the open door, turned, and paced back to the bed.

He'd been in here about twenty times in the past two and a half hours. It helped—a little. He sank down on the chair he'd pulled up beside the bed hours ago.

The sheets and blankets were pulled taut, waiting. Just as he was waiting. He rested his burning eyes on the heels of his hands, elbows balanced on his knees.

He rose, paced, closed the blinds, opened them, then closed them again. Paced.

There had never been this much excitement in the small clinic. Jake's face flushed with both chagrin and embarrassment. God, what a damned fiasco. By the time he was bandaged and in a sterile white room Marnie had been in surgery.

The wait for her to come out of the operating room was interminable. He grabbed the phone. He could accomplish a few things while he waited.

After making a couple of calls, Jake got up to sit on the bed. With a wince, he leaned back against the pillows and swung his legs up onto the tight blankets. He couldn't close his eyes because a picture kept forming, a picture he would never forget as long as he lived and beyond.

He'd seen Marnie running toward him, a rictus of terror contorting her face. She'd thrown her healthy, supple young body against him, taking the bullets meant for him. Her slight weight had thrown him backward out of harm's way.

The combination of the painkillers and too many sleepless nights dragged Jake and his dreams down, until his weighted lids closed over bloodshot eyes.

The sound of a squeaking wheel woke him. He was up on his feet in seconds. The door bumped against the wall as they wheeled Marnie into the room. She lay as still as death under a blue surgical sheet, her hair covered by a paper cap.

"What are you doing in my patient's room, pal?" the doctor asked gruffly, eyeing Jake's gaunt, unshaven face and wild eyes.

Jake gave the good doctor a brief speaking look before coming to stand over the gurney. Her left arm was in a too bright white cast. His finger traced the faint blue lines in her closed eyelids. Her face was parchment pale. He pushed back the paper cap gently. The bandage on her head looked small considering the pain the bullet had caused.

"How is she?"

"She's going to be fine." The doctor motioned for the waiting orderlies to move Marnie to the bed. "Woke up for a few minutes in recovery, asked about you, said howdy to her family, then decided to take another little nap and told them to push off."

The doctor glanced around the room, then smiled at the banks of roses, drifts of pastel balloons, and jungle of foliage. Jake had bought out the only florist in town. One phone call and they'd delivered the entire shop to her room. Her brothers had had to go to the local grocery store for their offerings.

He wanted her to see only beauty. If he could, he'd have her memories of the last few days blocked from her mind forever. But then she wouldn't remember him. And he'd spend his life trying to make her fall in love with him. A fresh start.

"You've been busy," the doctor said. "And I see you managed to get yourself some clothes."

"No offense, Doc." Jake watched every move the other two

men made as they transferred her to the bed. "Careful, there! But that hospital outfit was beginning to get a little breezy. And frankly, after the impression I made this morning, I thought I better clean up my act."

The doctor chuckled. "Everyone understood your concern. It was the most excitement we've had around here for a while."

Jake walked over to stroke Marnie's cheek. Warm. Smooth. Alive. He looked up through blurred eyes at the doctor. "You did good. Thanks."

"Hey, pal, I told you I'm a pro. Remember?"

"Yeah, right before you slipped me that mickey," Jake said without heat. "I owe you big, Doc."

Jake sat very still, listening to the soft, even breathing of the woman beside him. A monitor beeped regularly on the other side of the bed. Tubes and wires hooked her up to various pieces of equipment. He couldn't restrain himself from touching her for the millionth time in the last two days. Her hand felt small and frail in his. But she wasn't frail, this small blond bombshell lying in this stark hospital room because she'd taken the bullet meant for him.

There was *nothing* frail or weak about her.

He'd give anything to switch places with her.

He stroked the back of her hand with his thumb. He shuddered remembering her grabbing hold of his jacket to prevent him tumbling off the rungs of the ladder perched sixty feet above a raging river, with absolutely no thought to her own safety.

She'd competently bandaged his bullet wound, *then* fainted because she couldn't bear the sight of blood. Circumstances had thrown her into a situation beyond her realm of experience. She'd faced each new challenge with unstinting bravery and her quirky sense of humor.

How the hell he could have compared her with Soledad, even in the beginning, was incomprehensible now. There was nothing similar. The two women were as different as night and day.

He touched her cheek. She wasn't hot. She wasn't feverish. She slept a deep, natural, healing sleep, just the way she was supposed to.

Her father and brothers had left word with the nurses' station to be called as soon as she woke up again.

They'd come and gone, gone and come, in the last forty-eight hours. They'd shoved food at him, brought him clothes, and sat vigil with him at her bedside.

Jake preferred his purgatory without witnesses, thank you very much. They'd taken off at last.

Which was fine with Jake. He didn't want them to spell him. He didn't want to talk to them, see the condemnation in their eyes, or hear what a son of a bitch he was for jeopardizing their daughter and sister. He *knew* all that.

Marnie had come swimming out of it several times, groggy and disoriented, calling his name, then fallen back to sleep. He hadn't left her side for more than ten minutes in the past two days.

He doubted she'd remember any of the brief conversations with him or her family. The anesthetic and loss of blood had knocked her for a loop. She'd spent a restful night last night, and Jake had laid his head beside hers on the pillow, his body twisted in the chair, just so he could breathe with her.

Damn. Am I a fool, or what?

"Good. You're still here."

Jake's head shot up as Michael Wright walked into the room. "I thought you guys went back to the hotel."

"The others went ahead. I wanted a word with you, alone. Outside."

It wasn't a request.

Jake rose from the uncomfortable chair, ready for the inevitable confrontation. In a way he was looking forward to it—to hearing out loud and in the open everything he'd been saying to himself for two days now. He followed the other man out into the hallway.

Tall, dark, and surly, Michael was the oldest and least charming of the brothers. His military training gave him the muscle and short haircut. He had his sister's blue eyes, but there was nothing either soft or feminine about the man leading the way through a side door to a small outside patio.

"If you're going to beat the crap outta me," Jake told the other man mildly, "better take it off hospital grounds."

He wasn't wearing a jacket, and icy air bit through his flannel shirt. His eyes burned from lack of sleep, his side hurt like hell, and he wasn't going to defend his actions to Marnie's brother either physically or verbally.

Not that the physical release wouldn't be a godsend, the way he was feeling. But there wasn't a damn thing the other man could possibly say that Jake hadn't thought himself multiplied to infinity.

"The family discussed the pros and cons of that action. We decided against it. For now." Michael stuffed his hands in the pockets of his jacket and narrowed his eyes, hunching his shoulders against the biting cold.

"I've heard of you before, you know." He looked out at the mountains beyond the manicured gardens of the hospital. "T-FLAC has quite a few ex-SEALs." He turned to look at Jake. "None of the men believed you were the mole."

When Jake responded with a disbelieving snort, Michael said flatly, "You have quite the rep, Tin Man. Quite the rep. Fair. Honest. Honorable. A veritable Boy Scout. You're also known to be hell on wheels when crossed. Antisocial. And relentless in your pursuit of the bad guys."

Michael leaned his hip against the low wall separating the patio from the brown lawn of the late fall garden. "In fact, you're precisely the kind of guy I'd like at my back in a dark alley. You and I could've been friends, if not for one thing."

"And that is?"

"You might choose to fight fair, Tin Man, but you're still a warrior. One we don't want anywhere near our sister. Marnie doesn't need a fighting man. *Capisce?*"

Oh, yeah. Only too well.

"I did some checking. They think highly of you at T-FLAC," Michael said grudgingly. "You're a hero for taking down Dancer, and with him SPA."

Jake had spoken to his boss already and resolved their conflict. All was set right with the spy world. It was his personal world that was FUBAR. He looked at Michael Wright and raised a brow. "That's nice to know. And your point is?"

"My point," Michael said grimly, pacing the narrow confines of the cement patio like a tightly leashed tiger, "is that Marnie needs someone who can take care of her. Something *you*, apparently, are incapable of doing."

And there it was. In the open. Short and sweet, and wrapped up in a neat package.

Jake would rather have taken the physical hit.

"Don't beat around the bush, do you?" Jake raised a hand when Michael stepped forward, blood in his eye. "Don't waste your energy. We both know you're right." Jake paused, torn. "Before I go, I have to have a promise from you."

"I don't owe you any goddamn promises, pal," Michael snarled, eyes blazing. "That's *my* kid sister in there. A girl with a bad heart you damn near got killed with your wet work. A kid who, no thanks to you, just had a bullet taken out of her. A kid who could have died without any of her family ever seeing her again.

"You want a promise? How about if I promise not to kill you if you're out of our lives in five? How about *that* for a promise?"

Jake wasn't about to go into the semantics of Michael's calling Marnie a kid. She might be that to her brothers, but she sure as hell was all woman to him.

"Two promises," he told Michael. "One. Find Duchess up there and get her home. Two—" Jake cleared his throat. "Two, stay with her until she's well enough to go home. Don't let her wake up alone in the hospital." He looked at the other man. "Please."

After a pause, Michael nodded.

Jake let out the breath he'd been holding and stuffed his fingertips in the front pocket of his new jeans. "I'll go in and say good-bye."

"She's sleeping."

"Then you won't mind staying out here until I'm gone, will you?"

Without waiting for an answer Jake walked inside, praying that she was indeed sleeping. He didn't think he could bear to see her eyes when he told her good-bye.

Three days later they reluctantly released her from the small mountain hospital. Marnie, taking the path of least resistance, went home to her father's house instead of her own small cottage a few miles away.

There she let the housekeeper tuck her into bed in her old room and lay staring at the ceiling for two days until she forced herself to snap out of her lethargy.

She showered, dressed, and went downstairs for breakfast on Monday morning to find her entire family at the kitchen table. There was much scraping of chairs as they all rose at the same time to hover over her.

Her father, big, rugged, and still handsome, his dark hair touched with silver, came over to give her a gentle bear hug. He was dressed for the office in a three-piece Armani suit and the tie she'd given him last year for his birthday. Marnie returned the hug. He felt big, safe, and infinitely dear.

"Morning, Daddy. Muskrats."

Her father let her go but looked down at her with keen eyes that read more into her expression than she would have liked. "It's good to have you up and about," he told her calmly. "Sit down and have some breakfast."

Kyle slung a brotherly arm around her shoulders and led her to a chair. "How're you doing, kidlet?"

"Just peachy, thank you." Since her brother the doctor had poked and prodded her endlessly for the last couple of days, he should know.

"Just like old times." Marnie took her place at the table and opened her napkin on her lap. "Are you all quite recovered from my injuries yet?" she asked mildly, looking around the table at her father and her Four Musketeers.

She thought how dear they were, with their worried eyes and grim expressions. They all loved her so much. She couldn't imagine her life without them. They'd always just *been* there, through all her highs and lows, through surgeries, through ghastly boyfriends. They'd been her wall of love. Protecting her. Treasuring her.

And she thought of Jake.

Jake, who'd never had anyone to care about him. Jake, who'd had his friends taken from him—twice in the case of Lurch. Jake, whose first love had betrayed him. Jake, alone. Isolated.

Tears sprang to her eyes. *Darn it.* She was still weak and weepy. She missed Jake so much it was a far worse physical ache than her injury.

"A bullet wound is nothing to take lightly, honey. Especially for a girl in your condition," her father told her, beckoning Hester, their housekeeper, to serve Marnie's breakfast. It was an unnecessary order, of course. The housekeeper had worked for them for almost twenty years and had X-ray ears and was already dishing up Marnie's food.

"Dad, I'm *twenty-seven* years old. Not a *girl* anymore. Second, I'm not in a *condition*. I'm as healthy as a horse. Yes, Daddy, I *am*." She prodded Kyle, sitting beside her. "Tell everyone, including yourself, Doc, how healthy I am."

"She's good," Kyle agreed.

Marnie looked around at the five large men taking up most of the room at the table. They might hear it. They might even agree with Kyle. That didn't mean they were going to treat her any differently than they had all her life. She sighed.

"Don't you have cows to punch?" she asked Derek, who lounged back in his chair cradling a cup of coffee between his long fingers. No one seeing her brother away from his ranch would guess he was a cattleman. He wore two-thousand-dollar suits and cashmere sweaters. Not a dark hair out of place. Yet she'd seen him soaked with sweat, a bandanna tied around his head as he castrated bulls, standing knee deep in cow poop.

"Things are under control." He grinned. "Don't sweat it."

"And you?" she demanded of his twin, Kane, the world-renowned photographer. They were identical in looks and opposites in personalities. While Derek was charm personified, Kane was quiet, kept to himself, and was almost antisocial. "Don't you have shutters to bug or something?"

Marnie glanced up and smiled as the housekeeper set a plate of eggs and bacon before her. "Thanks, Hessie." She looked back at Kane. "Well?"

"I'm between assignments right now."

"You, too?" she asked Michael, who sat brooding beside their father and searching her face for God only knows what.

"Yeah," he said, reaching for the coffeepot to fill her mug. He ladled two spoons of sugar into the brew, then added milk and picked up a spoon. "Between assignments."

Marnie watched him stir her coffee. "Have you by any chancc noticed what you're doing, Michael Dominic Wright?"

"What?"

"You just fixed my coffee as if I were a handicapped two-year-old."

"You're hurt."

"Yeah, Michael. I was *shot*. You've been shot before. Being alive beats the alternative, doesn't it? Nevertheless, I'm quite capable of putting milk and sugar in my own coffee." Marnie sighed as she looked around the table. "Look, you guys, I appreciate your going up there to help us. Thank you for worrying about me. But I'm fine now. Really, I am. Not talking about it isn't going to make what happened up there go away."

Her father leaned over and took her hand. "We tried talking you out of going up there alone, honey. We're not blaming you, but look what happened."

"Dad, guys, I hate to shock you all, but I wouldn't have missed going up there, and experiencing what I did, for all the tea in China. The getting shot part wasn't so hot," she added wryly, adding more milk to her mug. "But everything else I experienced was worth it."

"I don't want to hear the details," Michael snarled, getting up and going to the toaster. Half a second after he put his hand over the slots the toast popped up. Marnie had no idea how he always knew something was going to happen before it happened, even down to something as simple as the toast popping. He tossed the hot toast onto a plate and strode back to the table.

"Trust me, I wasn't going to give you details. Look, I went up to Grammy's cottage to think some things through. And despite all the running around and the dramatics, I've resolved some of those things in my mind." She glanced at their faces.

Behind Kane's shoulder the housekeeper gave her an encouraging smile and a thumbs-up.

"Dad, as much as I love you, I quit. I don't want to be a programmer. I don't want to work in an office behind a computer all day."

"Sure, honey. What about if I move you to—"

"No, Dad. I *quit* quit."

"You'll feel better after you get back into your routine and—"

"No, I won't. I'm going to try my hand at illustrating full time. After breakfast I'm going back home. I'm going to convert my second bedroom into a studio. Then I'm going to put together a portfolio of my work and make some calls, and see what happens."

"Great idea, kidlet," Kane told her. "I always said you have terrific talent. Why don't I drive you back and see what we can do about getting that studio set up?"

"I'll take the ride, thanks. But the studio I'll take care of myself."

There was a chorus of protests.

Marnie raised her hand. "*Stop*. You guys have to let me sink or swim on my own. I know you all love me, but you're smothering me. I have to take a big part of that blame. I've made excuses all my life and taken the path of least resistance. One, because I love you all and I didn't want to hurt any feelings. And two, because it was so much easier not to swim against the tide. But that's *got* to stop. I'm a big girl. I have to do things on my own. Please help me by not helping me so much. Okay?"

Without waiting for their answer—after all, it wouldn't make any difference at this point—Marnie said briskly, "Now, which of you got rid of the man I love? The man who could very well be the father of my baby?"

Chapter Eighteen

Nine-thirty-nine La Mesa Terrace was at the end of a cul-de-sac in a quiet residential neighborhood. At three-thirty in the afternoon a few kids, bundled to their noses in heavy outerwear, jostled each other on the sidewalk on their way home from school as Jake drove slowly down the street.

It was typical northern California winter weather. Bright and sunny. Not a cloud in the sky. Not as cold as the mountains, but fresh and crisp as a green apple. He'd left the window down and let the wind blow on his face for the five-hour trip down from the mountains.

He'd realized a little too late that she'd probably be at work. Or recuperating at her father's house. Or in a Paris art school studying some young stud's form.

"Glad to be home, girl?" he asked Duchess, who sat regally in the front seat, ears perked, tongue lolling. She'd been good company. No complaints, and a good listener.

Even at under five miles per, he was at the end of the street in about a minute and a half. Jake's heart had raced here in double time. He eased Marnie's little red Beamer alongside the curb.

The small house was painted daffodil yellow, with dark green shutters and front door. The lawn was a little long, but the beds were filled with a wild profusion of end-of-season autumn flowers.

It looked homey. Loved. Welcoming. *Damn, I've got it bad.*

Duchess stuck her head out of her open window, then looked back at him sitting there, steering wheel clenched between white-knuckled fists. She made a polite noise of inquiry.

A cigarette would be nice. He didn't smoke.

A drink would be great. He didn't drink.

It's good to want things, Jake reminded himself.

"Did I mention I was possibly a tad nervous here?" he asked the dog, who'd heard this before. Ad nauseum.

This was really stupid. All he wanted to do was fulfill his promise to Marnie to return her car and her dog. No big deal. And he wanted to make sure she was okay after taking a bullet meant for him. He owed her that much.

Like hell that was all he wanted.

Denial wasn't just a river in Egypt, Jake thought morosely. Denial had always been a form of self-preservation.

It had crept up on him full blown.

He loved the infuriating woman.

It was that simple, and that damn complicated.

Love. *Judas.* What did he know about love? Not a damn thing other than that he was crazy about Marnie Wright and would do anything it took to get her to admit she felt the same way.

The shocker was, he wanted it all. Love. Marriage. Commitment.

Ah, man . . . She wants to study art in Paris. Hell, she's probably in Paris right now. So would it be fair to bust in there and declare myself when she wants to fly free? Shit.

After the age of sixteen, when he'd left home to join the navy, he hadn't had a moment's indecision in his life. Yet here he was. Wanting her. *Starving* for her. Trying to be altruistic and do what was best for her.

I want to be *what's best for her, damn it!*

He wondered desperately what the pink flowers along her walkway were called. He admired the white tubs filled with droopy little blue flowers by the front door. He watched a kid scuffing his new school shoes as he kicked a plastic cup along the gutter.

Duchess sat patiently waiting for him to act. "I'm getting there," he said, a little irritated that she had so little faith in him. He had to get this right. One shot. He didn't want to screw it up. He couldn't barge in there half cocked and make demands.

Even though he wanted to. Bad.

Duchess was the perfect opening.

While Jake was being debriefed in Montana, where T-FLAC's headquarters were, Michael Wright had managed to get a message to him. He hadn't been able to locate the dog. Jake had hired someone in Gray Feather to pick up Marnie's car, then flown back to California, chartered a chopper, and gone to look for her mutt.

As promised.

It had taken the better part of the day to find her, cold and shivering, near the burnt-out ruin of the cabin. Having been on her own for several days, Duchess had been ecstatic to see him. Jake had left the chopper in Gray Feather, picked up the car, and headed out.

Judas. He'd faced down the world's most feared terrorists, in the world's worst places, with zero fear. He'd interrogated drugged up junkies on the docks with less trepidation. He'd been shot, stabbed, beaten, and tortured with less anxiety.

All he had to do was get his ass out of the car, lift the shiny brass knocker on her green front door, and tell her how he felt.

Piece of cake.

Then why the hell was he sweating?

He raked his fingers through his hair, thinking maybe he should have had it cut. When had he last had a haircut? He couldn't remember.

The dog looked at him pityingly.

Jake drummed his finger on the leather-covered steering wheel. "Get the lead out, huh?"

He'd never felt this way before. It felt terrifying . . . but *right*. And strangely comfortable.

What he'd felt for Soledad was so faint a copy as to be unrecognizable. Because, God help him, being ripped apart by Soledad's betrayal was nothing compared to how he'd feel if Marnie told him to get lost.

The thought terrified him.

Maybe he should have worn a suit. "Do you think a suit would have been better?" Man, he was talking to a dog. Okay, Duchess was smart, but she was still a dog. And he was so damn scared his hands were sweaty and his right eyelid kept twitching.

Hell, there was a first for everything.

He pulled the handle to release the door and got out. He held the door open until Duchess daintily walked across Marnie's leather seats to exit on the driver's side.

Doorbell or knocker? He rang the bell. He heard it chime inside the house. He tried to guess where she might be, and how long he'd wa—

"Jake," she said. No surprise. She'd probably wondered what the hell he'd been doing just sitting in her parked car staring at her house.

Her fluffy pale blue sweater matched the color of her eyes. "Here's your dog." *Brilliant. Really brilliant, Dolan.*

"So I see, thanks," she said with perfect calm. As though he hadn't almost killed himself getting here in a hurry. As though he hadn't walked all over God's creation to find her dog. As though he hadn't—

Get a grip here, pal, Jake cautioned himself while his heart raced and his eyelid continued to twitch. He wanted to hold her. Feel her warmth. Inhale her unique fragrance. Taste her mouth.

Marnie crouched down to fuss over the dog one-handed. "Hi, puppy girl, I missed you so much." A sling made out of a purple scarf with yellow happy faces on it supported her plaster-of-Paris-encased arm.

Signatures and drawings covered the cast, reminders of the fullness of her life. She had family. Friends.

"Are you going to invite me in or leave me out here freezing my ass off?" It came out more harshly than he'd planned.

She rose. "Yes, come in. You're letting five hundred dollars' worth of heat out."

She looked so beautiful his heart ached. It'd been only a

little over a week since he'd seen her. But she'd been groggy or sleeping, and that picture had stayed with him night and day since then.

Now, despite the broken wing, she looked pink-cheeked and breathtakingly alive. *Thank you, God.*

He never again wanted to see her blood staining his hands or hear the hideous noise as she gasped for air. He never again wanted to see her wheeled into an operating room or lying in a stark hospital bed, frail and helpless. He couldn't bear thinking about her bum heart.

He never wanted to see her hurt. Either physically or emotionally.

He wanted to love her.

Jake went absolutely tomb cold. What in God's name did he know about love? Answer? Not a damn thing.

Dispirited as he'd never before been in his life, Jake followed her through the house. He belatedly remembered her telling him she was more interested in finding herself than in finding a man.

A convenient memory lapse.

How *he* felt was immaterial.

But he wanted all or nothing.

Bullshit.

If she wanted to live in Paris, he'd live in her garret with her. He just had to persuade Marnie that was what she wanted, too.

The house smelled of tomato and lemon. He had a peripheral view of the rooms as they passed. Bright, primary colors, lots of open spaces, a jungle of plants, but Jake was more interested in watching her sweet little bottom.

"Let's go in the kitchen. I want to stir my sauce."

"Smells good."

"I had a craving for Italian. Coffee?"

"Yeah. Sure. Fine." Craving? Jake took a surreptitious glance at her flat stomach. "Are you pregnant?" As soon as the words were out he did a mental forehead slap. *Judas Priest!* He used to be known for his subtlety.

The mug she thumped down on the oak table before him

had a pink flamingo with bulging eyes as the handle. Coffee sloshed over the edge.

"Is that why you're here?" She tossed him a paper towel. It landed between them. *Like a gauntlet? Uh-oh.*

Jake obediently wiped up the spill and crumpled the napkin in his fist. He knew a trick question when he heard one. "I told you I'd deliver your car and Duchess."

"It's hard to believe you were such a chicken liver," Marnie said, sounding exasperated. "You let my brothers chase you away."

"They didn't."

"Then why did you leave me in that damned hospital without saying good-bye?" Marnie demanded, cheeks pink, eyes flashing.

"In my profession one doesn't *say* good-bye."

"Your profession stinks."

"I had to report in for debriefing." He remembered her comment when they'd made love the first time and wanted to smile. He'd kill to debrief her right now. Out of those jeans and that fluffy sweater and onto a soft bed . . .

He took a sip of coffee. Fixed just the way he liked it.

Marnie sipped hers. Too hot. It burned her tongue. She was going to win an Emmy for this. Or was it an Oscar?

Wearing jeans and an unfamiliar dark brown leather jacket over a cream fisherman's sweater, Jake looked disreputable and dangerously sexy. His hair was loose around his shoulders, shiny clean, and begging her fingers to explore.

She rose to stir the spaghetti sauce. Duchess, having inspected the house for intruders, wandered over to Jake and put her head on his knee.

"So what did you decide?" Jake asked casually, fondling Duchess's ear as Marnie resumed her seat. "Are you going to Paris?"

"No. I decided not to go."

"Because you're pregnant?"

She'd heard him the first time. It was like trying not to notice an elephant in the middle of the room. "What if I am?"

"*Are* you?"

"No. I—I don't know. It's too soon." *I'm praying that I am.* She wasn't going to beg him to stay. "I don't feel as though I am. Probably not."

"So why aren't you going to Paris, then?"

"I decided to convert my spare room into a studio." She took another sip of coffee, not tasting it. She longed to go around the table, sit on his lap, and pull his mouth to hers. Her lips actually tingled. "There's a local children's book author I've done some stuff with before. We've been talking about collaborating on a series of children's books."

How was it possible that after knowing Jake Dolan less than two weeks, she felt as though colors were brighter when he was in the room? She'd known how desperately she'd missed him, but until she'd seen him sitting in the car outside with Duchess, she'd had no idea how monochromatic her life was without him.

Jake Dolan made her heart glow in Technicolor.

"That's good. Sounds like you've made some choices." He drained his mug, set it down carefully, and shifted his big feet.

Her heart skittered, then thudded in sudden dread. Was he leaving? Just like that? *Here's the dog, your car, bye?*

"Yes." She licked dry lips. "I talked to my dad and the Musketeers. They say they understand. They promised they'll try to let me make my own choices about things."

"That's good." He picked up his empty mug and stared into its depth as though it were a crystal ball.

"Yes."

The kitchen clock ticked, and the sauce bubbled and plopped and filled the kitchen with its spicy fragrance.

I can't bear this. I can't bear *it,* Marnie thought as the silence dragged on. It hurt to breathe. At least on the mountain he'd been able to talk to her. This was horrible. Awkward. Stilted. Marnie knew he was trying to find a graceful way to say good-bye.

Please, Jake . . .

She stared at the reflected image of the overhead light fixture in her murky coffee. What was she pleading for? He was a man who didn't even know he *had* a heart.

What had been a life-changing experience for her had obviously been nothing more than a short sexual interlude for him. He couldn't wait to leave. She got up blindly and headed for the stove. She leaned her hip against the counter, picked up the wooden spoon from its rest, but didn't stir the bubbling sauce. Tears blurred her vision.

This was killing her.

From the second she'd opened her eyes in the hospital to find Jake gone, she planned what she'd say when she saw him again. *If* she saw him again. In none of her fantasies had her heart ached or her chest hurt with the pressure of unshed tears. In none of her fantasies had he sat looking at her with cool eyes and a hurry-the-hell-up-and-say-what-you-have-to-say expression.

"Did you sort out everything with your boss?" she asked, not looking at him. The sauce was going to burn on the bottom of the pot, but she didn't have the energy to stir. It was all she could do to hold her tears at bay.

"Yeah. It was Lurch all along. After faking his own death in San Cristóbal he started SPA. He knew terrorism from the inside out, making it easy to stay one step ahead of us. Then he trained his people just as we were trained in T-FLAC, blurring the lines even further."

"I'm sorry, Jake," she whispered in a tight voice. "How awful for you to be betrayed by your best friend like that. What happened to him? Was he . . . Is he . . . ?"

"He's the one who shot you." A muscle jumped in his cheek. "I shot him and ended it." He shrugged. "To me, he died years ago."

"Well, I guess that's that, then," she said, trying to sound brisk. "I'm really sorry about your cabin, Jake, but you'll rebuild that, won't you? What a hassle that'll be, dragging everything up the mountain."

Please stay. I won't ask anything of you, just that you love me a little. A bleak future loomed before her. She took half a breath, then scowled.

What was she *thinking*? Damn it! She'd reverted to type. That was the *old* Marnie, who did what other people thought was best for her.

Well, Jake Dolan was what was best for her, and she was what was best for him. But darn it, he was going to have to come to that realization himself. And he'd better do it *fast*. Before she had to resort to drastic measures.

Which she'd have to come up with soon.

She turned to stir her sauce, then removed the pot from the burner and turned off the stove. Narrow-eyed, she looked at Jake. He hadn't moved.

"I don't need you, you know." It sounded a little belligerent. Fine. She felt a *lot* belligerent.

Jake studied her, the muscle in his right eye ticked frantically. She didn't look loverlike. She didn't appear to be about to fling herself into his arms. In fact, she was starting to look pissed off.

He wasn't quite sure where this meeting had veered off course, only that it had.

"That's obvious," he said cautiously. "You have a nice house. A new career. Your family." He got to his feet. "I'd better get out of here, I have a plane to catch." *A plane to nowhere.*

He knew a dozen ways to get the truth out of a man, none of them pleasant. He spoke seven languages fluently, was a proficient marksman, and could use a knife with the skill and precision of a surgeon. He was considered one of the best at what he did. Yet he couldn't get one small, frail blonde to love him.

His mother and Soledad should both have been considered trial runs. He was batting a thousand.

"Oh?" Marnie asked, sounding only mildly interested. "How are you getting to the airport? You came in my car."

Jake gritted his teeth. "I'll call a cab."

"The nearest phone is at the mall. Six miles away."

Jake glanced at the yellow phone on the wall. "I don't want

a phone. Or a cab. Damn it, I want . . ." He raked his fingers through his hair.

"What *do* you want, Jake Dolan?"

"You."

"You've *had* me." She cocked her head, her eyes reflecting the pretty blue of her sweater.

Jake looked at her mouth, at that full, sexy lower lip. And he remembered the taste of her. The texture. The feel of her skin sliding against his . . .

"Is that what you thought?" she demanded, crossing her arms and glaring at him. "That you could drop off my car and dog, have a quickie, and be on your way?"

He kept his expression inscrutable. "I want to marry you." Surely she'd understand now. She was the air he breathed. He'd die without her.

"Because we had sex and I might be pregnant?"

"*Great* sex. People have married for less."

"Not the people *I* know."

"So the answer is no?"

She hesitated two beats. "Yes. I mean, yes, the answer is no."

He stared at her. It was a damn good thing he had no heart. It would be crushed beneath her dainty tennis shoes right now. *Judas, it hurts to breathe.*

Jake stared at her. At her smooth skin. Her wonderful hair. Her mouth, and her eyes, and her throat, and her slender wrists, and her . . .

This was agony. He had to get the hell out of here, before he . . . before he . . . He needed to leave. *Now.*

This was obviously what she wanted. He'd told her how he felt. She'd said no, hadn't she? He had to do what was best for Marnie. The right thing, God help him, was to stroll out that door and let her get on with her life.

"Well," he said, his voice strangely hollow, "I'll see myself out."

"Out?"

"I just wanted to see how you were doing, and to bring Duchess back."

"And to ask me to marry you," she added quietly, a look of frustration flitting across her beautiful face. She jumped up from the table, and the noise of the chair legs scraping across the linoleum made Jake's teeth ache.

"I'll see you to the door." Marnie stormed ahead, leading the way to the small entry. She snatched open the front door and stood back, shoulders military straight. Her eyes glittered feverishly as she glared up at him.

The cold air felt good on his face. The only good thing in the universe. He turned to look at her as she stood there, one hand on the brass handle, ready to slam the door in his face.

He frowned. "Are you okay?" He automatically put his palm to her forehead. Her silky hair brushed his skin before she pulled away.

"Just damn peachy, thank you very much."

He made a frustrated sound and dropped his hand. "Have a good life, Marnie Wright. You deserve it. I'll be on the lookout for those books of yours."

"Will you?" She licked her lower lip, her eyes shadowed. A breeze blew her hair about her face and she brushed it back. "Will you read my books to your children, Jake?"

Direct hit. Neat. Hardly any blood. A mortal wound. "There won't *be* any children."

"Why not?"

"Because . . . Damn it. Because the only person I can imagine being their mother is—you."

Marnie stared at him for a second, then grabbed him by the front of his jacket and pulled him back into her warm, tomato-and-lemon scented house.

She slammed the door behind him, then, clutching his lapels in white-knuckled fists, stood on tiptoe and brought him eye to eye. Almost.

"Tell me how you feel about me, Dolan."

"I told you how I feel."

"When?" Neither the snarl nor the mean eyes changed one iota.

Jake thumbed over his shoulder. "Five seconds ago. In the kitchen."

"You asked me to *marry* you."

"I'm sorry," he said stiffly. "I must have been out of civilian life too long. I thought that said something."

"In this case it could mean you want someone live-in for sex," Marnie said irritably.

"I don't. Hell, yes, I do. But that's not what I— Damn it, woman. You're making me insane. What do you want me to say? God only knows I *feel* it. I *taste* it. I *want* it." Jake rested his forehead on hers. "Please, tell me what you want me to say. I'll do, or say, whatever it takes to hold on to you. Anything."

Marnie let go of one lapel and poked him in the chest. "Tell." Poke. "Me." Poke. Poke. "You." Poke. "*Love* me."

"I do." Jake frowned, totally baffled as he nabbed her poking finger and brought it to his mouth for an experimental nibble.

"You do?"

He kissed her palm, then sneakily managed to get her hands around his neck and pull her a little off balance. "Of course."

"You *love* me?"

He hoped to God their children turned out just like her. "Hell, yes."

Her eyes were a little crossed in such close proximity. "*Say* it."

"I, Jake Dolan, love you, Marnie Christine—ha! you thought I wouldn't remember!—Wright."

Marnie pulled back and punched him in the solar plexus.

A warm summer breeze flirted between the leaves, filtering the sounds in the clearing. From behind the almost completed cabin, Jake heard the high-pitched whine of Michael Wright's Skil saw and the bass of Kyle's radio underscored by male voices. Someone had started the grill, and the pungent smell of briquettes mixed with the piney fragrance of the trees.

Hammer in hand, Jake paused, one foot on the first tread of the stepladder braced against the outside wall. He breathed deeply, drawing the fragrance of freshly cut lumber and contentment deep into his lungs.

Tomorrow he'd bring Marnie up to see what'd been done with the cabin. He thought she'd be pleased. Of course she hadn't been pleased with his caveman tactics yesterday, when he'd insisted she remain in Gray Feather. Arguing with Marnie had its own rewards, however.

Damn, life is good. Real good.

Married life suited him.

They'd had a small wedding in her father's backyard six months ago, Jake uncomfortable in a tux and Marnie so beautiful in her traditional white gown that she'd taken his breath away.

If anyone had told him a year ago he'd be in this emotional place, he would never have believed so much happiness possible. Or even probable.

His life before Marnie had been proof of the old adage You get what you pay for. He'd given his soul to what had passed for his life. He'd paid by becoming emotionally bankrupt. Cynical. Distancing himself from emotion to become immune to the human condition.

One small, sassy blonde had changed all that.

Marnie grounded him in a way he'd never thought possible. For the first time in his life Jake felt like an authentic human being.

Yes, married life suited him. It had also come with a few unexpected perks. Like family. A connection to others he'd only imagined.

Jake surveyed the building project with satisfaction. Many hands did make light work.

The cabin was almost complete. Hell, he could easily have torn down the burned timbers and constructed it by himself. God only knew he was used to doing things alone.

But he hadn't had to.

He'd erroneously thought himself incapable of being surprised. But once the dust had settled at T-FLAC, the powers that be had refused his resignation. And he'd discovered support from the most unexpected sources. People, he thought, still puzzled by it, who had been pissed when he hadn't called on them for help with Dancer. They considered themselves friends and had been ticked he'd been too blockheaded to realize it. Several of them had volunteered this weekend, helping to put the cabin together, along with all four of Marnie's brothers.

"That one bears watching." Hunt St. John, one of the T-FLAC operatives who'd given him grief over Dancer, gestured with his chin as Kane Wright rounded the corner. "What makes me think the guy's more than a fashion photographer?"

"In the seven months I've known him I've wondered the same thing."

"Ask."

Jake laughed. "Not if I want peace in my house, I won't."

"Henpecked? You?" The corner of Hunt's mouth kicked up slightly as he crouched to sift through the toolbox at his feet.

"You have no idea."

"No." Hunt's eyes darkened. "I don't. Gotta get these hinges on the bathroom door. Later."

Jake liked St. John. But he had a feeling few people knew the other man well, despite his laid-back style and easy smile. As for the Wright brothers, Jake had a strong suspicion *none* of them was quite what he seemed, either.

Judas, I've been around black ops and nefarious characters for far too long.

He'd managed an alliance with Marnie's family, although he sometimes still caught Michael watching him as though he was about to screw up.

Four Musketeers, and the guys from T-FLAC.

Friends.

Jake shook his head.

Damned if they weren't starting to grow on him. All these new friendships still felt a little like an ill-fitting suit, but they were becoming easier all the time.

The brothers and five guys from T-FLAC were all hard at work, kidding around as they hammered and nailed, ragging him unmercifully as they contributed ideas to the larger version of the cabin. Hearing laughter from some of these men was almost incongruous. Most of them were as Jake himself had been not that long ago—loners by choice.

How things had changed.

He and Marnie had bought a huge, hundred-year-old farmhouse on the outskirts of Gray Feather. Close enough to civilization, but distant enough for the discretion required for his work. He hadn't quit T-FLAC, he'd just changed direction. His interest in inventing private security and the existence of the lair had given him the opportunity to train new operatives on-site. He didn't miss fieldwork. His life was filled with enough intrigue and heart pounding for any man. Jake grinned.

"Hey, Dolan, you bringing my nails up here or what?" Derek yelled from the roof above him.

"On my way." Jake quickly clambered to the top of the ladder. "Judas, man," he grumbled, handing his brother-in-law the box of nails from his back pocket. "You and St. John! Don't you guys have sweat glands like the rest of us?"

Derek, not a hair out of place, white shirt spotless and still neatly tucked into his jeans, grinned. "I sweat when the occasion warrants it. Come see me sometime when I'm castrating bulls."

Jake shuddered. "I'll pass." He ran an expert eye over the roofline layered with new shingles. "Nice work."

Derek gave him a two-finger salute, then went back to work. The noise from the nail gun made further conversation impossible.

Jake skimmed down the ladder, then lightly ran his hand over the boards comprising the front wall of the new cabin.

The back of his neck prickled.

He turned, scanned the clearing, and reached in his back pocket for a weapon.

He wasn't carrying. But old habits died hard. Jake scrutinized the area anyway, left to right and back again.

There were no alarms to warn him when anyone approached. Everyone was either inside or out back. Not that anyone else was expected up here this weekend.

Jake did another visual scan.

Pine trees streaked with sunlight, grasses, a jacket tossed over a protruding branch on the downed tree across the clearing, a fawn-colored Great Dane . . .

Duchess wagged her tail and gave him a doggy grin.

Jake's heart gave an unexpected lurch.

The dog had been hiding her.

The slender blonde in a filmy pale green dress sat in the middle of the log, thirty feet from their almost completed cabin. Fair hair, all the colors of the sun and fingered by the summer breeze, danced in joyous spiral curls around her face and hunched shoulders. Her lips moved silently as she concentrated on something in her lap.

The second she heard his footfalls on the soft earth, Marnie's head shot up and a soul-warming smile blossomed on her lips, filling Jake to the brim with joy.

The word *love* didn't even begin to cover what he felt for this woman. Being loved by Marnie made him feel like a parched sponge soaking in liquid sunlight. Her love lit up even the darkest corners of his soul.

"What are you doing here?" he demanded, unable to control his smile as he took her hand to help her to her feet.

"I was lonely for my husband."

"You were supposed to stay in Gray Feather with your dad until tomorrow, when I was coming to get you. I don't like you wandering around up here alone right now. What if you fell, or—"

Marnie wrapped an arm about his waist and grinned up at him, blue eyes sparkling and unrepentant. "Pooh. That little stroll was nothing. I've run up and down this mountain with bad guys shooting at me in snow, sleet, and pouring rain. With all you tough guys up here, I'm as safe as could be. Besides"—she plucked a leaf off his T-shirt and twirled it under his nose—"I couldn't stand waiting till then to see what you've done. I sneaked out while Dad was taking a nap. For once I eluded his eagle eye."

"No, you didn't," Jake said laconically, waving to his father-in-law, who was trudging up the hill looking disgruntled.

Geoffrey Wright waved back, shot his son-in-law a sympathetic glance, and didn't pause until he disappeared inside the cabin.

"Can I have a tour now?" Marnie demanded.

Jake wrapped an arm about her waist, resting his hand gently on her very large belly. "It's hardly the romantic weekend I'd anticipated," he said dryly as the saw started up again and someone shouted for more nails. "I wanted to wait until it was just the two and a half of us."

She smiled. "One and a half of us don't mind company. We can always go home for quiet." She cast an appreciative gaze over the cabin. "It looks fabulous, Jake. Really terrific. And so *big*."

Arms about each other, they strolled up the slight incline to the front door.

"You didn't mention you'd been able to salvage any of the old cabin."

"I wasn't able to." Jake followed her gaze to the darker, weathered timbers comprising the front wall. "I used as much lumber as I could from your grandmother's cottage. Eventually the weathered timbers will blend with the new—Are you crying?"

Eyes bright with tears, Marnie turned to slide her arms around his neck, their baby nestled between them. "Oh, Jake. That is the sweetest, most dear thing. She'll always be in my heart, but I love knowing that part of her cottage will shelter us, too. Thank you, my love."

"My pleasure," he said gruffly against her hair. "Want to go inside?"

"In a minute." She rested her head against his chest with a sigh of contentment. "Just hold us like this a bit longer."

"My pleasure." Jake rested a possessive hand on her rounded tummy. "What were you saying to our daughter while you were sitting over there?"

Covering his stroking hand with hers, Marnie looked up at him with all her love in her eyes. "I was telling our future spy king of the universe what a lucky little boy he is to have such a wonderful daddy."

A son or daughter. Another Marnie miracle. Their lives were filled with them.

She'd given him her family, her trust, her absolute, unadulterated love.

She'd given him his heart.

Read on for a sneak peek at the next thrilling and sexy contemporary romance by Cherry Adair

Coming soon from Ivy Books

The noise and the yeasty smell of beer hit her the moment Taylor Kincaid opened the heavy front door of the Neon Armadillo and stepped into the blessed coolness of the air-conditioned interior. She paused a moment to let her eyes adjust to the dimness; then, waving at a few people she recognized, she crossed the postage stamp–sized dance floor to the long oak bar on the other side of the room.

"Busman's holiday?" Taylor smiled as she rounded the counter to toss her purse on a shelf behind the bar. Annie Macmillan was the Armadillo's other part-time waitress, but tonight she sat at the customer side of the bar, sipping a beer and watching the cowboys behind her in the mirror.

Cute with her slightly crooked eyeteeth and blond gamin haircut, Annie was five months pregnant. And everyone, Taylor included, tried to take care of her, much to Annie's annoyance. She probably shouldn't be drinking, but Taylor kept quiet. Their friendship was still too tentative to make waves.

Annie grinned back. "Checking out the scenery. If that Ray didn't have his eye on you, I'd take him for a whirl myself."

"Have at it. I'm not in the market." Taylor told her absently. "Hi, Charlie," she called to the owner playing liar's dice with an old crony at the other end of the counter. Charlie Mayher waved without looking up. Annie and Taylor shared a grin.

Charlie was the proverbial grouch with a heart of gold. Taylor got out a fresh bag of peanuts in their shells and started to refill the small wooden bowls scattered about the bar.

"You really dig working here, don't you?" Annie leaned her elbows on the oak counter and scrutinized her friend.

"Yeah, I do." Taylor loved the noise, the smells, and the camaraderie of the patrons. She loved everything about Matterhorn. She loved her new job, her new friends, and her sweet little house.

Life was abso-damn-lutely perfect.

"Heyya, sweetpea. How're my gals doin'?" Ruby Gardner slid a tray of empties onto the counter, then snatched a pack of unfiltered cigarettes out of the ashtray and lit up.

Taylor gave her a pointed look, and Ruby moved the ashtray slightly to the left so the smoke didn't blow in Annie's face. Not that the smoke seemed to bother Annie. The bar was always full of cigarette smoke.

Taylor tapped her foot in time with "I feel Lucky" playing on the jukebox. "I'm good." She smiled as she took the tray to dispose of the empty bottles and glasses behind the bar.

"Thanks," Ruby blew out a plume of gray smoke. She was the first person Taylor had met in Matterhorn. One couldn't get any more real than Ruby. She was quite a character, with a contagious zest for life that was delightful to be around, and a heart as big as Texas.

The first thing she'd asked Taylor was where she was staying, and she'd offered her own spare room. She'd done the same with unmarried and "all-on-her-lonesome" Annie. Taylor had her own house. Annie had opted for moving into the motor court motel south of town. Taylor'd thought Ruby must be lonely in her little blue house on the edge of town.

The jukebox conked out, and the click of pool balls, the low hum of voices, and the clink of glasses took its place. A ball game on the TV at the far end of the bar added more noise. A typical Monday night at the Neon Armadillo. Two guys played pool in back, a dozen or so people sat at the small wooden tables scattered about, and a few more were seated at the bar.

"You weren't kidding. It *is* quiet tonight."

"I told— Yo! Ray!" Ruby raised her voice at the cowboy kicking the temperamental jukebox. "That thing ain't gonna work until it's good and ready, so go sit down and drink your beer and stop kickin' the furniture!" She turned back to Taylor without missing a beat.

"Like I said on the phone this afternoon, sugah, you didn't need to come in. I told Missy Momma here the same thing. But she's busy lookin' for a daddy for junior."

Annie shifted slightly away from Ruby's tummy-patting hand and pulled a face. "Not."

She'd told Taylor all she wanted was companionship, not a relationship. She had enough problems already. She hadn't been much more forthcoming than that. And Taylor, who'd never had a real friend in her life, wasn't sure what was acceptable to ask.

"Pour me a Coke while you're back there, will ya, sug?" Ruby perched a jean-clad hip on a barstool and took another drag before pinching a piece of tobacco off her tongue with two nicotine-stained fingers.

Taylor drew two sodas, motioned to Annie's glass, and slid one of the glasses to Ruby when Annie indicated she was good.

On the shady side of forty, beanpole skinny, chain-smoking Ruby had her own sense of style. Tonight an enormous flame-colored hibiscus stuck at a jaunty angle into the crinkly mass of her improbably orange hair. Like Taylor, she wore a red T-shirt and jeans, but she'd added a dozen chunky bead necklaces to her ensemble, and her CFM heels were high enough to cause a nosebleed.

Half a dozen charm bracelets tinkled as Ruby took another drag of her cigarette and squinted her kohl-lined blue eyes at Taylor through the smoke. "Monday nights is always quiet. 'Specially when it's this dad-blasted hot. Everyone's home in their underoos catching a cold breeze off the AC."

She wiggled pencil-thin red eyebrows and shot Taylor a wicked look. "Except for Ray and his buddies over there giving you the eye. That boy sure has a mighty big crush on you, sweetcheeks."

Taylor gave a noncommittal shrug. She'd been considering Ray Adler as candidate for number one on her list. But so far something had held her back. And it wasn't fair to hold him off while she thought about it, not if Annie was interested.

Ruby gave her a sympathetic look. "Got lonesome out at your granny's place, did you, sugah?"

"I *like* working." Taylor inhaled a deep breath of smoky, beer-scented air. "Even if I just sit here all night watching everyone . . . I don't expect Charlie to pay me for sitting around," she added quickly.

Ruby chucked her under the chin. "Charlie'd pay ya for just sittin' any day of the week, sug. Fellas come from miles around to see that pretty face of yours." She rounded the end of the bar. "Yours, and our Annie, here. Besides, look at the old coot sittin' over there yakkin' away while we get our own orders." She held a glass under the spigot and drew a draft, grumbling under her breath about doing the bartender's job.

Taylor chuckled. "It's obvious who runs the Neon Armadillo, and it isn't Charlie."

"Yeah, well *his* name's the one on the deed." Ruby wiped her hands. "And don't change the subject. We were talkin' about you. Did you find any more pictures of your daddy and your granny?"

"I'm not sure. I've found a bunch more old photographs, but it's hard to tell. There are about a zillion boxes to go through, and I've barely started. Is it okay to bring another pile for you to identify when I come in on Wednesday?"

"Oh, honey, of course. I told ya. It's kinda fun to go through some of those and remember the old days."

"Old days? You're not old, Ruby."

"True. I'm feelin' younger every day havin' you two as my gal pals, sweetcheeks. And talkin' about you—"

"They're playing our song." Ray stood beside Annie, his eyes on Taylor. His shirt needed ironing, and his hair was a bit too long for her taste. But he had an engaging smile, twin dimples, and an easy charm she really liked.

He held out his hand, his blue eyes twinkling. "Care to take a twirl with me, honey?"

"No thanks, Ray." Taylor smiled. "I just got here."

A beat later Annie slid off her stool and took his hand. She didn't look five months pregnant in her pretty pink top and jeans. She looked fresh and young, and very eager, as she batted her eyelashes and clung to Ray's arm. "You lucky devil you, *I* just happen to be free."

Ray laughed and wrapped an arm about her slender shoulders to lead her to the small clearing made for dancing.

"As sweet as that gal is, she's gonna steal that boy away if you don't tell him yes for a change," Ruby told her, watching the couple rub together slowly on the dance floor.

"It's okay; Annie's welcome to him."

Ruby searched her face. "Yeah, you're probably right. You're too classy for a cowboy, sug. Set your sights high."

"Oh, no. That's not what I meant at all—"

One of the guys shooting pool yelled for a beer. Ruby shouted back, "Hold your horses, cowboy, I'm comin'!" With slow deliberation, she filled three more glasses and loaded her tray; then, with a wink, she teetered off on her high heels.

Smiling, Taylor closed her eyes for a second, and sent up a little thank-you prayer for her terrific new life and caring friends.

"Life is *good*," she whispered to herself, feeling invincible and ridiculously happy.

A shot of hot, creosote-scented, night air swirled through the bar as the front door opened. Still grinning, Taylor glanced up, mildly curious.

A broad-shouldered man, backlit by the streetlight, stepped inside, then let the door swing closed behind him.

The hair on the back of her neck lifted as a sudden awareness of impending danger washed over her. Her smile dissolved.

"Oh, shit, shit. *Shit!*"

He wore jeans and a black T-shirt; his dark hair was scraped back ruthlessly from his face and tied at the nape of his neck. Something about the guy screamed trouble with a capital T. Although Taylor didn't know him, she knew the type only too well. Cocky, used to getting his own way, and arrogant as hell. Six-foot-plus of attitude. The kind of guy she'd scraped off her shoes when she'd left L.A.

She couldn't figure out why, when he was dressed pretty

much the same as every other man in the room, she *knew* he was different. Dangerous. A disaster waiting to happen. And there wasn't a doubt in Taylor's mind that this guy was here for *her*.

Yet how? Why? She'd covered her tracks well. No one had followed her. She'd made damn sure of that. She'd paid cash for everything. Taken a circuitous route. She'd worn colored contacts the moment she'd left L.A. She'd whacked off her hair. She wore no makeup. No, he wasn't here for her. It was just paranoia rearing its ugly head.

If the folks of Matterhorn hadn't recognized her in broad daylight, there was no way this stranger could identify her in a dimly lit barroom.

Taylor took a deep, calming breath and tried to place him. He didn't look like a reporter, or a private eye. She wiped her suddenly sweaty hands on a napkin, then drummed a tattoo with her finger on the edge of the bar, and waited. Eventually he'd spot her. She wasn't going to hide, but she didn't plan on going up to introduce herself either.

The Red Dog Beer sign flickered over his head, casting a menacing glitter in the predatory shift of his gaze as he probed the shadows. His features were too rawly masculine to be particularly good-looking—his face too austere, his taut jaw too stubborn and unyielding.

Black brows winged over dark, hooded eyes as he scanned the room. He was as focused as a laser, oblivious to the noise and low, dense cloud of cigarette smoke suspended in the slow-moving air. Thank God the bar wasn't full—still, people stared openly, wondering who he was and what he was doing here. Just the sight of him twisted Taylor's stomach in a knot.

She felt the exact moment he spotted her. Like a guidance missile his gaze suddenly locked with hers. Recognition gleamed. A heartbeat later, he was in motion.

Damn!

Wishing him to Hades, she reminded herself that no matter who, or what, he was, he couldn't force her to do anything. As long as she figured out how to hustle him away from here before he spilled the beans, everything would be fine. For some reason that thought didn't calm the butterflies swooping around in her stomach.

Six-feet-plus of potent, virile, dangerous male strode toward her with purpose. A broad smile enhanced the glint in his eyes. She took an involuntary step back, and covered her throat with her hand. God—she'd seen feral smiles like his on Predator's Week on the Nature Channel.

"Darling!"

Darling?

Now that he was closer he looked vaguely familiar. But not "darling" familiar. She took a step back. Her retreat didn't bother him a bit. Before she could react, he came toe to toe, wrapped an arm around her waist, pulled her flush against him, and tilted her chin up with his free hand.

Shocked at the electrical jolt as he pressed her to the hard length of his body, Taylor nearly came out of her red, fake-skin boots. "W—"

The arm about her waist tightened as his mouth came down on hers, effectively shutting her up.

Stunned, she stood stock-still, arms at her sides, breath nonexistent as the stranger proceeded to kiss her like there was no tomorrow. He kissed her with the familiarity of a long-time lover. He kissed her as if she were his water in the desert. He kissed her as if he had the right to lave her mouth with the wet heat of his tongue and to draw her body so close to his that they cast one shadow.

Stunned by the sudden rush of raw desire surging through her like a Texas tornado, Taylor went deaf and blind. Impressions came at her with lightning speed. The smooth glide of his tongue against hers, the compelling smell of his skin, the heat and hardness of his large body crowding hers. Her blood thrummed through her veins with a fast, almost violent beat as his hand skimmed her back, down to her bottom, and pulled her hard against him.

Catcalls and whistles eventually pierced the veil of insanity shrouding her brain. Taylor tore her lips from under his and swiped the back of her hand across her hot, puffy mouth. Boggled by the actions of a complete stranger, she looked up.

And met the gaze of a feral panther, one paw on the heart of his prey, partially retracted claws ready to sink through her tender flesh.

God. I'm being fanciful. He's just a man. But a chill coursed through her overheated body, and the faint tang of his spicy after-shave made her light-headed. Disoriented, she looked from his eyes to his mouth. . . .

A chair leg scraped. Voices intruded. Suddenly aware that every eye in the place was fixed on them, Taylor managed to get her arms between them to push at his chest with her elbows.

"Are you nuts?" she hissed. "Let me go!"

"Ah, darling, can you forgive me?" The words came from behind clenched teeth. A thread of menace wove through his smooth baritone like a dark underground river. He didn't release her. Instead, he gave her a meaningful look, his arms like iron bands around her.

"Don't be angry, sweetheart." His voice was low and resonant. The voice of a man used to giving orders and having them obeyed. *Immediately.*

"I know you said you needed more time, but I was so blue without you, I had to come."

Like the commercial for the investment company, everyone in the bar stopped to listen to their every word. Taylor felt as though she was stuck inside the *Twilight Zone*. The situation got weirder by the minute. She suppressed a shiver and gave him a cool look.

"Pleasant as that was, sugah, you've mistaken me for someone else."

There was nothing pleasant about the half smile barely curving the sensuous line of his mouth as he watched her with dark, opaque eyes.

He lowered his voice to a breath. "I don't *make* mistakes. Blue."

Taylor swore under her breath. His arms were still wrapped about her, but she lost all feeling, as a bone-deep chill pervaded her body. He towered over her own five-foot-eight inches by at least six inches. Tall, implacable, intimidating.

Bluff or bolt? She straightened her shoulders under the steel band of his arm and locked her gaze on his face.

"I'm not the gal you're lookin' for, so that was just a plumb waste of time, now wasn't it? All I am is a lil ol' waitress—"

Eyes hard, voice light and mocking, he shook his head. "Knock it off. The tabloids didn't exaggerate when they said you couldn't act worth a damn. Despite the haircut, and the brown contacts, I recognized you immediately. Don't waste my time pretending you aren't who you are."

Quite a neat trick. If she could've figured that out years ago, she would have.

Feeling returned in a rush. The knot in her tummy turned to lead. Blood surged in her ears. The temperamental jukebox burst into song with Johnny Cash's "Ring of Fire."

When Ruby, who religiously read the tabloids, hadn't recognized her, Taylor had thought herself gloriously incognito. Then in walks *this* guy, and her lovely life goes to hell in a handbasket.

His arm tightened around her back, reminding her that he still had her clasped like a boa constrictor. She shifted in his embrace. More a breath than tactical retreat. Surprisingly, he released her. His arms dropped to his sides, but his eyes kept her firmly in place.

Taylor tucked her fingers into the front pockets of her jeans. "Y'know, sugar, folks have been tellin' me I look a bit like that singer gal for years, but nobody ever thought I was *really* her before. Thanks for the compliment."

She cocked her head, trying to read his expression. The man must be damn good at poker. "I read in the tabloids that Blue's in Aspen or someplace." A pretty feeble bluff, but worth a shot.

"*Marcy Stewart*'s in Aspen." His gaze slid impersonally down her body, taking in her plain, red cotton T-shirt, loose jeans, and inexpensive boots, then traveled back up again, just as slowly.

"Your doppelganger might have the press snowed, but she didn't fool me." His lips quirked in a parody of a smile.

"Although Miss Stewart looks a lot more like the Blue the world knows than you do at the moment."

"Whatever you're selling, I'm not interested." She dropped the phony accent and pivoted to go.

"Stay right where you are." A chilly command couched in jaw-clenched courtesy. "I've gone to a lot of trouble to find you."

They stared at each other like cobra and mongoose.

He made her feel prickly-hot, then shivery-cold. How did a guy she'd never met know the difference between herself and Marcy?

Her heart beat much too fast for a simple encounter with a stranger. Even a kissing stranger. For years Taylor had experienced life through a plate-glass window. Separated from reality by her celebrity. This man was more reality than she was ready for. Everything about him made her feel defenseless and vulnerable.

She didn't like the feeling any more than she liked the way he arrogantly expected her to stand there and hang on his every word while he toyed with her.

"Who the hell *are* you," Taylor demanded, teeth clenched, "and what do you want? Spit it out, and let's get this over with."

"The name's Huntington St. John." He braced his hand against the bar behind her, effectively blocking any retreat. "I have a request. And an offer you won't want to refuse."

She raised a brow.

"I want Blackman," he told her. "You'll be doing us both a favor if you tell me where your uncle is. Before his friends come looking for *him*, and find *you*, as I did."

Taylor's heart contracted at the casual reference to her uncle. If he was looking for Uncle Toby, he was involved with major-league gambling. And as far as Toby went, gambling meant Las Vegas. Realization prodded her fear into high gear. This man had nothing to lose by revealing her identity. Taylor took a calming breath. It didn't work.

"You came all the way from Las Vegas for nothing," she

told him flatly. "My uncle died in a plane crash two months ago."

"No," St. John said coldly. "He did not."

Nonplussed, she stared back at him.

"Blackman is alive. I know it. You know it. And it won't take long for his associates in Las Vegas to know it, too. They aren't nearly as civilized as I am about things. Trust me. They won't ask politely."

"Look," she held on to her composure by a fraying thread. If this guy considered himself civilized, he was delusional, and she was in bigger trouble than she'd thought. "Believe me, Toby died in that plane crash. I wish it were otherwise, but it's not."

A quick glance showed Ray and Annie standing together across the room. Annie laid a hand on the cowboy's arm as he shot St. John a menacing scowl. Damn it! This was all she needed.

"Everyone's staring. Don't you dare make a scene."

"You're used to people staring at you."

She could actually hear her molars grinding. "No one here knows who I am."

"Is that so?" he said smoothly. "Then I'm sure you'd rather not discuss this in your place of employment."

"I'd rather not discuss it at all."

"Any more than you want the paparazzi to descend en mass on your nice quiet little hideaway. Then everyone in the free world would know who, and where, you are. Why don't I start by telling the cowboys over there how privileged they are to have the famous Blue in their midst?"

"Better people than you have tried, and *failed*, to blackmail me." Taylor set her chin and regarded his implacable face with hostility. Life was too short, *her* life was too short, to put up with this crap.

"Consider this conversation over." If the bastard alerted the press, she'd deal with it. Just as she'd dealt with everything else.

"I'm willing to cut you a little slack," he said, his voice cool. "If you're determined to maintain the fiction of being a waitress, I'd suggest somewhere private to finish this conversation. But finish it, we will."

Taylor snorted inelegantly. "Oh, please! You walk in here, grab me in a lip lock, threaten my privacy, tell me my dead uncle is alive, and then demand to take me somewhere *private*? And you think I'll go . . . *willingly*? Buster, get a reality check." She pushed at his arm so she could get past him.

He didn't budge, didn't even have the graciousness to acknowledge her efforts.

Out of the corner of her eye, Taylor noticed Charlie had joined Ruby, Annie, and Ray. God only knew what they must be thinking right now. Ruby said something to Charlie, then started walking toward them. The cavalry was moving in.

"I'm not interested in anything else you have to say," Taylor told him with finality. "Move so I— Mmmpf."

He kissed her again. And damn it, he was good.

Really good.

She gave him a few more seconds to cut it out . . . then slammed down her heel, hard, on his instep.

Look for these page-turning novels

by Suzanne Brockmann

THE UNSUNG HERO

After a head injury, navy SEAL lieutenant Tom Paoletti catches a terrifying glimpse of an international terrorist in his New England hometown. When the navy dismisses the danger, Tom creates his own makeshift counterterrorist team, assembling his most loyal officers, two elderly war veterans, a couple of misfit teenagers, and Dr. Kelly Ashton—the sweet "girl next door" who has grown into a remarkable woman. The town's infamous bad boy, Tom has always longed for Kelly. Now he has one final chance for happiness, one last chance to win her heart, and one desperate chance to save the day . . .

HEARTTHROB

Once voted the "Sexiest Man Alive," Jericho Beaumont had dominated the box office before his fall from grace. Now poised for a comeback, he wants the role of Laramie bad enough to sign an outrageous contract with top producer Kate O'Laughlin—one that gives her authority to supervise JB's every move, twenty-four hours a day, seven days a week.

BODYGUARD

Threatened by underworld boss Michael Trotta, Alessandra Lamont is nearly blown to pieces in a mob hit. The last thing she wants is to put what's left of her life in the hands of the sexy, loose-cannon federal agent who seems to look right through her yet won't let her out of his sight. But the explosive attraction that threatens to consume them both puts them into the greatest danger of all...falling in love.

Don't miss these wonderful novels

by Patricia Rice

IMPOSSIBLE DREAMS

Maya Alyssum's impossible dream is to open a school where kids can find unconditional love and acceptance, the very things she never had as a child. The town council of Wadeville, North Carolina, is determined to stop her until the day Axell Holm walks into her shop. He's the kind of uptight authority figure she loves to hate . . . and hates to love.

VOLCANO

After landing in gorgeous St. Lucia on business, Penelope Albright receives the shock of her life: She is accused of smuggling drugs. Then a sexy stranger appears claiming to be her husband, "kidnapping" her before trouble begins. Or so she thinks. Trouble and Charlie Smith have met. He needs a wife—temporarily—to help him keep a low profile while snooping into the mysterious disappearance of his partner. And like it or not, Penny is already involved. . . .

More marvelous fiction
by Patricia Rice

BLUE CLOUDS

Around the small California town where Pippa Cochran has fled to escape an abusive boyfriend, Seth Wyatt is called the Grim Reaper—and not just because he's a best-selling author of horror novels. He's an imposing presence, battling more inner demons than even an indefatigable woman like Pippa cares to handle. Yet, while in his employ, she can't resist the emotional pull of his damaged son or the chance to hide in the fortress he calls a home.

GARDEN OF DREAMS

JD Marshall is on the run with his sixteen-year-old son, his computers, and his raw nerve—trying to stay alive and finish creating a hot new software program. But an accident derails him in Madrid, Kentucky, and his angel of mercy is Nina Toon, a sassy blond pixie who stirs his blood. Nina is equally unsettled by this gorgeous stranger who is negotiating his way into her life . . . and her heart.

Sometimes you have to lose everything to find what really matters...

ON MYSTIC LAKE

by Kristin Hannah

Annie Colewater's life fell apart the day her eighteen-year-old daughter left home and her husband of twenty years abandoned her for a younger woman. Shattered, she returns home to the small Washington town of Mystic, seeking solace to the haunting emptiness of her own soul. Here, a broken woman will open her heart to a shattered little girl and her father, Nick Delacroix, an embittered, grieving widower. These three lost hearts find the courage to trust in love again—never expecting the turn of events that will force Annie to make a harrowing choice between what is . . . and what could be.